ACHE
FOR
YOU

ACHE FOR YOU

A
SLOW BURN
NOVEL

J.T. GEISSINGER

Montlake
Romance

Published by Montlake Romance, Seattle

www.apub.com

Amazon, the Amazon logo, and Montlake Romance are trademarks of Amazon.com, Inc., or its affiliates.

ISBN-13: 9781503904385
ISBN-10: 1503904385

Cover design by Letitia Hasser

Printed in the United States of America

ACHE
FOR
YOU

ONE

KIMBER

No matter how plump, plain, or poor a woman is, the right wedding gown will make her feel more beautiful than any fairy-tale princess.

Right about now, I'm thinking Cinderella can kiss my beautiful ass.

My heart pounding, I step out from behind the dressing room door in an extravagant cloud of silk and lace that took me three months to make, and wait for Jenner's reaction.

It's even better than I hoped.

"Winston Churchill's hairy balls!"

He jolts to his feet from the ugly chintz divan he's been lounging on while I've been getting ready for the ceremony. Sleek as a seal in his perfectly tailored Armani tuxedo, he looks me up and down slowly. "You're an angel! A vision! A fucking *goddess*!"

That makes me blush. I take compliments about as comfortably as enemas. "Thank you."

Pursing his lips, he frowns and folds his arms over his chest. "Would it be very wrong if I got an erection? Things are getting a bit heavy downstairs."

Delighted, I laugh. "You always were a slut for French lace."

He waves a hand in the air, imperious as the queen. "Twirl, darling. We need to see this dress in action."

I pick up the hem of my dress and spin around in a ballerina's twirl. My veil floats around my shoulders like the finest of halos, spun from pure clouds. When I stop and face Jenner again, he's pretending to be misty-eyed, covering his mouth with a fist.

"My little girl's all grown-up."

I sigh, looking at the ceiling. "Oh my God. You're *one* month older than me."

"I'm being metaphorical!" Hands out, he strides toward me with his elegant gait and takes me in his arms, careful not to wrinkle my dress or smudge my makeup when he kisses my cheeks. "Now, I admit I didn't always have faith that Brad would marry you—"

"You literally told me, and I quote, 'That shitstick will never marry you.'"

He groans. "Mary Poppins, you've got a memory like an elephant! As I was *saying*, I didn't always have faith, but I'm so happy to be proven wrong. For your sake."

He pulls away and grasps me gently by my shoulders. Because he gets twitchy when things aren't just so, he tucks a rogue curl that's escaped from its updo behind my ear. When his voice hardens, his British accent becomes even more clipped. "But if he does a single thing that makes you unhappy, if he so much as makes you *frown*, I'll neuter that shitstick with a rusty butter knife."

Gazing at Jenner's stern face, I smile. I say softly, "I love you, too."

"You're disgustingly sentimental."

He says that dismissively, but I see how his lower lip quivers. "I'm gonna throw that right back at you when you're weeping into your hankie as I take my vows, girlfriend."

He's quiet for a moment, thinking, then he starts to fiddle with the edge of my veil. "Any last-minute jitters?"

"No."

I've been waiting for this moment for three years. Since the second I laid eyes on Bradley Hamilton Wingate III, I've been madly in love with him. This is the happiest day of my life. The only thing that would make it more perfect is if my father were walking me down the aisle, but since his intense claustrophobia makes a transatlantic flight impossible, my handsome, elegant Jenner will do the job almost as well.

Still thoughtfully toying with my veil, Jenner says, "I've got the Jag right outside, you know. We could be in wine country getting massages and ogling the pool boys at Meadowood in under two hours."

I glare at him. "I know Brad's not your favorite person, but if you ruin my wedding day by talking shit about my husband, I'll light your collection of vintage Gucci scarves on fire."

He quirks his mouth into a wry pucker. "Don't get your knickers in a twist, *Bridezilla*. My lips are henceforth sealed." He pretends to turn a lock and throw away the key, then pauses. "But I want to be on the record as saying that you could do so much better—"

"Jenner!"

He takes in my clenched jaw and fists, my bulging eyes. "You're right," he says softly. "My bad. I just want what's best for you, that's all."

He leaves unspoken all the times I cried on his shoulder after one of my fights with Brad about how emotionally unavailable he was, all the teary phone calls when I agonized over why he wouldn't commit and get me a ring, all the soul-searching over mimosas about what I might be lacking.

But all that's over now. We were just going through what we needed to go through to get to our happily ever after, where we were supposed to be all along.

3

Everything will be different once we're married.

I'm just about to tell Jenner that when the wedding coordinator bursts into the room in a flurry of flailing hands and breathless gasps, her dark hair frizzing in the August humidity.

"It's time! It's time! Is everyone ready?" She sees us, pulls up short, and puts a hand to her throat. "Holy Christmas, you look stunning."

"Thanks, Miranda."

When she blinks and says, "Oh, uh—you, too!" I realize she was referring to Jenner.

He chuckles when he sees the sour look on my face. "Don't worry, darling, I'll slouch and pout as we go down the aisle so you'll look even more glorious in comparison."

I say drily, "Yeah, except slouching and pouting make you look prettier, not worse. I can't believe I was dumb enough to ask a model to be my maid of honor. I rue the day I met you."

"You're *lucky* you met me. If I hadn't pretended to be your boyfriend to save you from that Neanderthal slobbering all over you in the shoe department at Neiman's ten years ago, you might still be there, trying to politely avoid his big, hairy hands."

"Be quiet and give me the damn bouquet."

He plucks it from a vase on the table beneath the window, his lip curled as he inspects it. "Calla lilies? Good God. They're a funeral flower."

I warn, "If you say anything even remotely close to *How apropos*, I'll gut you like a fish."

He regards me with cool disdain, which is the British version of affection. "Ah, more threats of violence. On the wedding day, no less. How very Don Corleone of you. Must be that Italian blood of yours."

"You're damn straight. Now let's go make that aisle our bitch." I turn back to the dressing room and holler, "Girls!"

Out come Brad's sister, Ginny—a Grace Kelly look-alike—and my girlfriend since high school, Danielle, who flew out from Ohio for the wedding. Both are gorgeous in bespoke champagne chiffon gowns, though Danielle's boobs are trying their hardest to escape from the bodice.

"You should've installed scaffolding for those things," says Jenner, eyeing Danielle's chest with alarm.

Danielle shakes her double Ds and blows Jenner a kiss. "She tried, but the girls need to be free. I made her take all the boning out."

Jenner looks disturbed. "Is this a wedding or a cabaret?"

"It's not only a wedding—it's *the* wedding," says Ginny, dabbing on a last-minute dollop of lip gloss. She caps the tube and sets it on a side table, then turns to Jenner with a smile. "Everyone who's anyone in San Francisco is here. I can't wait to see the coverage in the press!"

I shudder. "The press. God, don't remind me."

"I know those jerks from the tabloids have been following you around, but the people Daddy hired to cover the wedding are totally legit. It'll be great for your company, Kimber." Ginny smooths a hand down the waist of her gown. "These dresses are gorgeous, and you look like a princess. Once the pictures come out, your obscure little dress shop will be famous."

"Knock wood."

"Please! Everyone, let's move!" shouts a hyperventilating Miranda.

I take the bouquet from Jenner's hands and inhale a deep breath to calm my screaming nerves. Not that it helps, but I have to try something. My antiperspirant is already failing, my stomach is in knots, and my hands are shaking so hard the callas look spastic.

Danielle and Ginny grab their bouquets and go ahead of us, then Jenner and I walk arm in arm from the room. "It's showtime, darling," Jenner murmurs as photographers swarm us and cameras start whirring. "Chin up. Back straight. Tits out."

I lift my chin, square my shoulders, and try hard not to gulp air like a guppy. When we round the corner and enter the narthex through a pair of heavy wooden doors, the classical strains of Pachelbel's "Canon in D" fill my ears. Miranda frantically motions us forward. Jenner squeezes my trembling hand. We take a few more steps and we're in the nave.

It's so beautiful, for a moment I'm overwhelmed. The flowers. The candles. The huge crowd of well-dressed guests, standing for my entrance.

And Brad, awaiting me at the altar, so tall and broad shouldered, wearing his tux with such ease it's as if he were born in it.

When our eyes meet across the distance, my heart swells. All-American apple-pie perfection is what he is. The square jaw, the golden tan, the wavy blond hair gleaming under the lights. The proud bearing and ridiculous good looks.

My Prince Charming. He's more beautiful than everything else put together, more perfect than my wildest dream.

Except for that look of abject terror on his face, which really clashes with his tux.

When my step falters, Jenner squeezes my hand again. "Steady, darling."

We start our trek down the aisle at the glacial pace we've been browbeaten during rehearsals by Miranda to adopt. One step—pause. Another step—pause. It heightens the drama, she said. She was certainly right, because with every step I take closer to him, Brad's face drains of blood until he could handily pass for a corpse.

Under my breastbone, my heart does a credible impersonation of a dying fish and flops wildly around, gasping.

Through his manufactured smile, Jenner quietly observes, "Your spoiled little frat boy looks even more douchey than usual."

My own smile is so wide it feels as if my face might crack. Two photographers lurk at the end of the aisle, snapping pictures, so I try not to move my lips when I answer. "He looks like he's facing a firing squad. Is that normal?"

"Maybe Satan got a drop of holy water on his skin, and he's trying not to turn to ash in front of all Daddy's constituents."

I'll kill Jenner later. Right now it's taking all my concentration to keep my smile alive.

By the time we make it to the end of the aisle, I can clearly see the sweat streaming down Brad's temples, the wild, trapped-animal panic in his eyes, and his deathly pallor. Beside him, his best man, Trent, grins like a fool as he ogles Danielle's chest.

So loudly I flinch, the priest says, "Who gives this woman to be married to this man?"

"She gives herself," replies Jenner smoothly, trashing his Miranda-approved answer of *I do.* Then he hands me off to Brad, who's obviously struggling to remain conscious.

Stepping forward with a tremulous smile, I whisper, "Honey? Are you okay?"

Blinking like a baby bird, Brad swallows. He makes a froggy croaking noise that doesn't sound anywhere close to a *yes.* I've seen victims of car crashes in better shape.

I shoot a desperate glance at his parents in the front row. Senator and Mrs. Wingate are dressed to the nines, like everyone else. Unlike everyone else, however, they appear almost as nervous as their son.

Something is terribly wrong.

Fear coils around my heart and squeezes.

The priest says something I can't hear over the crashing of my heartbeat. It's all *words, words, words,* a nonsensical soundtrack underscoring my choking sense of doom as I stare in rising horror at my intended, who so clearly is a breath away from vomiting or fainting.

Or both.

The priest finishes whatever he was saying, then turns to Brad. "Bradley Hamilton Wingate, do you take this woman to be your lawfully wedded wife? To have and to hold from this day forward, for better, for worse, for richer, for poorer, in sickness and in health, until death do you part?"

A cavernous silence follows in which Brad stares at me with all the whites of his eyes showing. A vein throbs frantically in his neck. It's so quiet the clicking and clacking of camera shutters sound like gunfire.

When the silence stretches uncomfortably long, the priest clears his throat. "Son?"

Brad's mouth works, but no words are forthcoming.

The air goes electric. Whispers and rustling make their way through the guests. A cold bead of sweat trickles down between my shoulder blades. I throw a desperate glance over my shoulder at Jenner, who's giving Brad a hard, dangerous stare.

Stout and red-faced in his tuxedo, Senator Wingate leans forward from the front row and hisses, *"Bradley!"*

It seems to break whatever spell Brad is under, because he finally speaks. "I . . . I . . ."

I nod frantically, my head bobbing like a doll's. Desperation lends my voice a hysterical pitch. "Yes, honey?"

He drags in a huge breath, lets it out in a gust, and—like a dam bursting—starts to babble incoherently. "I can't do it I just can't I'm sorry this isn't happening, Dad . . ." He turns to his father, who is already rising from the pew. "I can't do it there's no way I can marry her!"

With the bellow of an enraged bull, his father charges. He crashes on top of Brad. They go down in a tangle of arms and legs, hitting the marble floor of the altar with a *boom* that topples a brass candelabrum and draws gasps of astonishment from the crowd.

Three hundred people leap to their feet.

Brad's mother lets out a pitiful wail.

Cameras click and whirr in glee.

Someone snickers and says under his breath, "So much for Brad's inheritance."

Then a piercing, anguished scream that seems to come from everywhere echoes painfully off the walls. It splinters into a thousand smaller screams as it bounces over hard marble surfaces, over and over again, conducted high into the rafters like a flock of shrieking birds startled into flight.

It's an awful sound. I've never heard anything so terrible in my life.

It isn't until Jenner grabs me and drags me off the altar steps that I realize that horrible scream is coming from me.

TWO

The pictures are catastrophic.

"Well, look on the bright side," says Jenner from my sofa, where he's reclining on a pile of pillows and snacking on low-fat chips. "That nose of Satan's will never be straight again."

I take little satisfaction that I shattered Brad's nose with one well-placed punch after I broke away from Jenner's arms. Blood sprayed from the squealing weasel's face like a fountain. Even his father looked impressed by my aim.

"Yeah," I say bitterly. "His nose, my heart. Same mush."

In the three days since the wedding that wasn't, I've cried constantly, gorged myself on ice cream, smashed all the wedding china, and gone almost hoarse screaming at the walls. What I haven't done is left my apartment or answered the phone. I'm going to add a ban on the internet, too, because photos of my public humiliation have made their way online.

The pic of me breaking Brad's nose is a keeper, though. I printed it out and taped it up on the fridge.

I flop over onto my stomach, adjusting the pillow under my chin. I'm lying on the floor in the middle of my living room, where I've spent most of the past three days. I can't stand to be near the bedroom because the bed Brad and I shared leers at me every time I walk by.

It'll be gone soon, anyway. I can't afford this place on my own. When the first of the month rolls around, I won't be moving into the charming Victorian in Ashbury Heights that Brad bought for us. I'll be moving into the back room of my shop until I can find a studio. Somewhere cheap, out of the city. Preferably underground, so I don't have to face people.

"The Jilted Dressmaker!" one headline screamed.

I've been reduced to a cheesy made-for-TV movie.

"Danielle texted me that she made it home safe. She wanted to know how you were holding up."

"What'd you tell her?"

"I lied and said you were doing fine. I knew if I didn't, she and those boobs of hers would turn around and get right back on a plane." He makes a retching sound. "How anyone could move to Cleveland after growing up in San Fran is beyond me. Ohio is the Florida of the Midwest."

"You're a terrible snob."

"Merci. When are you going to call your father?"

I groan, burying my face in the pillow. When I think of all the money my father sent me for the wedding, I want to die. The fabric for the gowns alone cost thousands.

My voice is muffled by the pillow when I speak. "He thinks I'm on my honeymoon. I've got another eleven days before I have to call him."

"Unless he sees the pictures online."

I consider that, but decide the likelihood that my technology-challenged father will be near enough to a computer to glimpse evidence of his only child being roundly mocked by the crème de la crème of San Francisco society is close to nil. I sent him a Kindle for Christmas one year, and he wanted to know how to open it. He thought it was a really flat book.

"Tell me again why we didn't go on your honeymoon like the girls did in *Sex and the City* after Carrie got dumped by Big at the altar?"

"Because two weeks at a dude ranch in Montana was Brad's idea of bliss, not mine. And you know very well Carrie didn't get dumped at the altar. She got dumped over the phone at the church *before* she had to walk down the aisle."

Lucky bitch.

Sounding wistful, Jenner sighs. "Au contraire. Two weeks at a dude ranch sounds like absolute *heaven*, darling. Just think—all those cowboys. And their lassos. Oh my."

When I look up at him, he's fanning his face with the empty bag of chips.

"No. No cowboys. No boys of any kind, for that matter. I don't care if I never see another man for the rest of my life!"

Jenner stops fanning and quirks his brows. "You do realize I'm the proud owner of a penis, yes?"

"You don't count."

"Ouch!"

"You know what I mean!" I flop back into the pillow, but pop back up when I hear a knock on the front door.

Jenner and I look at each other. My heart starts to pound. The knock comes again, this time louder.

Half-terrified and half-furious, I whisper, "Do you think it's Brad?"

Very droll, Jenner says, "I rather doubt it, darling, since he has a key. He's probably still picking bits of cartilage out of his teeth, anyway." As the knocking continues, Jenner sits up and looks toward the door. "Do you want me to get it?"

"Why are they knocking and not ringing the bell?" For some reason, that strikes me as an ominous sign. What kind of person would rather pound a fist on the door over and over than press a nice civilized button?

"I'll just go look through the peephole and see who it is."

Before I can protest, Jenner has glided out of the room. In a moment, his voice drifts down the hallway. "It appears to be a courier. Should I open up?"

A courier? More likely another member of the paparazzi trying to snap a candid picture of the senator's poor, cast-off daughter-in-law-to-never-be.

My curiosity gets the better of me. I trot barefoot to the front door in my ice cream–stained sweats and push Jenner aside so I can press my face against the door and look through the peephole.

Sure enough, it's a uniformed courier, holding a small envelope and a clipboard.

I whisper, "Do you think it's a trap? Like is that really a guy from TMZ and that clipboard is a camera?"

"Oh, yes," says Jenner, his voice dripping sarcasm. "The infamous clipboard camera. I hear they're all the rage these days."

"What about the guy yesterday who knocked on the door and said he was from the electric company but turned out to be a journalist from *The Examiner* wanting to know if the reports that I was suicidal were true?"

Jenner purses his lips. "You have a point."

"I know I do!"

Jenner sighs. "If this is a man trying to take your picture to sell to the tabloids, I'll divest him of his testicles. Happy?" He sweeps me out of the way and pulls open the door. "Hello. How may I help you?"

"Got a package for Miss DiSanto." The courier looks Jenner up and down. "That you?"

It would be a ridiculous question, but considering Jenner is wearing my fuzzy purple bathrobe and a long red wig I bought for Halloween a few years ago that he dug out of my closet, it's a legitimate question.

Jenner is prettier than most women I know. Strike that—*all* the women I know.

"Although that has a lovely ring to it," says Jenner, "I'm sorry to have to tell you that I'm not, in fact, Miss DiSanto." He points to me.

"Here is the lady in question." He pauses. "And I'm using the term *lady* loosely, mind you."

The courier thrusts the envelope at me. When I take it, he shoves the clipboard at me and says, "Sign on number twelve."

I sign, the courier leaves, and Jenner closes the door. Then I rip open the thin cardboard envelope and look inside. There's another envelope, this one square and ivory. On the outside my full name is written in scratchy black ink, the handwriting slanting and loopy.

Peering over my shoulder, Jenner says, "Ooh. Fancy. Do you think it's an invitation to a ball?"

"Ha." I tear open the glued flap, withdraw the piece of thick note paper inside, and read aloud, *"I have been unable to reach you. Come at once. Your father is gravely ill."*

The card flutters to the floor as I tear off down the hallway, headed for the phone.

On the best of days, San Francisco International Airport is a nightmare. But on the day you're desperately trying to get to Italy before your father dies, it's absolute hell.

By the time I'm smashed into my economy seat between a three-hundred-pound woman with a crying baby on her lap and a college student with a head cold and a tattoo on the back of his left hand that reads *Fuck the police*, I've been in a fender bender that almost made me miss the flight, been jostled by irate travelers and smacked by carry-ons too many times to count, and endured a grueling second-tier screening from a hostile TSA agent who seemed convinced I was hiding contraband in a bodily orifice.

The earliest flight out I could book has a layover in New York. When my flight arrives at JFK, I stumble bleary-eyed from the plane in search of coffee and extra-strength hand sanitizer.

Whatever bug that college student had, it produced a lot of phlegm.

I'm just about to get at the back of the long line at Starbucks when I spot a discreet silver plaque on the wall next to an elevator across the corridor from where I'm standing. It reads *Centurion Lounge*.

Sweet Jesus, it's an American Express members' lounge!

I run so fast to that elevator I almost trample a family of four in my rush. Ignoring the father's grumble of displeasure, I stab my finger on the elevator call button. My mouth salivates at the thought of the oasis of luxury and tranquility I'm about to enjoy, thanks to Satan.

My shiny new platinum card in the name of Mrs. Bradley Hamilton Wingate arrived in the mail only last week.

The woman at the check-in desk smiles pleasantly, sweeps the card through a reader to confirm I'm a member, then says, "Thank you for joining us, Mrs. Wingate. All food and beverages in the lounge are complimentary. You're welcome to take advantage of the massage and facial services offered in the private spa room near the back. Those are also complimentary."

I want to kiss her.

She tells me to enjoy my stay, and I wander out of the check-in area into a large, attractively decorated room. Seating areas, tables, and comfortable-looking chairs dot the carpeted floor. A bar dominates one end of the space. Beside it stretches a buffet where a few travelers browse, holding plates. Classical music plays softly on hidden speakers, and I'm in heaven.

I drop into a big comfy armchair beside the wall of windows that overlooks the runways. Onto the chair next to me, I deposit my carry-on, coat, and handbag. A smiling waitress approaches with a tray of drinks.

"Champagne, ma'am?"

"Yes, thank you." I take the flute from her hands with near-religious gratitude, like she's offered me the Holy Grail. I proceed to guzzle the contents in one go, then slump down in the chair and exhale a huge, exhausted sigh.

Which is when I spot him.

He's so breath-stealingly beautiful I think I must be hallucinating. That's literally my first thought when I glimpse the god striding toward the bar—*I'm hallucinating.* I must be, because not only is he masculine perfection personified, it appears he's moving in slow motion.

Either his beauty has changed the laws of physics or there was something funny in that champagne.

He's tall and dark haired, with that unstudied, aristocratic elegance certain men are born with. I decide he's European. I'm not sure which is more gorgeous, his face or his outfit. In stark contrast to all the other travelers in the lounge, who are dressed for comfort, he looks as if he stepped off a fashion show runway.

His bespoke navy blue suit is molded perfectly to his muscular body. The collar of his dress shirt is so white it glows, setting off the gorgeous olive hue of his skin. A cashmere overcoat the color of butterscotch hangs from his broad shoulders. I catch a glimpse of a silk pocket square, a chunky silver watch, and a pair of shoes that look made from the kind of buttery soft leather you want to rub your cheek against.

The urge to throw myself at his feet and nuzzle his loafers seizes me.

I watch as he approaches the bar and says something to the bartender. Polishing a glass, she turns, catches sight of him, and freezes. Her eyes bulge.

Euro Hunk must get that a lot.

He has to repeat himself twice before the poor woman finds the presence of mind to respond. Then she pours him a drink, hands it to him with a shaky hand and an even shakier smile, and starts blinking as if she's trying to signal someone for help.

I'd laugh, but I feel sorry for her. The man is too stunning for words, let alone rational behavior.

He takes a swallow of the amber liquid in his glass, then turns and sweeps his gaze over the room.

I quickly look away. Although I'm a pathetic jilted bride who's the laughingstock of the internet, I still have enough pride not to be caught drooling at a stranger.

No other female in sight has such scruples. I've never seen so many gaping people in my life. Even some of the men are staring in awe.

My fascination with Euro Hunk fizzles as fast as it came.

This guy makes Brad look like Homer Simpson—and Brad's gorgeous. So if Brad's ego and self-confidence were at stratospheric levels, I can't even imagine what a pompous, conceited ass Euro Hunk must be. He's probably got a woman in every city around the globe.

I decide I hate him.

Him and his perfect hair and his superhero's jaw and his stupid cashmere overcoat.

Who even wears one of those, anyway? What is he, a count? Actually, he does look like he could be a count. I bet he's totally entitled. I bet he has twelve mistresses and is cheap with his servants and beats his dog.

Like they do when I'm irritated, my lips pinch into the dried-prune shape that used to get on Brad's last nerve. When I look up again, Euro Hunk is staring straight at me with intense scrutiny.

Shit.

With as much nonchalance as I can muster, I turn to the chair beside mine and dig through my carry-on for my sketch pad and pencil. Without lifting my gaze above my lap, I start to sketch. It's something I've done since I was a little girl, and it never fails to calm and focus me.

Within moments, the lines of a beautiful gown are taking shape. Mermaid shaped, it's skin revealing but chic, with a low scoop back, elaborate crystal-and-seed-pearl embellishments on the shoulder straps and bodice, and a long French-lace train.

I stop abruptly, horrified to realize I'm drawing my own wedding dress.

From behind me, a man says, "*Che bella*. You're very talented."

God, his voice. My panties erupt into flames.

As rich and buttery soft as his shoes, his voice also has a slight Italian accent that manages to sound suave and sexual at the same time. I bet he could make me orgasm just by whispering the phone book in my ear.

But I hate him, so forget that.

I say coolly, "Thank you," and try to project a haughty don't-disturb-me-you-perfect-stupid-dog-beating-Euro-jerk vibe. It doesn't work.

"Are you an artist?"

"No."

"Hmm."

I keep sketching, ignoring him, waiting for him to walk away. He doesn't take the hint. I grow more and more uncomfortable as he stands watching my hand move over the page.

Why isn't he saying anything? Why doesn't he leave? What the hell is that delicious cologne he's wearing? Holy shit, is my mouth watering?

Cursing myself for my stupidity, I swallow and sketch faster.

"It needs ruching in the small of the back." He leans over my chair and taps his long, elegant finger on my sketch pad. "Here."

Though I was about to add the ruching—which the real dress has—I'm so aggravated by his presumption that I care about his opinion that I scribble a big ugly bow instead.

He chuckles.

The sound is so sexy all the tiny hairs on the back of my neck stand on end.

I stuff my sketch pad back into my carry-on, grab my handbag and coat, and launch myself from the chair. Without looking back, I head over to the bar and install myself on a stool, dropping all my stuff at my feet. I order an espresso from the bartender who was robbed of speech by Euro Hunk's beauty, then prop my elbows on the bar top and rest my aching head in my hands.

"I've offended you."

I jerk my head up. The Italian stallion stands beside me, gazing down at me with eyes the exact color of the water on the tiny island of Bali where I wanted to honeymoon with Brad—clear, brilliant aquamarine. They're rimmed with a thicket of lashes so lush and black I want to smack him.

He says, "How?"

I draw my eyebrows together, squinting at him because he's blinding me with his stupid, perfect face. Then he repeats himself, just in case my uterus didn't already explode.

"How have I offended you?"

Your beauty offends me. The effect you have on women offends me. The fact that you own a penis offends me. You, sir, are a man—the epitome *of a man—and therefore I hate your guts.*

I say, "I don't speak English," and drop my head back into my hands.

"Really?" he muses. "Odd—you seemed to understand me a few moments ago. Let me try again."

He repeats his question in French. Then German, then Italian, then Spanish. When I don't respond, he says it in a language I don't recognize but that could be Dutch.

Now he's just showing off.

I lift my head and level him with my most lethal stare. "I don't want to talk to you."

He doesn't even blink. "Ah. You are a lesbian."

"No, Count Egotistico, I'm not a lesbian! I'm just not in the mood for conversation, okay?"

"Okay." His gaze drops to my mouth, and his voice drops an octave. "What *are* you in the mood for?"

I want to be furious. I want to be outraged. I want to slap him across the face. However, a thermonuclear blast has detonated between my legs, so all I can do is stare at him for a moment as a scalding wave of heat envelops me, and my nipples start to tingle.

Finally, when his full, sculpted lips lift into a carnal smile—because he obviously sees the effect he's having on me—the anger I'd hoped for makes an appearance.

Holding his gaze, I say through gritted teeth, "You arrogant, stuck-up, cocky, self-important, sexist *peacock*. You wanna know what I'm in the mood for?" I lean closer to him. *"Murder."*

If I hoped that psychotic little speech would turn him off, I'm wrong. His eyes flare, his carnal smile turns absolutely filthy, and he produces another chuckle that makes the bartender, who's arrived with my espresso, emit a tiny gurgle of lust.

Staring intently into my eyes, he says softly, "Yes, *bella*. I want you, too."

THREE

For a moment, my mind wipes blank. If someone asked me my name, I wouldn't know it.

Then a light bulb goes on over my head, and I realize what's happening.

"Oh, I get it." My laugh is so acidic it could corrode steel. "You're hilarious, pal. Very funny." I peer at his silk pocket square. "Where's the camera hidden? In there? Or is it one of the buttons on your jacket?"

I lean into his chest and say deliberately to the top button on his suit, "Go fuck yourself."

He doesn't even have the good manners to look embarrassed that I've caught him. He simply watches me with a look of amusement in those blistering aquamarine eyes, like he's waiting to see what strange and adorable thing I'll do next.

I wave my hand dismissively. "Off with you. I don't have time for this shit."

"Which shit is that? Being desired by a man?"

I glare at him. Now I'm getting really mad. "Look. You've had your fun. You've got your pictures, or your video, now you can go back to whatever rock you crawled out from under and post all that crap online so everyone can laugh at me some more. And just for the record, I can't *believe* you'd stoop so low as to find out my itinerary and stalk me all the way to New York. I swear to God, if any of your buddies are waiting for me when I get off my next flight, I'll cut a bitch."

He cocks his head, studying me.

"Oh, you're going with the silent treatment? The last guy who did that to me ended up with a broken nose. You've been warned."

I chug my espresso, glaring over the rim of the tiny porcelain cup at the bartender, who never left and has been standing there the entire time, listening. She looks so scandalized that I've rebuffed Euro Hunk, I feel an explanation is in order. "He's a paparazzi," I tell her, jerking my chin at him.

He says calmly, "The word *paparazzi* is plural."

I breathe in and out slowly, gripping the cup so hard it might shatter. "So is the word *fists*."

Sliding onto the stool next to mine, he addresses the gaping bartender. "I'll take another Glenlivet, please. The lady will have another champagne."

The look on her face is priceless. Seriously, if I were Euro Hunk, I'd be taking pictures of her, not me.

She turns and walks away, leaving me alone with my choking anger and an Italian hell-bent on humiliating me.

"Wait." I look him over. "You're probably not even really Italian, are you?"

He smiles, showing off a set of perfect white teeth. Then he says something in Italian.

"That's not proof of anything. If I started speaking Mandarin right now, it wouldn't make me Chinese."

He lifts his dark brows. "You speak Mandarin?"

"That's not my point."

"So you'd like some other kind of proof?"

I narrow my eyes at the suggestive tone in his voice. "Short of a DNA test, there's nothing that can prove you're Italian."

"Of course there is."

Grinding my jaw, I say, "Okay. I'll play your silly little game. What would prove you're Italian?"

His voice drops an octave, and his blue eyes burn. "Have you ever made love with an Italian man?"

I roll my eyes and exhale. "Oh, for fuck's sake."

He gifts me with that insanely sexy chuckle again. "Exactly."

The bartender returns, sets our drinks down, then stands there looking at us eagerly. I'm surprised she doesn't pull up a chair. When I scowl at her, she moves two feet down the bar and pretends to polish the counter.

"So," says Euro Hunk, picking up his glass. "You're being followed by the paparazzi."

More games. This guy is unbelievable. "Let's just call them what they are: scum."

He brings the glass to his lips, tips back his head, and swallows. I watch his Adam's apple bob and fight the urge to lick it.

"Even scum has its uses."

I snort in disgust. "God, how do you sleep at night?"

"Like a baby, thank you."

I glare at his perfect profile, willing his head to explode. Unfortunately, I haven't recently gained any supernatural powers, so his dumb, pretty head stays intact.

He slides the flute of champagne toward me, giving me a good view of his watch as the cuff of his shirt rides up over his wrist. Brad is a watch whore—"timepieces," he insisted on calling his collection—so I've seen my fair share of ridiculously overpriced watches.

The one Euro Hunk sports makes Brad's look like kiddie prizes from a gumball machine.

"This is an interesting outfit you're wearing, Count. Pricey. Do you and your compatriots draw straws for the cashmere overcoat and the

Patek Philippe, or is there like a schedule for who gets to wear the rich playboy disguise when you're out stalking innocent people?"

Very seriously, he says, "I'm not a count."

"Hello! Obviously!"

"I'm a marchese."

His ruse is so stupid I can't resist baiting him. "What is that, like a cheese?"

His gaze drifts over my face, taking in all my features and my expression of disdain. With his eyes lingering on my mouth, he says, "It's one rank above an earl."

I say drily, "Ah yes. One rank above an earl. Good place to be, I suppose."

"It's also one rank below a duke, if that makes you feel any better."

"Oh, *much*." Fuming, I drink my champagne. *The nerve of this idiot, pretending to be a titled Italian supermodel. I should kick him in his balls.* "How did you get into this lounge, anyway? Bat your baby blues at the lady at the front desk? Give her the ol' razzle dazzle until her brain was a soggy mound of spaghetti? God, you must be really useful for all kinds of jobs. Hey—was it you who got past security at Paris Hilton's New Year's Eve party and got all those shots up her skirt?"

"You are very charming," he says in his formal English, smiling. "Very American. My mother would love you."

"Ha! I bet she would! Where is she, in a federal correctional facility?"

For the first time, his face wears an expression that isn't pleasant. He glowers at me, suddenly intimidating, and says something sharply in Italian.

"Sorry, I didn't get that."

"I said, *'Do not disrespect my mother.'*"

Astonished, I stare at him for a moment before bursting into laughter. "Well, you're dedicated to your job, I'll give you that. You know, you should go into acting. Or modeling! You could make bank. My best friend is a male model, and it's *ridiculous* how much—"

"Why are you sad?"

He might as well have stabbed me in the heart with a dagger for how much that hurts. My laughter dies, my throat closes, and the hot prick of tears comes to my eyes.

"That's just mean," I whisper. "That's just downright mean of you."

"I'm sorry, I don't understand—"

"Leave me alone. Go away."

I can't bear to look at him, so I stare at the tiny bubbles rising in my flute of champagne instead.

After a moment, he quietly exhales, then rises. He murmurs another apology before walking away.

I can't believe I even spoke a word to him. He probably has the entire conversation on tape. These ruthless bastards have been following me for months, ever since my engagement to Brad was announced. "Kimberella Gets Her Prince," one article sneered. The plucky, penniless seamstress marrying American royalty, the golden son of a political dynasty.

Yeah, it's a real Cinderella story all right. Except her prince wasn't being forced by his father to marry on the threat of losing his inheritance.

But the worst part, the absolute heart-smashing, soul-killing part, is that everyone knew but me.

Everyone knew he gambled, and ran up huge debts on his father's credit, and had women all over town. Everyone knew he was the biggest threat to his father's political career and the family's good name, and everyone knew Daddy had given him an ultimatum.

Get married and settle down or be cut off.

How convenient for Brad that I was so trusting and blind. And so desperately in love with him. I made it all so easy.

Not everyone was convinced of my innocence, however. Several online articles theorized I knew all about Brad's problems and had swooped in like a vulture to pick at the helpless corpse of his playboy days while stuffing my pockets with his money.

As if I cared about his money. When I think of all the times I told him I loved him and he'd mumbled, "You too," and looked away, it makes me sick.

Screw love. And screw *men*. From now on, I'm focusing on work. But first I have to get to Italy.

"No. That can't be right. I have to be on this flight."

"I'm so sorry, ma'am. Unfortunately, the flight was oversold. Your seat has been given to another passenger. There's really nothing I can do."

The woman in the red vest at the gate looks apologetic, I'll give her that. But if she thinks I'm going to let her and her airline bump me off this flight, she's nuts.

I lean over the counter and say emphatically, "You're not listening to me. I *have* to be on this flight."

"We can put you on standby for the next flight, which is . . ." She checks her computer screen. "Tomorrow at ten o'clock."

"*Tomorrow?* Are you kidding me?"

For the first time in the few minutes since I was called over the loudspeaker to approach the gate agent, she begins to look uncomfortable.

Reaching under the counter, she says, "Here's a pamphlet regarding your rights—"

"I don't want your pamphlet. I want my seat."

She holds the folded paper out like a peace offering. "We can offer you denied boarding compensation in the form of cash, check, or vouchers for a future flight, but I cannot get you on *this* flight. I'm sorry."

Sweat dampens my underarms. My heart starts to thump, and my pulse skyrockets. Trying to maintain a demeanor of calm so I don't get arrested by airport security, I say, "You don't understand. My father is dying. If I have to wait until tomorrow to get on a flight to Italy, he might already be dead when I get there."

She loses patience with me and turns curt. "Miss, I have other customers I have to assist. I really can't do anything for you except what I've already offered."

I think it's being demoted from "ma'am" to "miss" that makes me snap. Or maybe it's everything else I've been through over the past few days. Either way, I grip the edge of the counter and thunder, *"My father is dying! I have to be on that flight!"*

"I understand you're frustrated—"

"No, I'm not frustrated, I'm angry! How can you just arbitrarily throw me off this plane? I paid for my ticket like everyone else! It's not fair!"

Her face flushes red. I feel bad for her because it's not her fault the airline oversold the flight, but it is her job to deal with irate customers, and it's also her job to make other arrangements for those irate customers when they're getting fucked in the ass by her employer.

Besides, she's the one who wanted a job at this dickish airline. If she wanted to avoid awkward confrontations with distraught customers, she could've been a dog trainer.

"You need to bump someone else off this flight—someone whose father didn't suffer a massive heart attack in another country! There has to be some kind of consideration for emergency situations, right?"

When her gaze turns stony, I plead, *"Right?"*

"Please step away from the counter, miss."

I become aware of all the people in the gate waiting area, staring at me, at the same time I become aware of the security guard eyeing me from his post beside the boarding door.

My anger turns to panic. *Shit. This can't be happening!* My voice wavering and my eyes filling with tears, I say, "Please. I'm begging you. I haven't seen my father in five years. He's the only family I have left. I have to be there for him. I have to get on this flight. If he dies and I'm not there, I'll never forgive myself."

The gate agent opens her mouth to shut me down, but a voice behind me says, "The lady can have my seat."

I don't have to turn around to know who it is. I'd recognize that panty-melting accent anywhere.

Plus, the gate agent looks as if she's been electrocuted.

"Oh, s-sir, that's very kind of you. Are you sure?" She glances at me and frowns, clearly thinking I don't deserve to even stand in Euro Hunk's general vicinity, let alone be the recipient of this magnanimous gesture.

"I'm sure."

He moves into view, coming around my left side to stand next to me. His arm brushes my shoulder, sending a rash of goose bumps cascading down my spine.

"Let me see if I can arrange it. We do allow transfers in some cases. May I have your boarding pass, please?"

Gazing down at me with a small smile, he pulls a boarding pass from the inside pocket of his overcoat and hands it to the gate agent, all without glancing away from my face.

In a strangled voice, I ask, "You're on this flight?"

He inclines his head in a kingly nod.

"You're not a paparazzi?"

"A paparazzo," he corrects. "Not the last time I checked."

I turn to face him fully. "And, um, the count thing—"

"Marchese." His eyes are bright with laughter. "No, it's not a cheese."

I put a hand over my chest and breathe, "Oh my God, I'm so sorry."

"Sir," chirps the gate agent.

Our gazes hold for a moment that feels like an eternity until he looks away from me and turns his attention to her. "Yes?"

"This is a first-class ticket."

I look at her in shock. She stares back at me with her brows lifted, like *We both know you don't deserve first class, sister.*

"Yes, it is," says Euro Hunk firmly. "Is there a problem?"

She looks at me, then back at him, then plasters a big fake smile on her face. "Not at all, sir. Your identification, please?"

He fishes a passport from another pocket of his coat and hands it over.

"Madam, may I have your boarding pass and identification again, please?" The gate agent smiles sweetly at me.

Unbelievable. I've been promoted to "madam."

In total disbelief, I watch the gate agent tap away on her keyboard, changing the reservations so I can get on the flight. I turn to find Euro Hunk gazing at me with that same laserlike intensity he had when I glanced up from my sketch pad and caught him staring.

I say, "I can't let you do this."

"Of course you can."

"It's a wonderful gesture, but that ticket must've cost a fortune."

The gate agent decides it's time to be helpful. "The full fare for a first-class nonstop flight to Florence is $10,608."

My jaw comes unhinged and hangs somewhere in the middle of my chest.

Euro Hunk sees my horror and tries to make me feel better. "That's the round-trip fare."

"I'm sorry, but there's no way I can pay you back for that. As much as I'd love to accept your generous offer, I can't."

He tilts his head as if he's considering something. His gaze drops to my carry-on. "Your sketch pad."

"What?" I'm so startled I say it too loudly, causing the gate agent to jump.

"Your sketch pad. I'll take it in trade for the ticket."

He says that like it's a completely rational thing to barter a $10,000 ticket for and he fully expects me to hand it over without another thought. But what he doesn't know is that my sketch pad doesn't contain the doodles of a hobbyist.

It contains the designs for my entire spring collection, which I was going to begin work on as soon as I returned from my honeymoon.

The honeymoon might be off, but the collection isn't—and I haven't yet scanned the images into my computer.

Which means that if I give Euro Hunk my sketch pad, those designs are gone forever.

I tighten my grip on my carry-on and pull it behind my back. "That's impossible."

A flash of irritation darkens his eyes, but they quickly regain their tropical-water tranquility. I can tell he isn't used to hearing *no*, but he does his best to cover it up with a tight smile.

"I see. Best of luck with your father." He turns his attention to the gate agent, who's watching our interaction as avidly as the bartender did. "It seems I won't be needing to transfer the ticket after—"

"Wait." Panicked, I grab a handful of his plush coat sleeve.

He looks down at me with a brow arched condescendingly.

"Why would you want the pad? Isn't there something else I can give you?"

When his carnal smile makes a reappearance, I know how bad that sounded. I quickly backtrack. "That wasn't a proposition."

"No? Pity."

We stare at each other, our gazes locked. The heat in his eyes is unmistakable. With a sinking feeling in my chest, I realize I have to make a choice between prostituting myself and losing my spring collection.

My panic turns into full-blown hysteria.

Inside my body, a tug-of-war breaks out between my hormones, my brain, and my moral compass, which—if I'm being totally honest—is the first one to lose the fight.

So it's logic versus hormones who commence a death match, while my uterus cheers on from the sidelines, waving pom-poms and jumping up and down in glee.

Logic tells me that I've been giving away my cookie for *free* for years to Brad with nothing to show for it. No, wait—those are my sneaky hormones, who are clearly on the side of Euro Hunk. What logic is *actually* telling me is that the flight is only moments away from boarding. If Euro Hunk wants some nookie, he'd probably settle for a quick blowie in a men's room stall. There's simply not enough time for anything else.

My hormones scream in happiness at the thought, but logic tells them sourly that if Euro Hunk is the kind of man who'd accept a blowie from a stranger in an airport restroom, he's most likely riddled with STDs.

Team Hormones reminds me that there will be a condom machine in the men's room.

Team Logic reminds me I could probably reconstruct the designs from memory. If not perfectly, enough to get by.

Team Hormones says yeah, *but just look at him.* His penis is probably as glorious as the rest of his body. He'd be doing us both a favor, sweetheart, *and* you'd get your sorry ass on that flight.

Team Logic sighs and reminds me that although my moral compass recused itself, I'd feel dirty and used, and haven't I had enough of that already this week?

I expel a huge gust of air, release Euro Hunk's cashmere sleeve from my death grip, and unzip my carry-on. I present him with the sketch pad with both hands, like the precious gift it is.

"Here. Take it. Nothing is worth missing this flight."

Not even the sight of your glorious penis.

He examines my face in silence for a beat, then takes the pad from my hands. He starts to flip through it. Distracted, he instructs the gate agent, "Carry on."

She shakes her head as if she can't believe this shit, either, and recommences typing into her computer.

"These are incredible," murmurs Euro Hunk, admiring a page with a drawing of an elegant one-shoulder crimson gown, the kind a sophisticated woman might wear to a formal party. The model's body is loosely sketched, but I spent a lot of time on the detail of the dress. It seems to leap from the page. I can almost hear the sigh of silk as the skirt sways around the model's legs.

"Yeah, well, they're yours now, so enjoy."

I try to keep the bitterness out of my voice when I say that because I'm getting what I wanted after all. I won't have to wait until tomorrow to get on another flight, and hopefully that will translate into getting to my father's bedside before the unthinkable happens.

"Just out of curiosity, why did you want them?"

Euro Hunk glances up at me. His mouth takes on a ruthless slant. "I'm an avid collector."

I frown at him. "Of sketch pads?"

His hesitation is split-second, so short I probably imagine it.

"Of art."

I'm flattered he thinks my drawings qualify as art, but I'm also crushed I've lost the sketch pad, and I'm also filled with gratitude that he's giving up his seat for me, and I'm also confused about how much I'd simultaneously like to kiss him and punch him in the face. So I'm not able to offer more of a response than a defeated, "Huh."

"Okay, we're all set!"

The gate agent's smile stretches from ear to ear. She hands me my ID and a new boarding pass. "I need both of you to sign these release forms, please. And I've just checked you in, madam, so you can go ahead and board. Right through those doors."

"Thanks." I sign on the paper where she indicates, then take the boarding pass and turn to Euro Hunk. "And thank you. Sincerely. This is really amazing." I add sheepishly, "And sorry again about my behavior in the AmEx lounge."

"If you really want to make it up to me, give me your phone number."

That stops me cold. He waits through my hesitation with eagle-sharp eyes, his impatience palpable. Not only is he a man who doesn't often hear *no*, he obviously doesn't have to wait for things, either.

Because he's aristocracy. An Italian marchese, a.k.a. the Big Cheese.

Who probably has twelve mistresses, is cheap with his servants, and beats his dog.

I go back to hating him with the speed of two fingers snapping.

"Sure," I say graciously, smiling. "Do you have a pen?"

He whisks out a silver Mont Blanc from his suit-jacket pocket while I hunt for a scrap of paper in my purse. Then I scribble my digits on the paper with my name underneath.

Well, not *my* name and number. I don't know who the number belongs to, but the name belongs to a woman who knows how to put a philandering asshole in his place.

FOUR

Matteo

I watch her walk through the glass doors of the boarding gate and down the gangway until she disappears around a bend. I'm not surprised when she doesn't look back.

I don't know why her foul mouth and dismissive attitude please me so much, but they do.

Go fuck yourself, she told me.

No one has ever spoken to me with such disrespect in my life.

It matters little that she thought I was a paparazzo at the time. I could be the king of Spain in coronation robes for all she'd care.

Che palle. The balls on that woman. I know *mafiosi* more meek.

I didn't know about the bad attitude when I first saw her, though. It wasn't her smart mouth that had me sucking in a breath.

It was that hair. Black, thick, pin straight, cascading like a brushstroke over one shoulder. That mouth. Red as a fucking strawberry. That milk-pale skin. Her colors were so vivid. So much contrast. It took me a moment to take her all in.

Then she looked up, caught me staring, and pinned me in place with the force of her gaze.

I've never seen eyes like hers. Green as the finest jade and canted up at the corners, like a cat's.

Yes, that's it exactly. She reminds me of a Siamese cat. Sleek and haughty. A sinuous walk and needle-sharp nails and teeth made to crunch bones.

Which made the pain she was so obviously in that much more interesting.

I'm not a man drawn to damsels in distress. I find weak women supremely boring. But the combination of tough talk and soft under-belly gave me an erection the likes of which I haven't had in years. Walking away from her at the bar after she told me to leave her alone was painful.

Literally. My cock throbbed so hard it felt like a medical emergency.

I imagined my hand was that strawberry mouth as I jerked myself to an unsatisfactory climax in the men's room.

Assuming our brief encounter would be our last, I was thrilled to see her at the gate of my outbound flight. Then not so thrilled when I heard the desperation in her voice as she begged the scowling woman behind the counter for help.

"My father is dying. I have to be there for him. If he dies and I'm not there, I'll never forgive myself."

It was the last part that gripped my heart and made me offer my seat. Because if anyone knows the lingering shame of that particular situation, it's me.

So I stepped in.

And she gave me those cat eyes again.

But this time she gave me something even more powerful.

Inspiration.

As the plane I was supposed to be on backs slowly away from the gate, I press a button on my cell phone. After a few rings, my right-hand man, Antonio, answers the phone at the atelier in Florence.

"Si."

In Italian, I say, "I have good news."

A relieved curse, followed by an exhalation. "You hired a new designer?"

I tap my finger against the cover of the sketch pad. A satisfied smile curves the corners of my mouth. The plane switches directions and pulls down the runway, picking up speed. "Something like that."

Antonio's silence echoes with questions, but he knows better than to ask if I don't offer answers.

"Tell everyone to be ready to get to work as soon as I'm back. Ciao."

I disconnect, then dial the number I've already memorized. Intending to leave a voice mail for my raven-haired siren to hear when she lands, I'm startled when the line is picked up by a man with a rough Brooklyn accent and a hacking cough.

"Yeah? Who's this?"

I don't like his voice. Or the strange feeling in the pit of my stomach. I snap, "This is Matteo, Signor Marchese Moretti. Who is *this*?"

A boozy cackle comes over the line. "Who, me? I'm the Baron von fuckin' Trapp, bro."

"Are you related to Miss Bobbitt?"

"Who?"

I grit my teeth. "Lorena Bobbitt. Does she live there?"

The man on the other end of the phone becomes belligerent. "Is this some kinda fuckin' joke, bro? You makin' a prank call? 'Cause I'll put my fist right through this phone and rip off ya fuckin'—"

"Sir!" I snap, livid. "Do you know the lady or not?"

He barks out a laugh. "Yeah, I know her. Everybody knows the broad who cut off her husband's dick while he was sleepin', bro. Hey— is this bein' recorded? Am I on the radio?" He shouts into the background, "Angie, I'm on the radio!"

I hang up, so angry my ears are hot. I type the name Lorena Bobbitt into the web browser on my phone, then read the Wikipedia article in astonishment.

Apparently my Siamese cat has a very dark sense of humor to go along with her smart mouth.

After a moment of shock, I throw back my head and laugh out loud.

Then I book the next flight to Florence, excitement building, and try to put the alluring stranger I'll never see again out of my mind. I've got the House of Moretti's spring collection to start working on.

Stroking the cover of the sketch pad, I smile. *And what a collection it will be.*

FIVE

KIMBER

As soon as the flight lands in Florence and I've collected my luggage, I take a taxi straight to the hospital, urging the driver to go faster so many times he curses at me. I check my voice mail on the way, hoping there won't be a message from Dominic. It was my father's oldest and closest friend who sent me the letter via courier to tell me the terrible news, and I know if he called again while I was on the plane, it would be more bad news.

Luckily, he didn't. I pick up messages from Danielle and Jenner, both telling me to call them when I get settled, then freeze when I hear Brad's voice on the next.

"Hey, Kimber. Uh, it's me. Can you, uh, call me when you get a chance? We need to talk."

Mother. Plucker.

Hearing his voice makes me so furious I almost throw my cell phone out the taxi window. I stick my head out and suck in a few deep breaths of warm Italian air instead.

It's the first time he's tried to reach me since our Hindenburg wedding. He's probably calling to find out when I'll have my things cleared out of the apartment. He can damn well wait. If I'm not back in San Fran by the first, I'll charge another month's rent on his blasted platinum card.

At the information desk inside the hospital, I ask a sleepy-looking staffer to direct me toward my father's room. He points down a hallway and yawns, and that's the end of our conversation. Weighed down by my luggage and a dark sense of doom, I hurry down the hall toward the room.

When I burst through the door, the first thing I see is Dominic slumped in a chair beside my father's bed. His head is bent. His lips move silently in prayer as he fingers the rosary in his hands. He looks up, catches sight of me, and leaps to his feet with open arms.

"Tesoro!"

I haven't seen him in five years, but his craggy face is as familiar to me as my own. His hair is completely white now, and his shoulders are rounded, but even in his mideighties, he retains his joyous energy.

I drop all my luggage inside the door, then run to Dominic and hug him as he kisses my hair. "God, it's good to see you," I whisper, squeezing him tight. "You haven't changed a bit."

In heavily accented English, Dominic says, "Eh, you're lying to an old man. But I forgive you. It's so good to see you, too. If only it were under happier circumstances."

When we break apart, we smile at each other for a moment. Then I turn my gaze to my father, lying motionless in the bed. He's thin, almost as white as the bedsheets that cover him, and hooked up to too many machines to count.

Tears springing to my eyes, I cover my mouth with my hand and grip Dominic's arm for support. "My God, he looks dead already!"

Dominic says quietly, "I think he's only been holding on for you to arrive."

I start to shake. The acid sting of bile rises in the back of my throat, and I have to swallow before I can speak. "There's nothing the doctors can do?"

Dominic's bright eyes are filled with sadness. "I'm so sorry, *tesoro*. His heart was irreparably damaged. The doctors are surprised he's made it this long. He could go at any moment."

A small cry of horror passes my lips. My legs shaking, I move to the side of the bed and take my father's cold, limp hand in mine. I whisper hoarsely, "Dad? Papa, can you hear me?"

My only answer is the heart monitor's faint, erratic beep.

Dominic drags a chair to me and motions for me to sit. I'm thankful because I'm not sure how much longer I can stand. I sink into the chair and fight the tears that threaten to crest my lower lids. I dash them away, determined to be brave.

Now isn't the time to cry. Not while his heart is still beating. There will be plenty of time for tears later.

Dominic rests his hand on my shoulder. He says softly, "Have you eaten?"

I shake my head, my gaze never leaving my father's face.

"I'll get you something." He tiptoes out of the room. In a while, he returns with a cold sandwich and coffee from a vending machine.

I unwrap the plastic around the sandwich, but the smell of meat turns my stomach. I place it on the little table beside me and tell Dominic I'll eat it later. I try the coffee, but can only get a sip past my lips.

Then we sit in silence, listening to the machines whirr and chirp, until he clears his throat. "Kimber, there's something you should know."

I glance at him sharply, worried by this new tone in his voice that portends more bad news. "What is it?"

"Your father . . ." He looks guilty, as if he's about to disclose a terrible secret.

My worry zooms closer to panic. I sit up straighter in my chair. "*My father* what?"

Dominic takes a breath, then meets my eyes. "He recently remarried."

My mouth opens, but no sound comes out. I stare at him in cold shock, all my limbs frozen. Finally, I find my tongue and say accusingly, "He would've told me."

Dominic shakes his head. "He didn't want to take any attention away from your wedding. He knew how excited you were, how long you'd waited, how busy you were with all the plans. He thought it would be better until after you returned from your honeymoon to tell you."

I'm horrified by that. "My God, am I that self-centered? My own father feels like he can't share his good news with me because I'll throw a tantrum?"

"No, *tesoro*," says Dominic gently. "It's not like that at all. You know better."

He's right. I do. My father thinks the sun shines out of my ass. I'm his pride and joy. He brags to anyone who'll listen about his daughter in America: what a success I am, what a genius with a needle, what a head for business.

All vast exaggerations, but he's always been my biggest champion. Even though the love of his life died giving birth to me, he's always made me feel like the world's most precious jewel.

"So I have a . . . stepmother." I try the word out hesitantly. It's got a lot of baggage, that word. I lift my head and stare at Dominic. "Where is she? Why isn't she here?"

Dominic's expression turns pained. "She's at the house with the girls."

I'm startled. "Girls? What girls?"

Dominic clears his throat again, like he does when he's nervous. He fidgets in his seat. "Cornelia and Beans."

Boom! goes that second bomb he just dropped in my lap. It's even more shocking than the stepmother one. I've always wanted a sister— and now I have two? And one of them is named *Beans*?

I try to think of anything to say, but can't. In the space of seconds, I've gained three new family members. I close my eyes, rub my temples, and draw a long breath, gathering my thoughts.

"Okay. This is good. This is *weird*, but it's good." I look at Dominic. "You know what? I'm really happy about this. He's been alone too long. It's great that he finally found someone. I just wish I would've known sooner. I would've come out for the wedding—"

"It was sudden," interrupts Dominic, slanting a look toward my father. "He didn't tell anyone it was happening." His gaze flashes back to mine, quiet anger kindling in his eyes.

"Not even you?"

Dominic shakes his head. "They were married at the town hall with no family or friends."

"What? That's crazy! How did he meet this woman?"

"She came into the shop and introduced herself."

There's a cynical undertone beneath the words *she introduced herself* that suggests cold calculation on her part, as if she were out husband hunting. The dislike in his voice is so obvious I'm taken aback by it. I can't imagine my father would marry anyone Dominic didn't like. The two men are so close in personality they're almost brothers. "So what's her deal?"

Dominic looks again at my father. He hesitates a moment, then stands and goes to a small desk near the restroom. He finds a piece of paper and scribbles something on it, then silently hands it to me.

The note reads *She is a barracuda.*

When I look up at him, he puts a finger to his lips and shakes his head.

He doesn't want to say anything negative about my new stepmother in front of my father, even when he's unconscious.

"I see." I fold the note, my stomach turning. "We'll discuss it more later."

He nods, then smoothly changes the subject. "Have you checked into your hotel?"

"Hotel? I planned to stay at the house." When Dominic grimaces, the sick feeling in my stomach gets worse. "But that was before I knew it would be so crowded." *With barracuda.*

Shit.

My sickness quickly turns to anger. If my father made the mistake of marrying a terrible woman who doesn't even have enough feeling for him to be at his bedside as he's about to die, I'm sure as hell not going to let her keep me away from the house I was born in. There's plenty of room for all us fish to swim in that bowl.

What eats barracuda? Killer whales? Yeah, I'm gonna be a killer whale. Here, fishie-fishie.

Watching me go through my mental gymnastics, Dominic smiles. "You're so much like her," he murmurs.

"Who?"

"Your mother." He makes the sign of the cross of his chest. "God rest her precious soul."

Tears leap back into my eyes as if they're spring-loaded. I swipe them angrily away, sniffing. "I wish I would've known her."

"She was a very loving, patient woman, but she had the heart of a lion." Dominic's eyes glimmer with moisture. "Your grandmother was the same way. Lionhearted. And the stories I've heard about your great-grandmother . . ." He chuckles and kisses his fingertips. "Fantastico."

I leap to my feet and start to pace at the foot of the bed, wrapping my arms around myself to ward off my sudden chill. "I need to talk to the doctor."

"I'll let the nurse know." He stands, giving me a wink. "I've asked her for a date half a dozen times, but she always tells me she has a boyfriend. Ladies in their sixties are such teases."

He leaves, patting me on the shoulder as he goes. As soon as the door closes behind him, a soft, scratchy voice says, "Kimberly."

I whirl around. My father's eyes are open. He's looking at me with a faint smile and a faraway look, like he's viewing me through a crystal ball from some distant, magical place.

"Papa!" I run to his bedside and collapse onto his chest, bursting into tears as soon as his hand rests on my head.

"Shh. Hush now, my angel. Everything is all right."

I lift my head and gaze at my father, his face swimming because of my tears. I whisper, "I'm so sorry."

Smiling dreamily, he strokes my hair. "There's nothing to be sorry for."

I cry, "But I haven't seen you in so long! I haven't been here for you—"

"You were living your life, angel," he interrupts. "Just as you should." His eyes drift shut, and he releases a soft, ragged breath, as if the conversation has exhausted him.

"I'll get the doctor!"

I start to move, but my father grips my wrist with surprising strength. His eyes fly open, and the look in them is sharper, more focused. For some reason that strikes a chord of terror deep in my heart.

"No. It's too late for doctors. Listen to me now, angel. I have something important to tell you." He pulls me closer, his breath leaving his chest in a wheeze.

"Papa, please, don't talk! Let me get the doctor—"

"Your mother was the love of my life."

I break down and start to sob, resting my forehead on my father's frail chest and clutching the cold bedsheets. I can't bear to listen, because I know deep in my bones that whatever he's about to tell me will be the last words he'll ever speak.

"From the day we met, I never looked at another woman. No one could compare. When she died, my heart became a wasteland where nothing could grow. You were the only thing that brought me joy, angel. The only thing that kept me going."

I cry and cry, unable to stop the flow of tears.

"But life is strange." His chuckle is faint, so faint I barely hear it. "Just when you think you've got it figured out, it throws you a curveball to make sure you know you're not the one making the decisions."

He strokes my hair off my face and smiles at my wet cheeks. "I found love again, angel. In the winter of life, this old man found love."

I lift my head and blink, tears streaming down my face and dripping from my chin. "I'm happy for you, Papa."

He nods, his eyes gaining that faraway look again. "I knew you would be. And I know you'll love her as I do." He draws a breath for strength, then focuses all his energy on his next words. "Just remember: nothing worthwhile is easy. That goes for everything. The easier it comes, the easier it goes. The truly valuable things and people will always test your mettle, but every bit of pain will be worth it in the end. Don't give up when something is difficult. Dig in your heels."

A delicate tremor runs through his chest. He closes his eyes, and he seems to sink down farther into the mattress, as if all his muscles have lost their fight against gravity. He gives my wrist one final, weak squeeze. A sigh slips past his lips. His mouth goes slack, as do his fingers on my arm.

Terror devours me. I whisper, "Papa?"

The heart monitor emits a long, flat electronic tone.

I scream, *"Papa?"*

Dominic and the doctor run into the room, but my father is already gone.

SIX

Hours later, after they've taken away my father's body and I've completed all the necessary paperwork, Dominic helps me out to his car and drives me to my father's house as I weep against the window, looking out into the starry night.

I'm an orphan now. No father, no mother, no other family except two stepsisters who are complete strangers and a stepmother who couldn't be bothered to be there for Papa in his final moments.

When Dominic tells me she never came to the hospital at all, I want to curl my hands around her throat and choke the life right out of the uncaring witch. She should've married Brad. They'd have been a far better match than she and my loving, sweet-tempered father.

Il Sogno, our family's ancestral villa, was built in the fifteenth century by an intrepid DiSanto who'd made a small fortune in textiles, then promptly lost it once construction was completed. Every other DiSanto who's inherited the place has suffered from the same bad financial luck, my father included. If you knew nothing about my family, you'd assume we were wealthy based on the majesty of our property alone.

But, as with so many things, appearances can be deceiving.

Boasting classical Italian gardens, a reflecting pool, and spectacular views of Florence, Il Sogno lies on a hill above the city while going about the business of quietly crumbling into ruins. When we round the bend of the long gravel drive and I catch a glimpse of the stately old building, I'm breathless with the realization that my father won't be running out from the front door to greet me like he always did when I arrived on my summer breaks from school.

For a moment the pain is so huge I can't breathe.

Then Dominic parks the car, shuts off the engine, and turns to me with a somber face.

"I'll come in with you," he says darkly, as if he's carrying a concealed firearm we might find ourselves in need of.

This stepmother of mine must be something else.

Gravel crunching underfoot, we trudge past the row of cypress trees that lines the driveway until we're standing in front of the tall wooden doors of the main house. I apply my knuckles to the wood, then we wait in silence unbroken except for the singing of crickets and a breeze whispering through the trees.

Finally, footsteps echo from inside the house. Unhurried, they grow closer. Then the door swings open to reveal a man I've never seen before.

He's tall, salt and pepper haired, impeccably dressed in a dark suit and tie. He appears wide awake, though it's after midnight. We obviously didn't wake him.

He bows slightly, says, "*Buonasera*, Signor Dominic," then turns his gaze to me. His eyes are an unusual shade of gray, like an overcast sky. With one swift up-and-down look, he takes me in. Then, in perfect English, he says, "And you must be the beautiful daughter your father so loves."

I burst into tears.

Sighing, Dominic settles his arm around my shoulder and gives me a squeeze. "Si, Lorenzo. This is Luca's daughter, Kimber. We've just come from the hospital."

Even through my tears I see the look that passes between the two men. When Lorenzo's face turns ashen, I decide not to dislike him as much as I already dislike my stepmother.

He crosses himself, murmuring, *"Mio Dio."* Then he waves us inside, stepping back quickly to open the door wider so we can pass. "Come in, come in. Let me help you with your luggage."

As Lorenzo takes my handbag and coat, he and Dominic have a quick, quiet discussion in Italian that must have something to do with the sleeping arrangements because at the end of it, Lorenzo says, "I'll make up the spare bedroom."

"Spare bedroom" is a running joke in the family. Il Sogno has ten bedrooms originally made to house the founder's large family, only three of which remain in use—a master suite and two smaller adjacent bedrooms on the main floor. All the other sleeping quarters are on the second floor, which was closed off years ago to save on cleaning and heating costs. Aside from overstuffed sofas and many uncomfortable, stiff-backed chairs, the only other place to sleep in the house is in the small, stuffy, windowless "spare bedroom," on a cot.

In the attic.

"What?" I say, dazed with grief. "No—I'll sleep in my old bedroom."

When Dominic and Lorenzo both freeze, I know before anyone says a word what's happened.

Lorenzo delicately clears his throat. "Ahem. Unfortunately, that's not possible, signorina, as that room is now occupied by Cornelia."

I'm stunned. My father gave my bedroom away.

My bedroom.

My face flushes so hot I feel it all the way to the roots of my hair. "Well, I'm not sleeping in the attic. Give me some blankets, and I'll be fine on the drawing room sofa for the night. I'll check into a hotel tomorrow."

Lorenzo makes another polite bow, murmuring apologies. When he leaves with my luggage, headed toward the drawing room at the back of the house, Dominic says, "It's not your father's fault." He sends me a pointed look. "He didn't have a choice."

I grind my back teeth together so hard they're in danger of shattering. *The wicked stepmother strikes again.* "So this Lorenzo is what—the house man?"

"Majordomo," replies Dominic. "At least that's what the marchesa calls him."

"Who's the marchesa?"

"Your father's new wife."

I'm dumbfounded. "She's *aristocracy*?"

"From what I understand, she comes from a titled but impoverished background." He waves a hand dismissively. "You know how it is in Europe, *tesoro*. There are as many destitute barons and counts as there are churches. Many of the old aristocratic families lost their fortunes, but no matter how poor you become, you get to keep the title." He adds sourly, "It impresses people who don't know any better."

"I know you want to add *like Americans*, but I'll have you know I met an aristocrat in New York and *wasn't* impressed."

Dominic pats my hand. "That's because you have a good head on your shoulders. Now let's get you settled so you can get some rest. You're going to need it."

With those ominous words ringing in my ears, I follow, exhausted and heartbroken, as he leads me deeper into the house.

I awaken hot and disoriented with a crick in my neck and a massive headache throbbing between my ears. I roll to my other side, open my eyes, and come nose to nose with an enormous black dog sitting on the floor next to the sofa.

Unmoving, unblinking, it stares down at me with a hungry look, as if it's about to crack open its massive jaws and gobble me up.

I scream.

Startled, the dog jumps, then scrambles backward clownishly, its big paws fumbling and flapping against the floor. Then it turns around and streaks from the room, ears flattened, tail tucked, whining.

Apparently, I scared it as much as it scared me.

My heart pounding, I throw off the blanket and sit up. It's still early. Sunlight streams through the windows and illuminates the polished wood floor to a blinding glow. Rising, I scrub my hands over my face and walk through the quiet house until I reach the kitchen, where I find Lorenzo sitting at the big wood table, sipping espresso and reading the papers. He's in another impeccable suit, this one charcoal gray. I wonder if he ever sleeps or if he just changes clothes and keeps working.

"Good morning." I yawn, taking a seat across from him at the table.

"Ah, good morning, signorina." He folds the paper and sets it beside his cup of espresso, then looks me up and down in that swift assessing way he has that suggests he never misses a thing. "What can I get you? Espresso? Eggs? Some toast and jam, perhaps?"

"You don't have to wait on me, Lorenzo."

He rises, smiling. "But it's my pleasure." He chuckles. "Also it's my job."

"In that case, I'll take an espresso."

I watch him walk across the kitchen to the sleek black coffee machine on the opposite counter. There's an economy in the way he moves, as if no energy is wasted, no step taken that isn't planned. He exudes efficiency. He must've been a godsend for my messy, scatter-brained father.

Papa.

I bite the inside of my cheek so I don't break down into tears, then struggle to compose myself as Lorenzo brews the espresso. By the time he sets the little white porcelain cup in front of me, I've regained most of my control, but my voice still comes out shaky.

"Thank you."

"You're welcome." He takes his seat across from me again, folds his hands, then simply gazes at me in silence.

"What?"

"Forgive me for staring, signorina. It's just that I feel as if I already know you. Your father spoke of you so often, I feel as if we're old friends."

Shit. I start to get choked up again and have to look away and blink hard to clear the water from my eyes. I gulp the espresso, wincing as it scalds my tongue. "How long did you work for my father, Lorenzo?"

"Since the marchesa and he were married, in June."

It's August. My father kept his marriage a secret from me for two months. I know it isn't the espresso that causes that bitter taste in my mouth.

Lorenzo says, "But I've been with the marchesa for more than thirty years."

That surprises me so much I almost drop the cup. "*Thirty* years?"

He inclines his head. "Since before her first husband died. It has been my honor to serve in her household for so long."

So this mysterious marchesa was a widow for thirty years before marrying my father. Almost exactly as long as my father was a widower. That bit of information seems important somehow, but I don't know why. Then something else strikes me as important. "You say it's been your *honor* to serve in her household?"

Lorenzo answers with quiet pride, "I've never known any other person as fine."

I inspect his face, but find no trace of sarcasm there. His opinion of the marchesa is certainly not in line with Dominic's. I don't know how to reconcile two such opposing viewpoints, especially since I'm inclined to hate her for not getting her fine ass to the hospital.

"Has she been told my father died?"

Lorenzo doesn't blink at my tone, which is just this side of hostile. "Yes, of course."

"And?"

Lorenzo draws his brows together in a quizzical frown. "I'm sorry, signorina?"

"Well . . . was she upset? What did she say? How did she react?"

A flicker of emotion rises in his gray eyes—there, then instantly gone. In a steady, quiet voice, he says, "The marchesa does not share her feelings with her servants. And—forgive me—even if she did, I wouldn't share them with anyone else."

He's in love with her.

It seems obvious that that's the reason he's been with her so long, the reason he speaks so highly of her, the reason for that momentary flash of emotion he had to smother so I wouldn't see it. Lorenzo is in love with my father's widow, and has been for—

Oh shit. Are they having an affair?

That would explain why the marchesa didn't show at the hospital. She was busy getting busy with someone else. Maybe she never loved my father at all. Maybe she only married him because she thought he had money.

Money that would support her and her lover, Lorenzo.

I'm abruptly so angry my cheeks start to burn.

Watching me, Lorenzo says, "I apologize if what I said angered you, signorina. It wasn't my intention to be disrespectful, only honest."

I set my cup on the table and take a breath, trying to control myself because there's no evidence what I've thought is true. My father's dead and I'm emotional, and I'll only make things worse by creating a scene or throwing around accusations based on nothing more than a hunch.

But there's a tiny voice in my head reminding me that I ignored all the blinking red signs of Brad's secrets, and I shouldn't make the same mistake again.

"I appreciate your honesty," I say stiffly, looking at my fingers clenched around the delicate handle of the cup. "And I'm sure *you* can appreciate how I might not be myself today." I look up and meet his eyes, and let him see all the emotion burning there. My voice comes out a raw scrape of pain. "The person I loved the most in the world is dead, and I'm not above letting *anyone* know how I feel about it."

A look of compassion comes into Lorenzo's eyes, but before he can say anything, a rustle of skirts makes us glance at the doorway. And there she stands with her chin held high and her back ramrod straight, regal as an empress.

The marchesa.

Lorenzo rises and bows, but I can't look away from my stepmother. It's not because she's so beautiful, exactly—she is, stunningly so—and it's not because of the finery of her clothing, or the way her mere presence makes the air crackle.

It's because I've never seen another person so chillingly cold.

She's brilliant icy perfection, from the top of her blonde head to the hem of her silvery Dupioni gown. Though she's obviously not young, her skin is dewy and unwrinkled. Her eyes are an inhuman shade of blue, as electric blue as a cyborg's.

She radiates a fierce, freezing intensity. She's an iceberg with eyeballs, draped in custom-cut silk.

"Lady Moretti," murmurs Lorenzo to the floor. "May I present signorina DiSanto." He lifts a hand in my direction.

The marchesa and I gaze at each other. Neither of us makes a move.

Lorenzo straightens and looks at me. "Kimber, this is Lady Moretti."

That's it? I'm supposed to address this woman like that? I don't even qualify to use her first name? And why does she go by Lady Moretti and not Mrs. DiSanto? She didn't take my father's last name?

Oh hell no.

I say flatly, "Hi."

"Hello, Kimber."

Her voice is like the rest of her: frigid. Since I addressed her in English, she replied in English. I get the sense the language feels dirty in her mouth, something reserved for the peasants that she wouldn't otherwise use.

As if someone is pointing a gun at her head and forcing her to speak, she says frostily, "Finally, I meet Luca's beloved daughter. Your father spoke of nothing else."

The verdict is in: I can't stand this bitch.

I send her my most acid smile. "Funny, he never mentioned you."

Her frozen perfection remains untouched by that. She simply stares at me with unnerving intensity, no trace of emotion in her arctic cyborg eyes.

Lorenzo clears his throat. "Ah, perhaps signorina DiSanto would like to meet Cornelia and Beans?"

The question is directed at the iceberg, but I'm not used to having other people make my decisions for me, so I answer before she can get anything past her frozen lips. "Yes, I'd like to meet my stepsisters."

A glimmer of surprise surfaces in the marchesa's eyes. She lifts a pale hand to her throat. Some distant relative to a smile touches her lips, but dies before it can find a home on such inhospitable ground. "Stepsisters," she murmurs. "That's very sweet."

What's so funny? Am I supposed to address them as "your royal highnesses" or something?

The mystery is quickly solved, however, when Lorenzo puts two fingers between his lips, then produces a whistle of such piercing volume I cringe.

The sound of nails clacking rapidly against wood grows closer and closer, until the huge black dog I saw earlier rounds the corner of the kitchen, tongue lolling. It bounds toward Lorenzo. Halfway there, it catches sight of me, skids to a comical stop, then runs and hides behind the marchesa's legs.

"Cornelia!" laughs Lorenzo. "Come now, silly girl, don't be afraid!"

My mouth drops open in shock. This is my stepsister? My stepsister is a *dog*?

Visibly worried, Cornelia timidly peers out from behind the marchesa's skirts and looks at me. The marchesa reaches down and reassuringly strokes a hand over the dog's massive head.

I shout, *"You gave a dog my bedroom?"*

With a whimper, Cornelia ducks back into hiding.

The marchesa looks at me sharply but gets distracted by the sight of a tiny peach-colored furball marching imperiously into the room, nose lifted high in the air, plumed tail quivering with pride. The pink studded collar it wears probably weighs more than it does. It parks itself next to the marchesa's right foot and glares at me with small black eyes that glitter with malice.

"Let me guess," I say flatly. "This must be Beans."

At the sound of its name, the tiny peach furball bares its teeth and growls.

"Yeah," I say, glaring back at it. "I know the feeling, sister."

SEVEN

"You're *shitting* me."

"I shit you not. They each have a bedroom of their own, and they eat their meals *at the table.* The big one's tall enough that it doesn't need a chair, it just sits on the floor and gobbles its food right off the plate, but the tiny evil one has a booster seat like they give kids at restaurants—only it's made of *silk.*"

"Dear God," says Jenner. I hear his shudder through the phone. "Dogs at the dining table? How obscene."

"What's really obscene are the dogs' wardrobes."

"Don't tell me. Your wicked stepmother has them wear dresses."

"I'll do you one better: my wicked stepmother has them wear dresses that my poor father *sewed by hand.*"

After a short silence, Jenner says, "Oh, honey. She must have a magical hoo-ha to be able to get a man to do that."

I mutter, "I'd like to kick her right in her magical hoo-ha, I'll tell you what."

After our disastrous meeting at breakfast, the marchesa and I retreated to opposite corners of the house. She and the dogs appeared again for lunch, this time in matching outfits. The four of us ate at the long oak table in the formal dining room in silence interrupted only by the sloppy chomping of Cornelia. The marchesa and Beans consumed their food with the same delicate manners, exuding the same royal disdain.

When Lorenzo came in to inform us that my father's attorney would be arriving later in the day to discuss some financial matters and read the will, I took the opportunity to excuse myself. I'd already researched local hotels and had booked one nearby so I didn't have to spend another night on the sofa.

Or near the WS, as I'd begun referring to my wicked stepmother in my head.

"So when's the funeral?"

"In three days. I made the arrangements this morning." With the help of Lorenzo, because I don't speak Italian and my father's doting widow retired to her bedroom at the mention of the funeral. Probably to do a happy dance at the thought of what she'd inherit.

Il Sogno may be old and crumbling, but the land is valuable. The view of the Duomo alone is priceless. I'm sure the WS has plans to sell it to the highest bidder the minute the funeral ends. I don't know anything about community property laws in this country, but judging by the way my father spoke of her, the WS will get everything, right down to the doormat.

Not that I care. Without Papa, this is just another old villa in the hills. He was the one who made it special. I didn't grow up here. I only visited once a year—there's nothing left to tie me to it except painful memories, and I've had enough of those to last a lifetime.

"And how are you holding up, Poppins?" Jenner asks gently. "This has been one hell of a week for you."

I close my eyes and turn my face to the hot afternoon sun. I'd come out to the overgrown back gardens to be with the butterflies and the hummingbirds, hoping I could head off my pending mental breakdown with a quiet stroll, but the heat is as oppressive as my jet lag, and the hummingbirds are nowhere to be seen.

The WS must've boiled them in her cauldron.

"I'm surviving." My sigh is heavy. "Actually, I think I'm in shock. It still doesn't seem real. Any of it. Brad, the wedding, my father, my father's secret wife . . . it all feels like a dream."

"Nightmare, more like," says Jenner with empathy.

"Enough about my problems." I wave a hand in the air to dispel the somber mood. "How are *you* doing? What's new in the modeling world?"

"You know, the usual: cocaine, bulimia, fake friends. I can hardly wait until I start to wrinkle so I can retire and do something meaningful with my life."

I know for a fact that he doesn't do drugs, have an eating disorder, or have fake friends. I've met all of them, and they're almost as awesome as he is. The stereotypes about models are depressingly wrong. You'd think the beautiful people would be more fucked-up than the rest of us, but as far as I've seen, that's not true. Jenner just enjoys pretending it is.

"You're too pretty to wrinkle. You've only gotten better looking since I met you."

He sighs as if his beauty is a terrible problem that's been vexing him for years. "I know. Let's talk about something else. Oh—tell me about all the gorgeous Italian men!"

Smiling, I walk deeper into the garden, meandering down the gravel path toward the stone fountain. After all these years in the elements, it's still beautiful, and still one of my favorite things. It depicts Aphrodite and her lover, Ares, in a passionate embrace. It was my father's wedding present to my mother. It's been dry since the day she died, twenty-nine years ago.

"I've only met one gorgeous Italian, but that was in New York. But damn, he was a doozy."

"I can hear the drool in your mouth, Poppins! Tell me everything!"

I give him a shortened version of the story, concentrating the details on what Euro Hunk looked like and what he wore, the two things I know are required. Jenner gasps and exclaims in all the right places, then asks excitedly when I'll be seeing him again.

"I didn't give him my real number, dummy."

"Why on earth *not*?"

"Because, *hello*, I was just dumped at the altar! I'm not exactly in a man-loving mood!"

"Who said anything about loving? Have revenge sex with him, silly! Hell, have revenge sex with every Italian stud you meet! What better way to get Brad out of your system? Seriously, you're swimming in an ocean of testosterone over there, darling, dip your vadge in that beautiful sea!"

I say drily, "I think the saying is 'Dip your *toe*.'"

He scoffs. "Toe, vadge, whatever. Get it in there! Swim in it! *Drown* in it! Good God, if it were me, I'd be running naked through the streets!"

"Yeah, I've seen the pictures."

His tone turns snippy. "Don't be judgey, darling. It was my first show in Paris. I was seventeen."

"Really? What's your excuse for what happened last year at the Issey Miyake show in Tokyo?"

Jenner says innocently, "It was my first time in Japan!"

"I see. Remind me not to go with you anywhere you haven't been before."

"It's not like you haven't seen me nude."

"The amount of people who haven't seen you nude is a very small number, my friend."

"Well," he says airily, "one does what one can to spread beauty into the lives of the less fortunate."

I laugh at that because I know he means it. "Have I told you lately that I love you?"

"You tell me alarmingly often, darling. For such a sharp, ball-busting businesswoman, you're awfully mushy."

He's trying to be condescending, but I know him too well. "Pfft. You adore it and you know it."

His chuckle is low and warm. "I adore *you*, Poppins."

I swallow, tears gathering in the corners of my eyes. My chest tight, I whisper, "You're the only family I have left now."

He sounds alarmed. "Oh God. Don't cry. You'll make *me* cry, and I've just applied a forty-dollar mascara."

I start to laugh. He makes it impossible not to.

"That's better. Now listen to me carefully, darling." His voice turns firm. "You're the baddest bitch I've ever known. You *will* get through this. All of it. And you'll come out stronger on the other side. Do you hear me?"

My voice is small when I answer, "Yes."

"I'm sorry, I didn't catch that. Is there a mouse on the other end of the line?"

"I said yes!"

He sounds satisfied by my shout and chuckles again. "Good. Stiff upper lip, Poppins. Tears are undignified. And remember—*revenge sex is good for the complexion.*"

He hangs up before I can tell him again that I love him, because there's nothing Jenner hates more than having to admit there's a real heart in his chest, instead of the shard of ice he pretends sits in its place.

When the attorney arrives a few hours later, the marchesa invites him into the library and asks Lorenzo to look after Cornelia. Beans, however, isn't banished from the meeting, and sits glaring at me from the marchesa's lap as the lawyer removes sheaves of papers from his briefcase and gets himself organized.

Muttering to himself, the attorney pats his coat pockets. He finds the pair of glasses he was looking for, settles them on his aquiline nose, then sits across from us on a leather sofa. Gesturing to the papers on the coffee table between us, he launches into a rapid-fire speech in Italian.

"Wait." I hold up a hand. The attorney peers at me over his glasses. "In English, please." When he squints at me, I get a bad feeling. "You do speak English?"

"Of course I speak English. But why would I, when Italian is so superior?"

Petting Beans as if the dog were a bag of diamonds, the marchesa smiles.

Heat crawls up my neck. Reminding myself murder is a capital crime, I say, "Because I don't speak Italian."

Now the attorney looks confused. He glances at the marchesa, then at me, as if he can't believe his ears.

"But you were born in this country, no? And your parents were both Italian. Why would you not know your mother tongue?"

There's a lead crystal paperweight on the table between us that would make a very nice dent in this idiot's skull. "Yes, I was born here, but I grew up in the States. I moved there when I was three years old and only came back for summer breaks from school."

When the attorney keeps right on gazing at me as if I'm making no sense whatsoever, I sigh heavily. "When I went to live with my aunt, my father wanted me to be a 'real' American, okay? He wanted me to fit in with all my friends, not be picked on for being a foreigner. He never spoke Italian to me."

The attorney looks as if I've informed him I shot his mother point-blank in the face. "Never spoke Italian to you?" Scandalized, he stares at the marchesa. "But this is child abuse!"

"Oh, for God's sake, just get on with it!"

Beans doesn't like my aggravated tone and growls deep in her throat.

I cut her a withering look. "One more peep out of you, dog, and I'll make you into a purse."

"*Per favore*, Signor Rossi, continue in English," says the marchesa, icy calm. She doesn't glance at me, but Beans looks as if she's about to explode with fury. I might not speak Italian, but apparently the dog understands English. If it weren't for the marchesa's hand on her back, I'd have a peach furball chewing off my nose.

I narrow my eyes at Beans, she bares her teeth at me, and Signor Rossi grunts in disbelief at my horrible shortcoming.

"Very well. In *English*, then," he says, sounding aggrieved. "Let us begin." He picks up a sheaf of stapled papers and launches into a long and terrifically boring outline of my father's business holdings, bank accounts, and various other financial instruments and the value thereof, all of which amount to a pittance.

This isn't news. Though he was an exceptional designer, Papa's business acumen was for shit. He was constantly lending cash to people who'd never pay it back, forgetting to pay taxes on time so the fines would be astronomical, and generally failing at managing his money. All he wanted to do was sketch, sew, and design. And though his creations were truly beautiful, he didn't price them correctly. He felt guilty for making a profit. He was an artist, not a businessman.

Then Signor Rossi says something that almost makes me fall out of my chair.

"Now, turning to the real estate. The house and property were recently assessed at fifteen million euro—"

"Whoa! Back up—did you say fifteen *million* euro?"

"That's roughly eighteen million dollars in your American money," sniffs the attorney.

I make a sound like a cat trying to expel a hairball and look at the marchesa. She gazes back at me in inscrutable silence, the smallest of smiles hovering over her lips.

Her smile doesn't falter when the attorney adds, "Of course, you can't sell the property while Lady Moretti is still alive. Without her permission, that is."

I whip my head around so fast I'm surprised it doesn't fly off my neck. "What? Me? Sell? Huh?"

Signor Rossi gazes at me over the rim of his glasses and speaks very slowly, as if to someone with limited mental capacity. "Your father left everything to you, Kimber. The business, the investments, Il Sogno—everything. The only stipulation on any of that being that you allow Lady Moretti to stay in the house until she dies, if she so wishes."

I stare at him for a while, then at the marchesa, who remains undisturbed.

Watching me with those frozen blue eyes, she says calmly, "I would prefer to stay in the house, but if my stepdaughter would prefer I did not, I will move."

She's talking to him, but she's looking at me. Looking right down into the bottom of my soul.

Daring me.

I whisper, "My father left me this house?"

Signor Rossi says, "Yes."

"But . . . I can't sell it until she dies?"

"Unless Lady Moretti agrees to leave, which—if I understand her correctly—she will do if you ask her to."

The marchesa says, "That is correct."

In her cold smile, I think I see a checkmate.

Damn. I have to hand it to her. That's a ballsy move.

She knows without my having to say so that I'd never disrespect my father's wishes. No matter how much I might dislike her, no matter how much I could use the money—*fifteen million euro!*—I'd never ask her to leave, because he wanted her to stay.

It's an incredible gamble on her part, but this is one crafty woman. She probably had my number at first glance. She probably saw exactly how this would play out, right down to the next words that leave my mouth.

"If my father wanted you to stay until you die, you're staying until you die."

The marchesa's small smile grows the tiniest bit wider.

Not so fast, WS. "But I can't guarantee you won't meet with any unfortunate accidents that might reduce your lifespan by a few decades."

My feeling of satisfaction at watching her smug smile disappear is one of the highlights of my life to date.

The attorney interrupts our stare-off with a rough throat clearing. "In regard to your father's business, DiSanto Couture has an excellent reputation for quality. However, based on a review of the books, it's operating at a loss. It's not sustainable at current levels of income versus debt, so the obvious course of action is to bring in a buyer." Signor Rossi glances up from the paperwork. "Unless you'd like to try to take it over and turn it around."

"No. I'm not staying here. I've got to get back to the States."

He nods. "We'll find a buyer. I recommend going through the inventory and repricing it to more competitive levels in order to boost the selling price. From what I can see, there's substantial room for improvement there."

The marchesa says, "I know someone who will be interested."

I just bet you do, Cruella.

"Bene," says the attorney, nodding. Then he looks at me. "That means *good.*"

"I know what it means."

He purses his lips as if he doesn't believe me.

I'm abruptly angry, because massive mood swings are my new normal. "Are we done here? Because I'd like to check into the hotel before dinner."

Before he can answer, my cell phone rings. I glance at the number, frowning when I see it's my landlord. "Excuse me for a sec." I rise, hitting the "Answer" button as I walk from the library into the hallway.

"Hey, Mr. Drummond."

"Hello, Kimber."

The man I rent my tiny but horrifically expensive shop from in the Castro district sounds unusually somber, which sets off alarm bells in my head. *What time is it in San Francisco, anyway? 6:00 a.m.?* I check my watch, and sure enough, it's just after dawn there.

"Is everything okay? My rent check cleared, right?"

"Yes, your check cleared. That's not why I'm calling."

When he draws a breath, my heart leaps into my throat. "What is it? What's wrong?"

I can tell by his heavy exhalation whatever he's about to tell me won't be good, but nothing can prepare me for the words that come out of his mouth.

"There's been a fire."

"A fire?" Panic like a chaos of wingbeats erupts inside my chest.

"The cause hasn't been determined yet, but it's bad. The whole block went up. I'm standing across the street as we speak. I'm sorry to be the one to tell you this, but your shop and everything in it is gone. There's nothing left but ashes."

I stand rooted to the spot, sick with disbelief, a high-pitched scream ricocheting inside my skull. My files, my computer, all the dresses I spent countless hours crafting so carefully are gone? My entire business has disappeared overnight?

This can't be happening.

"Under the terms of your lease, you're responsible for your rent until you've been cleared of any liability. I have no idea how long it'll take the authorities to determine what happened, so"—he laughs uncomfortably—"I'm still gonna need another check on the first."

And the hits just keep on coming.

EIGHT

MATTEO

I don't believe in fate, but when I see her walk into the hotel bar, I can't help but think something more than coincidence is at play.

She looks angry. Angry, fierce, and beautiful, like a vengeful goddess. All that black hair I'd like to wrap around my wrist spills over her shoulders in tangles. Her cheeks are red. Her eyes are wild. She exudes a dangerous, frantic energy, as if she recently escaped from prison.

"Matteo? Are you listening?"

"Excuse me for a moment, Antonio."

Without another word, I rise from the table—the one I always sit at, the best one, in the back of the room—and stroll toward the bar.

She's taken a seat at the end. Her back is to me. She drags her hands through her hair, props her elbows on the bar, then drops her head into her hands.

I stop beside her, admiring the way the lights glint blue in her hair. "You're upset."

She jerks her head up. When she sees me, her eyes widen. She stares at me with her lips parted and a look of disbelief on her face.

It quickly turns to fury.

"You," she says, as if it's a curse.

I smile down at her, enjoying everything about this moment, including how much she'd obviously like to stab me in the eye with a cocktail fork. *"Buonasera,* Miss Bobbitt. Cut off anyone's cock since I last saw you?"

She narrows her gorgeous green eyes at me. "The night's still young."

Stifling my laughter, I take the seat next to hers.

"What're you doing here?"

"I live here."

"In this bar?"

"In this city. But I do come here often for drinks."

She exhales slowly, then says with quiet sarcasm, "Get a little lonely up in your castle, do you?"

"I'm never lonely," I lie, holding her fierce gaze.

It's unsettling how easily she pegged that, and how uncomfortable I am that she might think me weak. I can't remember the last time I gave a damn about what someone else thought.

Until right now.

Moistening her lips, she looks me over like a warlord might look over a kingdom he's about to invade. It's electrifying.

"I want my sketch pad back."

I smile at her. "Too bad you already traded it for a plane ticket." Then I remember why she was so desperate to get on that flight. "How is your father?"

All the color drains from her face. She winces and turns away.

"I'm so sorry." Moved by her pain, I'm overwhelmed by the sudden urge to take her in my arms. I have to fight to keep my hands by my sides. "If there's anything I can do—"

She whips her head around. "You can give me back my damn sketch pad!" she says loudly, causing the bartender to turn and squint at us. When he sees it's me she's shouting at, he smiles, nods, and turns away.

"What will you give me in return?" I smile. "Since you enjoy bartering so much."

Through gritted teeth, she says, "You know what—never mind." She folds her arms over her chest and shakes her head, muttering darkly about people with stupid titles and men with oversize egos and various other things until I interrupt her.

"How long will you be in Florence?"

"None of your business."

Dio mio, this attitude makes me hard. "I want to take you to dinner."

She snorts. Somehow it sounds elegant. "No."

That shocks me. Not only the finality of it, but the word itself: *no.* Women don't say *no* to me.

Ever.

My dick throbs and lengthens, straining to get free from my trousers.

"Breakfast?"

"No."

"Hmm. I suppose lunch is also out of the question?"

"I'm not interested in eating food with you, Count Egotistico."

"I've already told you I'm not a count."

"Yeah, I heard. Whoop-dee-do."

I drop my voice and lean toward her. "So if you're not interested in eating food with me, bella, what *are* you interested in doing with me?"

When she snaps her head around and glares at me, I look directly into her eyes. "Because we both know you're interested in something. And so am I."

A flush darkens her cheeks. She chews the inside of her lip. Something crackles in the air, as sharp as danger.

"I don't do one-night stands."

"How many nights will you be here?"

Our gazes hold. A vein throbs in the hollow of her throat. Her breath quickens, and my erection is so hard there must be no blood left anywhere else in my body.

As if she's not sure she should be answering, she says, "Five. Maybe six."

The heat that flashes over me is intense. I can't remember the last time I've wanted a woman so much. "Plenty of time to show me exactly how much you dislike men with oversize . . . egos."

Silence stretches between us, not long but cavernously wide, filled with tension and unspoken need. Then, in a throaty voice, she says, "I dislike them *a lot*."

It's so blatantly sexual I almost groan. I lean closer, so close I can smell her skin. She smells like sunshine. Like the outdoors. Like honeysuckle and citrus and something else indefinable I want very badly to eat. Into her ear, I say, "Then you're really going to hate me. You'll hate me over and over and over. I'll make sure, bella, that you'll hate me more than any other man you'll ever meet."

She inhales against my throat. Resting on my arm, her fingers tremble. She takes a breath, then slowly blows it out. "Okay, fancypants, you're on. I'm in room four-twelve. Give me ten minutes."

She pulls away and meets my eyes. In the candlelight, her skin is flushed and rosy, her eyes shine, and her lips are darkest red against that pale skin.

I've never seen anything so lovely.

When I nod, she rises and walks away without looking back. It isn't until she's gone that I realize I still don't know her name.

I take a moment to gather myself, then head back to my table. Antonio has obviously been watching our interaction, because he asks, "Someone you know?"

I smile, thinking of all the ways I'm about to get to know that gorgeous creature. All the delicious, dirty ways. "Let's call it a night. Something came up."

Antonio looks at the bulge straining the front of my trousers and lifts his brows. "Evidently."

Without another word, I pull money from my wallet, leave it on the table, nod a farewell to Antonio, then head to the lobby, because even though she said ten minutes, that's nine-and-a-half minutes too long to wait.

NINE

KIMBER

A fact I've recently come to understand: Womanizers are all alike. They're arrogant, selfish, and convinced they're doing you a favor when they throw their pretty peen in your direction.

I'm so over it.

When I get back to my room, I get the water hot for a bath and raid the minibar while the tub is filling. Fortified with a hefty rum and Coke, I strip, wind my hair into a messy bun, and slip into the hot water with a groan of pleasure.

What a shit day. *Week.*

I close my eyes and let my mind drift, taking the occasional sip from my drink. *How could Papa have married that woman? That heartless ice cube of a woman?* I start to get angry thinking about it and chug the rest of my drink. Then my mind wanders into Euro Hunk territory, and I get even angrier.

So he's beautiful. So what? He's obviously a letch. If he acts that aggressively with me, I'm sure he acts that way with every woman he encounters. And hell if I'll ever be so naive again the way I was with Brad.

I don't know who's in room 412, but I hope it's someone with a short temper and a fondness for fistfights.

Imagining Euro Hunk getting punched in the face by a surly hotel guest upset at being disturbed makes a bitter smile curve my lips. Then I feel guilty because without him, I wouldn't have made it to the hospital in time to hear my father's last words.

Then, without warning, I burst into tears.

I lie in the tub and let the pain wash over me. There's so much of it I feel as if I'm suffocating. I have to set the glass on the edge of the tub because my hand is shaking so hard I can't hold it. I sit up, wrap my arms around my knees, and ugly cry until I've wrung myself out and the water has grown cold.

Then I dry off and make myself another drink.

Then the phone rings.

"Hello?"

"Buonasera," says a husky voice I'd recognize anywhere.

"How did you get this number?" I demand, my face going hot.

A chuckle, even sexier than the voice. "I have friends at the front desk. Apparently you made quite an impression when you checked in. All I had to say was 'Beautiful American,' and they connected me to your room straightaway. Speaking of rooms, the lady in four-twelve was very nice, but I prefer my women to have their real teeth and be able to walk without a cane."

Apparently the privacy laws in this country are as lax as the traffic laws. I say tartly, "Really? I'd have thought as long as a woman was breathing, you'd be good to go."

"You'd have thought wrong. I'm very particular. My last serious relationship was three years ago."

I roll my eyes. "Sure. Listen—I'm grateful to you for that ticket. Sincerely, I am. And if you'll give me your address, I swear I'll find a way to pay you back. But I'm not interested in sleeping with you." *Okay, that's a teeny lie, but whatever.* "I'm burying my father in a few days—I'm not in the mood for . . . whatever this is." *Why am I explaining this to him? Hang up!*

But I can't hang up, because I'm conflicted. Giving me his ticket was an incredible gesture of generosity. Even if he *was* hoping for a blowie in the men's room, it was still generous.

Even though I had to surrender my sketch pad with my entire spring collection, it was still generous.

Also, he's incredibly hot, and my uterus is shrieking at me that she'll never forgive me if I hang up on him first.

So I don't hang up. I wait, breathing shallowly, listening to static crackle over the line. After a long pause, Euro Hunk speaks again. "I understand. And I'm sorry about your father. I know how hard it is to lose someone you love."

With a soft click the line goes dead.

I stand frowning at the receiver in my hand, wondering why that felt weird. Like, wrong weird.

Like a mistake.

"Because you're an idiot," I say aloud to the empty room. Then I get ready for bed and put the whole thing out of my mind.

I toss and turn all night, dreaming of boiling cauldrons and cackling witches and handsome princes riding white steeds. When I wake up, I'm disoriented. It takes a good thirty seconds of staring blankly around the hotel room until I realize where I am. Then I get so depressed I lie there staring at the ceiling, mentally sifting through the shambles of my life.

Where am I going to live? What am I going to do for money? How did I lose my fiancé, my father, and my business within the space of a few days?

I enjoy a good solid ten minutes of imagining throwing the WS and her ridiculous dogs out on their asses and living at Il Sogno myself, but I can't keep up the anger for long and end up crying again.

My pity party is interrupted by the arrival of a text.

We really need to talk. Please call me.

I text Brad back that I'll break his jaw next time if he tries to contact me again, then block his number.

I sit there seething until I can't stand it anymore, then drag myself out of bed and take a shower. I'm supposed to be back at the house at noon to meet with the potential buyer of DiSanto Couture who the marchesa set a meeting with, so though I'd love nothing more than to lie in bed and wallow, I'm forced into adulting. On the cab ride to Il Sogno, I check my bank account, choking out a sick laugh when I see the balance.

By the time I arrive at the house, my mood is black. The WS better watch out because this morning, I'm capable of murder.

"Buongiorno," says Lorenzo when he answers the door. "You look lovely this morning."

I think I look like something a cat coughed up, but decide to be pleasant since he's being so nice. "Thank you. And you look very dapper, as always."

He smiles, pleased by the compliment. "Come in. Lady Moretti is waiting for you in the library." He swings the door wide, allowing me to pass, then ushers me through the house to where the marchesa awaits. Wearing a gorgeous plum dress and matching lipstick, she's immaculate.

She looks up when I come in. Setting aside the book she'd been reading, she greets me with a muted "Hello."

I'm surprised she didn't speak in Italian, but simply nod in response.

"Kimber, what can I offer you? Coffee? Water? Anything to eat?"

It's so weird that I'm being treated as a guest in a house that belongs to me. But Lorenzo's only doing his job. I can't hold it against him. "Nothing, thank you."

He bows and retreats. I take a seat on the opposite side of the coffee table from the marchesa, and we commence gazing at each other in unblinking silence like it's some kind of competition.

She breaks first. "I'm sorry your husband didn't come with you. I would have liked to have met him."

It's a slap across the face. My cheeks sting exactly as if she'd cracked her open palm against them. "The wedding was called off."

"Called off?"

When my only response is a freezing stare, she says, "I assume your father didn't know, or he would have told me."

It's her way of letting me know Papa told her everything, that there were no secrets between them. Unlike the whopper of a secret he kept from me—namely, *her.*

It's another checkmate for the marchesa. I swallow around the lump in my throat and look away. "It only happened a few days ago."

The following pause is filled with tension. "You called off the wedding . . . because of . . ."

"No," I say sharply, understanding that she thinks I dumped Brad because Papa was sick. "I wasn't the one who called it off."

As soon as it's out of my mouth, I regret it. I clamp my lips together and wait for the smirk I'm sure is coming. But for whatever reason, the marchesa seems affected by this new piece of information. She goes very still.

She says slowly, "Your fiancé left you because your father was sick?"

Is she acting? Joking? What is this? It's not like she cares! "It was before that. Brad didn't know Papa was sick. *I* didn't know Papa was sick. I got Dominic's letter a few days after we broke up."

At the mention of Dominic's name, she clenches her hand into a fist, as if she wants to hit something. When she sees me notice it, she flexes the hand open and smooths it over her dress.

I watch all that with interest, wondering what it means. I guess the dislike Dominic feels for her is mutual. *And why did she seem upset about Brad? What am I missing?*

The mystery of the marchesa's strange reactions will have to wait because Lorenzo has returned and is bowing again. It seems like a reflex, the way some people sneeze when they look at the sun.

He addresses the marchesa in Italian.

She replies, "Bene. *Grazie.*"

It doesn't take a genius to know that the potential buyer has arrived. The faint blush of color rising in the marchesa's marble-pale cheek gives proof of her excitement. There's a gleam in her cyborg-blue eyes, too, the mercenary. If I didn't already know my father left his business to me, I'd assume her sudden good mood had to do with the prospect of money. I'm confused and instantly on guard.

But then I figure it out. She must have made a deal with this buyer, whoever he or she is. *Yes—that's it! She made some kind of back-end deal where she'll get a referral fee, or maybe even a percentage!* I smile grimly. *Not so fast, WS. You might think I'm a dumb American, but you've got another—*

"Ciao, Mamma," says a voice.

That voice.

Shocked, I whip my head around. And there he stands, all hunky, cocky six-and-a-hella-sexy-inches of him, dressed in a drop-dead gorgeous navy suit and his usual air of entitled superiority.

Euro Hunk. In the flesh.

The marchesa says, "Ciao, Matteo. Come in, son."

Oh, dear God in heaven, you are one sick mofo.

Because not only is the man standing in the doorway the man who took the inspiration for my entire spring collection. Not only is he the man who gave me his ticket so I could get to this country before my father died. Not only is he the man who propositioned me—twice—and inspired lust in me the likes of which I've never felt.

He's also my stepbrother.

Why does God hate me?

TEN

When those aquamarine eyes slice to mine, I can tell by the look in them that he's as shocked as I am. He's stunned speechless and simply stands staring at me with his lips parted and his eyes wide until the marchesa clears her throat.

"Matteo, this is Kimber. Luca's daughter."

After a beat, Matteo recovers his wits. "We've met." He walks slowly toward me, his gaze trapping mine. When he's a few feet away, close enough for me to smell his cologne, he stops. In a low voice, he says, "Your father was a wonderful man. I'm so sorry for your loss."

Electricity jolts through me. *Oh my God. Of course he knew my father! His mother was married to him!*

"You've already met?" says the marchesa, confused.

Matteo stares at me with such burning intensity I'm surprised the room doesn't burst into flames.

I whisper, "Your son is the reason I was able to see my father before he died."

What are the odds? What are the ever-loving odds? What kind of universal mind fuckery is this?

The marchesa says something to Matteo in Italian. He responds in kind, keeping his gaze locked to mine. I can tell he thinks this coincidence is anything but convenient, but I'm not sure if he's angry or simply surprised.

Then it dawns on me that the reason he wanted my sketch pad wasn't because he was an art collector.

"Wait," I say, horrified. "You knew about ruching. You told me to add ruching to the sketch of the dress I was drawing. And your clothes . . ." I stare at his gorgeous bespoke suit, and it all comes together with the speed of two fingers snapping.

He's a fashion designer.

Outraged, I leap to my feet and glare at him. "If you use any of the designs I gave you, I'll sue you so fast your head will spin!"

His burning gaze doesn't flinch, but a grim little smile curves his lips. "Faster than your mood swings?"

"Those are *my* designs!"

"Incorrect. They're mine. As you just said, you gave them to me."

"Under duress! From necessity!"

"So you don't think it was a fair trade? You'd rather have your sketch pad back than to have seen your father before he died?"

That's so ruthless I gasp. In a low, shaking voice, I say, "You son of a bitch."

The marchesa intervenes before I can find something to stab her son with. "I don't quite understand what's happening, but let's all calm down, shall we?"

"Lady, I'm so far from calm I'd have to send out a search party to find it." I point at Matteo. "Why didn't you tell me the buyer was your son?"

She's placid in the face of my fury, folding her hands at her waist and gazing at me in cool composure. "Why does that make a difference?"

"Gee, where should I start?" I say bitingly. "It's a pretty crafty way to get your hands on some of Papa's money, I'll give you that."

Her lips thin to a slash of plum that looks like a stab wound. "I would never have mentioned the sale to Matteo if he weren't capable of handling the business and honoring Luca's artistic vision. The House of Moretti is among the most respected ateliers in fashion. Perhaps you've heard of it?"

She's smug, the witch, because of course I've heard of it. Hell, everyone in fashion has heard of Moretti! They're the hottest thing in the industry at the moment. But I won't give either one of them the satisfaction.

"Can't say that I have."

Matteo crosses his arms over his broad chest and gazes at me from under hooded lids. I look back and forth between him and his mother, who's wearing the exact same hard, emotionless expression.

Everything inside me says, *Fuck this.*

The sale isn't going to happen.

"Not that you'd care to know," I say in a voice that sounds like I've swallowed a handful of gravel, "but my father's last words to me were about you."

A muscle in the corner of her eyelid twitches, but that's all the reaction I get from the marchesa. I turn my gaze to Matteo.

"And he gave me a piece of advice I didn't realize would come in handy so soon. He told me not to give up when things get difficult. His exact words were '*Dig in your heels.*' So this is me digging in my heels."

I take a breath, amazed at what's about to come out of my mouth. But what the hell. I've got literally nothing left to lose.

"I'm not selling the business. I'm going to run it myself."

The marchesa sputters, "What?" but my attention is focused on Matteo.

Beautiful, ruthless Matteo, who bartered a plane ticket he could probably pay for a million times over for a sketch pad chock-full of inspiration for new designs for his clothing line.

I say acidly, "Oh, wait. I think I *have* heard of you—didn't I read somewhere that the House of Moretti recently lost its head designer?"

He's got an eye twitch like his mother's. He says stiffly, "*I* am the head designer."

My gaze rakes over his spotless suit, the platinum cuff links, the shoes made from the skin of veal calves massaged by virgins and hand stitched by a cloister of nuns singing hymns in a Tibetan mountaintop abbey. "Not really hands on, though, I'd guess. I can't picture you with rolled-up sleeves, pinning cloth on mannequins, working deep into the night. Probably too busy running around with supermodels."

The marchesa sniffs. "My son doesn't date models."

I lift my brows and look at her. "Do you pick out his underwear for him, too?"

Matteo barks, "Stop with the disrespect!"

My temper snaps. "Don't you *dare* talk to me about disrespect! Your precious mother didn't have enough respect for my father to visit him in the hospital while he was dying, did you know that?"

My shout dies in echoes that linger in the air like poison gas. No one speaks for what feels like an eternity. Then the marchesa says quietly, "Please excuse me," and walks out of the room, head high.

Matteo watches her go, a muscle flexing in his jaw, but doesn't try to stop her. When he turns his gaze back to me, I feel a primal urge to run away. I never knew blue eyes could burn with so much fire. It's like looking into an incinerator.

"You and your mouth," he says, stalking closer. He looms over me, glaring down at me like he's fighting himself not to curl his hands around my neck. He leans into my face. "And your attitude, and your selfishness—"

I gasp, infuriated. "*My* selfishness?"

"And your bad manners!" he thunders. "Did it ever occur to you that not everyone wants the whole world to know when they're in pain?"

I was in a fight once, in grade school. I stuck up for a kid who was being bullied by a group of girls, and one of those girls had a strong right arm. Matteo's words feel exactly like that punch I took to the gut all those years ago.

I stand staring at him breathlessly, my heart beating fast, tears welling in my eyes. I swallow, then say bitterly, "I'm sorry my grief is so offensive to you. I have this thing called a heart. I'm not the kind of person who's able to pretend everything is fine when it's bleeding."

I start to brush past him, but he stops me with his hand gripped lightly around my shoulder. "Wait."

"Get your hands off me." I try to twist away, but he doesn't let go. He pulls me even closer.

"Kimber, stop. *Stop.* Please."

I stand stiffly, vibrating rage, staring at the third button on his white dress shirt while breathing hard and trying not to cry. He exhales a slow breath and loosens his grip on my shoulder but doesn't release me.

"Look at me."

"Go to hell."

"Stop acting like a child. Look at me."

Heat pulses in my cheeks. I close my eyes and take a brimming lungful of air, then do it again because I'm trembling all over and feel like I might pass out.

He mutters some kind of Italian oath under his breath, then puts his thumb under my chin and tilts my head up. I open my eyes to find him staring at me with thinned lips and a tight jaw, those thermonuclear eyes still blazing.

We breathe angrily at each other. I try not to smell him but it's impossible. He's a gorgeous noseful of cedar and smoke and male musk, with a crisp top note of clean linen. I give in and inhale like a perfumer, flaring my nostrils so my weird little fetish might pass for outrage.

If he's nose porn for me, I'm eye candy for him. He looks like he wants to peel off my clothes with his teeth.

"You're my stepbrother. You shouldn't be looking at me like that." I was aiming for disdain, but my breathy voice probably gives me away.

He doubles down and stares at my mouth as if he's about to make a meal of it. "Stepbrother," he muses, his face all hard angles and dangerous speculation. Unexpectedly, he laughs, but it lacks any trace of humor. "What an interesting development."

He releases me suddenly, as if I've burned him, and turns away. He drags his hands through his hair, then props them on his hips, muttering again under his breath. He stands with his back to me while I try desperately to regain control of my breathing. I'm shaking so hard I should probably lie down on the floor for a while.

I sit on the sofa instead. Wiping my sweaty palms on my thighs, I watch as Matteo starts to pace back and forth over the Turkish rug. Even angry he's elegant. He's as sleek and gorgeous as a thoroughbred, and I wish I had a riding crop handy because damn. I'd like to ride that pony hard.

I drop my face into my hands and gnash my teeth.

"Where is your husband?" he asks, agitated. "Didn't your father tell me you were getting married? You're not wearing a ring."

Oh great. Yeah, let's get all up into this *now.* I speak into my palms. "There's no husband."

When the silence stretches too long, I glance up to find him staring at me with narrowed eyes, like he thinks I'm lying. That pisses me off all over again.

"I pushed him off a cliff," I say, wishing it were true. "He took something of mine and wouldn't give it back." I'm talking about my trust, but I might as well be talking about my sketch pad.

Matteo's smile could burn a hole through steel it's so acid. "Ah. So that's what happened to your dignity."

Blood creeps up my neck and floods my cheeks, but I refuse to look away. "That's right. He humiliated me completely. But he did it because he's immature. You just did it because it made you feel good. Which is worse?"

He's not happy with my question. He starts to pace again, all flashing eyes and an angry jaw, his perfect hair rumpled from running his hands through it.

I like him better like this. Undone. Imperfect. It makes him seem a little more human.

The heartless bastard.

He says abruptly, "You can't be serious about keeping the company."

I cock a brow at him. "And why is that?"

He sweeps me with a look, up and down, dismissive. Before he can open his mouth, I say, "If you're about to make a nasty comment about my gender, my brains, or my style, I'm about to neuter your smug ass."

His eyes are cutting. His lip is curled. Him looking at me is like being assaulted by a volley of flying arrows. "What is it with your hostility?"

"What is it with your arrogance?"

"There's a big difference between self-confidence and arrogance."

"Yeah, there is, and any man who propositions a woman in an airport lounge after a thirty-second conversation lands squarely on the arrogance side of that equation."

"I didn't proposition you. I said I wanted you."

"You're splitting hairs. The intent was clear."

He studies me for a long moment. "You think I do that all the time, is that it?"

"I honestly don't care one way or the other."

"You'll have to learn to lie better than that if you're going to succeed in fashion here, bella."

He smirks, and I want to knock him out. The urge is surprisingly strong. I'm not normally a violent person, but the man brings out the insane-o little cavewoman in me. "I don't need business advice from you."

"This isn't America." He says *America* like you'd say *Ew, poop.* "This is Italy. The fashion capital of the planet—"

"Tell that to the French."

He waves me off like I'm being ridiculous. "And a girl from San Francisco—not even New York—who owns a sweet little dress shop is in no way prepared to compete *here*."

"Wow. I'm not sure which was worse: the sexism in that statement, or the sheer snobbism. I'm insulted on behalf of my gender *and* my country. And how do you know so much about me, anyway?"

His expression turns grave. "Your father spoke of you often."

My throat tightens. "You . . . spent time with him?"

"Yes. There were dinners, visits here, or to my home. We became close."

Hearing that is so painful I have to close my eyes and concentrate on simply breathing for a moment. All the time I was clueless about my father's new wife and stepson, they were enjoying time together. They ate meals together. Like a family. They "became close." While I was wasting time planning a wedding that would never happen with a man who didn't love me.

Why didn't you tell me, Papa? Why?

I'm gripped by a jealousy so strong it leaves me shaking. For the past two months, this arrogant jerk was spending quality time with my father. Precious time that I'd never be able to spend with him again.

His tone more gentle, Matteo says, "I'll give you a good price for the company. Better than anyone else would offer."

"So you can turn around and give all the money to your mother? No thanks."

"My mother doesn't need money," he says flatly, all the gentleness gone.

I glance up at him and can tell I've offended him again. Good. "That's not what I heard."

He grinds out, "Who told you that?"

"It doesn't make any difference. You're not getting the business either way. Go back to your castle and holler at your servants. I'm done with this conversation."

We engage in another round of hate staring.

I break first, because it's taking too much energy and this entire exchange has exhausted me. I push off the couch and exhale loudly, dying for a drink. And maybe a rock to hurl in his general direction.

"So your plan is to give up your entire life in America just to spite me? And my mother, whom you obviously dislike? You're going to move here, to a country whose language you don't even speak—"

I whirl on him. "How do you know I don't speak Italian?"

"Your father told me. He told me many things about you. He spoke of your kindness. And your strength. And your intelligence. He made you sound like Wonder Woman." A hard look comes into his eyes. "The only thing to wonder is how well he knew you."

He moves closer, a panther stalking his prey. I move back, one step for each of his, until I bump into a table and can't retreat any farther. Matteo does away with any consideration for personal space and gets right up in my face so our bodies are almost touching.

"He never mentioned your temper. Or the way you make snap judgments before you get to know people." His gaze drops to my lips, and his voice drops with it. "Or that mouth."

My nipples tighten, the traitors. A wave of heat dampens my skin. I stare at him, willing myself not to pant, then push him slowly away using the tip of one finger.

His chest is so hard he could be wearing a Kevlar vest.

"I guess he left out the bad parts. Like Mommy Dearest would no doubt do when talking about you." His eyes flash with anger at the mention of his mother, but I'm not finished. "I'm happy to fill you in, though. I'm stubborn. Like a mule. I'm *super* competitive. My friends won't play Scrabble with me anymore because of all the screaming. And when I die, I'll need two caskets—one for me and one for all my grudges. And the only thing keeping *you*"—I stab my angry finger into his bulletproof chest—"off my permanent shit list is that plane ticket.

Which I *will* pay you back for, even if it kills me, because I'd rather be down to my last cent than be indebted to a rival in business."

I already am down to my last cent, but he doesn't have to know that. I'm going for the biggest dramatic impact here, not a prize for truth telling.

Matteo stares at me for a long time, measuring my anger, letting his gaze rove over my face. He says thoughtfully, "A rival in business."

It sounds like he's plotting a war.

The slow smile that spreads over his mouth is even worse.

"All right. Rivals it is. Best of luck with your new endeavor." He leans in close, so close his warm breath fans down my neck as he whispers into my ear, "And technically, since your father died, I'm your *ex*-stepbrother. I'll look at you however I want." With a dark chuckle, he spins on his heel and is gone.

I listen to the sound of his footsteps echoing off the wood floor and my heartbeat crashing in my ears, hating myself for the pulse of heat throbbing between my legs.

Whatever this thing is between us, I can tell it's gonna get ugly.

ELEVEN

"Dominic, I need a lift to my hotel, then Papa's shop. Are you available?"

"*Certo.* When?"

"Now."

There's a pause. "Er, now?"

I look up at the late-summer Italian sky. It's an indescribable shade of Technicolor blue, so vivid it hurts to look. All the colors of this country are so saturated, so alive. Even the bowl of the heavens looks like something from a Disney movie, endless and electric and perfect, whimsically painted with the faint crescent slice of a new moon.

"I'm sorry. I know it's short notice."

It's also the *riposo*, the traditional daily afternoon shutdown of business, Italy's version of the siesta. I can tell by Dominic's sleepy voice that I woke him. Italians take the riposo very seriously, but this is an emergency.

I'm at war.

I'd take my father's car, but I'm afraid I'd wreck it within two blocks. Italians drive like psychos.

I hear a sigh over the line, then Dominic says, "Give me twenty minutes."

"Thank you! See you soon." I hang up and call Jenner. As soon as he picks up, I say, "I'm moving to Florence."

Silence.

"Did you hear what I said?"

"Yes. I'm just trying to picture what the kidnapper holding a gun to your head looks like. I've always had a fantasy about being held hostage by a brute of a man with too many tattoos and a limited vocabulary."

"Don't be silly. There's no kidnapper."

"So it's drugs, then. You're on drugs."

"You know I don't do drugs."

More silence. "You're not actually serious, Poppins."

He sounds affronted, as if moving to Florence is a ridiculous idea. Okay, it might be a tiny bit ridiculous, but I haven't told him why yet.

"Are you ready to hear something really freaky?"

"I'm waiting with bated breath."

I can practically hear his eyes rolling. "Remember the guy I told you about, the gorgeous Italian who I met in New York and gave the fake phone number to?"

"Yes. Your description of his suit gave me an erection. What about him?"

"He's here. In Florence."

Jenner gasps. "You saw him again?"

"Oh, honey, that's not even the best part."

I have to smile when Jenner shrieks. *"Revenge sex?"*

"Kinkier."

His voice comes low and thrilled. "Oh my God—are we talking Christian Grey kinky?"

"Waay kinkier than that."

"Tell me before I *die*! Is he a sadist? A dominant? A genius with knotting ropes?"

"He's my stepbrother."

In the ensuing pause, I hear Gordon Ramsay shouting at someone in the background. Jenner loves watching cooking shows. "Did you say . . . stepbrother?"

"I did. Well, technically speaking, he's my ex-stepbrother now."

"Hold on. Let me make sure I'm following. What you're telling me is that you met a gorgeous man at the airport in New York whom you had an instant sexual attraction to, gave a fake phone number to, whom you then met again in Florence . . . and turned out to be related to?"

"I'm saving the best part for last."

"There's more?" Jenner shouts.

"I didn't tell you that I was bumped off my flight to Florence . . . but got on the flight because he gave me his plane ticket. His *first-class* ticket."

"Rubbish!"

"It's true!"

"*Why* would he give you his ticket?"

"Because he overheard me arguing with the gate agent. I told her I had to be on the flight because my father was dying. He stepped in to save the day."

"That's just about the most romantic thing I've ever heard." Jenner sounds as if he's about to faint.

My voice is dry. "Don't pass out yet, because in trade for this ticket, he made me give him . . ."

Jenner sucks in a hard breath. "What? What did he make you give him?"

I know he's picturing all kinds of hot, sweaty stranger sex in a hallway closet, so I wait a beat, just to torture him. Then I say flatly, "He made me give him my sketch pad."

Jenner's silence throbs with confusion. "I've lost the plot."

"You know, my sketch pad. The one I always use to design my dresses—"

"Yes, yes, of course I know. You're always carrying the wretched thing around like a security blanket. Why would he want that dreadful tattered book?"

"Are you still sitting down?"

"Not only am I sitting down, I'm ruining my manicure gnawing on my cuticles! Spill, bitch, spill!"

"He's a fashion designer."

There's a strangled sound on the other end of the line, like maybe Jenner's choking on his tongue.

"And not just *any* fashion designer. You'll recognize his name. You own a few of his suits."

"Oh." He pants like an overexcited puppy. "I'm having a stroke. I'm having a heart attack. I've burst a vessel in my brain. Who is it, Poppins? *Who?*"

I'm starting to enjoy this and grimly smile. "Matteo Moretti."

A brief silence, then from Jenner's throat bursts a long, wavering shriek that could rouse the dead from their graves. *"Shut. Up!"*

"I'm telling you."

"You. Liar!"

"Swear to God."

"No!"

"Yes, honey. One thousand percent yes." I hear a loud *thud* and worry I've killed my best friend. "Jenner! Are you there?"

"Do you have any idea," he begins faintly, "any *idea* how many times I've masturbated to the thought of Matteo Moretti?"

I wrinkle my nose. "Dude. TMI."

"My God, Poppins, he's *the* most *beautiful* man who ever *lived*. Did you see the spread of him in Italian *GQ* when he first launched his company?"

"No. I'd never seen a picture of him before. I had no idea what he looked like, which is why I didn't recognize him at the airport!"

Jenner's sigh is heavy and full of longing. "Matteo. Oh, my dear sweet Matteo. *J'taime. J'adore. Tu es tout pour moi—*"

"Please tell me you're not touching yourself right now."

He grumbles, "Puritan."

"Can we get this train back on track? My point of this story is that I'm moving to Florence!"

I hear another sigh, but this one is different. Jenner has an entire vocabulary of sighs, each one nuanced, each one articulate. This one is what I imagine a mother disappointed in her daughter's choice of husband would sound like. It's all *Where did I go wrong?* and *How could she be so stupid?* and *I ruined my vaginal canal for* this?

"Darling," he says gently, "it's best not to make such huge life decisions when you're grieving. Moving to another country on a whim isn't like you. You're dependable. Reliable. Grounded. What you need right now is therapy, not Italy."

"Give me one reason why I should come back to the States."

"Me."

He says it like *What other reason would anyone need?* It makes me smile. "I happen to know for a fact that you come to Italy twice a year for Fashion Week. It's not like we'd never see each other again. You'll be here next month."

He makes a noise of impatience. "Need I remind you that you already have a business to run *here*?"

"Oh yeah. I didn't tell you about what happened yet."

My hollow laugh causes Jenner to say, "Uh-oh."

"Uh-oh is right. There was this fire, see . . ."

When I don't continue the sentence because my throat has closed, Jenner says, "No. The universe can't possibly hate you that much."

I sit on the concrete bench across from the fountain and drop my head into my hand. "Apparently the universe has put me at the top of its most-hated list. I got a call from my landlord yesterday. The shop went up in flames, along with everything in it. My entire life there is gone. Even if I did come back, what would I return to? All that's left is an apartment that isn't mine and a reputation as Bradley Wingate's sloppy seconds. Who'd want me? I'll always be the girl who was dumped at the altar. I'll never be able to live that down."

We're quiet for several minutes as Jenner absorbs that. "I suppose this is as good a time as any to tell you I saw him."

I jerk my head up. My heart explodes like a grenade inside my chest. "When? How?"

"He came to my apartment. I made the mistake of opening the door without asking who it was."

I stand and start to pace to try to work off the tension that's gripped me. "What did he want?"

"To talk to you."

When Jenner hesitates, I demand, "What are you leaving out?"

He exhales heavily. "I debated whether I should tell you this, but he looked wrecked. Like he hadn't slept since the wedding."

"The nonwedding," I bite back, furious. How dare Brad stalk Jenner to try to get to me? "And good, I'm glad!"

When Jenner doesn't respond, I start to get a bad feeling. "What else?"

"He cried."

I stop pacing abruptly, hold the phone out and look at it, then put it back to my ear. "I'm sorry, I thought I just heard you tell me that Brad *cried*."

"I did."

I scoff. "Brad doesn't cry! I don't think he even owns tear ducts! He yawned through his grandmother's funeral! When the family dog got hit by a car, Brad suggested his mother turn it into mulch for her roses!"

"Well, darling, unless the man recently took up method acting, these tears were bona fide. He sat on my sofa and sobbed like a baby. When I told him your father had died, I thought he'd pass out. He even tried to hug me when he left, if you can imagine."

I'm so angry I have to stand still and drag deep breaths into my lungs in order to stop myself from kicking the bench over and over and breaking my foot. "Why would you tell him about my father? Why would you tell that asshole anything? Why would you even let him through your door?"

"Because the first thing out of his mouth was that he knew he cocked the whole thing up. And the second thing out of his mouth was that he was the biggest idiot on the planet and didn't deserve you. Since we were in such agreement about the basics, I thought I'd hear him out."

"He left me at the altar!" I shout into the phone, my face burning. "He humiliated me! I hate his guts and wish he was dead!"

"Except you don't," says Jenner softly.

When I don't say anything—because I'm too emotional to speak—Jenner continues, "Do you remember what you said when I told you that I'd never seen you so happy after you and Brad started dating? You said, 'Every time I look at him, I feel like it's the first time I've seen the sun.'"

"I was a fool," I whisper bitterly, angrily swiping at the tear cresting my lower lid.

"Maybe. And maybe so was he."

When I growl at this betrayal, Jenner rushes to add, "I'm not saying give him a second chance. I know it's beyond that. I'm saying maybe just . . . listen to what he has to say. For your own peace of mind. For closure, if nothing else. If he really didn't care about your feelings, he never would've sat there and let me vomit my disdain all over him. He took it for half an hour, darling, nodding and crying the entire time."

I try to picture it but can't. Brad was obviously the victim of a body snatcher. There's no way in hell he'd allow Jenner to give him a dressing down, or cry, never in a million years.

Yet apparently he did.

"I can't deal with this shit right now. I've got a wicked stepmother, canine stepsisters, and an arrogant, infuriating stepbrother I'd like to do all kinds of dirty things with. I've got my father's funeral to attend, his business to salvage, and my former life to kiss goodbye. I've got no money and nowhere to live except under the same roof as the woman who refused to visit my father when he was dying."

I start to get teary. "I am *not* living my best life right now, okay? The last thing I need to hear about is fucking Brad and his fucking regrets. If you see him again, tell him that if he really wants to make it up to me, he can slice off his balls, put them in a blender, and live stream it on the internet! Then maybe he'll start to have an idea how I feel!"

I disconnect the call before Jenner can hear me break down.

Then I sit on the bench and cry until I hear Dominic's car driving up the gravel road to the house. When I stand, wiping my face with the backs of my hands, I happen to glance up at the house.

The marchesa stands at her bedroom window, gazing down at me with an expression of intense concentration. When she sees me looking, she turns and disappears, the drapes swinging closed behind her like the folds of a shroud.

TWELVE

Though Dominic keeps trying to engage me in conversation on the drive to Papa's shop after I collect my luggage from the hotel, I'm silent. Seething. My hands balled into fists on my legs, I can't stop thinking about Brad and his visit to Jenner, no matter how hard I try.

By the time we pull up in front of the shop, I've got a headache from gritting my teeth so hard.

"You're quiet today," says Dominic gently, unlocking the door.

It's an invitation to talk, but talking is the last thing I want to do. Right now, I need to work.

Dominic hits the switch on the wall beside the door, flooding the room with light. The front of the shop is a small retail space, with racks of elegant dresses in all colors of the rainbow, two small fitting rooms behind hanging curtains, and a counter with an old-fashioned cash register. Lead-paned windows overlook the cobblestone street outside. It smells of new fabric and old wood. The spicy aftershave Papa always wore lingers faintly in the air, like a ghost.

"It's exactly the same as I remember," I say, looking around. *How did he manage to do all this alone?*

As if he can read my thoughts, Dominic says, "Your father recently hired helpers, three ladies he trained to take orders and measurements, cut the cloth. The sewing he always did himself, of course." He crosses to the counter with the register, jingling the keys in his hand. "Still no answering machine, though." He catches my eye and smiles. "Or computer."

"Or website. It's like he didn't believe the twenty-first century was a thing."

Dominic chuckles. "He only got an email address so he could communicate with you. If they didn't have computers for public use at the library, he would've kept sending letters."

I drift over to a headless mannequin situated on a dais between the two single dressing rooms. She wears a gown of palest pink, cinched at the waist and cut generously through the hips, with a plunging neckline and cap sleeves. It's feminine to the extreme, exquisitely chic. When I look at the tag, I sigh in exasperation.

"No wonder he was broke."

An examination of several more dresses reveals a truth I've known all my life: My father should've had a business partner. Some artists can successfully create and deal with money, but he wasn't one of them.

"I offered many times to assist, but you know how stubborn he was." Dominic shakes his head at the price of a gorgeous silk scarf draped on a stand next to the counter. It's probably missing a few digits, like everything else.

I look around for a moment, taking stock of the situation. "Okay. First I've got to go through the inventory and reprice everything. Then we need to look at the advertising budget—"

"Advertising?" Dominic snorts.

"Don't tell me he was still relying only on word of mouth?"

Dominic lifts a shoulder. "Old dog. No new tricks."

I drag my hands through my hair, knowing it's gonna be a long night. "Can you drop my luggage off at the house for me? I'm not sure how late I'll get back, and it'll be easier for me to come in without all my stuff."

Dominic hesitates, looking confused. "You're not moving to another hotel?"

"Nope. I'm moving in with the marchesa." His expression is so horrified I have to laugh. "It's a long story. The bottom line is that I've decided I'm not selling Papa's business. I'm going to stay here and run it."

Dominic blinks slowly, standing stock-still behind the counter. "Is your husband moving here, too?"

God. How many times am I going to have to tell this story? "We broke up."

He's stunned. Apparently he also feels the need to ward away any evil I might be carrying because he makes the sign of the cross over his chest.

Annoyed, I walk past him and through the door leading to the production area in the back of the shop. It's much messier back here, with bolts of cloth and color sketches strewn across work tables, dozens of mannequins in various stages of undress standing around like headless party guests, and sewing stations, file cabinets, and boxes waiting to be unpacked.

Pinned to a corkboard on the wall above a workstation hang photographs of me at various stages of my life. The latest one is a Polaroid from the last time I visited, five years ago. Papa had me laughing at some terrible joke he'd made and took the picture before I could stop him. My head is thrown back. My eyes are closed. My mouth is wide open. I look happy.

I'm seized by a terrible feeling of guilt. *Five years.* I spent that time trying to build my business and going gaga over Brad, and what was my father doing?

Slowly going broke and falling in love with a vulture.

So, samesies.

"I'm so sorry to hear that." Dominic sounds rattled. He's followed me in from the other room and stands in the doorway, looking disturbed. "Do you want to talk about it?"

I shake my head and leave it at that.

He opens his mouth to say something else, but we're interrupted by loud knocking from the front room. Someone's at the door.

Not just anyone, I see as I move past Dominic into the front room. *Him.*

I jerk open the door and glare at Matteo. "What're you doing here?"

He smiles, looking me over with hungry eyes like I'm a cupcake on display in a bakery case and he'd like to lick off all my icing. "I was in the neighborhood and saw the lights on."

"Liar."

His smile deepens, dimpling his cheeks. "You know what they say. Keep your friends close and your enemies closer."

"They also say you don't have to be a cactus expert to know a prick when you see one."

His eyes flash. "Is it just my dick you're obsessed with, or dicks in general?"

"Don't flatter yourself. And while you're busy not flattering your-self, *leave*."

He purses his lips, as if he's considering it. Then he says casually, "No," and strolls past me into the shop.

I slam the door and turn to him with my arms crossed over my chest. "Oh, I get it. On the lookout for more designs to steal, is that it?" I smile sweetly at his withering look.

"You seem to have a mental block about the facts, so let me remind you that you *gave* me that sketch pad, bella."

I hate the way goose bumps form over my arms when he calls me that. There's something so intimate about it. A note of secret knowledge hums in it, an undertone of sensuality, as if he knows how I sound when I come.

"I'm not going over this with you again. Get out."

"Oh. Ciao." Ignoring my request, Matteo addresses Dominic, standing in the doorway to the back room.

Dominic looks back and forth between us with his brows drawn together. I can't tell exactly what his expression is, but I'm sure it's not happiness.

"Ciao." Dominic's tone is curt. I guess he likes my ex-stepbrother as much as he likes my ex-stepmother.

The two men size each other up for a beat, until Matteo says darkly, "A pleasure to see you again."

It's both a lie and a dismissal. Dominic can tell, too, because he bristles like a cat. He says something sharply in Italian. Matteo snaps a response. Then they stand there glaring at each other like two pistoleros about to whip out their guns and shoot.

"Well, this has been fun. Glad to see I'm not the only person you annoy. Bye!"

Matteo's eyes cut to me. They're brilliant, blistering blue, two light-sabers slicing the air with a whiz. It's all I can do not to step back from the electric force of their impact.

He says stiffly, "You really should learn to speak Italian."

Intrigued, I glance at Dominic, who's scowling. "I will. I mean, I am. Soon." *Shut up, Kimber!* I straighten my shoulders and pretend nonchalance, while Matteo watches me with his crackling light-beam eyes. After only a moment under his scrutiny, I want to jump out of my skin.

Making a show of solidarity with Dominic, I walk over to him, then stand shoulder to shoulder with him as I coolly regard Matteo. "Was there something in particular you wanted? Because I've got a lot of work to do."

Matteo roasts me with his look. I'm a pig turning over hot coals, getting a nice crackly crunch to my skin. "Yes," he says, holding my gaze. "There *is* something I want. And you know exactly what it is."

Quivering, I think the word is. Yes, that's what my vagina is doing right now. *Quivering*.

When I swallow, heat scorching my cheeks, Matteo's gaze turns ruthlessly satisfied. He lifts a hand, indicating all the dresses around us. "You know this shop should be mine."

I hate him. I hate him with the heat of a thousand suns. I hate him with the force of gravity on—what's that planet that has all the crushing gravity? Jupiter. Yes. I hate him with the gravity of Jupiter.

"This shop will never be yours," I say, enunciating each word. Just to get back at him for making my lady bits resemble Jell-O, I add, "Neither will anything else of mine."

Oh so softly, Matteo answers, "We'll see." Then he smiles.

The smug SOB *smiles*.

As if he can sense I'm about to rip the cash register off the counter and commit murder with it, Dominic drapes his arm over my shoulder and lightly squeezes me closer. Drawing strength from his support, I draw a breath through my nose, then point at the door. "Out."

I should've known Matteo isn't one to take direction. He strolls over to the mannequin in the pink dress on the dais and touches the skirt. He traces his finger along a seam and muses to no one in particular, "I wonder what Luca would think to hear the way his daughter speaks to me."

He couldn't have found a more tender spot if he searched with a bloodhound. I'm stabbed in the chest by a knife of pain, not only because Matteo used my father's first name so casually, indicating how close they were, but also because I know he's right.

My father would be appalled at my hostility. He raised me to be considerate of others, even if I didn't like them.

But that was before I was publicly humiliated and decided to hate all men under the age of sixty. Especially gorgeous, arrogant, rich ones who treat women like everything they're good for is between their legs.

I turn to Dominic. "Will you please excuse us? Matteo and I need to talk privately."

Dominic cuts a stony glare at my archnemesis, then gives me a hug. He murmurs into my ear, "I can tell you don't like him. Smart girl." He pulls away, eyes me meaningfully, then turns his back on Matteo and leaves.

As soon as the door closes behind him, I turn to Matteo. "I owe you an apology."

He inspects my face in narrow-eyed silence, his expression assessing.

I know this crow I'm about to eat is gonna taste really shitty, but it's what my father would want. He always told me that anything could be forgiven in a person's character except lack of kindness. So I grit my teeth and get it over with.

"For how I talk to you. I'm normally not this . . . ragey."

After looking at me for a long moment, he says, "You're hurting. I'm just a convenient target."

Shit. I was expecting a snappy comeback, not understanding. And *especially* not insightfulness. If he's going to be this observant all the time, I won't be able to be around him. No one likes to feel as if her soul is hanging out for everyone to see, like an untucked shirt.

I arrange my face into an emotionless mask and focus on a spot on the wall over his shoulder so I don't have to contend with those soul-piercing eyes. "I suppose you're right. The sketch pad situation didn't help, but it was more than a fair trade. That plane ticket is probably the best gift I've ever been given."

I have to stop because my voice cracks and water is welling in my eyes. I turn away before Matteo can see and mock me for my lack of dignity. I refuse to be anyone's kicking bag.

But he surprises me again.

"I envy you," he says quietly.

When I jerk around in surprise, I find Matteo staring at me with a strange expression. It's something like longing, only darker.

"What do you mean?"

He turns his attention back to the pink dress. In profile, he's even more appealing, all ruler-straight lines and sculpted angles, impossibly long lashes swept downward to a smudge on his golden cheeks.

"My father died when I was very young."

His voice is hollow, edged with regret. There's something he's not saying. Though my curiosity is intense, I won't ask what it is.

"At least you knew him. My mother died when I was born."

He turns his head. His gaze locks onto mine and doesn't let go. I feel exposed and vulnerable and have to fight the strong urge to flee. We stare at each other across the small room while my heartbeat goes haywire and the walls seem to grow closer.

"Your father showed me a picture of her once," says Matteo in a hesitant voice, as if he's afraid to spook me, or kick-start another bout of anger. "You look so much like her."

There's a bitter taste in my mouth. Must be all the tears I'm swallowing. "I know. I mean, from all the photographs I've seen, we're like twins. As I got older, sometimes I'd catch Papa staring at me with this haunted look, like he was seeing a ghost."

Matteo moves closer. Slowly, as if drawn by a force he's fighting against. "Do you think that's why the only pictures of you in the house are from when you were a child?"

Whoa. The man notices everything. I look at the floor, hiding my eyes, and nod. I think of the Polaroid of me laughing tacked to the corkboard in the back of the shop and wonder how often Papa looked at it and saw someone else in the shape of my face. How often he put it away, only to take it out and tack it up again.

How much pain it must have caused him.

"Hair as black as night. Skin as white as snow. Lips as red as blood."

When I look up, startled, Matteo says, "That's how your father described you. Like Snow White, he said, only too smart to take a poison apple from a witch."

How can someone smell so good? How can someone be so beautiful? Look at him. He's like a walking piece of art.

Then it's like a switch gets thrown. Remembering how I let Brad's good looks and pedigree blind me to reality, my voice hardens. "If there's one thing fairy tales have taught me, it's that the most tempting, perfect-looking apples are always the ones that are rotten to the core."

He stops. We're feet apart. His tone, so soft only moments ago, turns cutting.

"Question: How much of your dislike of me is actually about me, and how much of it is about your ex-fiancé?"

I feel as if he can see through me, like every thought I have is floating in a bubble over my head and there's a gauge stuck on my nose that's broadcasting my temperature. Hot, cold, boiling, freezing, want you, hate you, about to cry. He sees it all, and it drives me crazy.

"My ex has nothing to do with anything."

"Really?" His eyes do their laser beam thing again. "Because I'm starting to think you decided to hate me before we ever spoke a word to each other. I'm starting to think that look of disgust you gave me at the airport lounge when you first saw me had nothing to do with me and everything to do with you getting dumped at the altar."

An atomic detonation of fury blasts through me. If I were Wolverine, this is the part where my long steel claws would unsheathe from my knuckles with a violent clang. "I never said I was dumped at the altar."

Here comes that condescending eyebrow arch. I'd like to slap a blob of wax on that thing and rip it clean off.

"You didn't have to. There are plenty of stories about it on the internet."

My mouth drops open. I stare at Matteo in horror. "You *googled* me?"

His lips curve into his signature ruthless smile. "I like to know all there is to know about my business rivals. 'The Lovelorn Seamstress'?

'The Cast-Away Couturier'? So many clever headlines. Maybe you can use one of them for the name of your new shop."

I'm so embarrassed I can't talk. I stand there staring at him, my cheeks blazing with heat. I'm living that awful moment all over again. I can't escape it, even thousands of miles away. In another country halfway around the world, I'm still the girl who wasn't good enough.

I think I'm going to be sick.

"Maybe I did decide to hate you before we spoke a word to each other, and maybe I had good reasons. The way you walk around like the world should throw itself at your feet. The way you smirk at everyone, so superior. The way you look at women—"

"You," he interrupts, his voice gruff. "The way I look at *you*, you mean."

"You're splitting hairs again. I'm sure I'm just one of millions of women you've given that look to."

"Which look?"

He steps closer. Now we're inches apart. Breathing each other's air. Feeling each other's body heat.

This guy has serious space issues.

I moisten my lips. His eyes follow the motion of my tongue. The smug smile is gone. All that's left on his face is blistering intensity.

"You know which look. And step back. You're crowding me."

"No. I want to talk about this look you're so upset by. I want you to tell me what you think it means."

I become mesmerized by the pulse beating in the hollow of his throat. It's hard and fast, and shocking. Is his heart pounding as hard as mine is?

"I don't know what it means," I say primly.

That makes him laugh, low and throaty, a sound that for some strange reason sends a flood of heat between my legs.

"Such a terrible liar," he murmurs. He takes a lock of my hair between two fingers and tugs on it.

It's a tease, like a schoolboy pulling a ponytail, but the heat in his eyes is anything but boyish.

I've never been looked at like this by a man. Never. I think he wants to devour me. I think he wants to do *really* bad things to me.

I think my ex-stepbrother wants to fuck my brains out.

When my uterus starts doing cartwheels, I have to remind her that not only is it gross to have sex with a relative, it's probably illegal. She shoots back that we're no longer relatives, so all bets are off, and all signs point to Go.

The cheeky bitch.

Matteo murmurs, "I'd love to be part of whatever conversation you're having in your head right now, bella."

My uterus sighs and melts into a pool of liquid. At least she shut up.

"I was thinking I have a lot of work to do. I was thinking you should leave now."

He brushes the ends of my hair over my cheek and jaw, trails it slowly down my neck as his gaze follows. My pulse kicks up a few thousand notches.

"I don't accept your apology." He leans closer, fogging my brain like a humid car window. "I don't think it was sincere. I think you should *show* me how sorry you are for the way you talk to me, bella. And I think you should do it like this."

He takes my face in his hands and kisses me.

THIRTEEN

His mouth is heaven. I've died and gone straight to heaven. I'm floating on clouds. Somewhere off in the distance, cherubs pluck harp strings and unicorns sail over rainbows.

He's gentle but firm, slow but dominant. His hands around my face are almost rough, but his mouth is as soft as cotton candy. He parts my lips with his tongue and makes a sound in his throat when he does it, a sound that instantly hardens my nipples and makes every nerve in my body glow with lust.

All thoughts of personal space are out the window. All thoughts about anything else but his mouth and hard body against mine are toast. I stand there and let him give me the hottest kiss of my life, not caring at all that I know after it's over, I'll be horrified with both of us.

It's too damn good to care about that right now.

I arch into him, grabbing at his suit. He slides one hand into my hair and makes a fist at the scruff of my neck, holding my head in place as his tongue probes deeper into my mouth. His other hand moves from my jaw to my ass. He grabs a handful of it, dragging me closer.

We stand there in front of the counter in my father's shop and feast on each other for what seems like hours. He kisses me for an eternity, licking and sucking, taking gentle nips of my lower lip, pinning me against him with an arm like a vise when I slide my hands up his chest and wind my arms around his shoulders so I can get even closer.

God, I needed this. How did I ever think I'd been kissed before? This kiss makes every other kiss I've ever had feel like a dry peck on the cheek from a granny.

This kiss makes me feel like a woman.

He says something roughly in Italian, breaking away from my mouth to drag his lips over my jaw and down my throat. Pulling my head back with that hand in my hair, he sucks on the ragged pulse in my neck, making me moan.

His voice hot at my ear, he whispers, "I want to hear you make that sound when I'm inside you."

My eyes roll back in my head. I'm starting to sweat. My heart pounds so hard it might be in danger of bursting. My body glows with heat, especially in the damp space between my legs, which is also howling with need.

We stagger back a step or two and bump into the counter. Matteo's erection presses into my crotch. I whimper, panting and delirious, and hear him make an animal noise, a growl, like a bear.

It's the sexiest sound I've ever heard.

Then he opens his mouth and ruins everything.

"You see? We don't have to be enemies. Let me buy the business, and we can be the best of friends."

I freeze. All the blood that was pumping through my veins so hotly falls to a complete standstill. I stare at him, at his beautiful face so close to mine, and wonder how strict the laws on murder are in this country.

"Wait. Wait—*did you just kiss me to try to get me to sell you my father's business?*"

He glowers at me from under dark brows but doesn't respond.

I push him away, wiping my mouth with the back of my hand. "Answer the question."

He inhales a slow breath, drags a hand through his hair, and straightens his jacket. Then he tosses his head back and stares at me down his nose.

"Oh my God. You . . . you . . . mercenary!"

A muscle flexes in his jaw. His eyes could make a cold pile of kindling explode into flame. "The company will be better off in my hands. If you want to honor your father's memory, let someone run it who can make it the success it deserves to be."

This is the second time he's made me feel like I've taken a punch to the gut. I'm determined it will be the last.

I straighten my shoulders, lift my chin, and dredge up what little dignity I have left. Then I stare him right in the eye and let him have it.

"Fuck you, Matteo Moretti. Fuck you and that high horse you rode in on, and fuck your ego, and fuck your fake kiss."

"Which you loved, by the way."

"And fuck that stupid smirk on your face," I say through gritted teeth, willing myself not to lose control and start screaming. "Now get out of my shop. And don't ever come back, or I'll make you wish you were never born."

He stares at me in blistering silence, his gaze raking over my face. He looks as if he wants to say something else, but instead he shakes his head, turns around, and stalks out. He slams the door behind him.

I lean on the counter, breathing hard, still dizzy from his kiss. How many more times will I let myself be humiliated before I learn my lesson?

Men can't be trusted.

Neither can my uterus.

From now on, I'll only allow logic to run the show.

Still shaking, I lock the door to the shop and get to work.

Nine hours later, I've conducted an audit of the books, catalogued and repriced the inventory, reorganized most of the work space in the back of the shop, and managed not to think about Matteo more than once every four or five minutes.

My mind keeps wandering back to that kiss. The adrenaline levels in my bloodstream still haven't returned to normal.

I make a list of things to buy—first being a computer—turn the lights off, and lock up. Then I walk down the street to the square, where I find a taxi to take me back to Il Sogno.

The house is dark when I arrive. I don't have a key, so I'm forced to knock on the front door, hoping Lorenzo will still be awake so I don't have to sneak through a window. I'm relieved when I hear a quick step approaching.

The door opens. "Sorry I'm so late, Loren—" I stop short because the man who opened the door isn't Lorenzo.

"Don't look so surprised to see me. My mother lives here, remember?"

Smirking, Matteo leans against the doorframe. He's dressed casually, in dark slacks and a white dress shirt rolled up his strong, tanned forearms. He looks like a billionaire supermodel posing for a spread in *Billionaire Supermodel* magazine.

Incandescent with anger, I brush past him into the house. *My house*, I remind myself, fuming.

I head straight to the kitchen because I'm starving. Lorenzo's there, sitting at the big wooden table, swirling a snifter of amber liquid in his hand. Another snifter sits on the table across from him. He looks up and smiles. "Ah. Signorina. We were just talking about you."

Behind me, Matteo strolls into the kitchen. I feel him standing there in the doorway, making all the atoms in the room vibrate at a dangerous frequency.

"Were you now?" I say acidly. "Sounds like fun."

Lorenzo blinks at the tone of my voice. He glances over at Matteo, who's probably flipping me off behind my back. He rises, following me over to the fridge. "Can I get you something to eat?"

"You can get me a gun," I mutter under my breath. I grab a yogurt, remember I hate yogurt, throw it back, and grab a hunk of salami and a block of cheese. The fridge is filled with all kinds of stuff, but I want something I can eat in my room, tearing apart with my teeth.

I've got to figure out a way to ban Matteo from the house.

Without another word to either of them, I leave Matteo and Lorenzo in the kitchen and head to my bedroom. It isn't until I throw open the door and flip the light switch that I remember it isn't mine anymore.

Cornelia is sprawled in the middle of the bed, snoring like a chainsaw.

She has a nightlight shaped like a giraffe. She has a water bowl that appears to be real china, elevated on a silver stand beside the bed. She has a pink blanket with frolicking bunnies that covers the lower half of her huge black body.

Her name is painted in flowery fucking letters on the wall.

"Get out of my bed, dog!" I shout.

Waking with a snort, Cornelia jerks and scrambles upright. She sees me standing in the doorway, throws back her head, and howls in fright.

Drama queen.

I stand aside and point into the hallway. "Out!"

The dog launches herself from the bed. She promptly gets tangled in the sheets and falls to the floor. Frantically struggling, she kicks the stand with the water bowl, which topples over and smashes against the floor.

"Oh my God. This is a frickin' circus."

I stride over to the flailing mass of blankets and legs and grab a handful of fabric. I pull, and the dog is released like a rock from a slingshot. She blasts from the room in a blur of fur and tears off down the hallway, baying like a banshee.

Leaving the cheese and salami on the dresser where Cornelia's wardrobe presumably resides, I stomp over to the bed and strip off the sheets. I wad them up and toss them into a corner. I sniff the mattress, certain it will reek of dog, but smell nothing. I don't spot any suspicious stains, either. Satisfied, I get fresh sheets from the linen closet in the en suite bathroom and make the bed.

It isn't until I'm finished that I realize I have company. Matteo's leaning in the doorway, watching me with a smile.

"Look who it is. Count Egotistico. Here to give me another fake kiss?"

"If you'll let me."

His smile grows wider, the prick. I smile back violently.

"I think I'll pass, thanks."

With my chin held high, I go over to him, push him out of the doorway, and slam the door in his face.

The door instantly swings back open.

Shit. No lock.

"You know, hate and love aren't so different, bella."

He's being philosophical now, pursing his pretty mouth and gazing at the ceiling, as if viewing the stars.

I could kill him.

"Why do you enjoy torturing me? Are you some kind of sadist?"

He ignores me, naturally, and continues his little Socratic speech. "They're two sides of the same coin, really. Passion, obsession, sweaty palms, and a racing heart. Lost sleep." He slides his gaze over to the cheese and salami on the dresser. "A poor appetite."

"You want a poor appetite? I'll give you a poor appetite. I'll take that salami and wedge it so far down your throat you won't be able to eat ever again."

Amused by my fury, he smiles. "Passion," he reminds me, smug as shit.

I look around for something to throw at him.

"Let's call a truce." He strolls forward, hands in his pockets.

As if I'll feel safer that way.

"No truce. No way. And you're the one who started this war, remember?"

He makes a face, like he's doubtful.

"Yes, *you*. Wait, why am I even talking to you? You fake kissed me!"

"Did I?"

"Yes! You admitted you did!"

"Hmm. I don't recall that."

"So we'll add dementia to your long list of problems."

By now he's trapped me at the edge of the bed, advancing so stealthily I hardly noticed it, which was probably his dastardly plan all along.

I stand my ground and flatten my hand in the center of his chest, bracing my arm so he can't move forward. "I'm not a joke," I say, my voice raw. "I'm not a plaything."

"I never said you were."

Under my palm, his heart is a jackhammer. We do the hate breathing at each other again, which apparently is becoming our thing. Then we do the hate eye fucking again, which is *definitely* becoming our thing.

He says softly, "You're giving me grief about how I look at you? You should see your eyes right now." His voice drops an octave. "So dirty, bella. So very, very dirty."

"I'm not selling the company, no matter how much you try to sex it out of me."

He quirks an eyebrow. "Sex it out of you?" As I watch with ragged breath, he sinks his teeth into his full lower lip. "Now *that* sounds interesting. Let's discuss."

"You're a pig."

"And yet you want me."

"You're unbelievable!"

"Yes, women have told me that before. Usually right after they come."

I can't even with this guy!

Then it's like he remembers something. He looks around, frowning. "What are you doing in here?"

"What does it look like I'm doing? Trying to get rid of you!"

He looks at the wad of sheets in the corner. He looks at the freshly made bed. Then he looks back at me. The smile that breaks over his face is breathtaking.

"My darling ex-stepsister. Are you *moving in*?"

Very deliberately, I slide my hand up his chest until I reach his neck. Then I grasp his throat—lightly, but enough to let him know I mean it.

His skin is hot to the touch, and his throat is strong. Thick. It makes me think of other hot, thick body parts.

I officially hate myself.

He lifts his brows, obviously amused. "You have the most interesting internal conversations. Are you going to choke me?"

I growl. It sounds silly, like a kitten trying to be scary.

Matteo leans forward. My arm is still locked at the elbow, so it puts more pressure around his throat. Holding my gaze, he says softly, "Go ahead. I know you want to."

Boy, do I. I curl my other hand around his neck so now I've got him good and surrounded. I feel his pulse, beating hard against my palms. It's weirdly arousing.

Intently watching my face, he whispers, "Those eyes."

Then from the doorway comes a sharp voice.

"What's going on here?"

"Nothing to worry about, only Kimber trying to strangle me." Matteo turns around and smiles at his mother as I whip my hands guiltily around my back.

The marchesa's frosty gaze cuts to me, then back to Matteo. In her arms, Beans is dressed in a white nightgown that matches her mistress's. She's baring her teeth.

"Ah. I see you're working your usual charm." The marchesa glances back at me. "If you really want to annoy him, make fun of his hair. He's obsessed he might lose it."

She turns on her heel and leaves, her nightgown billowing like a sail behind her.

I gape after her, breath leaking from my lungs like a tire leaking air. "Did your mother just *diss* you?"

Matteo regards me with a sour twist to his lips. "No."

"She totally did! Oh my God, I need to buy a lottery ticket. Do they have the lottery in this country? 'Cause this has got to be some kind of sign from the universe that my luck is changing."

The rest of Matteo's face turns sour, and now I'm gloating. "Aw, whassa matter, Mattie? Did Mommy hurt widdle Mattie's feewings?"

The stare he sends me smolders with annoyance.

It's the most fantastic thing I've ever seen.

I smile at him and bat my lashes. This game of tit for tat wasn't fun, up until now. "Do I detect a chink in your glossy shining armor, stepbrother dearest? Have I finally found your Achilles' heel? Mumsy-Wumsy despises you as much as I do, is that it?"

He says darkly, "Careful."

For some reason, that particular word, spoken in that particular tone, gives me pause. "Oh. You actually think she does?"

Matteo says nothing. He simply stares at me with his hands clenched, a muscle jumping in his jaw.

I'm tempted to tell him how her eyes lit up when Lorenzo announced his arrival, but keep my mouth shut. He doesn't deserve peace of mind. *He fake kissed me.*

"Well, this has been real. But it's late, and I need to get to bed."

Matteo's gaze drifts to the bed. I picture us together on it, writhing around in a sweaty, moaning tangle. I swallow so loudly it sounds like a cartoon.

"Certo," says Matteo gruffly, still staring at the bed. Then he turns and heads to the door. Just as he's about to pass through it, he stops, puts a hand on the doorframe, and turns back. "Since you're going to be living in Italy now, I assume you'll be attending Fashion Week in Milan next month?"

His face is impassive, but there's something I don't trust simmering in his eyes. "I'd have to get an invitation. Why do you ask?"

He allows himself a smile, but there's not a trace of humor in it. "I think you'll be interested to see the House of Moretti's spring collection. We have some truly incredible new designs."

He lets that sink in for a moment. When I realize his meaning and suck in a breath, his humorless smile grows wider.

He raps on the frame with his knuckles. "Sweet dreams."

Then he leaves, taking the last of my faith in humanity with him.

FOURTEEN

MATTEO

Luca told me his daughter was stubborn. But there's stubborn, and then there's Kimber DiSanto.

Thank God she's even more competitive than she is pigheaded. What I've got planned for her counts on both.

Smiling at the curse she hollers at my back as I walk out of her bedroom, I make my way to the kitchen. I swallow the rest of the Frangelico in my glass, say a brief farewell to Lorenzo, and leave.

My work here is done.

For tonight.

FIFTEEN

KIMBER

I'm back at the shop before the sun's up, sketching out a new collection.

If that bastard thinks I'm going down without a fight, he's about to get the surprise of his life.

It's impossible for an unknown designer to book a runway show in Milan for Fashion Week, but there is *one* way for me to make myself known. One risky, go-broke-or-go-home way.

But I'm going to need help to pull this off.

Once I've got about a dozen rough sketches, I take a break and call Jenner. He answers on the fifth ring, just as I'm about to hang up.

"*Moshi moshi.*"

"Mo—what?"

"It's how they answer the telephone in Japan, darling. Haven't you been anywhere?"

"Are you currently in Japan?"

"Unfortunately, no. But I *am* currently in bed with a lovely Japanese lad who I was inside of earlier, so it's practically the same thing."

"Oh shit. What time is it there? I keep forgetting about time zones."

"Never mind, I've been up all night anyway. How are you? What's happening with my darling love Matteo? Tell me everything and hurry up about it."

In the background there's a sleepy male voice asking Jenner something. I catch the words "please" and "squeeze" and stop listening.

"Ugh. Your 'darling love' is the worst. We're total enemies. I'm gonna crush him like a bug!"

"Oh dear." Jenner chuckles. "Have you been playing Scrabble again?"

"No. I've got a bigger game in mind. A game with much higher stakes."

"Hmm. This sounds interesting. Continue."

I take a breath and let it out in a gust. "I'm gonna crash his show at Fashion Week."

There's a loaded pause, then Jenner says, "It's all that Mediterranean sun. It's gone to your head."

"I haven't been out in the sun!"

"The wine, then. You're having wine for breakfast, lunch, and dinner, right? They push it on you over there like it's Vitamin Water."

"I'm completely sober."

"Wonderful," he says drily. "That means you're serious, which means you're seriously deluded."

"I'm not deluded!"

Ignoring me, he sighs. "You're really starting to worry me, darling. First it was moving to Florence, now it's crashing an exclusive invite-only event that will be crawling with security. The next thing I know you'll be telling me you want me to model one of your dresses on the catwalk or some such nonsense."

When I remain silent, Jenner says, "Oh no. No, no, no."

"If you love me, you'll do this for me."

"That's emotional blackmail!"

"I need you, Jenner. Not only are you a professional model—an amazing model—you're the prettiest person I know. No one has cheekbones or a pout like you."

He grumbles something, but I know I've got his attention. Flattery works on him every time.

"I know how you love making a spectacular entrance, and what I've got planned will be *super* spectacular." I don't have anything planned yet, but I'm appealing to his sense of drama and love of the limelight. I'll work out the particulars later. "And you'll already be in Milan next month for the shows, so it's perfect."

He laughs. "Oh, Poppins. You're delightfully bonkers."

"So you'll do it?"

"Prance around in one of your daintily exquisite, frothy creations and make an utter fool of myself while simultaneously jeopardizing my career by being involved in an ill-conceived and quite possibly illegal harebrained scheme to disrupt one of the most prestigious fashion shows on the planet? Of course not. One of us still has his sanity."

I grouse, "Danielle would do it for me."

"Please. No one would let that woman *near* a catwalk with those enormous boobs of hers. I'm not even sure they'd let her in the front door—they'd turn her around and shuttle her off to the nearest Hooters! Honestly, how you people can walk around with those things, I'll never know."

"I'll have you know my boobs are my favorite part of my body."

"That's because you have lovely little B-cups, darling. They'll still be perky when you're in the old folks' home. I can just see you now, shakin' your moneymakers for all the drooling old gents in their wheelchairs! Oh, I can hardly wait. We should pick out your stripper name now so we'll be ready. How does it go, the name of your first pet and the street you lived on growing up? Yes, that's it." He laughs, delighted. "My stripper name is Frisky Broadmoor!"

This always happens in a conversation with him. We'll be discussing politics or current events and wind up on boobs or blow jobs. It's like his superpower.

"Getting back to the matter at hand . . . I also need a few of your model friends."

Silence.

"Before you say no, you should know that the pay will be great."

More silence, except for in the background, where Jenner's friend is giggling. I hear rustling noises and try not to imagine what might be going on under the sheets.

"Okay, not *great* great, but . . . um . . . actually, how much does a model make per hour?"

"You can't afford me," he says flatly, then says to his friend, "Stop batting at it, love, it isn't a cat toy. Here. Like this." He comes back on the line sounding practical. "Listen to me now. I know this is a terrible time for you. A terrible, trying time. It's normal that you're a little off-kilter."

Crushed, I close my eyes. *Of all the people in the world, you're the last one I thought would ever patronize me.*

"I know what you're thinking," he says when I'm quiet too long.

"No you don't."

"You're thinking I'm being patronizing."

Fine. So he knows. Big whoop.

"And maybe you're right. For that I apologize. What I'm trying so poorly to say is that I'm worried about you, and I'm here for you for anything that doesn't involve ending my career." His voice grows quieter. "Do you want me to fly out for the funeral?"

At the mention of the *F* word, the energy drains from my body. I slump into the nearest chair and throw an arm over my eyes. "No. Yes. I don't know."

"I can be on a plane in three hours. Just say the word."

In the background, Jenner's playdate complains about the possibility of him leaving and is crossly shushed.

"No," I say more firmly. "I'm okay. Thanks for the offer, though. I appreciate it."

The last thing I want is to be a burden on him. He's happy and having fun, and I'm ruining everything with all my disasters. "You know something? You're right. I'm off-kilter. I'm not thinking straight. It's been a really bizarre, emotional week, and all the wires in my brain are crossed." I laugh. It sounds about as cheerful as if I'd just slit my wrists. "I'm gonna go. Sorry for calling you so early. Or late. Whatever it is there."

"Hey. You. Greta Garbo."

"I'm not Greta Garbo," I mutter. "I'm Katharine Hepburn."

"Right. The feisty, independent one, not the moody 'I want to be alone' one."

"Exactly."

"I think you're a bit of both, but what I was saying before I was so rudely interrupted is that I love you."

"I know," I whisper, trying not to sound too teary and broken. "I love you, too."

"Oh, Poppins. It gets better. I promise."

"You sound like one of those PSAs for teen suicide."

"Call me anytime you need a pep talk, yes? And I'm serious about the funeral. Say the word and I'm there."

We say our goodbyes and hang up.

Then I go back to my sketches. If Jenner won't help me steal Matteo's thunder, I'll just have to find someone else who will.

At eight o'clock that night, I stumble bleary-eyed and starving out of the taxi and into the house. The door's open, so I let myself in.

Right in the middle of family dinner time.

At the formal dining table sit the marchesa, Cornelia, and Beans. They all look up when I walk in.

"Buonasera," says the marchesa, setting her fork down.

She's resplendent in a black silk suit. It sets off her pale hair and skin and makes her cyborg eyes glow like the Terminator's. She looks as if she's about to execute someone. To her left, Beans sits in her booster seat, trembling with malice. To her right, Cornelia is creeping down under the table with big scaredy-cat eyes, trying to be invisible.

At the other end of the table sits Matteo, lounging in his chair like the king of the universe.

He smiles, looks me up and down with a starkly sexual gaze, and winks.

It's a challenge. He's throwing down. He wants to see how I'll handle him hanging out here. I'd bet a million bucks he's hoping I'll throw a fit.

Without a shred of emotion in my voice or on my face, I say to the marchesa, "I realized I didn't tell you."

"Tell me what?"

"I'm moving in."

She delicately pats her lips with her napkin, leaving her lipstick undisturbed, then smooths the napkin over her lap. "I assumed that when Dominic brought your luggage back yesterday."

That's it? I wait for her to say something else, but she just gazes at me with that unnerving calm of hers.

From the corner of my eye, I see Matteo cover his mouth with his hand. He's trying not to laugh. I'm sure there's steam visibly shooting from my ears, but I force myself to stay under control.

"I took my room back. Cornelia will have to share with Beans from now on."

At the mention of her name, Cornelia whimpers quietly from under the table. I swear that giant dog is nothing but a giant wimp.

"I'm sure we'll make do." The marchesa picks up her fork and resumes eating.

When it becomes obvious that was the end of the conversation, I say, "Okay, then. Great talk."

Fuming, I leave the dining room and head straight to the kitchen. I know there are soups, stews, and all kinds of other food brought over by Papa's friends, but right now I need something else. I rummage through the cabinets until I find what I'm looking for, then grab a bottle of whiskey and pour myself a drink.

What could Papa have seen in her? She's so cold! Sleeping with her would be like sleeping with an ice block! Inside an igloo! In the middle of a blizzard in Antarctica!

I finish the drink and pour myself another. I can't believe she didn't ask me a single question. No *How long will you be staying?* No *What's your plan for the business?* No nothing!

Actually that might be better. I mull it over, finally deciding that yes, it will definitely be better if she doesn't ask questions. She obviously doesn't want to get to know me, and I definitely don't want to get to know her. We'll just stay out of each other's hair. I can do my thing and she can do hers.

Whatever her thing might be. Probably casting evil spells on the villagers.

"Working late, were you?"

Matteo strolls into the kitchen, smirking, looking like a god in a perfectly fitted midnight-blue suit and white dress shirt open at the collar.

"None of your business." I wish I knew a few of his mother's evil spells. I'd give him a hairy wart on the end of his nose and a hump on his back to tear down that ego a few notches.

Standing next to the wooden table, he slowly unbuttons his suit jacket, casually fingering it open until it parts under his hand. He slides it off, drapes it over the back of a chair, unhooks his cuff links, sets them on the table, and rolls up the cuffs of his shirt, staring at me the whole time.

I can't look away. It's like porn. You know you shouldn't watch it, but you can't stop.

Tailored suits were made for bodies like his. Everything about him is elegant, proportionate, finely made. He's muscular but not overly so, strong but not bulky. His skin is golden and poreless. It looks airbrushed. He's got cheekbones even Jenner would be jealous of, and a jawline so sharp it could cut glass.

The man is haute couture.

And my God, those eyes. Achingly blue, hauntingly sensual, they're the kind of eyes a woman never forgets. The kind of eyes you could drown in.

The kind of eyes that could ruin your life.

I guzzle the rest of my drink, coughing when the fumes sear my nose. "You need to start having these cheerful little family dinners at *your* house."

"Oh? Is that what I need?"

Smiling like he has a secret, Matteo strolls over to the cupboard, gets a glass, and pours himself a measure of whiskey. Then he leans against the counter and gazes at me, all lord of the manor and king of the hill, setting every nerve I own on edge.

"I don't want to have to deal with you every time I get home from work."

"Deal with me? Interesting choice of words. Brings to mind some kind of punishment."

When his smile turns smoldering, I've had enough.

I set my glass down with a clatter on the counter and level him my most lethal look. "I don't want you here, all right? Is that clear enough for you? I don't like you, I don't trust you, and I want you to stay out of my house."

The fleeting frown that crosses his face is quickly replaced by a sharky smile that would make his mother proud. "Perhaps we can negotiate."

I sigh heavily, overwhelmed by so many different emotions I can't pick one to focus on. I'm a melting pot of feelings. I'm goo. "Please. Just go. I can't do this right now."

His look sharpens. "What's wrong? Did something happen today?"

Is he kidding? "Leave," I say firmly, staring him down.

"You haven't heard my offer yet."

I'm about to stupidly ask, "What offer?" but snap my mouth closed just in time. I fold my arms over my chest and clamp my lips together.

Matteo drifts closer, swirling his drink. "But I suppose if you're not interested in getting your sketch pad back, we can forget about it."

I freeze. My neck goes hot, the flush slowly creeping up into my face. "You already said you're using my designs in your new collection, so it doesn't make a difference if I get the sketch pad back or not."

"Is that what I said?" His gaze is piercing. The faintest of smiles plays at the corners of his lips.

He's toying with me, like a cat with a mouse.

Except I'm no mouse. I'm a motherfucking lion.

"I'm not playing this game with you," I say, staring him right in the eye. "I've had enough of your bullshit. I want you to get the hell out of my house and stay out. If you don't, I'll call the police. I own this property. Not your mother, *me*. If I don't want you here, that means you're trespassing."

He's still for a moment, just looking at me, then he exhales. With quiet intensity, he says, "Do you have any idea how beautiful you are?"

My laugh is small and bitter. "I have a lot of experience with lying playboys. You can take your fake compliment and stick it up your ass with your fake kiss."

His jaw flexes. He says something in Italian, his voice husky, his eyes on my mouth.

I wish my heart would stop doing that thing it does whenever he looks at me like that. I'm determined to hate him, and all this fluttery butterfly bullshit going on inside my chest is really starting to annoy me.

"I'll tell you what." He goes over to the opposite counter, where a pad of paper and a cup of pens sit beside a telephone. He scribbles something on a piece of paper, folds it in half, then walks back to me and holds it out. "If you decide you'd like to hear my offer, here's my number. If you don't"—he shrugs—"I won't bring it up again."

I look at the piece of paper in his hand with my nose wrinkled, but say nothing.

He sets the paper on the counter, walks over to the chair where he draped his coat, and picks it up. He slings it over his shoulder.

On his way out the door, he says over his shoulder, "For the record, it wasn't a compliment. It was a question."

I shout after him, "When are you going to do us all a favor and jump off a building?"

His dark chuckle is the single most infuriating thing I've heard in my life.

SIXTEEN

I come awake in stages. It's early, probably just after dawn. Gray light filters between a crack in the drapes. The room is quiet and cool, which makes the heat at my back all the more strange.

I turn my head and find a giant black head on the pillow next to mine.

Cornelia's mouth is open. She's gently snoring, her long pink tongue lolling out of her mouth onto the pillow. One of her paws is draped over my side.

The damn dog is spooning me!

Trying not to startle her so I don't accidentally get mauled, I quietly say, "Yo, dog."

She doesn't wake up. I nudge her in the belly with my elbow.

Nothing. This animal sleeps like the dead.

A little louder, I say, "Wakey-wakey, Cornelia."

Her big black eyes flutter open. She blinks slowly, then cracks open her massive jaws and yawns in my face.

Ugh. Dog breath. Grimacing, I wave my hand in front of my nose. "Thanks for that."

She falls perfectly still. Her eyes go wide. She looks at me with an expression of terror, as if she just realized who I am and where she is.

"Don't freak out," I say gently. "I'm not gonna yell at you."

She looks at her paw slung over my waist, looks guiltily back at me, then slowly withdraws her leg.

It's adorable. So of course I feel bad. "Did Beans kick you out of her room?"

Cornelia buries her face in the pillow.

"Yeah. She's a real meanie, that one."

Cornelia's log of a tail starts to wag, tentatively at first, until after a few seconds it's thumping the mattress so hard the bed jiggles.

I have a terrible feeling I'm going to be waking up next to this horse every day from now on, and sigh. "Okay, dog. We'll be friends. But we're not sleeping together. I'll get you a proper doggie bed. Deal?"

Cornelia gets so excited I think she might pee herself. She leaps up onto all fours, wriggling like a puppy, panting and pawing at the covers, raining slobber onto my face.

"Gross." I wipe my face with the sheets and flip off the covers. Cornelia jumps off the bed and waits in the corner, watching me with worry as I yawn and stretch. When I stand, she turns in a circle, knocking over a floor lamp. She's so frantic with excitement she doesn't know what to do with herself.

I look at her sternly and point at the floor. "Sit."

She promptly falls down and plays dead.

"That'll do. Good dog."

I head into the bathroom and take a shower, wondering how I'm going to make it through this day.

The funeral is at eleven o'clock.

The only black clothing I brought with me is a pair of slacks. I had no thoughts of funeral wardrobes when I was packing in San Francisco.

I have a gray cashmere sweater that will have to do for a top, but I don't have heels, and there's no time to go out and buy anything.

I would've altered one of the dresses at my father's shop, but none of them were black. He always said a woman should never wear black unless she was grieving because it leeched all the color from her skin.

Papa.

Grief passes through me in a wave so strong it leaves me breathless. I have to flatten my hand against the shower wall to steady myself. I swallow hard, again and again, until the sob that wants to break from my throat subsides. Then I promise myself I'll hold it together until I can be alone again. I refuse to break down in front of the WS.

Or *him.*

I turn off the water and dry off. After I'm finished blow drying my hair, I go back into the bedroom. Cornelia's gone, but something new has appeared that makes me stop in shock.

Laid out on the bed is a dress. It's black, made of stiff silk organza overlaid with lace. It's knee length, with a sweetheart neckline, a nipped waist, a full skirt, and a matching jacket.

I don't have to look at the tag to recognize it's Dior couture.

"I thought you might need something to wear."

The marchesa stands in the doorway of my bedroom. She's pale and somber in a housecoat and slippers, both black. Her hair is down, and she doesn't have any makeup on. Dark shadows lurk in the hollows beneath her eyes.

It's the first time I've seen her look like a human being.

I don't know what else to say except, "Thank you."

She gazes at the dress. "It was my mother's. Dior, circa 1950s."

"The New Look," I murmur, unsure how to act. She's being nice to me!

"Yes. My mother loved French couture. It was all she wore. This dress was only worn once." She glances up at me. "To my father's funeral."

Okay, that is totally fucking weird. "Um . . ."

"You're a size six, correct?"

I nod.

"It should fit perfectly. Your figures are very similar."

I exhale the breath I didn't know I was holding. "Are you sure you don't want to wear it? I mean, it has sentimental value for you, so . . ."

"I'm too broad in the shoulders, and my waist hasn't been that small since before Matteo was born." Her eyes grow distant, as if she's lost in some old memory. "After she died, I donated all her clothing to the haute couture exhibition at the Palais Galliera. She had the most incredible collection. Practically priceless, by today's standards. This one I kept because the one time she wore it was the only time in my life I ever saw her cry."

Her voice grows quiet and sad. "She hated to show emotions. She said it was undignified. Weak. Whenever I cried as a child, I'd get a beating."

Our eyes meet across the room. The silence pounds between us, deafeningly loud.

Then she turns on her heel and disappears.

I sit on the edge of the bed and rest my hand on the dress, which isn't really a dress but an olive branch.

I can already tell this is going to be one hell of a day.

I'm in the kitchen with Lorenzo, nervously waiting for the limo to pick us up, when Matteo arrives.

He walks into the room and all the air goes out.

It's not fair that someone should be so beautiful. The light treats him differently than it does the rest of us, caressing the bones in his face, adding a loving sheen to his hair. He's wearing a gorgeous black suit and tie, black shoes polished to a mirror gleam, and a chunky silver watch that probably cost more than my college education.

His expression is somber. So is his voice when he says hello.

"Hey." I look at my fingernails, in dire need of a manicure. I decide this is the last time I'll let him in this house without calling the cops, and almost mean it.

Lorenzo murmurs a greeting, then we're all silent.

Finally Matteo says, "Has she come down yet?"

"No," answers Lorenzo. "She's not ready."

I glance up in time to see the two of them share a strange, meaningful look, which irritates me because I don't understand it.

"You're in the limo with us, Lorenzo."

His eyes widen. "Oh no, signorina, that wouldn't be proper. I will drive behind."

I say flatly, "Family rides in the limo. You're riding in the limo."

I get the feeling he doesn't want to contradict me, so he looks to Matteo for help. But Matteo simply inclines his head in agreement.

Lorenzo implores him in Italian, in answer to which Matteo waves a dismissive hand. Then he flicks an inscrutable gaze in my direction and says a few curt, quiet words.

I really have to learn that damn language.

When the doorbell rings, I stand, my heart thumping. "It's time."

Lorenzo says, "I'll get Lady Moretti," but Matteo quickly puts the kibosh on that.

"No. Wait for us outside."

He walks out of the room, leaving Lorenzo and me alone. He offers his arm. "Signorina."

Outside, we're greeted by the limo driver, a small man with black hair and a nose the size of a cabbage. I get in, but Lorenzo stands outside, waiting.

And waiting.

It's ten minutes before the marchesa arrives with Matteo, and by then my ears are burning with anger. I can't believe she'd make us all wait for her, today of all days. What could she be doing, anyway? Drinking champagne? Then Matteo assists her into the limo and I see her face, and my anger vanishes.

She looks stricken. She's as white as a sheet. Her hands are shaking. She swallows and looks out the window, avoiding my eyes.

Matteo instructs Lorenzo to sit beside her, then he climbs in beside me on the long bench seat opposite them. I feel him looking at me, but I won't look back. As the driver shuts the doors, Matteo reaches over and squeezes my hand.

He doesn't let go until we arrive at the church.

The church is three hundred years old, and so is the priest.

I sit beside the marchesa in the front pew, staring at my father's casket. On my other side is Matteo, and on his other side is Lorenzo. Dominic kneels in the pew on the other side of the aisle, his head bent in prayer.

All the pews are full, which isn't surprising. My father was always the most popular person wherever he went. Outgoing, kind, with a permanent smile, he made friends everywhere.

When I visited him on my summer vacations from school, the house was always swarming with people. Neighbors dropped by unannounced. There were impromptu dinner parties and afternoon picnics on the lawn. On Sundays after church he always put out a big brunch with champagne and everyone was invited.

When I think of it now, I realize that maybe he didn't have bad money-management skills. Maybe saving it and making it wasn't as important to him as how he spent it.

Maybe he simply had different priorities.

The ancient priest dodders over to the pulpit, signaling the start of the service. When he starts to speak in Italian, I stop listening to the words. Instead I close my eyes and listen to the cadence. To the responses from the crowd. To the painful beating of my heart.

There's a full mass, including communion. Hymns are sung, bible passages are read, people stand, sit, and kneel at the appropriate times.

I do, too, aware always of Matteo on my right and his mother on my left. Aware of his constant, grounding presence. Aware of his gaze, which doesn't stray from me for too long.

There are no eulogies, because my father thought it was morbid to talk about the dead. Then it's over.

I survived. Barely. The scream inside my chest survived, too, and is impatiently clawing for escape from my throat.

I'll let it have its moment later, when I'm alone.

Matteo, Dominic, and Lorenzo are three of the six pallbearers who bear my father's casket out of the church to the waiting hearse and to the gravesite. The service at the grave is a blur. All I remember is that at one point, I swayed and Matteo caught me before I fell. He kept his arm clamped around my shoulders for the rest of the service, which was lucky for me. I doubt if I would have been able to stand unsupported.

I throw a fistful of dirt on my father's casket, then it's over.

I don't remember walking back to the limo.

I don't remember the drive back to the house.

I don't remember anything, until I look up when the limo pulls to a stop and I see a familiar figure pacing back and forth in agitation in front of the front door of Il Sogno.

When I gasp in horror, Matteo whips his head around and looks at me, then follows my gaze through the window and narrows his eyes.

"Who's that?"

Though my mouth has gone bone-dry, I manage to answer, "It's Brad. My ex."

When Matteo makes a terrifying sound in his chest—like a bear's growl, only more lethal—I wonder if we'll be having more than one funeral today.

SEVENTEEN

I'm the first one out of the limo because I launch myself from it like a rocket.

Brad spots me and freezes. He's as handsome as ever in faded jeans and a navy blazer, though he looks bone tired. The bruises beneath his eyes and the white strip of tape over the bridge of his nose don't help.

With a pleading look on his face and a crack in his voice, he says, "Babe."

I whip off my right shoe and hurl it at him.

It lands in the middle of his forehead with a satisfying *thwack*, then bounces off into the bushes.

I really wish I'd brought a pair of heels. He could be missing an eye right now.

"Ow!" Clutching his forehead, he staggers back and stares at me with big eyes. "Babe!"

I shout, "Call me *babe* one more time, you lying, cheating, gigantic piece of shit! *I dare you!*"

Matteo exits the car behind me. He grips my arm, stopping me from flying across the driveway and clawing out Brad's eyes. In the most dangerous tone I've ever heard a person who isn't Clint Eastwood use, Matteo says, "You have ten seconds to get off this property before I kill you."

I blink up at him, surprised. Is he standing up for my honor?

Then I remind myself this is the same person who's stealing all my designs to use in his upcoming collection and shake my head to clear it. Matteo isn't concerned with my honor. Matteo doesn't *have* honor. He's concerned with avoiding a scene in front of Mumsy-Wumsy.

Either way, if it ends up with Brad dead, I'm on board.

"What the hell are you doing here?" I spit it out, beyond livid.

"You wouldn't take my calls. I had to reach you—I—we have to talk."

Lorenzo and the marchesa have exited the limo and stand with the limo driver, staring at our tawdry little tableau with expressions ranging from mild interest on the driver's part to extreme distaste on the marchesa's part.

For someone who dislikes shows of emotion, this must be akin to surgery without anesthesia for her.

But she surprises me by saying, "So this is the man who left my stepdaughter at the altar." She looks him up and down carefully, then sniffs. "You ought to be shot."

With Lorenzo on her heels, she lifts her head and breezes past Brad into the house.

Wow. That was a beautiful thing.

Hurt, Brad looks at me. "She's mean."

Deadly soft, Matteo says, "Your ten seconds are up."

I look at Brad and can't help the vicious smile that curves my lips. "You really don't want to talk shit about this guy's mother."

"Please, Kimber, I was wrong. I was stupid and wrong, and I freaked out, and it was a total mistake, and . . . can we please just talk for a minute? I came all this way. I have so much I need to tell you."

At first I think that scary grumbling noise is coming from my chest, but then I realize it's Matteo. He's about to blow a gasket. His face is so hard it looks like it's made of stone.

Murder stone.

When he drops his hand from my arm and takes a step forward, I grab his sleeve. "Wait."

He slants me a look. His nostrils are flared. That muscle in his jaw is jumping. He's got violence written all over him, and I'm a teeny bit uncertain now about how much of this is for Mumsy-Wumsy's sake and how much mine. I mean, she's already gone.

What is he doing?

I exhale a hard breath, glower at Brad for a moment, then lower my voice. "I know this idiot. If I don't give him a chance to speak his piece, he'll never leave me alone."

"If I remove his tongue, the problem will be solved."

Matteo's answer comes fast and quiet. It's even scarier than if he'd shouted it to the hills. He's serious. If I said the word, he'd take Brad apart limb by limb right here in the driveway.

Why that should give me such a thrill, I don't want to know.

"I'll keep that in mind."

He makes a small gesture indicating the rolling hills and woods around us. "There's a lot of property here."

"Are you saying it's good for burying a body?"

"Say the word and you'll find out."

We stare at each other in a strange kind of violent, intense Brad-hating bubble until Brad clears his throat.

"Uh, you guys? Still here."

Matteo says through gritted teeth, "You were going to *marry* this idiot?"

"I know, right?"

We turn our heads and glare at Brad.

He takes a step back. "Uh, okay, I'll just . . ." He points down the driveway. "I'll just wait for you over there."

He takes off walking at a brisk clip. Watching him go, the limo driver says, "Good hair, though. Robert Redford hair. You know Robert Redford? He's my favorite American movie star. Good actor. Good teeth. Great hair."

When he sees the look Matteo sends him, his eyes widen. He jumps back into the limo and takes off down the driveway, roaring past Brad with a wave.

"If you're not back in five minutes, I'm coming to get you. I won't be responsible for what happens then."

I lift my eyebrows, taking in Matteo's expression. His gaze is on Brad. The look in his eyes has gone from murder to genocide.

God, I'm so sick. I'm actually finding this show of protective machismo incredibly hot.

"Hey. Psycho."

Matteo cuts his eyes back to me.

"What's this caveman thing you're doing?"

"He hurt you."

"Yeah? So? How is that your business?"

His jaw works back and forth as if he's grinding walnuts between his molars. Finally he says, "We're family."

"Ex-family," I correct, watching his face. "You're the one who so helpfully pointed that out to me."

He draws a breath through his nose, straightens to his full height, folds his arms over his chest, and stares down his nose at me.

"Oh, this again? The snooty silent treatment? Great. That's just great. That's exactly what I need right now."

I hate myself for how my voice wavers, but I hate myself even more for letting anything he does affect me. It shouldn't matter.

It doesn't matter!

So why does it?

"Go be with your mother. She needs you more right now than I do."

Dashing away the water springing up in my eyes, I turn and start to walk away. Matteo takes hold of my arm and turns me back.

He drops his head so we're nose to nose. "Did you just say you need me?"

I frantically try to recall the specific words I just spoke, but with him so close and his damn delicious, brain-melting scent in my nose, and the scream trapped in my throat, and the tears filling up behind my eyes so fast, I can't.

I whisper, "I don't know what I just said. This is the worst day of my life. Last week I had the second worst day of my life, caused by that douchebag waiting for me at the end of the driveway. My brain isn't really working right at the moment."

We stare at each other until he exhales. He looks at my mouth, then briefly closes his eyes. When he speaks again, he sounds exhausted. "Let me get your other shoe."

He leaves me standing there while he fishes my shoe out of the bushes. Then, when he comes back and kneels down in front of me in the gravel, it's all I can do not to fall flat on my face.

He gently takes my ankle in his hand and slips my foot into my shoe. Then he looks up at me.

And my heart stops. It just stops, like you hear stories of when people first glimpse the love of their life . . . or in that split second after they stepped off a curb and realize they're about to get hit by an oncoming bus.

Yeah, probably more like the second one.

Matteo kneels at my feet with his big warm hand wrapped around my small cold ankle, and just looks at me while I stare back at him with a nonfunctioning heart and a barely functioning brain and try to remember how to breathe.

His voice thick, he says, "No matter what he says, remember who you are."

Before I can ask *Who am I?* Matteo has risen and is walking away with stiff shoulders and his hands clenched into fists.

I watch him until he disappears into the house, then I turn and walk down the driveway to where Brad awaits. He's pacing again, kicking at the gravel like a four-year-old.

I stop ten feet away, fold my arms over my chest, and send him a death glare.

He exhales loudly. "Okay. Okay, um . . . you're mad. I know you're mad. And you probably never want to talk to me again." He's still pacing. Pacing and wringing his hands, which is so unlike him I frown.

He glances at me, quickly glances away, then shakes his head and laughs. It's a horrible laugh, the kind that isn't funny at all. The kind that bursts out of you like a groan or a bark, or like the sound an animal makes when it's in pain.

Honestly, it freaks me out a little.

"Brad, stop."

He stops in place and looks at my feet. He inhales, his chest heaving, then finds the nerve to meet my eyes.

I've never seen anyone with that wild, awful look in his eyes. It's similar to the look he had when I was walking down the aisle toward him at the church, but there's more than sheer panic there. Now I see pain and fear and visceral dread, like someone being tortured.

Like someone about to die.

"You could've just written me a letter."

"You would've torn it up."

He has me there. I definitely would have torn it up. Then lit it on fire. Then stomped on the ashes and sent them back to him in a box marked *Fragile: Broken Heart Inside.*

"You have sixty seconds to tell me what you need to say. Then we're never going to speak again. Go."

He swallows, his Adam's apple bobbing, and shoves his hands into the front pockets of his jeans. He squints up at the sun, closes his eyes, and releases a pent-up breath.

Then he looks me dead in the eye and whispers, "I'm gay."

It doesn't hit me right away. I stand there waiting for him to say something, until I realize he did say something . . . and what it was that he said.

Slowly, I repeat, "You're gay."

He nods.

"Gay."

When he nods again, I'm *this close* to killing him with my bare hands. But I don't want to go to jail, so I'll kill him with sarcasm instead.

"So gay you slept with half the female population of San Francisco behind my back, huh? Was that just you making *sure* you didn't enjoy vagina? Just putting the lid on it?"

"Listen—"

"So gay you constantly made fun of Jenner and his boyfriends? *That* gay?"

"Kimber—"

I take a step toward him, my entire body shaking with fury. "So gay you had to, what, make up all those stories you told me about the amazing sex you had before you met me? All those crazy threesomes in your college days, all those kinky things you wanted me to try, all the ways you made me feel like I wasn't measuring up to your expectations in bed?"

The last part is shouted into his face. I'm so angry I can feel my pulse in every cell in my body.

In a defeated whisper, Brad says, "Yes."

I blink. "What do you mean, *yes?*"

"I mean . . ." He presses his lips together for a moment, his eyes fierce with unshed tears.

I'm shocked to realize he's going to cry.

"I mean yes. I did all that. I slept around with women because I was desperate no one would know. I said those things about Jenner and his boyfriends and made up those stories about all the sex I had in college and did pretty much anything else I could think of—*everything* I could think of—so I wouldn't have to admit it to myself."

He chokes out a sob right as the first fat tear rolls down his cheek. In a strangled voice, he says, "But mostly so I wouldn't have to admit it to my father."

Then he drops his face into his hands and starts to bawl. Shoulders shaking, body trembling, boo-hooing and carrying on in that totally over-the-top, out-of-control way you just can't fake.

I'm so overwhelmed I plop right down on the gravel driveway in my vintage Christian Dior couture dress and sit there with my legs stuck out in front of me, staring at my shoes.

"But nobody stays in the closet anymore," I say, bewildered, to my feet. "I'm no expert, but, I mean . . . do they? He's a grown man . . . a grown man who lives in San Francisco, the LGBTQ capital of the universe. Why on earth would he pretend to be straight?"

"I'm sorry. I'm so sorry!" Brad wails between his fingers. "I never meant to hurt you!"

"Oh, well, good job with that, Wingate." I'm too stunned to be furious at the moment, so it comes out as sarcasm, as dry as a crust of old bread.

Brad drops down beside me and folds his legs. He then proceeds to wail and cry in a cross-legged position, and now I'm getting a migraine.

"If anyone should be bawling here, it should be me, asshole. Do you have any idea how much you hurt me? How what you did absolutely *devastated* me? How I will never, ever get over that shit *for the rest of my life?*"

He wails louder. At this rate the authorities will show up soon to find out who's being murdered.

"Okay." I sigh, exhausted. "Hey, calm down, it's gonna be okay."

He grabs me and buries his face in my neck, clinging to me like a lost little boy, hiccupping between sobs.

I look up at the clear blue sky. I want to remember this moment. I want to let it sink in before I go numb. I want to be able to take it out later and look at it, examine it, try to understand what it means and how I ended up within it. Because maybe if I can understand, I'll be able to find some deeper meaning in it.

Something that doesn't make me feel so worthless and small.

"I buried my father today." I watch a fluffy white cloud float by overhead. In the branches of the trees, birds are singing.

"God, I'm so sorry." Brad's sobs have turned to sniffles. He's drying his face with his hands, wiping his fingers on his jeans. "I know how much he meant to you."

I look at him, this man I wanted to spend the rest of my life with. Really look at him. How could I have been so blind? "I spent three years of my life with you. *Three years.* You're telling me it was all a lie?"

"No, no, it wasn't." He's desperate, grabbing my hand and imploring me with his eyes. "I loved you! I did! I *do*. You're my best friend. You're the only person I ever felt safe with."

We stare at each other. His face is blotchy. His lashes are wet, stuck together in clumps. He looks as close to haggard as I've ever seen him. Haggard, hopeless, and lost.

"I don't understand. You could've told me at the beginning. I would've supported you. You didn't have to *steal* three years of my life. Because if what you're telling me is true, that's what you did. You stole three years of my life because you were too much of a coward to live yours. I can never get that time back. All that time and all that love I gave you . . . and you repaid it with disloyalty and public humiliation. And now you're here to what? Ask my forgiveness?"

He starts to cry again, this time silently. Tears flow down his cheeks and drip from his jaw. "I know," he whispers brokenly. "It's unforgiveable, I know."

He's so pitiful I just don't have it in me to hate his guts. I mean, I *do* hate his guts, but part of me also feels sorry for him.

Part of me remembers what a judgmental prick his father is and how nothing Brad ever did quite measured up.

A strange detachment overcomes me, as if my soul has left my body. It's peaceful. Alarming, but peaceful. I sit there and look at him as if he were a stranger until my curiosity rears its head.

"How could you have sex with me? Did you have to imagine I had a dick so you could get it up?"

He winces. "No, I just . . ." When he swallows, hesitating, I'm not sure I want to hear. But then he blows out a breath and goes on, his voice soft. Embarrassed. "It wasn't hard to be with you. You're pretty. And you always smell good. And you're a really good kisser . . ."

He's starting to look scared. I have no idea what my face is doing, and I don't care.

Something terrible has occurred to me.

I grab his arm. "Please tell me you used protection. All these other people you were having sex with—"

"I was always safe, I swear."

I examine his face for any hint of deception, but he seems sincere. On the other hand, he's so skilled at hiding the truth I'd be stupid all over again to believe him now.

I'm not sure who I'm angrier with, myself or him. I wanted the fairy tale so badly I let myself believe this frog I was kissing was really a prince.

I knew it when I read all those horrible articles about his side chicks, but I got distracted by my grief about my father. Now the reality floods back with sickening urgency: I need to get checked for STDs.

Brad might have given me something far worse than a broken heart.

I leap to my feet. Brad scrambles to his, staring at me with big horrified eyes, like a deer on the business end of a shotgun. When I point my finger at him, he shrinks back.

"Stay away from me. I don't ever want to see your face again, do you understand?"

"Please, Kimber, listen to me—"

"I don't ever want to hear your voice. I don't care what you have to say. Nothing can make it better. Nothing can undo what you've done. Stay the hell away from me, Bradley, or so help me God I won't be responsible for my actions."

I swing around and stride away, my chest so tight it burns. My eyes burn, too. I think I might vomit.

Brad calls after me, "I still want to marry you!"

I stop dead in my tracks. My chest heaving with ragged breaths, I whirl around and stare at him in disbelief.

He walks closer, one careful step at a time. "You can have the life you always wanted. I'll give you anything you want, babe, anything."

"Are you insane?" I shout. "What the hell are you talking about? You just told me you're gay!"

The words begin to tumble out of him in a rush. "You're the only person I've told. No one else has to know! We could have it all—think about it! The house, the lifestyle, all the money!"

I know my mouth is hanging open. I can feel the breeze playing around my teeth. "You're suggesting we *pretend to be a real couple*?"

He lifts his hands in a helpless gesture. "We'd be rich. And you could do whatever you wanted. You could expand your shop, travel, whatever. Think of the life we'd have. Think of the possibilities."

He moves closer. His voice drops to a conspiratorial whisper. "I never told you this, but the trust my father set up for me when I was born stipulates I get a lump sum of five million when I marry. You can have it all to do whatever you want with. Think of it, babe—five million dollars. Think how that could change your life."

He's serious. He's actually serious. The man doesn't know me at all.

My voice shaking with anger, I say, "I see you've thought this through."

He nods, swallowing, his face registering the first signs of hope. "We'd still be best friends. We'd still live together. We'd do everything together, except . . ."

"Except the one thing married people are supposed to do together. Namely, fuck."

He looks slightly offended at my flat, hostile tone. "I mean, you could have as many boyfriends as you wanted."

It happens before I'm conscious of making the decision. One minute I'm listening to his outrageous proposition that I give up any possibility of an authentic life with a man who actually loves me, the next my open hand is making hard contact with the side of his face.

Crack.

He staggers back, shocked, holding his face, his eyes as round as his open mouth.

"I took it easy on you this time because it looks like that nose of yours is still healing," I say, struggling for air. "But so help me God, one more word out of you and I'll knock all your teeth out. And by the way, I'm not a prostitute!"

"I never said you were!"

"You already left me at the altar! You think I'm crazy enough to sign up for that *twice*?"

"I panicked! I swear it wouldn't happen again! Now that you know, everything could be different!"

My laugh is bitter, just this side of hysterical. "You know, you almost had me. I felt sorry for you there for a minute. But now I just feel like ripping your intestines out through your nose."

He stops talking. Smart of him, because my fingers are itching to do some irreparable damage to his GI tract.

I turn around and run all the way back to the house.

EIGHTEEN

MATTEO

She bursts into the kitchen like an explosion of dynamite.

"Get me a drink," she orders, her voice rough. She sits down at the kitchen table and pounds her fist on it, once. Hard.

Her color is high. Her lips are thinned to a white line. She's so furious she's trembling.

Alarmed, Lorenzo looks at me. He leaves without a word.

He has no experience dealing with a woman's anger. My mother is far too skilled at keeping everything bottled up.

I force myself not to grill Kimber about what happened in the driveway. Not to ask all the questions crowding my throat. Instead I obey her wish and pour a stiff measure of whiskey into a glass. I set it in front of her silently, sit across from her, and wait.

It's one of the more difficult things I've ever done.

From the moment I set eyes on that preppy blond bastard, I wanted to commit murder.

I know what that means, unfortunately. It means I'm fucked.

But I knew that already. From the moment I saw her sitting on the sofa in the living room and realized who she was, I've been fucked.

No. That's not it, either. I was fucked from the first time I saw her at the airport.

She shoots the whiskey in one gulp. When she sets the glass down on the table, her hand shakes. She stares at that shaking hand as if she'd like to cut if off. "Another."

When I hesitate, she looks at me. Entire planets are burning in her eyes.

I pour her another drink.

She shoots that one, too. Then we sit in silence as the clock ticks on the wall and I fight myself from knocking the table aside and taking her in my arms.

Finally she says, "He wants me to go back to San Francisco and marry him. He still wants me to be his wife."

She laughs, a small anguished laugh that flames the rage crawling up my throat.

"What did you tell him?"

She moistens her lips, shakes her head, and closes her eyes. She's in so much pain it leaks out of her pores. She's breathing it out like flames.

"I'll hurt him if you want me to."

"Yes, I want you to."

I'm up on my feet before the next beat of my heart, but she grabs my wrist and tugs. I stop, breathing hard, waiting.

"You really would, wouldn't you?" she says softly, gazing up at me with those lucid cat eyes.

Slowly, my voice hard and full of violence, I say, "With pleasure."

We stare at each other for a beat. I'm aware of her hand wrapped around my wrist, that small shaking hand. I want to kiss her so badly I almost groan.

"Sit." She tugs on my wrist again but doesn't release it.

I blow out a hard breath and take my seat across from her.

She's still holding my wrist. I think she's measuring my heartbeat in the pulse beating wildly under her thumb. After a moment, she sighs and releases me. She tucks her hands under her armpits and looks at the tabletop.

She whispers, "I have to get out of here."

When she looks up at me, her eyes beseeching, my heart skips a beat.

When she adds, "Please," it takes off in a gallop. Blood surges through my body. My nerves start to sing.

"Where do you want to go?" I ask gruffly.

"Anywhere. Just . . . anywhere else."

Her voice is small. She sounds so lost. Lost and in pain. It's like a punch in my stomach.

I stand, pulling her gently along with me. When she wobbles, I steady her with my hand on her shoulder. "You're going to be all right," I say. "Look at me."

She looks up at me, those cat eyes so green and wide. It becomes impossible to breathe. I whisper, "I promise."

It's a vow. An oath. There's nothing on this earth or outside of it that could make me break it. I'll do anything in my power to protect her from harm.

She blinks slowly, as if clearing her eyes. Then she says with cold, quiet vehemence, "You men and your *promises*. By the way, how's that new collection of yours coming along?"

She sears me with her gaze, then shrugs off my hand and walks out.

Like I said.

Fucked.

NINETEEN

KIMBER

In my room, I carefully remove the Dior dress and hang it up in the closet, brushing the dust off the back. I change into jeans and a T-shirt and slip on my leather jacket, then head back out.

Arrested by a strange sound, I stop in the hallway and cock my ear. *What's that?*

It's a soft noise. Intermittent. It's only after a few moments of listening to it that I realize the sound is muffled crying.

I stare at the door at the end of the hall, shocked to my core.

The marchesa's room is behind that door. *The marchesa is crying.*

I put a hand over my throbbing heart and shake my head, pressing my lips together so I don't sob. I can't take anything else today. I don't think I'll survive one more surprise. My poor heart will burst into a million tiny bloody pieces, and I'll drop dead where I stand.

Might be a blessing, now that I think of it.

My eyes stinging, I run through the house, throw open the front door, and immediately come to a skidding stop.

Across the driveway, Matteo leans against a black Maserati. His arms are folded over his chest. He's staring at me from under lowered brows.

The passenger door is open.

Screw it.

I stride angrily across the distance, throw myself into the passenger seat, and slam the door shut. I sit slumped down with my arms crossed over my chest, not bothering to fasten the seat belt, breathing so hard it sounds as if I've been running.

Gravel crunches, then Matteo opens the driver's door and gets in. Without a word, he leans over me and fastens my seat belt. Then he starts the car, closes his door, puts the car into gear, and pulls away.

We drive. I have no idea where. We simply drive in silence as the landscape slips by in a colorful blur, and I try so hard not to cry I dig bloody little crescents into my palms with my fingernails.

The whole time, Matteo's knuckles are white around the steering wheel.

To the window and the passing view, I say faintly, "I always wanted to be married. When I was a little girl, I dreamed of how it would be. The flowers. The music. My wedding gown. I had this fantasy built up in my head of this perfect, beautiful day . . . and the perfect, beautiful man I'd marry. He'd be so in love with me, he'd die just for a kiss . . ."

Like my father was with my mother. That's all I ever wanted—a man to love me so much he couldn't see anything else. Instead it was me who couldn't see. I'd like to kick my own ass for being so blind.

As the first of the tears crest my lower lids, I suck in a hitching breath. I whisper, "I'm so ashamed."

"Don't be stupid," comes the hard response. "You have nothing to be ashamed of."

I close my eyes, letting the tears flow because I know there's no stopping them now. "Stupid to trust. Stupid to dream. Stupid to believe in the fairy tale."

"I could kill him just for this," Matteo mutters, taking a corner too fast. "Just for making you cry."

He growls something in Italian. It sounds super murdery and makes me feel a little better.

"I heard your mother crying. Behind her closed bedroom door."

His gaze on my face is burning. "Did you think she wouldn't?"

I thought she didn't know how, but keep my mouth shut. As I'm beginning to realize, I don't know much of anything.

We drive for another ten minutes in silence until we pull up to a tall ancient stone wall covered in ivy. The wall breaks, revealing a massive iron gate flanked by a pair of enormous stone lions. Beside the gate is a small metal box on a stand that Matteo punches a code into. The gates swing open slowly, and we pull into a cobbled driveway. On my right is a sunken cloister with formal Italian gardens. On my left are lighted fountains and a rolling green lawn.

Directly ahead is a massive neo-Gothic castle, complete with crenellated tower.

Squinting out the windshield, I ask, "What is this place?"

"Castello di Moretti."

I turn to him slowly as shock spreads throughout my body.

He smiles at the look on my face. "Home sweet home."

He makes it sound like a double-wide trailer. "You *live* here?"

"I grew up here. This has been the seat of the Moretti family for more than eight hundred years."

"Uh-huh." I stare at him.

"Why are you looking at me like that?"

I point at the monster castle. "This explains a lot."

Shaking his head, he maneuvers the car into a courtyard and kills the engine. He gets out of the car and comes around and opens my door, something Brad never managed to do the entire time we were together.

I blink hard to clear the water suddenly pooling in my eyes. *Don't start crying again. Don't you dare.*

"Come," Matteo says softly. "There are many old, priceless objects inside you'll no doubt enjoy breaking." He extends his hand.

I shouldn't do this, but I'm feeling reckless. So I take his hand and let him help me out of the car. He closes the door behind me but doesn't let go of my hand.

He leads me through a stone archway into another smaller courtyard. I don't know all the technical terms for what I'm seeing, but suffice it to say that it's all very castlelike. Fortified stone walls, towers, those little slits in the walls medieval archers could shoot through, all that.

When we enter through a small wooden side door into the main part of the building, a laugh unexpectedly bursts out of me and echoes up into the rafters.

Matteo glances back at me.

"Total shithole," I say with a straight face.

He turns away, but not before I see his smile.

We walk, and walk, and walk. The place is a maze of marble and stone and hanging tapestries, heavily carved wood furniture and gilt mirrors, flowers spilling from porcelain urns. We pass what I decide to call the Wall of Death, which features a variety of medieval axes, swords, spears, and other items designed to deprive a person of life in the most painful of ways in a giant glass cabinet lit from underneath just to make it all the more creepy.

"You grew up *here*?" I mutter under my breath, unable to imagine a young child wandering around this place. It's a miracle he didn't accidentally kill himself running into one of the thousand sharp edges everywhere or falling down and cracking open his skull on the slippery and unforgivingly hard marble floor.

"When I wasn't away at boarding school."

There's a dark undertone in his voice that suggests boarding school wasn't all fun and games. I want to ask him about it but am distracted by the smell of baking bread. It seems we're headed toward a kitchen. I hear women laughing and the sound of clanging pans. Then we pass through an open arched doorway into an enormous room that makes the word *kitchen* seem insufficient.

There are bread ovens and two wood-burning fireplaces and a long sink built right into the thick stone walls. Three large oak tables command the center space on the floor. There's a hearth so large it could fit several cauldrons, and a long row of shelves filled with pantry goods.

The two women I heard laughing fall silent when we walk in. Plump and grandmotherly with identical uniforms of black with starched white aprons, they could be sisters.

In unison, they curtsey.

"Mio signore."

I barely know any Italian, but I do know they just called Matteo "My lord."

When I snort, he slants me an irritated look. He says something to the ladies, gesturing toward the stainless-steel refrigerator on the other side of the room. Then he nods at them in farewell and leads me away as they gape after us in surprise.

As soon as we're out of earshot, I snicker. "Where are you taking me, *my lord?*"

He's still holding my hand, which he uses to pull me around a corner. Then he whirls on me and presses me against the wall.

Shocked, I stare up at him. His eyes are dark, and that muscle in his jaw is jumping.

I'm in trouble.

He says roughly, "If it were up to me, I'd be taking you to bed and putting that mouth of yours to good use. Now I can see why your attitude is so bad—there's no way in hell that *boy* you were going to marry could ever satisfy a woman like you."

His blistering gaze drops to my mouth.

Surely he must be able to hear the scream of sheer joy my uterus is making. It's so loud I'm deafened for a moment.

My body erupts into flames. I can't catch my breath. My armpits go damp, and so do my panties. The wall is cool and hard against my back, but Matteo is all heat against my front. Heat and muscle and palpable desire.

My hands are somehow flattened against his stomach. His hands are flattened on the wall on either side of my head. Neither of us moves, except for our chests, which are both heaving.

"You think you can do better?"

It's out of my mouth before I have any idea I'm going to say it, a husky whisper that sounds like I'm auditioning for a role in a porno. Apparently my uterus has taken control of all my bodily functions because though I *should* be pushing him away, what I really want to do is let him show me exactly what his eyes are saying he wants to do to me.

All the dirty, wonderful things.

He lowers his head and puts his mouth next to my ear. "Bella," he chides. "You know I can." Then he takes my earlobe into his mouth and gently suckles it as if it's my clitoris.

I almost die from the blast of lust that explodes inside my body. His mouth is wet and soft, his breath down my neck is hot, his stomach under my hands is as hard as steel. The little gasp that leaves my lips makes him chuckle.

He whispers, "Don't you?" and bites me on the neck.

It's not hard, not enough to break the skin or even leave a mark, just enough to be dominant. To let me know that he's the man. He'd be in control of whatever we did in bed, and he'd make sure I fucking loved every second of it.

It's a good thing my knees are locked because there's no way they'd be holding me up otherwise. He's turned my bones to gelatin.

He shifts his weight forward so I know he's as aroused as I am. I feel every long, thick inch of him, and exhale a breath that inconveniently sounds exactly like a moan.

Matteo takes my face in his hands. I take fistfuls of his shirt. He holds me there against the wall with his hard cock pressed into my crotch and looks deep into my eyes.

"Don't you."

This time it's not a question. It's a promise and a dare and above all an invitation. An invitation to say yes, to admit I know that if I had sex with him, he'd ruin me for all other men. That I know he'd pay close attention to my every arch and moan and shudder, that he'd read my body like a book and make it sing like a violin under his patient, plying hands.

That he'd break me and make me beg before he'd give me everything I never knew I needed.

When I'm silent too long, he softly warns, "Kimber."

My uterus pulls the final plug on my brain functions. I breathe, "Yes," and stand on my toes and kiss him.

He allows it just long enough for my nipples to tighten and begin to ache until he takes control back and pulls away. He keeps my face in one of his hands. The other he flattens against my chest. He spreads his big hand wide, the heel of his palm resting at the top swell of my breasts and his fingers flared out, as if he's claiming the space.

When he kisses the corner of my mouth, I close my eyes and give myself over to sensation.

He nips my lower lip, taking it between his teeth and then gently sucking on it. He slips his tongue into my mouth with soft, delicious suction, using that hand on my chest to hold me back when I become impatient, leaning into him because I want more. I want it deeper.

Against my mouth, he murmurs, *"Sei così dolce."*

I'm wet and throbbing between my legs. I want him to do the earlobe-sucking thing down there. I squeeze my thighs together restlessly, and he chuckles again.

"Voglio mettere la mia faccia tra le tue gambe."

"Are you . . . are you talking dirty to me?"

He slants me a heated look and smiles.

Oh dear sweet lord in heaven. That burning smell is my panties going up in smoke.

He takes my mouth again. This time his kiss is deeper, the way I wanted it. It's searching. Needing. I slide my arms up his chest and over his shoulders and sink my fingers into all that glorious thick hair, using it to pull him even closer. We're both breathing hard through our noses.

He slides his hand down from my chest to the side of my ribs. When his thumb nudges my hard nipple, it sends a shock wave through my lower body. I moan into his mouth.

He breaks the kiss and nuzzles his nose into my hair. "I want to suck on this," he whispers, breathing raggedly, stroking his thumb lazily back and forth across my nipple. "I want to pinch it and suck on it and lick it. I want to test it with my teeth, see how much pressure you can take before you squirm."

I'm panting now. Literally panting, like a dog. Cornelia's got nothin' on me.

But Mr. Hot Dirty Talk isn't done yet.

Right into my ear, in a tone somehow both hard and soft, he says, "I want to take off all your clothes and get you naked underneath me, spread you out on a bed so I can see all that beautiful skin. I want to put my face between your legs and eat your sweet pussy until you're hoarse from screaming and limp from coming. Then I want to slide my hard cock deep inside you and fuck you, *bella*."

His hand tightens around my breast. He flexes his hips, dragging the fabric of my panties across my engorged clitoris, making me shudder.

His voice turns rough. "I want to fuck you until you forget everyone and everything else but me. Until you're satisfied. Until you're mine."

The kiss we share is explosive. It's hard and passionate and almost sloppy, our teeth clashing and both of us making animal sounds as we claw at each other in greed.

"Wait—*wait*."

Panting, I push him away. We stare at each other for a beat as my brain reboots and I once more become capable of rational thought. "You're using my designs."

He licks his lips, shakes his head a little as if to clear it. "What?"

"My designs. From my sketch pad. You're using them in your new collection. Right?"

There's a long silent moment where he simply looks at me and breathes raggedly. Then, through gritted teeth, he says, "Yes."

I shove him away, wipe my mouth with the back of my hand, and curse. Loudly. It echoes off the stone walls. "I don't want you to. Don't."

He straightens his tie. Smooths his hair. Says casually, "Are we negotiating?"

Between him and Brad, it's a miracle I haven't committed murder already. "You know, you have to go to sleep at some point. But you don't necessarily have to wake up."

He ignores my threat on his life. "Here's my offer you didn't want to hear earlier: a kiss for every page I return."

When I don't respond, because I'm too breathless, he smirks. "Not a peck on the cheek, either. A kiss like the one we just shared."

A wave of hurt makes tears well in my eyes. *How could he? How could he do this to me? Today, of all days, when I'm the most vulnerable I've ever been?*

I whisper, "When I'm telling my best friend the story of the exact moment I went from disliking you and distrusting you to hating you, this will be it."

His eyes flash with emotion, but he quickly regains control of whatever he was feeling. His handsome face becomes a cold mask. He says flatly, "There are twenty-six designs in that sketch pad. I'll give you credit for the kiss we just had, plus the kiss at your father's shop. That leaves twenty-four. I'll leave it up to you when we start, but we'll have to be done by the night before the shows in Milan."

I stare at him with my mouth open. "That's three weeks."

One corner of his mouth lifts. "Better get started."

I'm somehow hot and cold at the same time. I'm sweating, but shivering. The shivering could be fury. "I'll tell everyone. I'll make sure everyone knows those designs are mine. I'll call the press—"

"Really? You want *more* press?" His gaze on mine is level.

The thought of the stories that would circulate on the internet makes me sick. He knows exactly which target to aim for, that's for sure.

"It doesn't matter. I can prove they're mine."

"How? Your name is nowhere on that pad."

Shit. He's right. I never wrote my name on the inside of the cover. I never thought I'd have to.

"And you didn't sign any of the sketches, so . . ." He shrugs.

My face is so hot it burns. Furious, I glare at him. "I have copies of everything. In San Francisco. On my computer. I always make copies of what I'm working on."

The smile that was flirting with one corner of his mouth blooms into a grin. "One of these days you'll learn how to lie convincingly. Today isn't it."

I want to hit him. I want to stab him. I want to set fire to his face. Spending the rest of my life in prison would be a fair price to pay to get rid of this ruthless prick once and for all. "I said I'd pay you back for the ticket, and I meant it. Once the shop is back on its feet—"

"I don't want your money, bella."

His voice is so soft, like fingertips lightly stroked down my cheek. It leaves no doubt as to his meaning.

Starting to get desperate, I try a different tactic. "You don't need my designs. Your company is the hottest thing going. Your menswear line alone is one of the most profitable—"

"We're expanding the ladies' evening wear line."

I can tell he'll have a comeback ready for anything I throw at him. I think he might have spent a considerable amount of time thinking this through.

Like Brad and his plan for us to live a lie.

My voice shakes with rage when I say, "My father would hate you for this."

He flinches. He recovers quickly, plastering the smile back on, but I know I got to him.

But he effortlessly checkmates me. "No. Your father would be disappointed that you're trying to go back on your word."

I gasp. That hurt so much he might as well have kicked me in the ovaries.

He speaks again before I can spit out some curse. "We made a trade. A fair trade. One you agreed to freely." His voice grows quieter. "A trade you admitted was the best gift you've ever been given, if you recall."

I can't look at him anymore. I just can't look at his awful, beautiful face one second longer.

I turn and run.

TWENTY

The problem with castles is that they're built to keep invaders out and the occupants safely in.

Which means they're annoyingly short on doors.

The few I do find are huge, made of thick wood fortified with iron, and locked. I could get one of the axes from the Wall of Death and try to chop my way out, but I don't have the energy. After wandering around for the better part of an hour, I finally give up and ascend a narrow winding stone staircase to a second floor. The staircase opens to a wide corridor lined with potted palms and ornate console tables, with the occasional ancient suit of armor standing vigilant in niches in the stone wall just to give you that warm, snuggly feeling of home.

The first room I come upon is a library. It's got overstuffed sofas and chairs, a cavernous fireplace at each end of the room, and heavy wooden bookcases fronted with glass that rise nearly to the ceiling. It looks like as good a place as any to hide for a while, so I flop into a tufted leather chair that could fit the Jolly Green Giant quite comfortably and stare morosely at my feet.

The stupid chair is so big they dangle off the edge like a kid's, not even touching the ground.

I'm there no more than five minutes when one of the uniformed ladies I saw in the kitchen enters the room carrying a large tray. Approaching, she smiles at me and says something in Italian.

"Oh, I'm sorry. I don't, um . . . *no comprende Italiano.*" I realize that was some kind of botched Spanish, but I'm hoping she'll get the gist.

She shrugs, as if she couldn't care less either way, and sets the platter on the coffee table in front of me. When I smell freshly baked bread, I perk up in my giant seat.

The nice lady pulls off the napkin covering the tray with a flourish and gives me an overview of everything on the tray, pointing out various breads, meats, and cheeses, and looking at me every so often to make sure I'm following.

Totally lost, I nod politely. *I really need to learn that damn language.*

When she's done, she asks me about something to do with the word *vino.*

Now she's talking. "Um . . . Chianti?"

It's the only Italian word I can think of other than vino that has to do with wine, but apparently it's enough because she nods briskly, says something I interpret as she'll be right back, then leaves.

I stare at the tray with my mouth watering. *As long as I'm here, I might as well let the asshole feed me.*

Before I can dig in, the telephone on the side table next to my giant chair rings. I hesitate, looking at it. There's an electronic readout beneath the buttons that displays *"Stanza di sicurezza."*

Sicurezza. Secure? Security?

On a whim, I decide to answer. Maybe it will be someone important trying to get hold of Matteo, and I can helpfully inform them that Matteo isn't available due to his unfortunate admittance into rehab. Or prison.

"Moshi moshi."

There's a pause, then Matteo's voice comes over the line. "I see you've been to Japan."

Of course he would know how they answer the phones in Japan. He's probably got a castle over there, too, the prick. "I'm sorry, Matteo isn't available at the moment. He's busy being a horrible human being. If you want to catch him when he's not being a massive asshole, you'll have to call back when pigs fly and hell has frozen over."

"You should try the chair next to the fireplace. It's a more appropriate size for you."

I look around suspiciously but don't spot him lurking in any doorways. "Where are you?"

"In the security room. Looking at you on a video screen."

I glance at the ceiling. Sure enough, there are two security cameras affixed on opposite ends of the room. I flip them both off and hang up the phone.

It rings again almost immediately. I look up at the ceiling and shake my head. After a moment, the phone falls silent. *Good. He got the hint.* I turn my attention to the platter of meats and cheeses. It looks fantastic. There are some dried fruits, too, and nuts, and some of that really yummy—

The phone starts to ring again.

I realize this could go on for quite a while. I'm starving, so I give in and pick up. "What?"

In a low, heartfelt voice, he says, "I hate seeing you unhappy."

"Are you bipolar? Is that the root issue here?"

"No. I'm telling you the truth—I hate seeing you unhappy."

"You can repeat that until the cows come home, but it doesn't change the fact that you're perfectly willing to be the source of my unhappiness. One of the sources, anyway."

I hear him exhale. In a lighter tone, he says, "Where do you think that saying originated?"

Confused, I make a face. "What?"

"Until the cows come home."

I sigh heavily, scrubbing a hand over my face. "Being around you is enough to drive anyone insane, you know that?"

His voice gets quiet again. "I know. I'm sorry."

"Seriously?" I grip the receiver so hard it could crack. "Stop it, then!"

"I can't."

I hang up, then take the receiver off the hook so he can't call back. In a few minutes, the nice lady returns with an open bottle of wine and a glass already filled. She sets the bottle on the coffee table next to the platter of food and hands me the glass.

"*Ecco.*"

"Thank you. Um, grazie."

She folds her hands over her apron, tilts her head, and examines me. Then she launches into a long and impassioned speech—about what I have no idea, because it's all in Italian.

At the end of it she sighs. Then, in English, she says, "But he's worth it."

She pats me on the shoulder, then turns around and leaves.

I guzzle the glass of wine and pour myself another.

I remember nothing else until I wake up with a pounding headache and a mouth that tastes like a homeless person took a dump in it.

Lifting my head sends spikes of pain shooting through the back of my skull. I crack open an eye and look around the room. *Where am I? And how did I get here?*

Cavernous yet cozy, the room is fit for a king. The ceiling is dark wood, crossed by thick beams. A circular iron chandelier hangs in the middle. The stone walls are warmed by colorful tapestries and framed landscapes in oils. Scattered over the floor are half a dozen thick tasseled area rugs. The furniture is also dark wood, heavy and masculine, and the fireplace is so big you could burn an SUV in it.

The massive four-poster bed I'm lying in is carved with elaborate scenes from a fox hunt. I find that vaguely disturbing.

Slightly more disturbing is the sight of Matteo asleep in a chair beside the bed.

He's sitting up, fully dressed, including his shoes. He's loosened his tie, but that's the only evidence he tried to get comfortable. His head is tilted back, exposing the strong line of his throat, and his hair is a little mussed, as if he were running his hands through it.

On the bedside table sits a glass of water and two aspirin.

As if he sensed me looking at him, his eyes flutter open. He turns his head and looks at me. His face is sleepy and soft, and his gaze is warm and hazy.

So this is what you look like when you wake up.

When he smiles, my heart hurts even more than my head.

His voice thick with sleep, he asks, "How do you feel?"

"Like shit. What happened?"

He stands, stretches his neck, then picks up the aspirin and holds them out to me. "You drank an entire bottle of wine in under thirty minutes, then passed out. Take these."

I allow him to tip the aspirin into my open palm. Then he hands me the glass of water. "Drink."

I pop the aspirin into my mouth and swallow some of the water, then hold the glass out for him to take. He shakes his head.

"Bossy," I grumble, and gulp a few more swallows of water.

When I hold out the glass this time, he takes it from my hand. He finishes what's left in it, sets it on the bedside table, and removes his suit jacket. He drapes it over the chair he was sitting in, unfastens his cuff links, and rolls up his sleeves.

Why do I find that so damn sexy?

Angry with both of us, I roll over onto my other side and burrow under the covers.

In a moment the mattress dips. Then I get his strong hands on my shoulders, kneading my aching muscles. It feels so good I groan.

He works his fingers between my shoulder blades, coaxing the knots until they relax. Then he squeezes my neck and rubs the base of my skull with his thumbs. I groan again, more faintly.

"Feel good?"

"I hate you," I mutter into the pillow.

He says softly, "I know."

His fingers work their way down my spine. His touch isn't sexual, only soothing, but of course my reproductive tract engages in an elaborate mating dance complete with drums and chanting. My head throbs in time with the pounding of the drums.

"How did I get here?"

"I carried you."

I try to picture that but can't. He doesn't appear to have any major muscle strains, so maybe when he says "carried" he means "dragged." Maybe he had one of the nice kitchen ladies bring up a cart so he could take me to . . .

Wait. Oh no. "Is this *your* bed?"

He must feel the sudden tension in my muscles because he chuckles. "I'll say no if it makes you feel better."

Oh my God. I'm in my stepbrother's bed. Ex-stepbrother. Bastard ex-stepbrother. Smoking hot, insanely sexy, arrogant, THIEF ex-stepbrother. Shit.

I should've known. The pillow smells like him. Stupid pillow.

I bury my face into it and suck in a deep breath. *Delicious.*

The bed dips again. An arm slides under my neck. A broad chest warms my back, and a pair of strong thighs pulls up behind mine.

"Don't freak out," he says as I start to freak out. "I don't take advantage of incapacitated women. I just need to rest my eyes for a minute. I was up most of the night watching to make sure you weren't dying."

He stayed up to watch over me? That's either the sweetest thing I've ever heard or a fabulous line of bullshit.

I get distracted from my contemplation of which one it might be due to the strong, steady thudding of his heartbeat between my shoulder blades. Then his other arm winds around my middle, and he pulls me gently against his body, fitting us perfectly together like a pair of Russian nesting dolls.

My swallow must be audible because he chuckles again.

"Bella. You think too much."

"I'm trying to decide how weird this is."

"On a scale of one to ten, you mean?"

"Yeah."

"Zero," he says confidently.

"But I'm mad at you."

His sigh is a big gust of warm air down the back of my neck. It gives me goose bumps.

"You're not mad. You're hurt. There's a difference."

"Believe me, Count Egotistico, I'm *mad*."

He starts to gently massage my neck again. The bastard.

When I grumble into the pillow, he says quietly, "It's all going to work out. I promise."

"Don't ever say the *P* word to me again. The next man who says the *P* word to me is gonna get a major beatdown."

"So violent," he whispers. I can hear the smile in his voice.

"You should believe me. I'm super scary."

"Oh I know. I saw what you did to blondie's face." His voice darkens. "It's an improvement."

We're quiet for a while. When he doesn't do anything alarming, I slowly begin to relax. It's deeply strange to be cuddling with Matteo, for a variety of reasons, not least of which is I'm determined he's my enemy. I never would've given him my sketch pad at the airport if I'd known who he was. And now he's *blackmailing* me to get it back, for the love of all that's holy.

My uterus decides this is a good time to interject an opposing viewpoint: *But look how supportive he was at the funeral! And how protective he was when Brad showed up!*

My ovaries chime in: *And he watched you while you were sleeping so you wouldn't die!*

"That was a very sad-sounding sigh. Care to share?"

I pick at the blanket, which feels like a cross between silk, velvet, and a newborn's bottom. I've never felt anything as soft. I squeeze my eyes shut and take a breath for courage. "So this offer of yours about getting my sketch pad back."

Matteo's hand falls still on my shoulder. I feel a new tension in him, then I feel him suppress it and force himself to relax. He waits patiently, seemingly calm, but his body betrays him. Between my shoulder blades, his heartbeat has started to pound like mad.

I think he really, *really* wants me to take him up on his offer. A flush of heat creeps into my cheeks.

When I'm quiet too long, he prompts, "What about it?"

There's a hint of impatience in his tone, and now the flush in my cheeks spreads to other parts of my body, far away from my face.

I clear my throat. "How do I know you won't use the designs even if I do agree to your . . . terms?"

Twenty-four kisses. Hot-as-fuck, panty-melting, toe-curling kisses. I try not to shiver at the thought.

"I'll give you a page back every time."

I frown at the thought of him handing me pages ripped and wrinkled, torn from the pad. "You could've already made copies of everything."

"I haven't. And I won't. And I'll destroy any dress we've made when I give you its sketch back."

I roll my eyes. "I'm supposed to believe that?"

"Short of saying the *P* word, how can I convince you?"

I try to think of something that would affect him as much as his using my designs in his collection would affect me. What would really get his goat? What would make him feel exactly as betrayed, angry, hurt, and powerless?

In a moment of brilliance, it comes to me. "I'll tell your mother everything."

Silence.

"She might not believe me, but—"

"She'll believe you."

He says it as if it's a foregone conclusion she'd take my word over his, even though she met me mere days ago and we haven't exactly become the best of friends. My intuition tells me I've stepped into all kinds of sticky, smelly ancient family poop, so deep I'd need an earthmover to get to the bottom of it.

Of course that makes me insanely intrigued and want to dive right in.

Aiming for nonchalance, I say, "You've blackmailed other designers before me, hmm?"

"No. She just doesn't expect me to be anything but disappointing."

That's so unexpected I have no response. *Disappointing? Her handsome, respectful, successful son is a disappointment to her?*

I become convinced there's a terrible, dark secret in his background that his mother had to cover up. Like an accidental death or a gnarly history of drug abuse. Some horrible scandal had to be hidden so they could continue to hold their heads high in the aristocratic circles they run in.

Maybe that's why he's always so quick to defend her honor! She holds the keys to his skeleton closet!

Or maybe it's more mundane than that. Maybe he's more like Brad than I realized. Not the gay thing—there's no way Matteo is batting for the other team. No, the gambling, running-up-debts, besmirching-the-family-name-with-douchebaggery thing.

Oh God. Maybe that's why I'm attracted to him. Maybe I have a *type*. Men Who Seem Like Catches but Are in Fact Giant Lying Pieces of Shit.

This is an awful realization, like finding out Santa Claus is a lie. *I wonder if I should try being a lesbian?*

"What are you thinking?"

My mouth is ahead of my brain. "About becoming a lesbian."

Without missing a beat, Matteo says, "You'd make a terrible lesbian."

"I think I'd make a great lesbian!"

"You like dick too much."

My face flames with heat. "I don't like dick any more or less than the next girl."

His arm tightens around me. Into my ear he says in a husky murmur, "Yes, you do. You just haven't ridden the right dick yet."

I want to fan myself, but I'm too busy hiding my face in the pillow. I have no idea how we went from revealing painful family dynamics to riding dicks so quickly, but here we are.

He punctuates his statement with a soft kiss on the nape of my neck. It sends a little tremor throughout my body, which he evidently knew it would because his chuckle is so smug I want to strangle him.

"You're an awful person."

"And yet you want me."

"We're back to *that* line? Your ego has its own atmosphere, you know that? God, I wish vanity were painful."

"I'm not vain, I'm merely stating the facts."

"Please stop talking now. You're making me want to commit murder."

His chest shakes with the laughter he's trying to suppress. "Remember what I told you about love and hate, bella. Two sides of the same coin."

He renders me useless by starting to massage my skull. It's heaven. His hands are big and strong, and the pleasure makes my eyes cross. I sigh again, caught between wanting to stand up and smother him with the pillow and wanting to live the rest of my life in this bed.

"Don't you have to go to work? It's Monday."

"I will. Eventually. Right now I've got more important things to do."

"Hmpf."

He whispers, "Go back to sleep."

"Like I could."

"Why not?"

"Gee, let's see. *We're in your bed*, for starters."

"Fully clothed. Which is how we'll stay." Pregnant pause. "Unless you're planning on undressing me."

"Shut up."

His fingers slide around my head and start to massage my temples. I make a noise like a pig digging for truffles.

"At least let the aspirin get to work. When you feel better, I'll drive you home. Then, later on or tomorrow, you can let me know what you decide about my offer."

It could be my imagination, but something in his voice makes me think he knows I've already decided to say yes.

Well, he's not the only one with a dastardly plan.

I knew this was gonna get ugly.

TWENTY-ONE

When I wake again, the angle of the light slanting through the windows high on the stone walls tells me it's no longer morning. My headache is better, but my mouth still tastes rank, and I really have to pee.

I'd move but there's a heavy arm thrown over me, pinning me in place.

Matteo and I are in the same position we were when I fell back to sleep, only now he's asleep, too. His breathing is deep and even. He doesn't snore, which makes me hate him even more.

One of these days I'll discover what faults he has other than egomania and a tendency toward the theft of intellectual property.

I carefully grasp his wrist and begin to move it so I can get up.

"Forget it. You're not sneaking off." His voice is deep and scratchy with sleep. He tightens his arm around me.

"I have to go to the bathroom."

A low noise of disagreement rumbles through his chest.

"Like . . . bad."

He withdraws his arm, gives my waist a squeeze, then a gentle push. "If you're not back in three minutes, I'm coming to look for you."

"Irritating," I mutter, and throw off the covers. I hop off the bed and head toward a door standing ajar on the other side of the room, hoping it's the bathroom. I'm relieved to find that it is and quickly shut the door behind me.

I give myself a fright when I catch a glimpse of my face in the mirror. I've got puffy raccoon eyes and something perched on my head that looks like roadkill. I take care of business, then wash my hands and attempt to smooth down my hair. I splash cold water on my face and find a tube of toothpaste in a drawer. I refuse to use Matteo's toothbrush, so I squeeze a blob onto my finger and do the best I can to smush it around in my mouth and get rid of some of the fur on my teeth.

When I'm done, I open the door to find Matteo standing in front of a big wooden armoire, removing a fresh white dress shirt from a hanger.

He's naked from the waist up.

I freeze like one of those pointer dogs when it finds the dead bird its master shot down. My eyes bulge out of my head. I exhale a long, unsteady breath.

He's so stunning I'm not sure I'll be able to remain standing if I continue to look at him.

He's art. Masculine, muscular, beautiful art. Those rippling muscles in his back. Those biceps, hard and meaty. That sleek, flat stomach.

That chiseled V leading down from his abs below the belt of his pants.

Crap. I think I just moaned out loud.

"You're staring," says Matteo, sounding amused. Slinging the shirt around his shoulders, he glances over at me. I want to look away as he slides one arm into the shirt, then the other, but I'm in pointer-dog mode and can't move an inch.

In a fantastic display of intelligence, I say, "Nuh-uh." And keep staring.

"Oh. My mistake." He turns to face me, leaving the shirt unbuttoned.

It's a gift. He's giving me a gift, is what he's doing. This might be the nicest present anyone has ever given me. Even his belly button is perfect. And my God! His chest! Michelangelo could've carved that chest!

My uterus slow claps, then faints.

After what could be several weeks, I manage to drag my gaze up from his magnificent body to his face. He's biting his lower lip. His gorgeous blue eyes are bright with laughter.

Shit. "Not a word, Moretti, unless you want a black eye."

He lifts his hands in a surrendering gesture and shakes his head, but his stomach clenches with silent laughter. Of course that makes every muscle stand out in 3-D, so now I'm looking at a tanned six-pack the likes of which I've never seen. It should be illegal for the effect it's having on my body.

The damn thing is an uncontrolled substance. His abdomen is a dangerous, dangerous drug.

I'd like to push my face into it and snort it up.

"I'll walk home," I pronounce, face flaming, and head toward the door.

"It would take hours. And you don't know the way."

"I'll call a taxi," I say over my shoulder. I stop at the door and look down at my bare feet.

"Your shoes are next to the bed."

I lift my chin and go on the hunt for my shoes, which are indeed next to the bed. I slip them on, avoiding Matteo's laughing gaze, and head to the door again.

He stops me with, "How are you going to get a taxi without a phone or money?"

When I turn and look at him, he smiles. "You didn't bring your purse with you."

"You're enjoying yourself, aren't you?"

"Just wait there a minute. I'll drive you."

He buttons his shirt. By that I mean he makes love to the shirt with his fingers, caressing each button with slow, sensual strokes as he slips them through the buttonholes at the speed at which honey would drip down a wall. It's a pornographic performance, one that could earn him an Oscar for hotness.

The entire time, he stares at me with a look. *That* look, the one that makes me weak in the knees.

"Those eyes," he murmurs, smiling.

I turn and leave before my uterus can revive itself and cause any more trouble.

Neither of us speaks on the ride back to Il Sogno. As soon as he slows to a stop, I leap from the car. I don't look back. I head inside and go straight up to my bedroom, where I flop facedown onto the bed and ponder the situation.

There's no denying it.

I want to jump Matteo's bones.

I'm disappointed in myself because he is—or was—a relative, so *ew.* He's another good-looking, entitled egomaniac like Brad, and I've sworn off those, and he's also a heartless jerk who wants to pass off my designs as his own. Unfortunately, none of that can be helped. The only thing I can control is how I deal with this whole debacle.

The main problem is proximity. If I'm going to be living in this house with his mother until she kicks the bucket, I'll be seeing a lot of him.

Maybe the idea of moving to Florence was a tad premature.

I suppose I could get my father's business back into the black and look for a buyer then. That would at least guarantee I'd get a fair price for it, instead of having to sell at a bargain-basement price because of all the current debt. That way I'd have some money to pay for the flight home, the rent I owe on my ash pile of a dress shop, and first and last month's rent on a new apartment.

That seems like a solid plan, until I remember what's waiting for me in San Francisco.

Humiliation galore.

How long would it be before I'd be comfortable showing my face in public? Do I have the strength to endure all the whispers and giggles I'd hear while standing in line at Starbucks waiting for my morning latte?

But maybe I'm being overly dramatic. I'm no celebrity, after all. Yes, the paparazzi were after me because I was the hot story of the moment, but surely some other scandal will soon come along and everyone will forget who I am. In fact, I could already be yesterday's news.

Excited at the thought, I jump up and snatch my handbag from the dresser. I dig out my phone and send Jenner a text.

> Nobody in San Fran will still be talking about me in like a month, right?

He texts back within a minute.

> I hate to tell you this, darling, but an executive from the Lifetime channel called my agent to see how they could contact you. They want to make a movie.

> OMFG. Please tell me that's a joke.

> I wish it were. How are you?

> Busy having a breakdown. I'll call you later.

I flop back onto the bed and stare at the ceiling in dismay.

Where could I get a new identity? They make it look so easy in the movies, but I don't know anyone even remotely criminal. Do I just walk into a passport photo place and drop hints about fleeing the country while flashing a wad of cash?

Maybe Lorenzo knows someone. Or Dominic. I bet he has ties to the mob—he knows everybody. Plus, he's Sicilian. They're super old school.

I'm deep in thought when my cell phone rings. It's a phone number I don't recognize. "Hello?"

"Please don't hang up."

It's Satan. Instantly my blood pressure shoots up a hundred points. "You have a death wish, don't you?"

He ignores my question and plows ahead with all the finesse of a bulldozer. "Five million cash *plus* the deed to the new house."

"In exchange for my soul and what's left of my self-respect? No."

"I'll throw in the apartment. The lease is up at the end of the month, but I'll keep paying it. You could use it as a studio."

"Or you could buy me a studio on Fillmore in Pacific Heights like I always wanted."

His shout is gleeful. "Yes! Totally! You pick the place!"

I sigh, amazed at this idiot. "That was a joke, dumbass."

"Oh. Okay." He has the nerve to sound crestfallen.

"Where are you calling me from? I want to make sure I block the number."

"I'm staying at a hotel downtown. And I'm gonna stay here until I can figure out how to make it up to you."

I picture his face as I walked down the aisle toward him, the horror in his eyes, and have to pinch the bridge of my nose hard enough so the pain distracts me from crying. "Here's an idea: light yourself on fire."

There's a pause, like he's considering it. I jerk upright in bed. "That was another joke!"

Big sigh. "Oh. Okay."

"What the hell is *wrong* with you?"

In a small, pathetic voice he says, "I'm lost without you. I didn't realize how much you meant to me until you were gone."

I throw a pillow across the room and shout into the phone, "Boo-frickin'-hoo, dickface! And by the way, *you're gay!*"

From somewhere downstairs, Cornelia whimpers.

Brad's quiet for a moment, then he heaves another big world-weary sigh. "Yeah. It's been really hard hiding it from everyone. I feel a lot better since I told you."

My eyes narrow. "I swear to God, dude, I'mma cut a bitch if you keep this shit up."

"It's the truth! I've known since I was like six or something, but you know how my dad's always going on about family values and homo-sexuality being from the devil and, y'know, all that stuff."

I do know. Once over brunch Senator Wingate lectured me for twenty minutes about the evils of "progressives" and their "backward" ideas about marriage. I think he's still bitter women got the vote.

"There are plenty of people with judgmental assholes for parents who don't go to the trouble of ruining an innocent person's life because they're too scared to stand up to Mommy and Daddy and live the life they really want."

He whispers, "I know."

Oh, for fuck's sake. Why am I listening to this? "If you really want to make it up to me, come out to your parents."

His silence is horrified. "No . . . no, what I'm saying—"

"I hear what you're saying. You need to hear what *I'm* saying: It's not gonna happen. I'm not gonna be your beard. I need love, Brad. *Real* love. A life to share and a strong shoulder to lean on, someone to build a future with. Have a family with. Grow old with. I wanted all that with you but you robbed me. And the really shitty part, the thing I just can't get over, is that you made me believe you wanted it all, too." My voice breaks. "You made me believe you loved me as much as I loved you."

"I do love you," he says urgently. "I swear I do."

"Even if you do, it's not the same and you know it."

We're silent for a while. I lie back down and close my eyes. I want to hang up, but I know we need to hash this out or he'll just keep badgering me. Like another irritating person I know, he isn't used to being told no.

"So who's the hottie?"

"What?"

"The dark-haired guy you were with yesterday with the amazing blue eyes who looks like a supermodel assassin."

One of the things I'd often overlooked in my mad scramble toward happily ever after is Brad's crippling lack of emotional intelligence. I know he's not deliberately trying to be hurtful, just as I know he needs an explanation to understand exactly why he is.

"Give me a break! You only told me *yesterday* that you're gay! We're not at the point where we're going to start talking about how hot other guys are!"

"Right. Sorry." He pauses for no more than three seconds before saying, "But who is he?"

So much for the explanation. "Not that it's any of your business, but he's my stepbrother."

"Is he single?"

"I'm gonna pretend I didn't hear that, you moron."

"It's just that he's probably the best-looking man I've ever seen. And so *intense*." He exhales a quiet breath. "You have no idea how good it feels to be able to say that out loud."

I clap a hand over my eyes and kick my heels against the mattress. "Can we *please* be done sharing?"

"Hold on—stepbrother? Your dad remarried?"

"Oh ho! Welcome to the conversation! Jesus, it's like you have selective hearing. Yes, he remarried."

"Why didn't you tell me?"

"Because I didn't know. From what I'm told, it was all hush-hush because my father didn't want to take any attention away from our wedding. He was planning on telling me after we got back from the honeymoon."

"That makes no sense whatsoever."

"Finally something on which we agree."

What sounds like the tearing of a plastic bag comes over the line, followed by the sound of crunching. Apparently Brad has decided it's time for a snack.

"So what's his wife like?"

"If Nurse Ratched and the iceberg that sank the Titanic had a love child, it would be her. She was the blonde yesterday who said you should be shot."

"Yikes. I'm surprised your dad would've married someone like that. He seemed so nice."

Brad and my father never met, but they talked on the phone a few times. We'd planned on coming to Italy after the honeymoon to see him, but like everything else, that plan is kaput.

"I guess falling in love with terrible people runs in the family."

He's hurt by the sarcasm in my tone. "I'm not terrible! I'm just—"

"Selfish? Immature? Cowardly? Shallow?"

He crunches another mouthful of whatever he's eating for a while. Then he swallows and sighs. "Yeah. I suppose I am terrible."

"So what're you gonna do about it?"

"I need your help!"

"Unless it's for castration, count me out. You're a big boy. Fix your own damn self."

"How about this—"

"No."

There must be something in my tone that sounds unequivocal because it shuts him up. Then in a quiet voice, he says, "I'm sorry. I know I messed up. I know I hurt you. I just got caught up in the whole thing. The planning, your excitement, my parents' excitement. I was so happy that everyone else was happy, but then it felt like I was riding a speeding train and there was no way to get off."

"You could've jumped and saved everyone a lot of trouble," I say, my tone cutting.

"If I could go back and change it, believe me, I would. I'd do everything differently."

He sounds so sincere I believe him. More than anything, that makes me sad.

"Please, if there's anything I can do for you, I will. I . . ." He takes a few deep breaths. When he speaks again, his voice is raw with emotion. "I do care about you. I do love you, in my way. More than anything in the world, I wanted to be what you wanted. I never thought anyone would ever want me for myself."

Tears again. Quiet, like he's trying to muffle them.

In spite of my rage, I feel sorry for him. There's nothing sadder than a grown man crying.

Except maybe a bride deserted at the altar on her wedding day in front of three hundred guests in a gown she sewed herself from fabric her dead father sent her.

What a clusterfuck.

"Look. If you really want to do something for me, have all my stuff at the apartment packed up and put it into storage. I'm not gonna be back in time to get that done before the lease is up."

"Done. What else?"

"Come out to your parents."

He groans theatrically, as if he's been stabbed. "I can't!"

"So what's your plan, then, genius? Troll some other stupid girl into falling in love with you so you can keep up this charade of being someone you're not? Because if I find out you do that, I'll out you myself."

There's a moment of shocked silence. Then he says in a tremulous whisper, "You wouldn't."

"Try me."

"Kimber!"

He has the audacity to sound offended. "You're lucky I won't do it anyway, you putz. I don't believe in revenge, but I won't let you do to anyone else what you did to me."

"But if I don't marry, my father will cut me off! Where am I gonna get money?"

"Try getting a job like the rest of us!"

"Doing what? You know the only things I'm good at are working out and planning vacations."

I think of all the time we spent together at the gym and researching trips we'd never end up taking, and get depressed all over again.

Sometimes what passes for a relationship is nothing more than having someone around to fill your free time.

"You're good at mixing cocktails and chatting up strangers, too. You could get a job on a cruise ship."

"Ha."

"I have a solution, but you're not going to like it."

He says cautiously, "What is it?"

"Marry a dude."

He scoffs. "Please."

"I'm serious. Ask your attorney what that trust actually says. Get a copy of it and read it. I'll bet your father didn't put anything in there that stipulates you have to marry a *woman*. The thought never would have even occurred to Mr. Family Values."

Brad's quiet for a while, then he starts munching again, furiously fast.

"Yeah, marinate on it. And while you're marinating, go back to the States."

"Before you hang up, I have one last thing to say."

"What is it?"

He takes a deep breath. "Do you think your stepbrother is into guys?"

This idiot. I'm not sure whether to laugh or cry. "It's a miracle you've made it this far in life without being murdered. You're the most clueless person I've ever met."

I hang up before he can ask me for Matteo's phone number.

TWENTY-TWO

MATTEO

Two days later, she still hasn't called me.

Forty-eight hours. Two thousand eight hundred and eighty minutes. One hundred seventy-two thousand eight hundred seconds. That kiss replays in my mind's eye the entire time. My erection has become a cliché.

By Wednesday afternoon I'm wound so tight I could snap.

"What's wrong with you?" scolds Antonio, frowning at me over the rims of his glasses. "You've been pacing like a caged tiger since yesterday!"

We're in the atelier, working on the new collection. Scratch that. One hundred full-time master sewers and technical staff are working on the new collection—I'm wearing grooves in the floor. "I have a lot on my mind."

Antonio watches me execute three more agitated passes in front of his desk. He's dressed in his never-changing outfit of black turtleneck, black slacks, and snowy-white athletic shoes. A measuring tape dangles from his neck, curling at the ends. An elastic pincushion bristling with needles hugs his wrist. He leans back in his chair, lights a cigarette, and exhales a cloud of smoke.

"What's her name?"

I don't bother asking how he knows my mood is due to a woman. His sixth sense is uncanny. His mother was a gypsy fortune-teller. I think it runs in the genes.

"Kimber."

He squints at me through the coils of gray fumes wafting around his head. "As in, *ly*?"

"She shortened it."

The squint deepens.

"There were five Kimberlys in her kindergarten class."

Her father told me the story over dinner one night of how his six-year-old daughter had informed her startled teacher she was to be addressed as Kimber from that day forward. Kims were everywhere, she'd said, and she was only willing to give up two letters in the name of distinctness.

I'd chuckled at the precociousness of it, never guessing I'd find myself on the other end of that formidable will soon enough.

Smoking thoughtfully, Antonio lets me make another few passes in front of his desk. Then he removes his glasses and folds his arms over his chest. "The woman in the bar the other night."

"Yes."

He murmurs, "Very beautiful." Then he waits, knowing silence is the most effective way to get me to speak.

I stop, prop my hands on my hips, and look up at the ceiling. I listen to sewing machines whirr and technicians conferring in hushed voice for a few moments before saying, "The new designs are hers."

He snaps his fingers, excited at the news. "Ah! Good! I need to ask her about the feathers on look number twenty. Valentina has ordered the bleached peacock, but there's a delicate floating accent on the hem that could either be ostrich or . . . what is this face you're making? You look like you ate a plate of bad clams."

I gaze at him meaningfully. "The designs are *hers*."

He jolts upright in his chair, staring at me with wide eyes. "You didn't buy them from her?"

"No."

"She hasn't given you permission to use them?"

"No."

Astonished, he gapes at me. His face drains of color. "That's theft! She'll sue! She'll ruin your name!"

"Not when I'm done with her, she won't."

He barks out a disbelieving laugh. "You're going to put her in a sex coma, is that it?"

Hopefully. "I'm going to convince her it's better to have me as a friend than an enemy."

That throws Antonio for a loop. His face goes through a series of interesting expressions, including confusion and suspicion, until finally it settles on dismay.

"You've *threatened* this poor woman?"

He says that too loud. Several people at workstations nearby stop sewing, lift their heads, and glance over at us. I glower at them, and they quickly go back to work.

"Of course not! You know me better than that."

"Then I don't understand what you mean."

"It's complicated."

Antonio takes a long drag from his cigarette. He's so agitated he doesn't notice when a fat clump of ash falls onto the middle of his chest and rolls down his shirt, bouncing off his belly and scattering. Then, as he does, he turns practical.

"Stealing isn't the way to compensate for the designs that snake Riccardo destroyed when he left. This is beneath the House of Moretti. This is beneath *you*. We'll scale down the show—"

"There has to be fifty pieces," I interrupt, starting to pace again. "We always show fifty new looks!"

"Of our *own*," he replies, his tone bone-dry.

I don't want to tell him exactly what I have planned, so I wave a hand dismissively in the air. "Think of it as a collaboration."

"I'll do no such thing!" he says, indignant. "We don't collaborate with anyone!"

"Interesting that's your takeaway on the situation."

He huffs and slumps down into his chair. "Eh, my takeaway. My takeaway is that you've lost your mind. I should look for a new job now, before word gets out that I work in a den of thieves and I'm unemployable." He *tsks*, muttering to himself. "To think of all the years of dedicated service I've given you. My loyalty repaid like this." He makes a resigned sweeping gesture with his arms, as if the *polizia* are closing in, guns drawn. "I'll die in disgrace. Ah!"

He throws an arm over his eyes and whimpers.

I think he gets his sense of melodrama from his mother, too.

I pull up a chair across from his desk, sink into it, and drag my hands through my hair. "You asked what was wrong with me. I told you."

"So accusing! You'd think *I* was the thief here!" he cries from behind his arm.

"I never said I stole the designs, you carping old woman. We traded."

He peeks out from beneath his arm and eyes me suspiciously. "Traded?"

"For a plane ticket."

"Well, why didn't you say so?" Casting off his air of doom, he straightens and breaks into a grin. "A trade! This is business! This is good!"

He's forgotten I told him I didn't get permission, so I have to clarify. "But I promised her I wouldn't use her designs in the show."

His expression goes from glee to horror. "This is bad. This is very bad."

"What if I said she's my stepsister?"

He doesn't react for a moment. Then I see him recall the state I was in when I returned to our table at the bar after I spoke to her, how the front of my trousers were tented, and he blanches. He makes the sign of the cross over his chest.

"Sorry—*ex*-stepsister."

"But . . . you're attracted to her."

"Of course I'm attracted to her. A man would have to be blind not to be attracted to her." *And that sweet red strawberry mouth. Fuck.*

I can tell Antonio is thinking hard because he always looks as if he's about to have a stroke when he's mulling over a problem.

Then he pronounces, "It still seems like a sin."

"It's not a sin," I say angrily. "Why does everything have to be a sin?"

He looks at me as if I'm an idiot. "I don't make the rules. Talk to the pope."

Exasperated, I jump to my feet and start another round of pacing. "I don't need to talk to the pope. It's not a sin. It's not illegal. It's not anything."

"If it's not anything, why are you so worked up?"

Good question. My tie feels like a noose. I yank at it angrily, manage to loosen it enough to breathe, and keep pacing. "She's ignoring me."

After a moment, Antonio says, "Oh."

I slide him a sideways look. There was more to that "oh" than simply "oh."

"What?"

"Ha!" He cackles, slapping the arm of his chair. "Ha ha! I never thought I'd see the day!"

"What the hell are you talking about?"

He jumps to his feet, points his finger at me, and shouts, *"You're in love!"*

As if an off switch has been thrown, everyone in the atelier stops what they're doing and stares at me.

I'm going to kill him.

"Back to work!" I'm instantly obeyed, but looks are flying around the room like arrows. I have a terrible feeling this will be the subject of gossip for months to come.

Antonio turns to the room and throws his arms wide. "He's in love with his stepsister!"

In unison, one hundred people swivel their heads and stare at me in unblinking silence, like an army of judgmental owls.

"*Ex!*" I shout, red-faced. I want to kick something. Especially Antonio's fat rear end. "Ex-stepsister! And I'm not in love with her! No one is in love with anyone!"

No one dares to make a peep, except Antonio, who turns back to me with little red hearts in his eyes. Sighing, he clasps his hands together at his chest.

"Ah, Matteo. You make a very handsome couple. The children—oh! They'll be beautiful. I've worried so long about you being alone. All you do is work, never taking time to meet a nice woman and settle down. I'm sure if you write the pope a letter explaining the entire situation, he won't let your souls burn in the eternal lake of fire."

I blow out a hard breath. "Jesus Christ."

Antonio nods. "Exactly."

I'm saved from the insanity of the conversation by my cell phone, which starts to ring. I yank it out of my pocket, hit "Answer," and snap, "*Pronto!*"

"Uh . . . *pronto* yourself. I guess."

There's a strange sense of relief at hearing her voice that I don't need to examine too closely. I already know what it means. "Kimber."

"Matteo. Now that we've confirmed we know each other's names, are you ready to talk? Or do you need a few minutes to finish skinning the cat or whatever you're doing that's got you so worked up?"

Through gritted teeth, I say, "I'm. Not. Worked. Up."

"Really? Hmm. 'Cause you sound kinda worked up."

I have to close my eyes and count to ten before I'm calm enough to answer. "Just dealing with some employee problems." I open my eyes and send a lethal glare Antonio's way.

He blows me a kiss and lights another cigarette.

"Okay. We'll do this some other time."

"Wait! Don't hang up! I need to talk to you!"

From the corner of my eye, I see Antonio's smile. It's so big it can probably be seen from outer space. I turn on my heel and stalk off the production room floor and into my office, slamming the door behind me.

"What was that noise?" asks Kimber.

"I closed a door."

"*Closed?* Sounded like you put some stank on it."

"I have no idea what that means. What have you decided about my offer?"

When she hesitates, I feel like my chest might explode.

"Well . . ." she drawls, torturing me. Then she relents. "I suppose I can survive two dozen kisses from you if it means getting my designs back."

I sink slowly into my desk chair. I loosen my tie another few inches, but still can't breathe, so I rip it off and toss it on the desk.

"I have some free time tomorrow. Say, from five o'clock to five-oh-one?"

"No. Today. And I'll need more than one minute."

"You never said anything about timing," she starts, sounding hostile, but I cut her off.

"A proper kiss takes more than one minute."

"That sounds ominous. I think we need to discuss the particulars before we go any further."

The particulars. My mind gifts me with a pornographic Technicolor show of each and every "particular" it wants. I open the top two buttons on my shirt, yanking aside the collar because it's stifling. "So. Discuss."

She's irritated by my curt response. I can tell because she says, "That tone is pissing me off, Count Egotistico."

I really hate it when she calls me that. I am a fucking *marchese.* "What doesn't piss you off?"

"The list is long. It includes all kinds of fun things, like rainbows, puppies, nonassholey men . . ."

"Very funny. I'm not an asshole."

She mutters, "That's what they all say."

I have to force myself to sound nonchalant and in control, though I'm anything but. "Let's get back to the subject at hand."

"Sure. One minute and not a second longer. That's my final offer."

"Five minutes."

"*What?* Who kisses for five minutes straight?"

I growl, "I'd like to kiss you for five hours straight, but we have to start somewhere."

That shuts her up for a while. Then she groans. "This is so weird."

"Don't forget you can tattle on me to my mother if I don't hold up my end of the bargain."

"Yeah, there is that."

She's imagining all the ways she'll humiliate me to my mother, I can hear it in her voice. I take advantage of her distraction to press my case. "Four minutes."

"Ugh. I can't even *look* at your face for four minutes at a time, let alone suck on it."

Remembering how she ogled me while I changed my shirt in my bedroom, I allow myself a smile. "Perhaps you'd rather look at my chest."

A sound like a snake's hiss comes over the line. "You know, every time I think you're not a complete dick, you do something to prove me wrong."

My smile grows larger. "And we're back to my dick."

"I never said anything about your dick!"

"You did. Just then."

"No, I did *not!*"

Maybe she's right. Maybe I am an asshole. Because winding this woman up is so much *fun.* "I distinctly heard you say the word—"

"Two minutes," she spits out. "That's it. Final, *final* offer."

Two minutes. Twenty-four kisses. That means her beautiful strawberry mouth is all mine for a total of forty-eight minutes.

It's more than I hoped.

If I were a supervillian, this is the part where I'd rub my hands together in glee and produce an evil laugh. "I accept your offer. I'll see you at your shop at five o'clock sharp."

"Not today! Matteo—"

I disconnect the call. Then I adjust my hard cock, grab my briefcase, and head out, the page I'd already removed from her sketch pad inside.

The full-color copy is pinned to the wall in the workroom, along with all the others.

Sometimes a man has to bend the truth in service of a greater cause.

TWENTY-THREE

KIMBER

I stare at the phone in my hand with my mouth hanging open and my heart impersonating a bongo inside my chest.

It's three o'clock. Matteo will be at my door in two hours.

Shit.

"Miss Kimber?"

Clara stands outside the doorway of my office. She's one of the three seamstresses my father hired to help him, and she's amazing. Since I met her two days ago, she's brought me homemade stromboli, homemade lasagne, homemade gnocchi, and about four thousand different kinds of homemade Italian desserts, just because she's a wonderful human being.

She has six children, fourteen grandchildren, nine great-grandchildren, and is built like Castello di Moretti. She could be anywhere from sixty to one hundred years old, but I'm not asking. I get the feeling Clara distributes head slaps as often as she distributes food.

"Come in."

I drop into my chair and wave her in, trying to put Matteo out of my mind. At least for a minute. I'm sure I'll go back to obsessing over him as soon as Clara leaves the room because it's all I've been doing for the past forty-eight hours.

Clara wedges herself through the door and stands in front of my desk. She's almost the same width. "The pleats are done."

"Already? Wow. You guys are fast."

She smiles. "We have to be."

She and the other two seamstresses—Amelia and Sofia, neither of whom speak English—have been working like lightning since I called them in to the shop on Monday to introduce myself and find out if they'd be able to help me finish the dresses in time for the show. As each dress requires somewhere in the neighborhood of one hundred fifty hours of work to complete, I wasn't sure if they'd be on board, much less capable of the task, but they surprised me by not only being enthusiastic about the idea, but far more skilled than anyone I'd worked with in the States.

These women take sewing *seriously*. More than once I've seen one of them say a prayer before starting work.

Hopefully the shop has enough cash to meet payroll at the end of all this, but we'll cross that bridge when we get to it.

"Okay. Let's take a look."

We go into the production room, which is the temperature of the sun. The old building doesn't have central A/C, so the air back here is like soup. Several floor fans are whirring, but that only means the soup is being stirred. Somehow I'm the only one sweating, despite all three other women wearing wool dresses.

Laid out on one of the large tables in back is a long piece of fabric, constructed of hand-dyed strips of grosgrain ribbon sewed together over a piece of tulle. It will eventually become the top layer of a voluminous skirt. Leaning over to pick up the edge, I inspect the stitching, which is flawless, the continuity of the pleats, also flawless, and the uniformity of color of the dyed grosgrain strips.

"Perfect," I murmur, awed. All by itself, this piece of fabric is a work of art.

Clara doesn't have to translate to Amelia and Sofia what I've said. They nod solemnly, as if perfection is simply the baseline standard, not the ultimate goal.

I'd like to kiss you for five hours straight, but we have to start somewhere.

Dammit. Matteo's in my head again. I can't seem to kick the fucker out. But God, his mouth! I want his mouth. I hate him for being such an incredible kisser. And for tasting and smelling so delicious, and for being so beautiful.

I just all around hate him.

"Miss Kimber, your face is a tomato," says Clara, looking at me with concern. "The heat, it gets to you. Maybe you should sit."

They're all gazing at me in grandmotherly concern, and now I'm embarrassed. "I'm fine, don't worry. Can we finish the underpinning in the next few hours?"

"Certo," says Clara, waving a hand like it's a silly question. "This is no big one."

I think she means no biggie, but I'm not about to correct her.

For the next hour and a half, I manage not to think of Matteo once. When I glance up from the piece of faille I'm embroidering with sequins and seed pearls, I'm surprised to see the time. Lying to myself that I'd do it even if I didn't have an appointment to kiss Matteo, I head to the bathroom and try to freshen up.

It's like trying to freshen a wilted piece of lettuce. I'm limp and unappealing, my hair frizzing, the rest of me misted with sweat. I run the water in the tap for what seems like forever until it finally comes out cold. I splash my face, hoping some of the color will subside in my cheeks by the time he arrives.

Thank God it's hot. I don't want Count Egotistico thinking my body temperature has anything to do with him.

Even though it has *everything* to do with him.

I could be lying nude on an ice floe in the middle of the Arctic Ocean right now and I'd still be on fire. All from the thought of his mouth.

I hate him. I hate him. I hate him.

I make it my mantra as I dry my face and smooth my hair. By the time I go into the front of the shop, cooler because all the windows are open and there's a cross breeze, I think I've got myself sorted.

Until he pulls up across the street in his sleek black sports car.

The moment he opens the door and steps out, his eyes find me. It's like they're tracking beams, homing in on my exact location behind the counter. He's spectacular in a dove-gray suit, but I barely notice that because his eyes have taken me hostage.

All my cells scream *He's here!* and start to party.

I hate him. I hate him. I hate him.

He closes the door of the car without looking away from me. Staring into my eyes, he slowly unbuttons his jacket. I have to grip the edge of the counter for support because my knees are doing their wobbly Jell-O routine again.

By the time he crosses the street and opens the shop door, my brain is scrambled eggs. The rest of me is one pulsing, incandescent beacon of lust.

I hate him. I hate him. I hate him.

He steps into the shop, and the air does that thing it does when he enters a room. It leaves in a *whoosh*, taking my breath with it.

"Kimber."

He says my name in a husky, possessive tone, as if he's already inside me.

Dear God, what is my uterus doing? I think it might be trying to escape from my body and fling itself across the room onto his face.

"Hey," I say with utter nonchalance. "What's up?"

He smiles. It's a secret smile, and completely unnerving. In his hand he holds a briefcase, which is where I suppose one of my purloined sketches resides.

"Did you bring it?"

"Of course."

We eye fuck each other for a while, until I want to run screaming from the room. "Let's see it."

He strolls across the space toward the counter as if he's got all the time in the world, that little unnerving smile hovering around his lips. He sets the briefcase on the counter, flicks open the locks, removes a folded sheet of paper, and hands it to me.

As soon as I have it between my fingers, I start to get emotional. I feel as if I've been reunited with my kidnapped child. Unfolding the paper, I press the sketch to my chest and blow out a shaky breath. "The red dress."

Matteo inclines his head. "It's one of my favorites."

Then I'm angry because he folded it!

He frowns at the look on my face. "What's the matter?"

I point accusingly at the crease in the page. "This. *This* is the matter."

I can tell he wants to roll his eyes, but he snaps the briefcase shut instead. Then he gets into this stance, the one he does when he's being the Big Cheese. He folds his arms over his chest, spreads his legs shoulder width, and looks at me down his nose.

He says, "Get over here, and give me my fucking kiss."

My heart stops. My mouth goes dry. In my hand, the sketch starts to tremble.

The son of a bitch smiles again.

"Not here. I have workers in the back."

His mouth takes on a ruthless slant. "You're stalling."

"No, I'm not. I just don't want everyone to see."

"If they're in the back, how are they going to see?"

"They could walk up front!"

He inhales through his nose, then exhales even slower, as if he's forcing himself to remain calm. "Kimber."

"Stop saying my name like that!"

He quirks an eyebrow. "Like what?"

"Oh my God. You're the most aggravating man on the planet, you know that?"

He growls, "You have ten seconds to get your ass around this counter and give me my kiss before I consider our deal null and void and set fire to the rest of your sketches."

I gasp in horror. "You wouldn't!"

His smirk tells me in no uncertain terms that yes, he certainly would.

Seething, I carefully place the sketch of the red dress on the counter. Then I straighten my shoulders, lift my chin, and march around the counter, reminding myself how much I hate him, to the very bottom of my soul.

As soon as I'm within arm's reach, Matteo grabs me and pulls me against his chest. He stares down hotly into my eyes. "I know," he says gruffly. "You hate me. Now give me that mouth. It's all I've thought about for two days."

Are uterine transplants a thing? Because mine is totally out of control.

"Fine. Here." I rise up on my toes and smash my lips against his in a clinical, close-lipped, extremely unsexy kiss that even a grandpa might find offensive.

Matteo and my uterus can both go to hell.

He turns his head enough to dislodge my dried prune of a mouth from his. Then he sends me a dangerous look. "Do that again and I'll bend you over this counter and make you regret it."

My feminist side is outraged. Ignoring all the other parts of me that are clamoring for a demonstration of exactly what he means, I sputter,

"Don't you dare threaten me! I'm not a child! I'm not your property to manhandle, you sexist, chauvinistic—"

Then his mouth is on mine, and he dissolves my anger with his lips, which are clearly laced with crack cocaine.

Because the high I'm getting must be drug induced. There's no other rational explanation.

He holds me up when I sag against him, dizzy and disoriented, intoxicated by his taste. Three seconds in and I'm addicted. I'm a helpless, filthy addict, and what's worse is I don't even care.

I always laughed when I read in romance novels how the hero "ravaged" the heroine's mouth. Now I know how accurate that description is. He kisses me senseless, wrecking not only my resistance but my ability for rational thought, taking what he wants without apology or hesitation.

Plundering. Like a pirate. Like an invader.

Like a boss.

"That's it, bella," he murmurs when I shudder. "Feel it."

Holy shit, do I.

He takes my mouth again, but just as quickly breaks away, leaving me panting and blinking in shock. Frowning, he looks at his watch. He presses a button on it, then turns back to me with a smile. "Sorry. Two minutes, you said."

"You started a timer?"

"Don't want to go over, do we?"

I shout, "How are you so irritating?"

He grins, and it's breathtaking. "Just lucky, I guess."

Then his mouth is on mine again, and I forget to be angry. I think the bastard knew he'd have that effect on me because he makes this sound deep in his throat, a little grunt of satisfaction.

I'll kill him later. Right now I'm swimming too deep in Horny Lake to pull off a murder.

His hand cradles my head while his other arm holds me tightly against his body. My arms wind around his neck. What started as a kiss turns into an incredible feedback loop of sensation as our bodies instinctively coordinate, our breathing falling into the same rhythm, our hearts thudding the same urgent beat.

His breath is my own.

My skin is on fire.

I never, *ever* want this to end.

Against my mouth, he says, "I think you needed this as much as I did."

I keep my eyes closed when I whisper, "I still hate you, but I have time left, so please shut the hell up."

His chuckle is dark and sends a bolt of pure lust straight down between my legs. His fingers curl into a fist in my hair, and he pulls my head back a little, angling my jaw to allow him better access to my neck, which he takes quick advantage of.

His mouth feels like velvet. His tongue sweeps against the pulse in my throat. He works his way down my neck, kissing and gently sucking, until he reaches the open collar of my blouse. When he dips the tip of his tongue into the hollow of my throat, it feels as if I'm being electrocuted.

Digging my fingers into his shoulders, I softly moan.

And, oh God, he starts to whisper in Italian, moving his mouth to the other side of my neck, slowly working his way back up until he's nuzzling the sensitive spot under my ear. He whispers something else and moves my body slightly so my pelvis is against his, and I feel his arousal.

A tremor runs through me, as fine as a breeze through grass.

When our lips meet again, I sink my fingers into his hair and pull him as close as I can get him, greedily sucking his tongue, unashamed at the little desperate noises I'm making, thinking of nothing except him. How big he is. How warm. How his chest feels against my breasts. How hard he is for me . . .

How I'd love to see the look on his face if I sank to my knees, unzipped his trousers, and took all that hardness as far as I could down my throat.

Beep. Beep. Beep.

Matteo pulls away so abruptly I gasp.

He glances at his watch. "Time's up." Then he looks back at me and says, "That was mediocre. If you're not going to put your heart into it, let's forget the whole thing."

He reaches around me for his briefcase, turns away, and *walks out the door.*

He doesn't even bother to close it behind him.

I'm not sure, but I think the blistering string of curses I shout after him can probably be heard all the way down the block.

TWENTY-FOUR

I don't get back to the house until almost midnight. By now I've managed to convince myself murder is a capital crime, and I really don't want to spend the rest of my life in an Italian prison.

But man, if it weren't against the law, there would be one dismembered marchese buried in the woods behind the house.

I stop by the kitchen to fix myself a plate of leftovers, then head to my room. When I flick on the light in the bedroom, I find Cornelia snoring in the makeshift doggie bed I created in one corner of the room using old blankets and pillows. She's snuggled up to one of my T-shirts that she must've dragged out of my open suitcase in the corner.

I haven't had the time or energy to unpack.

Trying to be quiet so I don't wake the dog, I set my handbag on the dresser. Then I sit cross-legged on the bed with my plate and laptop and munch while looking online for a local clinic where I can get an STD test.

I find a place with a nearby address, have Google translate their webpage to English so I can read it, then book an appointment. That awful task completed, I decide to google my name since I'm already in a bad mood.

I should've known better.

After reading every article on the first four pages of results, I'm convinced I can't move back to San Francisco, at least not without changing my name and having some major plastic surgery. Those pictures are never going away. Never. When I'm a hundred years old, there will still be full-color photos floating out in cyberspace of me punching Brad in the nose at the altar of Grace Cathedral.

Any man I'll ever date in the future will be able to see those pictures. He'll be able to read every smarmy detail about the worst humiliation of my life.

"I won't date," I tell the computer, getting teary. "I'll become a nun. I'll marry Jesus. He won't care that I'm the laughingstock of San Francisco. He won't care that I'm damaged goods."

He might care that I'm about as religious as a head of lettuce, but whatever.

I snap shut the computer and flop back onto the bed. After a minute or two of staring at the ceiling, I'm so angry I can't lie still anymore. I set the plate aside, hop out of bed, and dig my cell phone from my purse. Then I call Satan.

He picks up on the first ring, sounding wide awake and hopeful. "Babe?"

"You're not allowed to call me that anymore!"

"Oh. Uh, sorry." He's quiet for a moment, listening to me breathe like a dragon. "Are you okay?"

"No. Are you still in Italy?"

"Yeah."

"Good. I've figured out how you can make it up to me."

"I can't come out to my parents," he says, his tone pleading. "Anything else but that!"

"This has nothing to do with your parents."

He heaves a relieved sigh. "Okay. What is it?"

"Come to DiSanto Couture in the morning, eight o'clock sharp." I give him the street address, then warn, "Don't be late."

"I won't! I'll be there right on time!" Then, hesitating, he says, "What're we doing?"

"Taking your measurements." I hang up, smiling.

He's gonna look amazing in the pleated dress.

True to his word, Satan shows up at eight on the nose. Speaking of noses, his seems to be healing quickly. The swelling is down, and so is the bruising under his eyes. By the time I need him to look pretty again for the show, he should be all set.

I have Clara take his measurements because there's no way in hell I'm holding a tape measure to his inseam. Watching him squirm in discomfort as she manhandles him and bosses him around is so much fun I make her recheck all her numbers and take his measurements again.

When it's over and he asks what it was all for, I tell him the truth. Sort of.

"I need you to model for me."

"Model? What, clothes?"

I deadpan, "No. Taxidermy animals. It's my new hobby."

He squints, confused. "Would I, like, hold them or something?"

"Dude. That was a joke. You've heard of those."

"Oh right. Ha ha. Good one."

He still looks confused. I stare at him, wondering how I never noticed his tendency to take everything literally.

It hits me in full force that I was so focused on the wedding I didn't spend enough time considering what marriage to Brad would actually be like day to day. I wasted years daydreaming about one magical event without paying enough attention to who the man behind the handsome face really was.

Whoever coined the phrase "love is blind" was only half-right.

It's deaf and stupid, too.

But could there be a silver lining to all the humiliation I suffered at his hands? Maybe instead of ruining my life, he actually did me a huge favor. Maybe he taught me the most important lesson of my life.

It isn't the wedding that matters. Getting that piece of paper and saying "I do" can't make right what's fundamentally wrong.

Another revelation rocks me: Maybe I wasn't in love with Brad himself . . . maybe I was in love with an idea. Maybe I was in love with being in love, the worst possible foundation on which to build a marriage.

Maybe Brad wasn't the one who screwed me over.

Oh God. I think I might have done that all by myself.

Watching me, Brad draws his blond brows together in worry and shifts his weight from foot to foot. "The way you're looking at me is, um, kinda scary. Did I say something wrong?"

He's a little kid. He's just a big, goofy, self-centered kid who's scared of his parents and can't be alone.

I stare at him, struck by how *obvious* it all suddenly seems. Bradley Hamilton Wingate III isn't a man. He's a child in a grown-up's body, playacting to get acceptance and love the only way he knows how, too insecure to stand on his own two feet.

Everything he's ever done has been motivated by fear.

What a miserable way to go through life.

Aw, shit. And here I was determined to hate him forever.

Reeling from my epiphany, I say, "I'm still mad at you for being dishonest. But it's not all your fault. I can't hang all the blame on you, because I was busy being an idiot, too, just in different ways." I take a deep breath. "So if you ever decide to come out to your parents, I'll go with you. You won't have to handle that conversation alone. Okay?"

His eyes round. His lower lip quivers. He stares at me in white-faced shock for what seems like a long time, then swallows. In a small voice, looking at his shoes, he says, "Okay."

Then bursts into tears.

I'm not one of those people who can watch someone cry without giving them a hug. It's an uncontrollable impulse. So, sighing, I put my arms around Brad and let him blubber on my shoulder until his tears have turned to sniffles and he's red with embarrassment.

"Sorry," he mumbles, wiping his nose with the back of his hand.

"I've seen you cry more in the last week than I have in the entire time we were together."

He whispers, "Tough guys aren't supposed to cry." He chews his lower lip and sniffles again, looking pathetic but also adorable.

He's always adorable. It's one of his best qualities. He's playful, good tempered, and lighthearted, and always wants everyone around him to have fun.

Unfortunately, the man is actually a decent human being.

When I groan, Brad glances up at me, his forehead crinkled with worry. "What's wrong?"

"It's inconvenient feeling empathy for someone you previously decided to hate."

He grabs my hands, his eyes full of desperation and hope. "So that means you *don't* hate me?"

Overwhelmed by a wave of exhaustion, I heave out a lungful of air and beseech the ceiling, "How is this my life, God? Did I do something to personally offend you?"

Brad is too busy getting excited by this new development in the conversation to pay attention to my pleas to a higher power.

"Because I'd do anything to stay friends with you, even if you don't want the money and stuff. I meant it when I said you were the only one I ever felt safe with. You're my best friend, and there's nothing I wouldn't do to—"

"We're not breaking out the BFF charm bracelets and matching outfits yet, pal," I interrupt sarcastically. "Let's wait until after I get the results from my STD test to see how things are going to go."

"I'm clean!"

I'm taken aback by the volume and confidence of that pronouncement. "You sound pretty sure."

"I am. I get tested every month!"

Watching my face, he immediately realizes that was a mistake. He cringes in that puppy-about-to-get-smacked-for-chewing-a-new-pair-of-shoes way and bites his lip.

But I don't care. I've flipped from empathy to murder in two seconds flat. I peer at him in narrow-eyed suspicion. "If you were 'safe,' like you said you always were, why would you need to get tested every month?"

He glances at my clenched fists. "I'm afraid if I tell you the truth, you'll deck me."

"I might deck you anyway. Talk."

He debates it for a moment, inhales a breath for courage, then blurts the words out in one long breathless rush. "Because nothing is one hundred percent effective there's always a chance you can pick up something bad even if you use protection and I was scared I might pass something on to you so I got tested a lot to make sure I was clean so you wouldn't catch anything."

He stops for a breath, bracing himself for a hit, but my head is spinning too fast for me to take a swing at him.

"You're telling me you were trying to protect me?"

He nods.

"From getting a sexually transmitted disease that you might unknowingly have had?"

He nods again, but has to think about it first.

My voice rises. "Because you were sleeping around so much, with so many different partners, that the risk of catching a nasty virus was so high you had to be tested once a *month*?"

He says defensively, "Sometimes more often than that, just to be sure." Then he brightens. "But I'm totally clean, so we're all good!"

I stare at him with my mouth open because there just aren't any words.

There are. No. Words.

He decides this would be a good time for us to share another hug, and throws his arms around me.

At that moment a man's hard voice comes from the doorway behind us.

"I hope I'm not interrupting."

I peek over Brad's shoulder and see Matteo standing in the open doorway of my shop, his back stiff and his eyes blazing, looking as if he's about to burn the place to the ground.

TWENTY-FIVE

MATTEO

She has her arms around him.

They're hugging.

He's touching her.

My stomach knots. A wave of heat engulfs my body. The room narrows until all I can see is her hands on his back and her beautiful green eyes gazing at me from over his shoulder. Those eyes widen when she spots me, then narrow.

She's not happy to see me. She's in *his* arms, and she's not happy to see me.

I'm going to break something. Probably his legs.

Kimber pulls away from her ex. It looks reluctant. He glances over his shoulder and does a double take.

His expression is more complicated than hers. He's surprised to see me, too, and afraid, that's obvious. But there's something else I don't understand. Something like . . . excitement?

Maybe he wants to fight me. If that's the case, I'm going to mop the floor with this preppy *pezzo di merda*.

"What're you doing here?" Kimber's tone is as unfriendly as the look in her eyes.

"I was on my way to work." That's as much of an explanation as I can give before the snarl starts creeping into my voice, and I have to stop.

Brad moves to stand beside Kimber, nervously wiping his palms on the front of his jeans. He stares at me with a wild look in his eyes, as if he's not sure if he's going to bolt or start throwing punches.

I scowl, looking back and forth between them. *What is this? Are they getting back together?*

The thought makes it hard to breathe.

Kimber tilts her head, studying my expression. "So continue on your way."

Beside her, Brad fidgets like a child waiting impatiently for a piece of candy.

Gazing steadily at him, I say, "You don't need me to stay?"

At the exact same time, she says "No," and Brad says, *"Yes."*

With emphasis.

"I wasn't asking you!"

With a sharp intake of breath, he puts his hand to his throat. Kimber looks at Brad's face and snorts like she thinks something's funny.

The last of my patience unravels. I snarl, "What the fuck is going on?"

Wide-eyed, Brad breathes, "So intense."

He's mocking me. This son of a bitch is *mocking* me.

I take a step forward, ready to knock him out, but Kimber rolls her eyes and throws her hands in the air. "Cool your jets, Count, he was just leaving!" She gives Brad a little shove. "I'll talk to you later. Go back to your hotel."

By this time I'm vibrating with anger. I don't know what's happening, but I don't like it one bit. She wanted to kill him when she saw him after the funeral. Now they're sharing hugs?

"Matteo."

At the sound of my name, I snap my gaze back to her. She stares back at me with an eyebrow arched in disdain.

"Step aside." She looks pointedly at the door, which I'm blocking.

I manage three steps to my right. Then I glare at Brad as he slowly makes his way across the shop. His pace quickens as he skitters sideways past me like a crab, then he's gone.

None of the tension leaves my body, but at least he's gone.

"Your turn," says Kimber, dismissing me.

Instead I close the door and lock it. When I turn back to her, she's got her arms folded over her chest and her jaw set.

"I'm not doing this with you now."

"Doing what?" I move closer.

"Don't play that game," she warns, glowering.

Oh, love. This isn't a game.

When I don't say anything, she inhales an agitated breath and taps her toe against the floor. "What do you want from me?"

Everything. I want everything from you. And I want it now. I stop a foot in front of her and stare down into her eyes. "Time to eat the frog."

She crinkles her forehead. "Excuse me?"

"It's something my father used to say. If eating a frog is the worst thing you have to do in a day, don't put it off. Do it first thing and get it out of the way."

Her gorgeous green eyes kindle with anger. "You're comparing kissing me to eating a fucking frog?"

God, I love that temper. I love that I don't intimidate her. I love that she never tries to impress me, never bites her tongue, never backs down.

I love that she doesn't care about my money, my title, or my family name. I've never met a woman who wasn't after at least one of those.

Most of all I love that though she'd rather die than admit it, she's enjoying this bargain of ours as much as I am. Those cheeks are pink from more than anger.

"It's a metaphor. But I was talking about you," I say, staring hungrily at her mouth. "*I'm* the frog *you* have to eat. Might as well get it over with early so you don't have to think about it for the rest of your day."

Her lips flatten. "You don't get to call all the shots here. You can't just show up unannounced, demanding kisses."

"Yes I can. I just did. And I'll do it again. Give me my kiss."

She says frostily, "For a guy who said I'm a mediocre kisser, you're awfully eager to shove your tongue down my throat."

I said it because I know there's nothing more she thrives on than a challenge, but now I see it was a mistake. I went too far. I hurt her feelings.

Fuck.

"I'm sorry. That was stupid. It won't happen again."

She blinks, taken aback. A shade of the hostility fades from her posture, but she's still upset. "Why did you say it, then?"

"I wanted to rile you up."

She's beginning to look confused, worrying her lower lip with her teeth and frowning. "So . . . you don't think I'm a bad kisser?"

That she cares what I think makes my chest tighten and my pulse start to pound. I can't tell her that I made myself come three times last night thinking about her mouth. Her body. The little sounds she makes when she's wrapped up in my arms. I can't tell her that she's my fucking wet dream, that I can't get her out of my head no matter what I try.

I can't tell her anything yet. I don't want to scare her off or overwhelm her. Because if I told her what I really want from her, she'd run for the hills.

She's a woman nursing a broken heart. Though there's nothing more I'd love to do than throw her over my shoulder, take her home with me, and make her mine, I have to tread lightly.

Good things come to those who wait.

So I say, "If I thought you were a bad kisser, I wouldn't be trying so hard to kiss you, now would I?"

She eyes me, cagey as a spy. I can't tell if she believes me or not, but I don't have time to ask because she blurts, "Okay, fine, let's get this over with."

I take her face in my hands and take her mouth before she has time to change her mind.

TWENTY-SIX

KIMBER

He doesn't set his watch this time, so I have no idea how long we go at it, standing in the middle of the shop, macking each other's faces off. It might've lasted forever if it wasn't for the sound of someone loudly clearing her throat.

Breathing hard, I break away from Matteo and glance over my shoulder. Clara stands at the doorway to the back of the shop, looking at us with her brows lifted and her lips pursed, one hand propped on her ample hip.

She does not approve.

"Clara. Uh. Whuz happenin'?"

I can barely speak, I'm so disoriented by lust. Matteo grasps my upper arm when I teeter, chuckling in satisfaction at how thoroughly he's crossed my wires.

At least I think that's why he's chuckling. Truth be told, I'm not sure of much of anything at the moment except I'm going to need to start bringing extra panties to work if he keeps showing up like this.

"I need your direction on the bodice of the blue gown." She glances at Matteo, giving him one swift up-and-down look that manages to convey her grudging admiration of his beautiful suit and even more beautiful self along with her obvious irritation that I'm futzing around with a man instead of working.

Clara believes men are good for only two things: lawn care and vehicle maintenance.

"Oh. Uh-huh." I nod like a bobblehead doll. "'Kay."

She rolls her eyes and trundles away, shaking her head.

As soon as she's out of sight, Matteo spins me around and comes at me.

"Whoa! Easy, tiger!" I push him away, afraid that if I don't I'll soon be tearing our clothes off and mounting him like a bull. "Nope. No way. No more. Gotta get to work. Clara needs me. You heard the woman." I giggle madly, as if I've recently escaped from an asylum. "Back to the trenches!"

His smile is so beautiful it could end wars. "Are you sure you're ready to go back to work? You seem disoriented."

"I am totally fine." *Except I sound drunk.* I stiffen my spine and lift my chin, hoping he doesn't notice how badly my hands are shaking from the adrenaline crashing through my veins. I feel as if I just won a Formula One race. My nervous system is popping corks and spraying champagne everywhere.

"Fine?" He watches me, those laser beam hawk's eyes shining with mirth. "I'll have to do better next time."

If he does any better, I might explode. I think I just spontaneously ovulated.

"We need to set a schedule," I say sternly, attempting to sound like a rational human being and not a woman whose clitoris has its own heartbeat. "I can't have you showing up like this, interrupting me whenever you feel like it."

He nods solemnly, but I suspect he's trying not to break out into laughter. "That's reasonable. How about after dinner every night? Say, eight o'clock? I'll drop by the house."

That seems late, and contradicts what he said earlier about eating the morning frog or whatever it was, but I'm in no condition to negotiate, so I mutter, "Okay. Good. See you then. Bye."

I spin on my heel, but he calls after me, "Why was your ex here?"

I slowly turn back to him. The laughter has died in his eyes. He's back to that dangerous look he had when he first came in, dark thunderclouds churning over his head.

Is he jealous?

Halo glowing, a little cartoon angel materializes on my left shoulder. "Tell him the truth," she whispers, gently flapping her wings. "Tell him Brad is gay and there's nothing going on between you."

A red cartoon devil pops up on my right. "Drag this smug asshole over the coals," he growls, spitting fire. "You think you're the only broad he's makin' a run for? Don't be naive. He's got tail all over town. You can't be this stupid again. And by the way, dipshit, you're supposed to be thinking with your brain, not your vagina, remember?"

After a brief hiatus to consider my mental health, I decide to go for the gray area between truth and fiction that admits nothing, but also makes nothing up.

"I asked him to come."

Matteo takes a step closer, bringing his thunderclouds with him. "Why?"

"We have unfinished business."

A few more steps and he's invading my personal space again, frazzling my nerves and cracking my atoms. "Unfinished business," he repeats, demanding more of an explanation with his eyes.

A fight breaks out between the angel and the devil. It's a complete bloodbath—the devil wins without even breaking a sweat.

"He's begged me to forgive him. He's apologized, and I believe he's truly sorry. And now . . . we're working it out."

Matteo's cheeks turn ruddy. His nostrils flare. He seems to expand somehow, like he's filling with air, and I'm an evil bitch because that makes me happier than I've been in quite some time.

He says, "What exactly are you working out?"

I know a bargaining chip when I see one and don't hesitate to use it. "Give me all my sketches back and I'll tell you."

When a dark mood settles over him like a fog, I send him what I hope is a spectacular smile. "You sure are crabby all of a sudden, Count. Are you feeling okay? You seem disoriented."

A low noise rumbles through his chest, and his mouth takes on the hard line that means he's about to say something I'll want to smack him for.

He leans in and whispers gruffly, "Not as disoriented as you were a moment ago, bella. I could've pushed you against the wall and taken you standing up, you were so ready for it."

Of course it's the truth, but hell if I'm going to admit it. I simply shrug, like *Maybe I was and maybe I wasn't*, and politely stifle a yawn.

His lips curve into a smile that gives me goose bumps, it's so dangerous. "Challenge accepted. See you at eight."

He watches me gulp, smirks, then turns and saunters out the door.

I go back to work and spend the rest of the day trying not to count the minutes until I see him again and telling myself it's all just a game.

The problem with games is that there's always a loser.

I work straight through dinner and arrive at the house at the same time Matteo does. He's getting out of his car as my taxi pulls to a stop in front of the door. I pay the driver, gather my handbag and my courage, and step out.

Matteo watches the taxi drive off with a look of consternation. "Do you not know how to drive?"

"You people drive like psychos. I don't want to get into an accident."

He strolls nearer, carrying his briefcase in one hand, smiling like he finds me amusing. "I'm happy to drive you to and from work. All you have to do is ask."

"So you can spy on me and see what new designs I'm creating? No thanks."

His smile turns into a scowl. "Is that why you think I came by this morning? To spy on you?"

"I find it hard to believe you'd go to all this trouble just to kiss me."

He stops a foot away, his scowl softening as he glances at my mouth. When he looks into my eyes, the air between us crackles. "It's no trouble."

My pulse ticks up a notch. We stare at each other for a moment as a warm breeze whispers through the trees, bringing the scent of jasmine and freshly baked bread with it. I tell myself my mouth is watering because of the bread and not the man standing in front of me.

"All right," I say, all business. "Let's get this over with." I sling my handbag over my shoulder, straighten my spine, and lift my chin.

Watching me steel myself for his kiss, Matteo smiles again. "Let's go inside. I haven't eaten yet."

"I haven't, either, but this isn't a dinner date."

He steps closer so I feel the warmth of his body and smell his skin. In a low voice, he says, "What is it, then?"

"A business deal."

As far as my hormones are concerned, it's more like foreplay, but I have to find a way to get through the next twenty-something kisses with my dignity intact, so I'm going with nonchalance.

"You want to conduct business in the driveway?" He glances meaningfully at the front windows of the house that are spilling golden light onto the gravel where we're standing.

I form an uncomfortable mental image of his mother watching in horror as we kiss, and decide he's right. "We can't do it inside, either."

He understands without me having to explain and suggests an alternative. "The garden."

I picture us sharing a passionate kiss under the moonlight beside the fountain of Aphrodite, picture Matteo pushing me down onto the grass and pushing himself between my naked thighs, and my nipples harden. Between my legs, there's a hollow ache, howling to be filled.

What the hell have I gotten myself into?

"It's only a kiss," murmurs Matteo, watching my face heat. "Two minutes. I'll time it again so you'll be safe."

I have an awful feeling I'll never be safe from him, but I swallow my fear and nod, then turn and head toward the garden without looking back.

I don't have to look to feel him following. I'm as aware of his presence as I am of my own crashing pulse. All the years I was with Brad, all the times he kissed me, I never felt this kind of anticipation. Or is it dread?

It's probably both. I want him but I hate myself for it, for letting him get under my skin.

For all the ways he can unravel me with nothing more than a look.

Moonlight filters through the boughs of the trees as I wind my way down the stone path through the garden that leads to the fountain. The crickets are out in full force, chirping away in cheerful oblivion as we pass. The air is warm but my skin is warmer. I'm all flushed and out of breath.

I stop abruptly and turn to him, convinced this bargain we've struck is a huge mistake.

My heart is already broken. I'd be a fool all over again to expect Matteo will do anything but shatter it for good.

"I can't do this," I say, looking at his shoes. They're leather, black, gleaming, and infinitely less dangerous than his eyes. I watch his feet approach, until his shoes and mine are touching at the tips.

He sets his briefcase on the ground, then slides my handbag off my shoulder and sets that down, too. Then he puts his thumb under my chin and tilts up my head.

He's quiet for a moment, examining my face, thoughtfully stroking his finger along the curve of my jaw. I stand trembling, wishing I were anywhere but here, wishing I were the kind of woman my father thought I was, strong and brave and capable.

But I'm not. I don't think I ever was, or ever will be. I'm just a girl who sees stars every time a handsome man pays her attention, and if that's not pathetic I don't know what is.

Matteo says softly, "Is it me you don't trust or yourself?"

I swallow and close my eyes, gutted by how easily he reads me. Three years with Brad and I'd have to chisel my feelings on a stone tablet for him to get a clue what I was thinking, but Matteo somehow correctly interprets every nuance of my expression.

I suppose it's because he's always looking so closely.

"Both," I admit, miserable.

Big warm hands wrap around my jaw. "Thank you for being honest," he whispers, and lightly touches his mouth to mine.

Electricity jolts through me, as if I've been plugged into a socket. I suck in a startled breath. My eyes fly open, and I stare up at him in a panic.

"Don't run away."

I groan. "That you knew I was about to makes it even harder to stay put!"

"You don't like that I know what you're feeling."

It's not a question, which makes me feel worse. I'm beginning to think there's nothing he doesn't see, the damn mind reader.

I turn my head, and he rests his cheek against mine. "But you know what I'm feeling, too, so we're even."

I whisper, "I don't know what you're feeling. I don't know anything."

He takes my hand and flattens it over his chest. Under my palm, his heart pounds hard and fast. "Yes you do. You just don't trust it."

"I can't trust it. Not only do I have questionable taste in men, we're enemies."

"Frenemies. With kissing benefits."

"That's not even a thing."

"It is now."

To prove his point, he kisses me.

But oh, this kiss. This kiss is different from any other we've shared because he goes so slowly, so carefully, his mouth skimming mine, his tongue the softest coaxing brush along the seam of my lips. He's gentle in a way he's never been, almost sweet, and the effect is devastatingly intimate.

I could fall for this man so easily. My heart wants nothing more than to let go and let it happen, but I can't be blind like I was with Brad ever again.

This could be nothing more than a manipulation for Matteo, a way to have his cake and eat it, too. At this very moment, his team could be working on my designs. Despite his promise to the contrary, he could have copied every page of my sketch pad. He might have zero intention of destroying the designs before the show. He could, in fact, be counting on my crushed ego and broken heart to muddy the waters of my common sense.

I could be playing right into his hands.

He pulls away and gazes down at me, his eyes hot and dark. "You're thinking. Stop it."

"I just realized you haven't given me a sketch yet. For this morning, either. You owe me two."

"When we're done," he says, and takes my mouth again.

I grab on to his shirt for balance. He winds his arms around my back and pulls me close. All my senses are overwhelmed by the scent of the night and of him, by the feel of his strong body against mine, by the dark edge of longing chipping away at my self-control. When I make a desperate noise in the back of my throat, Matteo kisses me deeper. One of his hands threads into my hair.

He must have other women. I can't be the only one. He's rich and famous and hot as sin, and who am I? A sad little nobody. The Jilted Dressmaker. The Cast-Away Couturier.

The woman who didn't have enough sense to realize her fiancé would rather eat dick than her.

I push Matteo away and hold him at arm's length with my elbows locked and my hands flattened on his chest. We stay like that for a moment as the night breathes quietly around us, until Matteo rests his hands on top of mine. His voice comes out low and rough.

"Whatever's happening between you and your ex, remember this: I'm not him."

God help me, he knows exactly what I'm thinking.

How am I supposed to handle this? What's the smart thing to do? Laugh? Tell him to go to hell? I need advice.

Out of nowhere, I miss my father so fiercely I want to cry.

Matteo releases my hands. Bending down to his briefcase, he snaps open the locks, withdraws two sheets of paper, and holds them up to me.

My sketches.

Of course he came prepared. He's always prepared for everything.

When I take them from him, he closes his briefcase and rises, grasping it in his hand.

"Tomorrow, then. Eight o'clock."

He turns and disappears into the night, leaving me to wonder if he knew I was about to tell him I want to call the whole thing off.

TWENTY-SEVEN

I walk into my bedroom to find a disaster zone.

Dragged from the open suitcase in the corner, my clothes are strewn all over the floor, shredded into pieces. In shock, I pick up a T-shirt and inspect the damage. Judging by the size of the rips and tears in the fabric, it was attacked by a rabid animal with small claws and tiny razor-sharp teeth.

"Beans," I mutter, fuming.

Evidently Matteo isn't the only member of the Moretti family I'm at war with.

I clean up the mess, fantasizing about capturing Beans and shaving her coat to resemble a poodle's. Cornelia is nowhere to be seen. I'm guessing she doesn't want to get in trouble for her sister's bad behavior.

I go to bed without dinner, too exhausted to eat. In the morning, I've got bags under my eyes and a headache that feels like someone's having a go at my skull with a sledgehammer. I shower and dress, grab an apple from the bowl on the kitchen table, and leave before the sun's up.

I work until eleven, then call a cab to take me to my appointment at the clinic. I'm in and out in twenty minutes, after having blood and urine drawn and examining all my life choices that led me to this moment. Back at the shop, I order lunch in for the ladies, but I'm too stressed over the thought of the test to eat.

I won't have the results for two days. So, depending on how things turn out, Brad may or may not have forty-eight hours left to live.

I unblock his number and text him that, so he can suffer along with me.

Within sixty seconds, my phone rings.

"You're gonna be totally fine," Brad says when I pick up. "Trust me. It's all good."

"*Trust* you? Really?"

After a pause, he sighs. "Yeah, that was an unfortunate choice of words."

"Speaking of unfortunate choices, you might want to dial back the swooneration if you ever see Matteo again."

"Why, is he homophobic?"

I grimace. "*Homophobia* is such an inaccurate word. It's not a phobia. No one's afraid. They're just an asshole."

Brad laughs. "I think Samuel L. Jackson might've said that."

"Probably. He's very wise."

"Back to the swooneration."

"Well, from the looks of things, it makes him want to kick your ass."

After a longer pause than before, he says, "Two things."

"Shoot."

"One: You didn't tell him I was gay, did you?"

"Nope."

"Why not?"

"You haven't even come out to your parents. It's not my place to be spilling your private business all over the world."

Brad makes a small sound of shock, exhaling quietly. "I can't believe you'd have my back like that, after what I did."

"I know. I'm amazing. You don't deserve me. But remember my silence doesn't apply to any female you might want to trick into marrying you by pretending you're straight. Where you like to stick your dick is your business until you try to ruin another poor girl's life, then all bets are off. What's number two?"

"How serious are you about him?"

That shocks me into silence. Since when did Brad get so observant? When it becomes obvious I'm not going to say anything, Brad fills in the gap.

"We were together for three years, Kimber. I know you think I'm clueless, but even I can see that you never looked at me the way you look at him."

Remembering the way Brad looked at me when I was walking down the aisle toward him, I suffer a pang of heartache. "Maybe someday we'll look back on this and laugh. Maybe someday, after a few years have passed and I've grown scar tissue over all the holes you tore in my heart, we can be friends again. But right now I have to be honest and say it's none of your damn business."

"It is, though, because I care about you."

"You've got a funny way of showing it," I mutter.

"I looked him up, you know."

"What's that supposed to mean?"

"On the internet. I researched him."

"Whatever you're about to tell me, I don't want to know."

He snorts like he thinks I'm funny. "Liar."

Chewing my lip, I sit up straighter in my chair and brace myself for the worst. "He's a womanizer, right?"

"More like a monk. He hasn't been photographed with anyone for years. According to the gossip sites, he's obsessed with work."

I say darkly, "Or he's just really good at keeping secrets."

"Not everyone has skeletons in their closets."

"Don't you dare talk to me about closets."

Brad laughs, sounding delighted. "Right. Oops. It's kinda funny, though, right?"

"Sure, like an inoperable brain tumor is funny. I'm hanging up on you now."

"Before you go, tell me when I'm doing this modeling thing for you."

I'm instantly suspicious of his motives. "Why?"

"My mom wants to know if I'll send her some pictures."

My eyes bulge out of my head. "You told your *mother* about it?"

"Well, yeah. I mean, my parents know I followed you to Italy to try to get you back."

Of course they do. Brad's parents always have to know his whereabouts. I used to think it was sweet they kept such close tabs on him, but now I know better. It was all about damage control.

And now I'm mad all over again.

"Tell your mother there will be *tons* of pictures. She won't miss a thing." I wish I could have a picture of her face when she sees her son in a couture gown. It still hasn't occurred to Brad to ask me what he'll be wearing, despite the fact that all I've ever made is ladies' wear. He probably thinks I'm going into men's fashion just for him.

"Awesome. Thanks, ba—uh, Kimber. And thanks for being so cool about everything. It really means a lot."

Don't thank me yet, idiot.

I hang up without saying goodbye. Then I block his number again because I have a feeling if I don't, I'll have thumbs-up and best friend emojis arriving via text at all hours of the day and night.

I should've let Matteo murder him and bury him in the backyard. Things would be so much simpler if all I had to deal with was a guilty conscience.

Assuming I'd have a guilty conscience over Brad's demise, which is far from a given.

When the taxi drops me off at seven o'clock, Matteo's black sports car is already in the driveway.

"Great," I say under my breath. "Why don't you just move in? We'll all be one big happy, backstabbing family."

I slam the taxi door with more force than necessary, then stomp into the house, trailing steam from my ears. This whole situation feels as if it's spiraling out of control, like I'm in a bad soap opera. Next I'll find out I have an evil twin I never knew who wants to lay claim to Il Sogno and my father's business.

At this point, I'd be tempted to say *Have at it!* and wash my hands of the whole mess.

When I walk into the dining room, Matteo and the marchesa are sitting next to each other, deep in conversation, their heads bent together and their voices low and urgent, as if they're plotting a government coup. They break apart when they see me. Matteo leans back in his chair, a sly gleam in his eyes, and his mother begins feeding morsels of food from her plate to Beans, who's sitting in her booster chair glaring at me with the burning heat of a thousand suns.

I prop a hand on my hip and glare back, including the other two overbred creatures at the table. "Don't let me interrupt whatever pernicious scheme you're hatching."

Matteo grins. "Pernicious? Have you been reading the dictionary?"

I smile back, but it could peel the paint from the walls. "Yes. There are so many interesting words that start with the letter *P. Pushy. Peacock. Pecker. Pompous.* I could go on."

With laughter in his eyes, Matteo retorts, *"Pact. Pattern. Paper."*

Leave it to him to work our damn agreement into the conversation. When I glance meaningfully at the knife beside his plate, he chuckles. "Bad day, stepsister dearest? You seem tense."

He's teasing me, the jerk. Why is he in such high spirits? "*Ex*-stepsister."

He says airily, "Yes, that's right. I know there's been some confusion over the fine print."

When the ghost of a smile lifts the marchesa's mouth, I consider replacing all her shampoo with hair remover. Without another word to either of them, I walk out and head straight to my bedroom. Cornelia's napping in the middle of my bed on her back with her legs stretched out, looking like she's been shot.

"Dog!"

She jerks, rolls over, and sits up. When she spots me, she barks and starts to wriggle in excitement like a puppy, pawing the bedcovers.

I point at the bed I made her from blankets in the corner. She stops wriggling, puts her ears down, looks at the blankets, then back at me. Then she flops onto her belly and sets her giant head on her paws, giving me big moon eyes, trying her best to look utterly pathetic.

"Cornelia," says Matteo from behind me. *"Go."*

He doesn't have to ask twice. She slinks off the bed with her tail between her legs and curls up into a big black ball on the blankets, hiding her eyes under a paw.

"It's not eight o'clock yet." I toss my handbag onto the dresser and turn around to look at him. He's leaning against the doorframe with his hands in his pockets, smiling like he's on vacation.

Ignoring my comment, he says, "I love you in that dress. You look like a movie star." His eyes take a stroll around my figure, lingering on my breasts and legs before wandering back up to my face. He murmurs, "The color matches your eyes."

Trying valiantly to ignore the words *I love you* hanging in the air like a lit stick of dynamite, I run my hands nervously down the cinched waist of the dress. "It's one of my father's. A certain tiny satanic ball of fur shredded most of my clothes. I think the taxi driver on my way into work thought I was homeless."

"I should've warned you about Beans. She has an oral fixation."

"Thanks for the heads-up," I say sourly. "Go back to your dinner."

"Did you eat yet?"

At the exact same time I say "Yes," my stomach lets out a loud, alarming groan that sounds like I'm hosting an alien life-form in my bowels.

Matteo smirks, shaking his head. "I'll be back."

He turns and leaves. I'm relieved because I think I'm getting a while to get myself together before he returns demanding kisses, but he's back in five minutes, holding a plate piled with food.

Cornelia lifts her head, eagerly sniffing the air. My stomach emits another monstrous grumble.

"Osso buco alla Milanese," says Matteo. "My mother's specialty."

"Your mother cooks?"

He chuckles at my disbelieving tone. "She's an incredible cook. Lorenzo usually does the honors, but on Fridays we always have a family meal she makes herself."

He holds the plate out to me. It's filled with veal shanks falling off the bone, polenta, and some small balls smothered in red sauce. I assume they're meatballs, until Matteo corrects me.

"Those are arancini. Rice balls stuffed with cheese and ragu, coated with breadcrumbs and fried. They're delicious."

They definitely smell delicious. The scent wafting up from the plate is making my mouth water. I take the plate from his hands and accept the fork he holds out. I take a tentative bite of the veal, not completely convinced it isn't poisoned, but groan in pleasure when the taste explodes on my tongue.

Matteo smiles. "Good?"

I swallow that mouthful, then stuff another in. "Oh my God. *So* fucking good."

I realize how sexual that sounded when his eyes darken. Looking at my mouth, he says softly, "So fucking good."

It sends a thrill straight through me, like I've stuck my finger into an electrical socket. We stare at each other for a beat, until I remember to swallow. When the plate trembles in my hand, Matteo takes it from me. He removes the fork from my other hand, spears a bit of meat from the plate, and holds it up to my mouth.

"I don't need you to feed me."

"You have no idea what you need. Open your mouth."

Okay, so my panties just exploded. So what? That doesn't mean he's in charge here.

"You're used to getting your way, aren't you?"

"Yes. Now open your mouth." He nudges my lips with the tines of the fork.

I want to kick him in the shin, but I'm too hungry to put up a fight. So I simply open my mouth and let him slide the fork between my lips.

Like a hawk, he watches me. When my tongue darts out to lick some sauce from my lower lip, his eyes flare. My breath catches, and though I want badly to look away, I can't.

I'm a deer caught in headlights. I'm a fox caught in a snare.

Next I get a mouthful of creamy polenta. He feeds it to me slowly, easing the fork into my mouth, focused on me with extraordinary attention. I feel my pulse everywhere in my body, even my fingertips.

When I swallow, he wipes the corner of my mouth with his thumb. Then he sucks on it, savoring it as if he can taste me, as if he's wishing his thumb were some intimate part of my body.

"So fucking good," he whispers, eyes blazing, and fills the fork again.

At this rate I'll orgasm before we even get to the fried balls. "Matteo—"

"Hush." He nudges my lips with the fork.

I close my eyes and let him feed me, swallowing everything he lifts to my lips as my heartbeat goes haywire and my skin heats. After three bites, I'm so turned on I can barely swallow.

He touches the throbbing pulse in the side of my neck, then leans in and kisses it.

My eyes fly open. I suck in a startled breath. He sets the plate on the dresser next to my hip with a clatter, then sinks his hands into my hair, angling his head to kiss me.

"The door's open!"

He growls, "Fuck the door," and crushes his mouth to mine.

TWENTY-EIGHT

He tastes like spices and wine and something indefinable that's all him, that mysterious, masculine drug his tongue is laced with. Off balance, I stumble back a step. My butt jostles the dresser and the fork clatters off the plate, but his mouth demands all my attention. As I cling to his biceps, he sinks his hands into my hair.

This kiss is harder than the one last night. More sexual. It's a kiss that says clearly *I want to do bad things to you*, and my body responds as if he's said it out loud.

My nipples harden. My breasts feel heavy and begin to ache. That restless burn starts between my legs, made hotter by Matteo flexing his hips against mine so his hardness is trapped between us, nudging so close to where I need him most.

I break away, worried about the open door and the thought of Mommy Dearest peering in, but Matteo doesn't let me go. We stand chest to chest, crotch to crotch, breathing hard and gripping each other, staring deep into each other's eyes.

My God. This man. He makes the word *sexy* inadequate.

He pulls my head back and inhales deeply against my throat. His cheek is hot and scratchy against my skin. When he nuzzles his nose into my hair, the rough scrape of stubble on his jaw raises a rash of goose bumps on my arms.

He says gruffly, "Tell me what you just thought that made you tremble."

"I want to feel that rough jaw on the inside of my thighs."

I don't realize I've said it aloud until Matteo turns to Cornelia and orders her out of the room. He follows her to the door and closes it behind her, then walks slowly back to me at the dresser, where I'm barely managing to hold myself up.

Without a word, he sinks to his knees on the carpet in front of me and pushes my dress up my bare thighs.

I only have time to squeak his name in shock before he puts his face between my legs. He inhales deeply there, too, makes a hungry sound in his chest, then opens his mouth and bites me through my panties.

Right. *There.*

It's not hard. It doesn't hurt. It's more like a mark of ownership, like *This is mine, and I'll do anything to it that I want.* It's so unexpected and utterly sexy I can't help but exhale a soft moan.

Matteo opens his eyes and gazes up at me as I stare down at him. The look in his eyes is so dark, so dangerous, it makes my heart pound. Keeping his gaze locked on mine, he slowly rubs his jaw along my inner thigh, chafing it with his stubble, then turns his head and presses a kiss to the same spot. When the tip of his tongue snakes out and licks my skin, a wave of heat engulfs my entire body.

He turns his head to my other thigh, rubs his jaw over it, kisses it, and licks it as he did on the other side. Only now he's using his hand, too, stroking his thumb over the naked flesh next to the edge of my panties, pinching it gently, testing it and learning its firmness, how it feels under his fingers and his teeth.

His erection makes a thick bulge down one leg of his trousers. My nipples are so hard they jut straight through the bodice of my dress, two taut points of sensation screaming for attention from the hot, wet pleasure of his mouth.

"Spread your legs." He runs the tip of his nose up and down the damp spot on the front of my underwear. When I don't obey him, he shakes his head and *tsk*s.

Then he opens his mouth and suckles my throbbing clit right through my panties.

I suck in a hard breath, my back stiffening, my eyes wide. This is so wrong, but it feels so right that all I want to do is grind my crotch into his face and let him make me come, just like this, dirty and quick.

He says something in Italian, his voice guttural, his eyes burning. Then he's up on his feet in a blinding-fast move. He drags me against him so my breasts are smashed against the hard expanse of his chest. He kisses me again, so forcefully it bends me back at the waist.

He cups my head in one hand and caresses my breast with the other, squeezing the fullness of it in his palm, stroking and pinching my aching nipple through the fabric. When I groan into his mouth, he shoves the plate of food aside and lifts me onto the dresser.

My dress is bunched up around my thighs. My legs are open around his hips. My brain blinks offline, so now it's nothing but sensation.

His fingers slide like butter through the buttons on the front of my dress. I'm exposed to him in seconds, flushed skin and rapid breathing, a pink bra that's no match for his expert hands. The clip is in the front. He finds the way of it without even breaking away from my mouth, and my breasts spill out into his hands.

When he pinches both my nipples, I arch and shudder, whimpering. He lowers his dark head to one of my breasts and sucks a hard nipple into his mouth, his cheeks hollowing. I dig my fingernails into his shoulders, gasping. Lost.

He moves to my other breast, licking and sucking, murmuring in English and Italian as I pant and writhe against him, my head thrown back and my eyes closed.

"Look at you."

"So sweet."

"Cosi perfetta."

"Il mio perfetta dolci amore."

His words are so soft, his tone so ardent and tender, I'm suddenly overwhelmed by emotion. The hot prick of tears stings my eyes. I suck in a ragged breath, trying desperately not to cry.

All those times I slept with Brad were fake. My life was a lie. And here I am in the arms of a man who could just as easily be playing me.

Am I being used again?

"Easy." He's hugging me now, cradling me against his chest with his cheek pressed to the side of my neck and his body curved into mine. He combs a hand through my hair, strokes my back, softly shushes me when I make a noise of distress. "Just breathe, bella. Shh."

"I'm okay."

"You're not. And don't lie to me again."

His voice is both soft and hard, a caress and a command, letting me know in no uncertain terms that I can't hide from him—and the next time I try, there will be consequences.

I push against his chest but he's immovable. His arms around me turn into an iron band. He lowers his mouth to my ear and says in a low voice, "Running away won't solve anything. Talk to me. What just happened?"

I hide my face in his chest, tucking my forehead under his collarbone. I blink hard and fast, trying to clear the water from my eyes. "I'm not as tough as I act."

The softest of chuckles passes his lips. "I know," he whispers, tracing his fingertips down my spine. "It's one of the things I adore about you."

Oh God. What that does to my poor heart. You'd think it would've had enough of sweet-talking men by now, but it does somersaults in my chest like the sad clown it is.

"I don't understand why you're doing this."

"Doing what?"

I lift my head and meet his gaze. He blinks in surprise when he sees my face, his brows drawing together. I imagine I look like a wild animal backed into a corner.

"You told me you wanted to buy my father's business. You made it clear you don't think I have what it takes to make it in fashion here. And this game you're playing, the kissing game—what's the point? Are you hoping I'll develop feelings for you so I'll sell? Are you trying to make me fall in love with you so you can get what you really want—the business?"

He's focused on me with startling intensity. His eyes drill down into mine. "*Do* you have feelings for me?"

His tone is emotionless. It reveals nothing about what he might be thinking or feeling, and neither does his face. All I can see for sure is his extreme focus and intensity, which tells me only that my answer is important to him but not why.

Don't be a fool. Don't let a beautiful liar break your heart again.

I decide to deflect and see how he'll handle it. "What were you and your mother talking about when I came in?"

His left eyelid twitches, but that's the only reaction I get. After a moment of silence, he says, "Nothing important."

"If it's not important you can share it with me. What was it?"

A muscle flexes in his jaw. He slowly inhales and exhales. I suspect he's buying time.

And just like that, I'm out. That moment of hesitation tells me all I need to know.

Looking him dead in the eyes, I say, "Step back."

His brows lower and he scowls, the way he does when he's displeased. I can see threats are needed.

"Unless you want me to turn your balls into pancakes with my knee, step back."

For a moment he doesn't move. Then he curses under his breath and steps away, folding his arms over his chest so he and his balls can glower at me from a safer distance.

I fasten the buttons of my bodice with clumsy fingers, ashamed at myself for letting him get to me so easily. *I can still feel his mouth on my skin.*

"Tell me if you have feelings for me." His voice is dangerously soft.

"Tell me if you're manipulating me."

Irritated by my answer, he shakes his head. "I told you—I'm not your ex."

"Which is exactly what a man trying to manipulate me would say. It would've been easier for you to simply say no. Unless the real answer is yes."

He rakes his hands through his hair, curses again, then starts to pace the room.

"Okay, you want me to talk to you? Here goes. I'll give you my worst-case scenario. Your mother—who, by your own admission, is disappointed in you—needs some insurance on my promise not to kick her out of the house. She got nothing from my father in his will, which must've really stung, but his dopey daughter was recently dumped in the most spectacular way, and she's vulnerable. She owns a business that you'd like to get your hands on and an expensive house your mother would like to legally get her hands on, so the two of you decide that you'll work your magic and make the dopey daughter fall in love with you so she'll hand over the keys to the kingdom with a smile.

"Conveniently, you're in possession of a sketch pad the dopey daughter desperately wants back, so you concoct a clever ploy that forces the two of you to spend time with your faces stuck together. What better way to get those hormones wreaking havoc on her brain? Once you've convinced her to sell you the business and put your mother on the title of the house, you'll be back in your mother's good graces and everyone lives happily ever after.

"Except me. The idiot Kimberella, screwed by another toad masquerading as a prince."

By this time, Matteo has stopped pacing. He stares at me with his arms hanging loose at his sides and his lips slightly parted, a strange expression on his face. "That's what you think?"

I can't tell if I've shocked him with my accuracy or if he's about to lunge at me and wrap his hands around my throat. His expression is unnerving.

"Tell me I'm wrong."

"That's the kind of man you think I am," he presses. "A lying, scheming, manipulative prick so desperate for his mother's approval he'd fake his attraction to you before he even knew who you were." When I look confused, he clarifies. "At the airport, I didn't know who you were. At the hotel, I still didn't know who you were. I only found out you were Luca's daughter when I walked into the living room of this house and you were sitting on the sofa."

That sound I'm hearing is a tiny hiss of air being released from the pin he just stuck into my balloon of paranoia. "Maybe you decided after you discovered who I was that the mutual attraction would make it easier all around."

"Easier to fuck you over, you mean," he says, his voice hollow.

My pulse is all over the place. My mouth has gone dry. I wish I could tell what his expression is saying, but I'm such a poor judge of character I'd probably decide it was acid reflux and offer the man a Tums.

"Tell me you're not. Tell me I've made the whole thing up in my head. Tell me what you and your mother were talking about when I came in."

He answers without hesitation. "We were talking about you."

I knew it! "What about me?" I snap.

His eyes flash. He snaps back, "You wouldn't believe me if I told you, so what's the point?"

"Maybe you should try me!"

"Maybe you should trust me!"

I laugh, but it sounds awful. Like I'm dying on the inside. "Sorry, Count, trust is something I'm fresh out of."

His face flushes red in a wave from his neck to his hairline. A vein pops out in his forehead. He inhales a slow deep breath, gritting his teeth. "I'm. A. Fucking. *Marchese.*"

He stalks over to the door, yanks it open, and slams it shut behind him, so hard the windows rattle.

I holler, "Way to put some stank on it!"

The only answer I hear is the sound of his footsteps pounding angrily down the hall.

TWENTY-NINE

I spend the next day in a daze, trying to concentrate on work, but the upsetting scene with Matteo plays in my head on a loop. It won't stop, no matter what I try to distract myself. Anxiety settles over me like a cloud. By the time I return home at seven-thirty, I'm so wound up I guzzle a glass of wine to settle my nerves. I don't know whether Matteo will strangle me straight off when he arrives at eight or wait until after he gets his kiss to do me in.

But he's a no-show.

I can't decide if I'm relieved or worried. What could his absence mean?

I'm out of the house before the sun's up the next day and back at work. In addition to the new designs we're making, there are several unfinished bespoke pieces clients had on order before my father died that need to be completed. The day is a flurry of activity. I'm so busy and distracted I forget to obsess over my test results. When I take a break for a late lunch, I check my email on my phone and find a new message instructing me to login to a secure website with the password included to get the results.

I start to sweat like a farm animal and almost throw up.

After splashing water on my face and giving myself a pep talk in the bathroom, I take a seat at my desk. I log on to the site and try to keep my hands steady as I type in the password.

My heart thumps so hard it's physically painful.

The page takes a hundred years to load. Then the type is so small I have to zoom in and scroll around, searching in a panic for anything resembling the word *positive*.

It takes a few terrifying minutes, but finally it's confirmed: I'm negative for everything.

Instead of giving in to the urge to burst into tears, I treat myself to an entire pint of pistachio gelato from the charming little *gelateria* down the block, then call Danielle, who's been leaving me increasingly hysterical phone messages. When she picks up, she bypasses a greeting and goes straight into guilt mode.

"I can't believe you haven't called me back in two weeks!"

"I know. I'm a terrible friend. But life has decided I'm great for target practice, and I've been busy dodging bullets."

"Your dad. Oh, honey, I'm so sorry."

"Jenner told you?"

"He did. Also about your shop, your hot stepbrother, your weird stepmother, and the two dress-wearing dogs who eat at the table. I've been pestering him constantly for updates. Your life has more plot twists than the subtitled Korean melodramas I watch."

"If it makes you feel any better, you're the first one to hear this: Brad followed me to Italy."

The shriek on the other end of the line is as pleasant as an ice pick jammed in my ear. *"What?"*

"And he's still here."

"No!"

"Yep."

"What does that rat want?"

"Redemption, I suppose." I sigh, exhausted by the thought of him. "He begged me to forgive him. He still wants to get married."

Danielle exhales, and it sounds like she's breathing fire. "That *dick*. The nerve! Have you hired the hitman yet?"

"I don't know any hitmen. Not every Italian is in the mafia."

"But every Italian probably *knows* someone in the mafia, right? Or someone who knows someone who knows someone."

"You've been watching too many crime shows."

"Oh right," she says after a pause. "You can't tell me. Plausible deniability. That's smart."

"There's no hitman, Danielle."

"Sure there isn't." She drops her voice to a whisper. "Do you think the line is tapped?"

"No, but I do think you should take up writing mystery novels. That imagination of yours is being wasted. How are Brian and the kids?"

Her voice brightens. "Everyone's good. The kids are back to school soon, which is lucky because I'm one mood change away from a meltdown. I don't remember us being so dramatic at that age."

Danielle has three daughters. She married her high school sweetheart, moved to the Midwest, and started producing babies before she was twenty, beating all the divorce statistics about marrying young.

At least one of us is lucky in love.

"We were too busy being dorky to be dramatic. Remember my hairstyle?"

"Sweet Jesus, the perm. You looked like you styled your hair by sticking your finger into an electrical outlet."

"Let's not forget your headgear."

"Four years of wandering around in public looking like I'd just arrived from outer space. I'm still not over the trauma."

"At least you got those beautiful straight teeth at the end of it. I'm still stuck with hair that refuses to hold a curl unless it's chemically forced to."

"Your hair is gorgeous! Do you know how many girls with frizzy hair would kill for it to be straight?"

Don't talk to me about being straight. I heave an enormous sigh. "I miss you."

"I miss you, too. When are you headed back to San Fran? I can probably arrange to come out for Labor Day."

"I'm not going back to San Francisco. I've decided to stay in Italy."

Danielle's silence rings with worry. "Does this have anything to do with the hot stepbrother?"

"No." *Maybe.* "It's just time for me to make a clean start."

"Did you tell Jenner that? I can't imagine he'd let you move thousands of miles away that easily. You two are attached at the hip."

"Yes, I told him. He doesn't approve. He'll be here in a few weeks for the Milan fashion shows. He'll browbeat me then."

"Good luck. I wouldn't want to be on the end of a browbeating from Jenner."

"He's more bark than bite."

"Are you kidding? I've seen him reduce people to tears with one look. He's terrifying."

"He's British. They're skilled at frightening the peasants." I hear the bell over the front door chime, and know someone's come into the shop. "Honey, I have to go, but I promise I'll call you soon, okay?"

"You better, or I'll send my girls to Italy for their next school break and let you deal with the little monsters."

"Speaking of terrifying."

"Love you, kiddo."

"Love you, too. Bye."

After we hang up, I head out to the front of the shop but stop dead in my tracks when I see who's there.

Matteo stands near the counter. He's wearing a gorgeous navy suit, and looking all kinds of sophisticated, angry, and hot.

He's got my sketch pad in his hand.

"Oh. Hi."

He lifts the pad. "This is yours." Onto the counter he tosses it, with a dismissive flick of his wrist like he couldn't wait to get it out of his hand.

I can tell by looking at the pad that the rest of the sketches he hasn't torn out are there. My nerves begin firing on all cylinders. "Okay. I'll bite. Why are you giving it back?"

"I don't want it anymore," he says, staring at me in a weirdly challenging way. "It's not worth the headache."

I do my absolute best to conceal the punch to the gut that was, but I must flinch a little because Matteo's eyes sharpen.

"I see." I don't know what else to say. I flatten a hand over my stomach, though it does nothing to settle the churning inside. "Thank you."

"You're welcome."

The weird challenging stare is starting to freak me out. It's like he's waiting for me to do something or say something, but I don't know what it is.

"So our deal is off?"

"I'm not going to use your designs and claim they're mine," he says with an edge to his voice.

I was talking about the kissing part, but I suppose it's obvious enough. If he doesn't have the sketches to withhold, he's got no bargaining chips. And the sketches are the important part, not the kissing.

I think.

"What brought about this sudden change of heart?"

"As if you don't know. It doesn't matter anyway." His eyes burn. "Right?"

I hurt him the other night. The thought stuns me. I accused him of manipulating me, and it hurt his feelings.

The little red devil taps me on the shoulder and reminds me that Matteo decided not to answer my questions, to turn them back on me, so he's not the only one with hurt feelings.

I moisten my lips, caught between anger and an apology. "It might matter."

"*Might* doesn't cut it," he says. When I bite my lip, his jaw hardens. "Don't do that."

He's got the hungry look in his eyes. Combined with the angry look, it's incredibly sexy.

I decide to venture into uncharted waters. "It does matter," I admit. "I'm just not sure what that means."

We stare at each other. Finally he says, "I understand. You have a lot to deal with right now. I'm making your life more complicated. The last thing I want is to be a problem for you."

Why does this feel like a breakup? And why do I care if it is?

"I don't want to be a problem for you, either."

He says, "You're not a problem. You're the best thing that's happened to me since I was ten years old."

The breath leaves my lungs in a whoosh that feels like two giant invisible hands clasped me front and back and squeezed. "Oh," I say, trying not to fall over. "Um. What happened when you were ten years old?"

"My mother finally bought me the puppy I'd been begging for. A Great Dane, like Cornelia. I named her Maria, after my favorite opera singer. I loved her with all my heart. She slept in my bed every night, even when she grew too big for it. I'd scoot all the way to the edge so she'd have room."

His voice is raw and his eyes are shining, and my heart is bursting at the seams. I think of how Cornelia spooned me, and imagine Matteo as a little boy cuddling with his dog in his bed in that soulless drafty castle he grew up in.

I'm in so much danger of falling in love with him right now that I bite the inside of my cheek in fear.

"You had a favorite opera singer when you were little?"

"Opera was all I was allowed to listen to. My parents wanted me to be cultured."

At *ten*. Dear God. Between that and the Wall of Death, he should've been taken away by social services.

"Maria got cancer and died, though," says Matteo forlornly, looking lost, and I have to bite my cheek harder.

"That's awful."

"Yes. She was my best friend. I was outside playing with her when my father died. My mother sent the nanny to get me, but I wouldn't come in. I didn't want to be inside his room, where it smelled like sickness and was dark all the time. So I refused to come in, and my father died, and my mother never forgave me. She sent me away to boarding school after that, but from then on she always had a Great Dane in the house."

His voice grows faint. "It was her way of making sure I never forgot what I did."

I'm devastated. He's struck me with a thunderbolt and burned my soul to a cinder. He's never been vulnerable like this with me before. It's always some variation of arrogant or smug, testy or sexy, teasing or bossy as hell. Even when he was tenderly massaging my shoulders when I was hung over, he was still in Big Cheese mode. He still had all his armor on. He was still in complete control.

But this.

This kind of softness and honesty from such a chest-thumping alpha male is absolute crack. My heart pounds so hard I might as well have mainlined cocaine. I'm instantly addicted and desperate for more.

Also, I'm going to strangle his mother.

"I had a hamster," I blurt. "Named Bugs. After my favorite cartoon character, Bugs Bunny. He lived a really long time, though. Way past the normal life expectancy."

Matteo slow blinks, as if he's waking from a dream. His forehead crinkles. He says, "Oh."

If there were any sharp objects within easy reach, I'd happily stab myself in the eye. The man bares his soul, and I repay him with the fascinating tale of my immortal hamster.

I can do better than that.

"It's just that I'm terrified you'll break my heart."

I say that in my tiny voice, the one I only use when I'm telling secrets about myself. I sound small and scared and I hate it, but tiny voice is the one that tells the biggest truths.

Matteo looks like he's holding his breath.

"You challenge me. It's never easy with you. And I like that. I think I need it. I feel more alive when I'm around you, even though mostly I'd like to smack you for being so annoying. I spend most of my time bitching at you when we're together, and all of my time thinking about you when we're not. I met you at the absolute worst time of my life, when everything I cared about was suddenly taken from me. And now I'm off balance. I can't trust my own judgment. I can't decide if you're a fantasy or a nightmare. A prince or a villain. The best thing that's ever happened to me, or the worst. So . . ."

I take a big breath for courage. "I'm scared. I'm scared, but I've never wanted anything more than I want you."

His beautiful blue eyes shining, Matteo says softly, "I'm not a prince, bella. How many times do I have to tell you? I'm a marchese."

Then he closes the distance between us and kisses me.

It feels as if I've jumped off a cliff. My stomach drops. My pulse races in terror. There's a loud rushing noise in my ears.

Cradling my head in his hands, he peppers kisses all over my face, murmuring everything I want to hear him say. *"I adore you,"* and *"You're safe with me,"* and *"That was so brave,"* and *"How soon can we get you out of this dress?"*

"Promise me you'll never lie to me," I say, gasping against his mouth as he bites my lip.

"You warned me never to say the *P* word."

I shout, "Promise me or lose your testicles!"

His eyes full of emotion, he chuckles. "In that case, I promise."

The kiss we share is so passionate I'm surprised all the clothing on racks around us doesn't explode into flames. My heart drums a beat of *I want you I want you oh God how I want you,* and I cling to him, feeling the last of my resistance slipping away.

The kissing game might be over, but the kissing-naked-in-bed game is about to begin.

Only it's not, because a loud throat clearing from somewhere behind me slices through my lovely little lust bubble like a knife. I turn, woozy, and find Clara in the doorway to the back of the shop, gazing at me over the rims of her glasses.

"We've finished look six," she says, emanating scorn. If she were one of those scented room sprays, she'd be called Breeze of Utter Disappointment.

"Okay. Be right in." My voice strangled, I attempt a reassuring smile, but judging by the heavy sigh I get in response, Clara isn't reassured. She returns to the workroom, shaking her head.

"She doesn't like me," says Matteo, sounding unconcerned.

"She doesn't like people with penises. Kiss me again."

He obliges, and soon I'm flushed everywhere and having trouble remaining upright. "Holy hell, your mouth is a drug factory. Do you gargle with heroin?"

All throaty and hot, he says, "Wait till you see what I can do with my hands."

I think I groan a little, dizzy with lust. If his hands and all his other parts are anywhere near as good as his mouth, I'll overdose instantly. Matteo laces his fingers in my hair and turns my head to the side so I can see the dressing rooms.

Into my ear he whispers, "Should I show you?"

One beat of my heart, then two, then I'm decided. Those test results couldn't have come at a better time. "You *betcha*."

Before my heart beats again, Matteo grabs my hand and pulls me away toward one of the curtained-off rooms.

THIRTY

The dressing room is barely big enough for one person to turn a full circle, never mind two horny people with a mind to get their freak on, but Matteo and I make the most of the small space by remaining standing.

He rips the curtain closed behind us, pushes me against the wall, and kisses me so hard I lose my breath. In a moment he pulls away, panting.

"Sorry."

"For what?"

"I bit you."

"I know. Do it again."

He grins, looking like a pirate with a horde of fresh booty, then lowers his mouth to mine and very deliberately takes my lower lip between his teeth. He gives it a gentle bite, then licks it as I begin to melt.

"You like it when I bite your mouth," he says, husky and victorious. "Let's see where else you like it."

He runs his hand over my ass, down the back of my thigh, then slides it up under my skirt. He removes my panties with some kind of ninja mind-trick move because one second they were in their proper place and the next they're around my ankles.

He palms me right between the legs and squeezes the way I squeeze a cantaloupe to see if it's ripe, then sinks to his knees in front of me and shoves my skirt up to my waist. Staring at my exposed flesh, he growls, "*Fuck*, I've wanted this."

Can a person spontaneously combust? Is that a thing? If so, I'm about to.

Then his mouth is on the most intimate part of me. He makes a deep humming sound, like the yummy noise I make when I have a mouthful of ice cream. It reverberates all the way through my pelvis. I have to bite my tongue so I don't shout.

His eyes drift closed. He grips my hips and feasts on me, sucking and licking, making a meal of it, swirling his magical tongue around the sensitive little bud at the top—then gently biting it.

Heat rockets through me like I'm channeling fire through my veins. I jerk and gasp, gripping his hair, my nipples tingling and my heart pounding like mad.

"You like that, too," he says with a low chuckle.

"No more talking." I rock my hips nearer to his mouth, desperate for it.

Matteo's blue eyes grow dark. "Yes, ma'am," he whispers, then slowly lowers his mouth to my sex, watching my face as he starts to suck again.

Waves of heat roll over me, blistering hot. His tongue is soft and warm, wet and knowing, quickly finding the right rhythm that makes me weak. The pleasure is so intense I can hardly breathe. Seeing this powerful, gorgeous man on his knees in front of me is its own kind of pleasure, too, incredibly intoxicating. His teeth scrape my clit again and I shudder, my head falling against the wall.

Matteo takes my hands and presses them to my waist, so now I'm holding the fabric of my skirt, freeing his hands. In one swift move, he yanks down the neckline of my dress, scoops my breasts out of my bra, and pinches my hard nipples. Sparks erupt throughout my body.

He strokes his thumbs back and forth over my nipples as he continues licking between my legs. I'm so turned on I moan, unable to stifle it.

He whispers roughly, "Fuck my mouth, bella. Come in my mouth."

Okay, he's allowed to talk a little.

I arch against his hands, my eyes sliding shut as I lose myself to pleasure. I'm starting to sweat, little beads of perspiration dampening my temples and neck, blood drumming under my skin. My body takes over, and I lose control of the motion of my hips. I begin to buck against Matteo's mouth, grinding, swiveling, my breath coming in short hard bursts and my body trembling.

He grunts into me, soft sounds of satisfaction that drive me even higher.

I can tell he loves this. He loves seeing me come undone, loves giving this to me as much as I love receiving it. He's the one on his knees, but I'm definitely not the one in control.

He uses one of his hands to pinch and stroke the flesh he isn't licking. I think I might die. Then he slides a thick finger inside me and starts to slide it in and out as he suckles my clit. He releases my breast and grips my ass, hard, pulling me closer to his face, digging his fingers into my skin, his tongue working faster and faster as my heartbeat goes arrhythmic.

His mouth is so good, so demanding, pulling and stroking and twisting. Deep inside me a coil begins to tighten. White-hot heat builds at the base of my spine. My nipples are throbbing and my clit is pulsing and he's sucking oh God he's sucking it so hard—

He bites my clit and I come.

My orgasm is so violent my entire body stiffens as it rips through me. My back arches. My mouth opens in a silent scream. Wave after wave of pleasure tears through me, and all I can do is gasp and jerk helplessly, hearing Matteo's chest-deep growls of approval as I wring myself out against his mouth.

When the last of the convulsions are over and I'm a shaking mass of gelatinous limbs, Matteo rises. He gathers me in his arms and kisses me deeply so I can taste myself in his mouth.

"You're so delicious." He nuzzles my neck, sliding his hands up and down my waist and rib cage, learning my shape. "So beautiful. So perfect. I could eat you for every meal."

I sigh lazily, boneless and satiated, the biggest, dumbest shit-eating grin on my face. "Oh stop. Stop it some more."

He shrugs off his suit jacket, hangs it on a peg, unbuttons his shirt, and smiles at me indulgently when I gape at his bare chest. "Here. You can even touch it." He takes my hands and flattens them over his stomach.

I stroke his skin, and it's like satin. Like muscular, hairless satin. *He certainly has beautiful breasts.* A giggle slips past my lips. I'm feeling heady.

"Oh, she's *laughing* at me," says Matteo, mock angrily. He pretends to glower. "That won't do." He wraps his hand around my wrist and drags my hand lower, until it rests on the impressive bulge straining against his trousers.

To Matteo's obvious satisfaction, my giggle vanishes.

He's big. Not just long, but girthy, if that's even a word. *Thick.* Suddenly I want to be the one on her knees, wielding the power.

"Those eyes," Matteo murmurs, just before I sink to the floor.

I unclasp his belt and unzip his zipper with a few ninja moves of my own, my blood rising again at the thought of what awaits me. When I pull down the elastic of his briefs, his erection springs out at me like a jack-in-the-box that's been wound one too many times.

"I see this big boy has as much patience as you do," I say, glancing up at Matteo's face.

He looks down at me with a tight jaw and avid eyes, but says nothing.

Turning my attention back to the important matter at hand, I wrap my fingers around his girth, fascinated by the pulsing vein running underneath, by the deep-red flush on the crown. His cock twitches impatiently in my hand, making me smile.

"All right, pal, hold your horses."

When I apply my mouth, I'm gratified to hear Matteo's sharp intake of breath above me. I'm even happier when I get a low groan as I take the length of him as far as I can down my throat. He curves his body over me, propping himself up against the wall with one hand and sinking the other into my hair to cradle the back of my head.

I withdraw slowly, furling my tongue around the crown, pleased with the taste and feel of him, pleased even more when he mutters something in Italian, his voice strained.

I want to make him feel as good as I do. I want to watch him unravel, too.

Using more suction on the head, I stroke his shaft. Both hands are required to do an adequate job. His hand in my hair starts to tremble.

"Strawberry mouth," he says, breathing hard. "I love that soft red—"

He cuts off with a groan when I swallow his length again, stopping for a moment to fondle the velvet heft of his balls.

I start up a rhythm. A steady stroke and slide, swirling my tongue around the head as I withdraw, opening my throat to take him deep. He flexes his hips in response, tentatively at first, as if he's trying to make sure it's not too much, then with more ease when I hum an encouragement. My knees are burning against the carpet, and my heart is flying in my chest. I'm soaked between my legs, from his mouth and my own arousal, skyrocketing again, making me squirm restlessly the longer I have him in my mouth.

"Touch yourself," he whispers hoarsely.

I slip my fingers under my skirt and stroke my wetness as I continue to suck him. I know he's watching me, and that gets me even hotter.

He shudders and moans as my head bobs, and I work my fingers between my legs. We're both getting close. The temperature in the dressing room has shot up at least twenty degrees.

"Not yet," he rasps, tightening his hand in my hair. "Fuck. Kimber. Not yet."

When I glance up at him, his face is strained. A vein throbs in his neck. His eyes are dark and hot, and a thrill sings through me, high and sweet, like a single chord played on a violin.

He pulls me to my feet and kisses me again, roughly, his chest pressed against mine so I feel how hard his heart beats, how his skin burns.

"Do you have—"

"Yes, here—"

"Hurry."

He fumbles in his pocket, withdraws his wallet, finds a condom, rips it open, and takes it out. I watch him roll it down the length of his erection with my heart in my throat. As soon as he's situated, he grabs my thigh, pushes me against the wall, pulls my leg up to his waist, and angles himself between my hips.

I feel him, hot and hard between my legs, hungry for me, and cling to his shoulders as he finds the way of it with one sure, hard thrust.

We both groan in relief as he slides inside.

Finally.

I feel him everywhere at once, in my fingers and toes, underneath my eyelids. He's the burning-hot center of me, the center of everything, my breath and my heartbeat, the life in my cells. I don't know how I ever imagined sex was adequate before this. His body is a revelation, but it's not that. It's this *feeling.* This earthquake of sensation, this detonation inside me that feels like I'm being ripped apart and put back together, all at once. Like I'm shedding my skin for something new and completely wonderful.

Like everything bad that's happened was worth it because it was all leading up to this.

We stare into each other's eyes as he thrusts inside me. His chest is slick with sweat. My breasts are still bared, jutting out from the shelf of my bra, and my nipples drag against his skin with every movement, sending shock waves of pleasure between my legs. He's supporting most of my weight with his hands under my ass because the one leg I'm standing on is Jell-O, but he shows no signs of fatigue as he pumps into me over and over, his breath coming in short, ragged bursts.

"Ever since I first saw you," he says hoarsely, his lids half-closed and his face flushed. Dark strands of hair are stuck to his forehead. He turns his face to my neck.

"What?" I breathe, arching into him, almost, almost there again.

Against my throat, he whispers, "I've been yours," and presses his teeth into my skin.

His next hard thrust takes me over the edge. I dig my fingers into his back and bite his shoulder to muffle my scream as I writhe against him.

With one final hard jerk, he comes. I feel him throb and pulse inside me, feel the length of him somehow grow longer. A shudder runs through his chest. He gasps, and it sounds like my name.

It's several long moments before I come back to myself. When I do, I blink up at Matteo. He smiles down at me in hazy, wonderful satisfaction, his face aglow.

I say, "If you tell me that was mediocre, I'll neuter you."

He laughs weakly, squeezing my butt. "All these threats against my poor testicles. You should be nicer to them." His voice softens, and so do his eyes. "They like you."

"Oh, lucky me." When he pinches my behind, I laugh and relent. "I like them, too."

Matteo lifts his brows.

"And some of your other parts."

He purses his lips, waiting, and I sigh. I take his face in my hands and kiss him. "And the guy all the parts are attached to."

"How romantic," he deadpans. "Stop or I'll blush."

"Listen, you just banged me senseless in a dressing room. I'm in no shape for witty repartee. Can I have my leg back now?"

He frowns at me. "Are you always like this after sex?"

"Amazingly adorable? Why, yes. Yes I am."

I send him a brilliant smile. He grins back at me. "I think I'm rubbing off on you."

I lower my lashes, my smile turning coy. "I think the rubbing has already been done, sir. Now give me back my leg. I'm cramping."

He doesn't give me back my leg. Instead he starts to massage my bottom, then my hips, working his thumbs into my muscles and staying buried inside me, smiling and gorgeous as a teenage dream. He whispers, "I could stand here like this forever."

He's going to give me atrial fibrillation if he keeps looking at me like that. His eyes are selling me a fairy tale, and though I know I'm crazy about him and there's no going back from this, I'm not ready to roll out the red carpet for another white knight just yet.

Considering the last one turned out to have rusted armor and a lame horse.

When I push lightly against his chest, Matteo reluctantly withdraws from my body. He kisses me again, with infinite tenderness, then adjusts my skirt before discarding the condom into the tiny wastebasket in the corner. He buttons his shirt and tucks it into his pants. As he zips up and buckles his belt, I put my boobs back inside my dress and smooth my hair. Then I look around the floor for my panties.

"Allow me." Matteo snatches them up, then takes one of my ankles and maneuvers it through the leg hole. He does the same with my other foot, then slides my panties over my knees and up my thighs, settling them in place.

"That was almost professional," I say, trying to hide how much his soft eyes are affecting me. *Take it slow, Kimber. This was beautiful, but be careful. Be smart. One day at a time. Eyes wide open. Plenty of time to fall madly in love with him down the road after you get to know him better.*

"You're thinking again."

When I look up at Matteo, I find him gazing down at me, the smile faded from his face. I'm about to make a wisecrack, but decide to be honest instead. It worked so well the last time.

"I was thinking that you're incredible, and this was incredible, and I hope we'll keep doing this as often as possible, and also that we should take it one day at a time because I need to be smart and not fall in love with you too fast."

He looks amused, thank God. I'd hate to have ruined everything.

"That's unfortunate, considering I'm already in love with you."

Boom! goes my heart. A wheezing sound passes my lips. "Wha . . . wha . . ."

Matteo kisses me firmly, winding an arm around my waist. Then he tilts my head back, lightly gripping my jaw. "I'm in love with you," he says, slowly and clearly, staring into my eyes. "I know it's ridiculous, and I know it's too soon, and I know I'm in love with you. I didn't plan on it. I didn't even want to admit it to myself until I figured out why I haven't been able to sleep or eat or think straight since I met you. It's either love or it's insanity, and I don't care which because either way it's irreversible. It's fatal. No other woman has ever moved me the way you do, and if you decide you don't want me, it will be the end of me.

"So whatever happens from now on, you can't say you didn't know. You can't say I didn't tell you. I'm telling you straight out: I'm in love with you, Kimber DiSanto. Even if the pope does think it's a sin."

I stare at him for a long time, searching his face, dizzy with disbelief. "The pope?" I say weakly.

"It's a long story. Are you all right?"

My laugh is semicrazed. "Oh sure. Of course. Beautiful men tell me every day how much they adore me—"

"Love you," Matteo growls. After a moment, he adds, "Why are you looking at me like that?"

"I'm trying not to pass out."

He kisses me again. "You're going to be fine."

"But what if I pass out?"

"I'll make sure you don't hit your head on anything."

I'm finding it really hard to breathe. "Okay, I need to say something now, and I hope you won't get mad."

He waits a beat before saying, "I'll try not to, but that doesn't sound good."

I swallow, moistening my lips. "Does this have anything to do with Brad?"

He cocks his head. "What do you mean?"

He doesn't look angry at the mention of my ex, so I take that as a good sign. "I mean you came in here the other day, saw us hugging, acted weirded out about it, then left."

"And?"

"And we haven't talked about it since. Which means you have no idea what's going on between us."

He considers it for a moment. "That's true. I don't. But I do know that there's no way in hell you would've come anywhere near this dressing room with me if there was any chance you and he were getting back together."

"Why not?"

He answers without having to think about it. "You're a one-man woman. You're too good to play that game. Too loyal."

A flush of pleasure spreads through my belly. My heart dissolves into a kaleidoscope of butterflies, flitting through my body on gossamer wings. I feel tipsy, as if I've spent the afternoon sipping champagne.

Oh no.

"You've got that funny look again."

I make a small groan of desperation. "I'm finding it very, very hard not to fall madly in love with you. Like, *now*."

His eyes blaze with emotion. He says gruffly, "Challenge accepted," and gives me a kiss so passionate and pure and full of emotion I know without doubt it can never be matched by another man.

The entire time, a bell of warning rings in a distant corner of my mind. If the debacle with Brad taught me anything, it's that things that seem too good to be true inevitably are.

"Keep your friends close and your enemies closer," Matteo once told me.

Was that a joke . . . or his master plan?

THIRTY-ONE

MATTEO

"If you're going to do this right, Matteo, you have to tell her, and you have to tell her in a way that can't be misunderstood. Forget about being the strong, silent type. Women need to hear the actual words."

I'd given my mother an exasperated look when she'd said that over dinner the other night. A man can't simply charge in with an "I'm in love with you" out of nowhere. Especially with our history. *Her* history. These things take finesse. Finesse is practically my middle name.

Except it turns out it isn't.

I charged.

I couldn't help myself. Being inside her proved too much for my self-control. Judging by her reaction, I've made a huge mistake.

Let's hope it's not a lethal one.

"Are you all right?"

"Yes," she says weakly. She sends me an unconvincing smile.

"Then I'll assume you're so pale because I've just given you the most earth-shattering orgasms of your life. Anything else will crush my ego."

"I seriously doubt your ego could even be dented."

It's getting massively dented right now, but I decline to share that. I also decline to share that her bringing up Brad not two minutes after we had sex for the first time is more than a little disturbing.

She regrets it.

The thought makes my blood run cold.

"I should probably get back to work."

She's running away. Trying to avoid my eyes. *Fuck.*

"Look at me."

She gives me those big green eyes, and for a moment I lose my breath. Everything I've ever wanted is there. It's all right there.

And I've probably screwed the whole thing up by opening my mouth and coming on too hard, too soon.

My voice thick, I say, "I didn't plan to declare myself like that. It just came out. I'm sorry it made you uncomfortable. I won't bring it up again."

A small furrow forms between her dark brows. She stares at me in silence for a moment, searching my face. "Don't be sorry," she murmurs, sliding her hands up my chest. "It was beautiful." She stands on her toes and kisses me, a soft, sweet kiss that almost manages to break my heart.

I can already feel her slipping through my fingers.

What a fucking idiot I am.

A bell jingles over the front door. Someone's come into the shop.

"Shit," whispers Kimber, panicking. "Someone's here!"

"Hello?" a man's voice calls out.

Son of a bitch. It's Dominic. I'd recognize that bastard's voice anywhere.

When a growl of anger rumbles through my chest, Kimber smacks me on the arm and puts a finger to her lips. I scowl at her, ready to rip open the curtain and stride out, but she pushes me back, shaking her head, her eyes blazing.

"Hello?" The sound of Dominic's voice grows fainter. He must have wandered into the back room.

"Stay here until I get rid of him."

"What? You're joking!" I'm red with anger at being forced to cower in the dressing room like a bad little boy, but she's already gone, whipping the curtain back in place and calling out in a cheerful voice.

"I'm here! Hello!"

I stand there in shock and disbelief as Dominic and Kimber share friendly greetings and start to chat.

She's hiding me in the fucking dressing room! She's ashamed to be seen with me!

I've never been this humiliated in my life.

"How are you, *tesoro*? I've been so worried about you, living up there with the barracuda."

My body stiffens with outrage. I'm going to kill him. I'm going to separate all his limbs from his body. No one calls my mother an ugly savage fish and gets away with it. We have our problems, but I won't allow her to be disrespected.

I reach for the curtain, but freeze when I hear Kimber's voice.

"You don't have to worry. Things are okay."

"Really?" Dominic sounds dubious.

Kimber laughs. It's a nervous laugh, and completely insincere. "Well, one of her dogs destroyed my entire wardrobe, but that's been the only skirmish so far."

"You need to be careful, Kimber. I didn't want to speak of it earlier. Things were already so upsetting with your father's passing . . ." His voice drops. "But you can't trust that woman for a moment. The son, either. They're a pair of real slick operators, those two. You should get rid of her before she figures out how to get the house."

There's a long silence. I have to fight myself from bursting out of the dressing room, but I need to hear what Kimber's going to say in response to this outrageous lie.

Tell him to go to hell. Tell him you don't believe it for a minute. Stand up for me, if not for her.

Instead, she says in a strange tone, "Why do you say that?"

It's like a dagger plunged straight through my heart.

Dominic scoffs. "Because I know them! He's vicious, and she's money hungry. The only reason she married your father is because she thought he had wealth. The house, the business—that's what she fell in love with. Not your father. Believe me, I saw how she bled him. And once she found out there wasn't much money to be had, she started pestering him to sell the business. Of course she had a buyer in mind."

Kimber says faintly, "Of course she did."

She believes him.

It hits me with the force of an avalanche. Just as suffocating. Just as cold.

She believes every word coming out of that bastard's mouth.

Hope surges through me when she pushes back, her tone brisk.

"How do you know about any of that?"

"Your father told me."

He sounds apologetic, the fucker.

After I tear off all his limbs, I'll set them on fire.

When Kimber speaks again, her tone is no longer brisk. It's confused, edged in desperation. "But . . . in the hospital . . . he told me he loved her. He said he was *happy*—"

"Your father was a romantic," Dominic says softly. "You know that. A romantic who only saw the best in people. He looked at life through rose-colored glasses. He was a lamb, no match for the Moretti lions."

Fury pulses through me like acid, corrosive and hot. There's nothing more I'd like to do than reveal myself and choke the truth out of him, but I'd look like a fool strolling out of my hiding place now. She wouldn't believe me anyway. He's her father's best friend, a man she's known her entire life, and I'm the untrustworthy ex-stepbrother who forced her to trade kisses for her own designs.

Who she disliked on first sight.

Who's done nothing but irritate her since, orgasms notwithstanding.

I already know how this story ends. It's not with a happily ever after.

THIRTY-TWO

KIMBER

I feel sick. I'm going to be sick all over my shoes, the floor, the front of Dominic's white linen shirt.

How could I have been so stupid?

Again?

"That's really upsetting to hear," I tell Dominic, my voice shaking. "I don't want to believe it."

His expression softens. He clucks in sympathy, patting my shoulder. "I know. You have a good heart, like your father. It's hard to hear such awful things about people. Believe me, *tesoro*, I hate to have to tell you. But you're like a daughter to me, and now that your father's gone, it's my job to look after you, yes? So. This is what you do." He turns businesslike, folding his arms over his chest. "First thing, you turn the marchesa out of the house."

"No."

We're both surprised by that. I had no idea it would come out so forcefully, and Dominic's rapid blinking tells me he didn't, either. I hurry on, talking over the pathetic groaning of my heart.

"My father specified in his will that she stays in the house until she dies. I have to honor that. It's what he wanted."

Dominic sputters, "But she cannot be trusted!"

"He loved her," I say firmly. "He was alone for almost thirty years after my mother died, and for whatever reason, the marchesa made him happy. I won't throw her out."

I can't believe I'm saying the words, but they feel right. The marchesa might be a snooty unlikeable witch, but she gave me a dress to wear to my father's funeral, and she gave birth to the god who made me understand what sex was *really* supposed to feel like, even if he is a lying jerk.

I know it's too soon, and I know it's ridiculous, and I know I'm in love with you.

I wonder if his mother coached him to say those words. How to say them, with such sincerity shining in his eyes. I wonder how soon he planned on bringing up the sale of the business again.

I wonder if he was eventually going to ask me to marry him, get everything squared away legally, get all the paperwork out of the way so he and Mumsy-Wumsy could have everything they wanted. My breath catches—returning the sketch pad was such a *clever* move.

"The longer she lives there, the better her case to make a claim of ownership on the property." Dominic is beside himself. He's not the only one who can't believe I'm taking the marchesa's side. "And the more she'll try to win you over with her wiles!"

"Trust me, she's not trying to win me over."

"No? She hasn't given you any gifts? Done anything special for you to make you like her?"

The dress. And she said Brad should be shot.

God, please just kill me now.

I squeeze the bridge of my nose, but it doesn't help the stabbing pain in my forehead. "Matteo's rich. He lives in a castle, for God's sake. *Their family owns a castle.* They can't be *that* hard up for money!"

Dominic looks at me as if I'm incredibly dim-witted. "Castello di Moretti is owned by the family only in name. The government has a lien on the property. Back taxes, my dear. The upkeep on the place is astronomical."

The wind has been knocked out of me. I should sit down before I fall. But first I have to ask one final question before I abandon all hope. "Lorenzo has such a high opinion of her. He seems like such a smart guy, and he's been with her for so long, how could he not see what she's really like?"

"Isn't it obvious?" Dominic says gently. "He's in love with her."

Yes, now that you mention it. It's as obvious as day. I had it pegged right from the beginning. I had *everything* pegged on the nose.

"Right," I whisper as the world crashes down around me.

I barely make it to the trash can under the register before my lunch comes back up in a Technicolor stream.

Dominic exclaims in surprise, hurrying over to hover over me like a mother hen. I wave him away as I retch, embarrassed and humiliated, wanting to get rid of him, Clara, and the other ladies as quickly as possible.

I need to be alone with Matteo. I need to look into his eyes when he comes out of that dressing room. I need to make him tell me the truth to my face.

"Sit, sit, you're as pale as a ghost!"

Gripping my arm, Dominic helps me onto the stool behind the counter. I collapse onto it, gasping and faint, wiping my mouth with the back of my hand. The peperoncini in the salad I had for lunch tasted much better going down. Now they're searing my throat and the inside of my nose and making my eyes water.

Yeah, that's it. The water in my eyes is from the peppers.

Dominic hands me his hankie. "Are you sick?"

Heartsick. Soul sick. Sick of men and their endless supply of bullshit. "I think I ate some bad fish at lunch," I say dully, though it was a vegetable salad. I can't have Dominic thinking my projectile vomiting has anything to do with the story he told me. I might have terrible taste in men, but I still have a shred left of my pride.

God, he'd be so disappointed to know what I was doing before he walked in the door.

"Let me take you home, Kimber. You should rest."

"I'm fine." I'm desperate to be rid of him. I can feel the burning presence of Matteo behind the dressing room curtain. I have to get Dominic out of the shop before something bad happens. I'm surprised Matteo hasn't burst out already, but that probably only means he's buying time to formulate his response.

"You're not fine," he presses. "You vomited. That's the opposite of fine."

I have to spend another five minutes convincing him I'm well enough to be left alone. He doesn't like the idea of me taking a taxi home, but I reassure him by saying Clara will drive me. After he extracts many promises from me that I'll call him later, he finally leaves. When I close the shop door behind him, my hands are shaking.

When I turn around, Matteo is standing outside the dressing room door.

He looks as sick as I feel.

"You believe him."

His voice is quiet, level, but an undercurrent of rage runs through it. That and his expression give me hope that everything that happened between us earlier was something more than a clinical business maneuver.

"I don't want to." I admit it openly, not trying to hide how upset I am, letting him see all the confusion and hurt I feel.

"But you do."

I can't deny it. Nor should I. Whatever's really happening here, it's best for everyone involved if we put all our cards on the table right now. "Put yourself in my shoes. How would you feel? What would you think?"

"Dominic has hated my mother for a very long time."

"Why?"

"She married another man."

That rocks me back on my heels. "They were together?"

"When they were very young. Before she met my father."

I have a flashback to the marchesa's reaction when I mentioned Dominic's name the afternoon at the house when I first found out Matteo was her son. She was upset but tried to hide it.

Whenever I cried as a child, I'd get a beating, she'd told me the day of my father's funeral. I was too distracted to think much of it at the time, but now that simple phrase seems to reveal so much about her personality.

Or is he making this up on the fly?

"What happened?"

He exhales a heavy breath. "Honestly, I don't know the details. The only reason I know at all is because I overheard a discussion between her and your father, shortly before they were married."

I jerk forward several steps, my heart beating faster. "And? What did they say?"

Matteo's jaw works. He's angry, obviously uncomfortable, disheveled from our incredible dressing room interlude, and so handsome it hurts.

It physically, painfully hurts to look at him.

"Your father wanted to lend Dominic money. Apparently it was a regular thing, but my mother insisted he'd been generous enough and should say no. When he asked why she didn't like Dominic, she said it wasn't that she didn't like him, but that she knew his character. After your father pressed her, she admitted they had a brief 'entanglement,' as she called it, before she married my father. My grandfather didn't approve of Dominic, so he intervened and separated them. Dominic never believed that it was her father. He blamed her. From then on he made it his mission to discredit her name whenever he could. He spread awful rumors. He never forgave her for breaking his heart."

I digest all that for a moment, my mind spinning. Dominic and the marchesa? I try to picture them as young people, in love, but can't.

"Dominic never married," I say, thinking hard, sifting through memories. "I remember he used to tell my father he found the only woman in Italy who didn't care about money."

"Yes," says Matteo sourly. "Dominic always makes a big deal about money. Who has it, who doesn't, why he doesn't have enough. Personally, I think the man never had feelings for my mother. I think he saw a paycheck. I think my grandfather realized it, too. My mother was his only child, and the light of his life. If he thought Dominic was a good man, he never would've separated them, no matter how small Dominic's fortune."

I stand staring at Matteo, feeling helpless and overwhelmed, unsure what to believe. "What about Castello di Moretti? Does the government really have a lien on it?"

Matteo doesn't flinch or break eye contact when he answers. "No."

I'm not sure if that's true, either, but I can probably look it up on the internet. There has to be some kind of government property portal where you can research outstanding liens and such.

"Miss Kimber." Clara stands in the doorway to the back room.

"Yes, Clara?"

"If you have a moment"—she sends Matteo a disgruntled glance—"we need you on look six." She turns and disappears again, muttering under her breath, leaving Matteo and I gazing at each other in painful silence.

Finally he says, "Well. I tried."

He crosses the room in a few long strides and winds his arms around me, giving me a hard squeeze. He kisses me on the temple, whispers gruffly, "I meant everything I said in the dressing room. At least believe that." Then he releases me and walks out the door without looking back.

Twenty minutes later I'm sitting on the stool, staring into space and trying to untangle the knots of my thoughts, when a courier drops off a paper bag from a nearby drug store. Inside are antacids, a travel toothbrush and toothpaste kit, and a big bottle of water, along with a note that reads *You didn't ask Dominic why he called me vicious. Ask.*

I groan. "My life is a Shakespearean drama!"

From behind me, Clara says, "Hopefully not the kind where everyone dies at the end. Are you coming, or should we all go home? We're getting old back here. My husband wants stromboli for dinner tonight, and it's not going to make itself."

I turn and look at her. "You know my father's friend, Dominic, right?"

"Yes."

"What do you think of him?"

She snorts. "He's a man. What's there to think? They're nothing but overgrown babies. If they don't have a woman around to cook for them and coo at them and tell them what to do, they're lost. But I don't think it's Dominic you need advice about." She drills me with a look.

I suddenly feel like a kid caught sneaking out of the house at midnight or ditching school.

"You're a smart girl, and your love life is none of my business. So I'll say this, then I'll say no more." Her gaze grows intense and a little frightening. She says darkly, "The egg does not swim to the sperm. *Never* chase a man. It goes against nature. If you want him, let him chase you until you catch him."

She pulls herself up to her full height of four-feet-eleven inches and sniffs. "And no more sex in the dressing rooms. Who do you think has to clean in there?"

She turns on her heel, calling over her shoulder, "If you want to meet a good man, read a book! Now let's get back to work!"

When I get home that night, the house is eerily dark and quiet. I flick on the light in the kitchen and find a note from Lorenzo on the small white pad near the telephone. It says the marchesa has gone to Milan in advance of Fashion Week as she does every season. There's a phone number where they can be reached in case of emergency and the name of a swanky hotel.

"The plot thickens," I mutter. A few weeks in Milan isn't cheap, especially with a butler and two dogs in tow. She'd need connecting suites in the hotel . . . *Unless she and Lorenzo are sharing a room.*

I realize with a jolt I never asked where Lorenzo sleeps. Probably because he never seems to. As far as I know, all the second-floor guest rooms are still closed off, as they have been for years. Does he sleep in the attic?

Ten minutes later, I have my answer. The second-floor rooms are still closed off, and no one has slept in the attic for years. There's a layer of dust on top of the dresser, the bedcovers smell musty, and judging by the droppings on the floor, a family of rodents is the only resident.

I trudge downstairs to my bedroom, lost in thought and aching to talk to Matteo.

Instead, I spend an hour online playing amateur detective. I hit the mother lode when I find a website offering title reports on Italian properties, but the kicker is the cost for the report and the wait: two hundred bucks and two days.

I already maxed out my credit card for the plane ticket I didn't use to get here, but there is one other option. From my purse, I pull out my shiny new Amex card in the name of Mrs. Bradley Hamilton Wingate III and stare at it.

"It's stealing," I say to the empty room. Or is it a small form of payback?

Probably stealing. I text Brad that I'm going to charge two hundred dollars on the card. It isn't a question. And I don't think it can technically be considered theft if I tell him about it in advance.

He texts me back that there's a fifty-thousand-dollar credit limit, so I should knock myself out.

That brings a dangerous smile to my face. *Fifty thousand. Good to know.*

I order the report, then call Dominic. He picks up after the first ring.

"Hello, *tesoro*. How are you feeling?"

Impatient to get to the point, I bypass a polite greeting. "I have to ask you something, and I need you to be completely honest with me."

After a short pause, Dominic says, "Of course. Anything."

"How much money did my father lend you?"

I was going to ask about the marchesa first, but decided at the last second to go with the money angle. I have an idea of what to say if he denies it.

Which he does. Vehemently.

"Your father never lent me money! Where did you get such an idea? Did that horrible woman tell you that?"

He sounds overly outraged and offended, the way guilty people do when charged with the truth. But his tone is proof of nothing. Unfortunately, there's only one way to get to the bottom of this, and it's with a white lie.

"I found a ledger my father kept."

I leave it at that, trusting Dominic's imagination to fill in the blanks.

I hold my breath, waiting for his answer with my heart in my throat. Finally he says, "I don't know anything about that."

Now his tone is flat and unequivocal, but there's something off about it. Something that makes me want to dig a little more. "That's very interesting because there's a lot of information here about dates, loan amounts . . ."

Convince me, Dominic. Tell me it's not true. Tell me you loved my father, you never took money from him, and I can trust you.

The moment I hear his heavy sigh, I know he's giving up the ruse of innocence, and my stomach falls.

"There might have been a few times I needed help here and there over the years."

"How many times?" I demand, my voice too loud. "How much money did he give you?"

"Doesn't your ledger say?" he asks, hedging.

I hedge back. "I want *you* to tell me."

Silence. Then another heavy sigh. Then he names a number so large I almost fall over in shock.

Then the jerk decides it's time to change tactics. He says sternly, "This was between your father and me, Kimberly. It's no business of yours. And it's disrespectful of you to ask me. Your poor father—"

"Don't you dare talk to me about my 'poor' father, or about disrespect! Not even two minutes ago you lied about never getting any money!"

He sniffs. "It's beneath me to speak of."

I swear, one of these days one of the men in my life is going to push me too far, and then my name will be in all the newspapers for a very different reason than being left at the altar: "The Cast-off Couturier Goes on a Murder Spree!"

"You're stonewalling me now? Then I guess you won't want to talk about your relationship with the marchesa."

There's a long icy pause. "She has poisoned you against me."

"Are you denying it?"

"Whatever she told you is a lie."

"Okay, then answer me this: Why did you say Matteo was vicious?"

Another pause, but this one is long and cavernous. I sense he's carefully choosing his words. "He wouldn't allow me to attend the wedding.

I tried to go, but he blocked me at the door. He threatened to rip off my head. He's an animal."

An animal who goes into beast mode when someone he cares about is disrespected. I wonder what Dominic said about the marchesa to make Matteo threaten him.

I bet it wasn't nice.

"At the hospital, you told me you weren't invited to the wedding. That no one attended. That it was done in secret. This sounds like a much different story."

Dominic decides he's had enough of my interrogation and launches into a full-blown rant.

"Your father and I were friends for fifty years! I was the only one who came to the hospital when he was sick! I was the only one who stood by him after your mother died and he fell into the bottom of a bottle for so long you had to be sent away to live with your aunt in the States! I was the one who cared for him during his depression and made sure he ate, and showered, and his business didn't go under! Me! If anything, I deserved the money he gave me! I *earned* it!"

My first thought is: *you dick.*

My next thought is: *Matteo.*

I already know the title search on Castello di Moretti will show no government lien.

I click end to disconnect with Dominic, then I make one more call, to the number Lorenzo left for the hotel in Milan.

THIRTY-THREE

"Pronto?"

"Lady Moretti." *Jesus, Mary, and Joseph, I can't believe I called her that.* "It's Kimber. I hope I'm not disturbing you."

"Kimber? Is everything all right? Is it Matteo? What's happened?"

Her tone is edged with panic. I don't blame her. If the roles were reversed and she were calling me, I'd assume the worst, too.

"Everything's okay. Matteo's fine. It's not about him. I wondered . . ." I have to clear my throat of the frog stuck in it. "I wondered if I could speak to you for a minute. If we could have a chat."

I was expecting anything but the soft surprise and warmth in her voice when she answers. "Of course. I'm happy to talk to you." After a moment of hesitation, she adds, "I'm glad you called."

Why don't I have a glass of wine in my hand? What was I thinking? This calls for a huge glass of alcohol!

Attempting to sound like a sane adult, I continue the conversation. "I think we got off on the wrong foot. Strike that—I *know* we got off on the wrong foot."

"Yes. I believe we did."

Her voice is quiet, but not hostile. So far, so good.

I start to pace. I think she must sense my agitation because she remains patiently silent until I gather my thoughts.

It takes longer than I thought it would.

"You're sure I'm not disturbing you?"

"I've just finished supper, and Lorenzo left a few minutes ago to walk the dogs. This is a good time."

Okay, we'll start there. "Where does Lorenzo sleep?" It comes out more accusatory than I intended. I might as well have called her a big slutty ho.

"I beg your pardon?"

Oh screw it. Let the chips fall where they may. "Are you and Lorenzo a couple?"

Her laugh is unexpected. "If we were, his wife would certainly have something to say about it!"

I stop pacing. "Wife? What wife?"

"His quite lovely wife of almost forty years, Barbara. She's a darling woman, but if she believed for one moment I had designs on her husband, I'd be missing my teeth. She's German. You should see her arms. The woman could pass for a professional wrestler. They live close to Il Sogno—it's the white cottage with the blue door at the bottom of the hill next to the bakery. You've seen it?"

I've seen it. I'm sure there's a nice bed for Lorenzo inside.

"Barbara works the night shift, which is why Lorenzo often stays late. Or comes early, depending how you look at it. And to answer your question directly: no. Lorenzo and I are not romantically involved. He is one of my truest friends, however. He's seen me through many difficult times."

She pauses to control the small tremor in her voice. "Barbara arrives tomorrow on the train. It's our annual tradition, a little holiday for all of us. I can get on quite well with the service in the hotel, and Lorenzo and Barbara take in the sights. Milan is so beautiful this time of year."

That's more than I've heard her say in the entire time I've known her. Apparently accusing a woman of sleeping with her butler is a great way to get her to talk.

I have to give her major props for not hollering at me and hanging up.

"I hope I get to meet her soon. I'm sorry I had to ask you that. I don't mean to be disrespectful, it's just that—"

"It's just that Dominic has been in your ear," she finishes, sounding sad but unsurprised.

"Yes." I feel guilty admitting it. *She's being so nice! Where has this nice lady been all along? Why has she been wearing an iceberg disguise?*

"I wondered how long it would take him. Is there anything else you'd like to ask me? Since we're having such a nice chat."

The warmth is back in her voice again. Maybe she's been drinking. She's on vacation, after all.

"Now that you mention it, I do have a few more questions."

"I'm listening."

I take a moment to wrangle open a wine bottle and pour myself a glass. Then I sit down at the kitchen table and fortify myself with a few sips. "Why didn't you come to the hospital when my father was sick?"

"Oh," she says faintly. "I see you've brought the big guns."

"I'm terrible with small talk."

"Evidently." She inhales a quiet breath. "My first husband suffered for more than two years before the cancer finally killed him. We were constantly in and out of the hospital. Everything in our lives revolved around him being sick. I'm not complaining, you understand, just explaining that was our reality. Waiting for him to die. Watching him get weaker and sicker. The helplessness I felt at not being able to do anything to stop it . . ."

She trails off into silence. I think I hear a faint sniffle, but can't be sure. Her voice is stronger when she comes back on the line.

"When I married your father, he vowed I'd never go through anything like that with him. He extracted a promise from me that if he were ever to fall sick and have to be hospitalized, I would stay away. I refused at first, but when he said it would be easier on him, not having to watch me watch him waste away, I agreed."

Her soft sigh is full of pain. "Since we're being so open, I have to tell you it was the hardest thing I've ever done. It nearly killed me to stay away, but that's what he wanted. So I honored my promise."

"And I yelled at you for it," I whisper, tears stinging my eyes.

Her voice turns gentle. "Oh, my dear. You didn't know."

"I nicknamed you the WS," I blurt as if it's a murder confession. "For Wicked Stepmother."

She chuckles. "That's rather clever, isn't it? I do enjoy a good nickname."

Definitely drinking.

She says, "You'll be wanting to know about Matteo, of course. He's dreadfully in love with you."

I almost spit out my mouthful of wine. Instead I gulp it down, gasping. "Uh—"

"It's been giving me such delight watching him try to manage it. He doesn't wear his heart on his sleeve, as you no doubt know." She chuckles again. "That runs in the family, I'm afraid."

Wine. Drink more wine. That's the only rational thing to do. I obey myself and guzzle.

"When you came in the other night at dinner, he was asking my advice on how to court you. Isn't that sweet? So old-fashioned. You wouldn't think it to look at him, but he really doesn't have much luck with women." She laughs. "Always trying to be so macho. He's like his father that way. Can't stand to be seen as weak. The ego! Ha! It's their Achilles' heel."

I drop my head to the table and proceed to repeatedly smack my forehead against the wood.

His face. Oh God, his face when I asked him what he was talking about with his mother. I'll have to get down on my knees when I beg him to forgive me.

"Speaking of ego, he's also terribly vain. Terribly. His morning routine takes a lifetime. The hair products alone . . ." She exhales, a great gust of air that conveys affection along with disappointment.

"He told me about Maria. About how you always had to have a Great Dane in the house so he would never forget how he refused to come in and see his father on his sickbed before he died."

There's a long awful pause, in which I imagine I can feel how much I've hurt her with my words.

"That's what he thinks? That I was punishing him? I thought it would *comfort* him to have the same breed as Maria around. He and that dog were so close."

I groan. "Oh crap."

"Indeed," agrees the marchesa. "It seems all of us have been operating under false assumptions."

I polish off the last of the wine in my glass. "One last question."

"Yes?"

"Do you know why my father didn't tell me about you?"

"I asked him to wait until we could meet face to face."

That startles me so much I freeze. "Why would you do that?"

She says softly, "Because you'd never had a mother, and I'd never had a daughter. I thought . . . it's silly, I know, but I thought we could both get what we'd always been missing at the same time. You'd arrive after your honeymoon and we'd meet, and we'd all be one big happy family. I had a big party planned. Like a surprise party." Her voice grows tight. "I'm sorry, it all seems so stupid now."

Tears roll down my cheeks. Big fat tears of sorrow and joy.

After I get done kicking my own butt for all the ways I've misjudged her, I'm going to give this woman a hug.

"It's not stupid. It's lovely. I'm sorry it didn't work out like you wanted."

Her laugh is small and sad. "That's life, I'm afraid. It keeps interrupting all our wonderful plans."

"I think I owe Matteo a big apology."

"Why? Did you insult his hair?"

"It's worse than that, I'm afraid."

She turns practical. "Just compliment his hair. It goes a long way, believe me. Anything else can be solved with a kiss."

I laugh, but I'm still crying, and holy guacamole my life is a mess.

I think it's going to be okay, though. Somehow I think everything's all going to turn out just fine.

When the taxi driver pulls up to the curb outside the main gate of Castello di Moretti, I'm out of the car before it slows to a complete stop and pressing my finger impatiently on the button of the call box.

A crackle comes through the speaker, then Matteo says, "Kimber."

I can tell by the tone in his voice I'm going to be groveling well into tomorrow morning.

"Yes, it's me." Grinning, I wave at the small camera mounted high on the stone wall, waiting for the gate to swing open.

Nothing happens.

Frowning, I press the button again. "Matteo? Hello?"

The following pause is so long the seed of worry in my stomach flowers into a bloom of terror the size of the Bermuda Triangle.

He's not going to let me in!

Finally the gate opens with a rusty metal groan, and I can breathe again. I push through the space between the two halves of wrought iron as soon as there's enough room to do so without injuring myself, then sprint past the sunken cloisters, the rolling green lawns, and the fountain lit in purple and blue lights, until I'm inside the first row of stone arches that encircle the courtyard.

I start to panic in earnest when Matteo walks through the big wooden door and I see his face.

It's not the face of a man who'll be swayed by compliments about his hair.

I slow from a run to a walk, my heart throbbing painfully hard, my stomach in knots. When I'm standing a few feet away from him, I stop. Only then do I become aware of the warm evening breeze and the scent of night-blooming jasmine, because we stare at each other in silence until my nerves are so highly strung I think I can hear my fingernails growing.

"Hi."

"Buonasera." He makes no move to invite me in.

"Um . . . can we go inside and talk?"

He looks away, inhales a big breath, and drags a hand through his hair, and now my heart is dying.

Then he opens his mouth and kills off the rest of me.

"I don't think that's a good idea."

Heat floods my cheeks. My chest constricts, as if a giant fist has clutched my lungs. "I just wanted to tell you that I'm sorry. I was confused—"

"It's understandable. Your life is chaotic right now."

"I spoke to Dominic—"

"You don't have to explain."

"Clearly I *do* have to explain because you're not—"

"I can't do this." He says it loudly, with force, his brows drawn down and his jaw hard.

It feels like a punch in the gut.

When I only stare at him with my mouth open, he looks at the ground and says softly, "Fuck."

Breathing is proving extremely difficult. When I speak I sound like Minnie Mouse. "You're breaking up with me. Is that what this is? You don't want to see me anymore?"

He props his hands on his hips, shaking his head, still looking at the ground.

"Matteo, talk to me."

When he raises his head and meets my eyes, breathing becomes impossible. He's a million miles away, and fading fast.

"You need time. Time to grieve your father. Time to grieve your ex. In six months, you'll probably feel very differently about everything. Right now, as you said, you're confused."

"*Was* confused," I whisper, trembling. "Was."

He closes his eyes briefly, his expression registering pain. "I forced this on you. All of it."

He sounds so full of regret I want to throw my arms around him and make him feel better. Except he's ending our nonrelationship, so I also want to break his head.

"Hey! You didn't force *anything* on me, pal!" I say heatedly. "Don't paint yourself as the bad guy! And don't paint *me* as some damsel in distress without any choice in the matter! What happened in the dressing room happened because we *both* wanted it. And all those kisses happened because we *both* wanted them to."

"I was *blackmailing* you," he says through gritted teeth.

"Yeah, you were! Newsflash—I loved every second of it! If I didn't, you'd have two black eyes and an empty hole between your legs where your dick used to be!"

He glares at me. I glare right back. "Don't you dare chicken out on me now, Moretti. I will be *so mad at you* if you chicken out on me now."

"Calling me poultry isn't going to help anything," he snaps, stepping closer.

"I'll call you a goddamn wet noodle if I want!"

His eyes blaze. He growls, "That mouth," and takes another step toward me, as if he wishes he wouldn't but can't help himself, his shoulders stiff and his lips flattened, his head turned slightly aside in protest.

Pinch your nose if you have to do it, Count Egotistico, but kiss me, dammit. Kiss me now.

We breathe angrily at each other.

We do our wonderful eye-fucking thing.

Then he tilts his head skyward and shouts, *"Fuck!"* He snaps his head back down and glowers at me. "I'll call you a taxi. Go wait by the gate."

The sound of a wooden castle door slamming is exactly as loud as you'd think it would be.

THIRTY-FOUR

By the time I get the phone call, I'm deep into a third glass of wine, a second bag of almond biscotti, and a hopelessness I suspect is soon to become the defining characteristic of my personality.

"Hello?"

"Hey, it's me."

"Now isn't a good time, Brad." I stuff another biscotti in my mouth and chomp loudly into the phone. Serves him right for calling in the middle of my breakdown.

"What's wrong? You sound weird."

"It's nothing much. Just an existential crisis that will undoubtedly leave some major scars on my heart, my psyche, and my ability to successfully interact with the rest of the human race."

"Good luck with that. What're you eating? It sounds good."

"You're as empathetic as a dirt clod," I say without heat.

"Sorry. Do you wanna talk about it?"

"I'd rather have my eyeteeth pulled. What do you want?"

"I wanted to find out when exactly this modeling thing I'm doing for you is going to happen."

I sigh heavily and take another swig of my wine. "It's not happening."

"What? Why not?"

Brad sounds unduly upset by this news, which makes me suspicious. "Because the reason I wanted to do it in the first place no longer exists. Why do you care?"

There's a split-second hesitation before he answers, "Because . . . it's how I'm supposed to be making it up to you. About the ditching-you-at-the-altar thing."

"I'm aware of why you're supposed to be making amends to me," I say drily. "Now tell me the real reason."

He drops the pretense, going glum in the process. "Fine. I had someone I wanted to invite."

I snort. "Your mother was going to fly all the way to Italy to watch you in a fashion show? I thought she only wanted pictures."

"It's someone else."

I'm about to lift the glass to my mouth again, but this piece of news stops me. "Really? Who?"

"Giancarlo."

"*Giancarlo?* Who the hell is Giancarlo?" When Brad takes too long to answer, I know. "Oh my God. You have a *boyfriend?* Already?"

"Don't act so scandalized! I'm not the only one with a new boyfriend, girlfriend!"

After a moment, I say, "Good point. And if you ever call me *girlfriend* again, I'll rebreak your nose." I finish off the glass of wine and pour myself another.

Brad grouses, "You let Jenner call you *girlfriend* all the time."

"Dig that hole any deeper and I'll bury you in it." My voice drops an octave. "And I don't have a boyfriend. Matteo and I . . . it's not happening."

"Why not? Did you have a fight?"

Brad sounds genuinely concerned. I can't decide whether that's hilarious or depressing. "We were never together in the first place. But now we're *really* not together."

"Oh, well, that makes perfect sense. Thanks for the explanation."

He's being flippant, the cad. "Not that I owe you an explanation, but . . . it's complicated."

Brad gasps. "You farted in bed, didn't you?"

"That happened *one time!*" I shout. "And you promised you'd never bring it up again!"

He tuts. "You know you shouldn't eat beans, Kimber. You can't digest them. If I were a weaker man, I'd be dead right now. That fart was, like, *killer*. It took months for my nose hair to regrow."

"This isn't happening." I groan, slumping down farther into my chair. "I'm not having this conversation right now. I'm somewhere in a locked room with padded walls, wearing a nice comfy straitjacket, having a respectable mental breakdown. *This* is *not* my life."

"I'm gonna call you right back. Don't go anywhere."

Without further explanation, Brad disconnects the call.

I figure Giancarlo showed up at his hotel room and I won't be hearing from him again anytime soon, so I'm surprised when my phone rings about ten minutes later. When I pick up, Brad sounds like an efficient secretary.

"I've got Jenner and Danielle on the line. I conferenced them in."

"You did what? What the—"

"Honey," says Danielle, sounding frantic. "Brad said you're in trouble—"

"Poppins?" interrupts Jenner. "What's all this about? Are you okay?"

Brad jumps in, and then they're all talking over each other. I sit listening in disbelief as Brad explains his version of our previous phone call and Jenner and Danielle pepper him with questions. Finally, after a few minutes, a pause ensues.

Jenner says, "I don't understand why *you're* calling us, though."

Brad replies, "She's my best friend. I want her to be happy."

Another pause, this one longer. Into the silence, I say, "I think there's a small piece of information the rest of the group is missing, Brad. Up to you if you want to share it or not."

"You didn't tell them?"

He's shocked. I can hear it in his voice. "Not my place. Already told you that."

"Not even Jenner?" he whispers, his voice wavering.

"Excuse me," says Jenner impatiently, "but what the bloody hell is going on?"

Brad says, "Um. I, um . . ." He makes a small panicked noise, then begs, "You tell them."

I don't bother to argue. Nothing makes any sense anyway. Why should this? "So, do you guys remember where Brad and I were going to go on our honeymoon?"

Danielle says, "The dude ranch?"

Jenner says, "What about it?"

"Two things. The first is that it's where *Brad* wanted to go. The second is that it's a. Dude. Ranch."

The silence only lasts for less than a few seconds before Jenner says flatly, "No."

Sounding sheepish, Brad chimes in. "Yeah."

More silence, then Danielle says, "What's happening?"

Jenner's the one who answers her. "If I'm not mistaken, what's happening is that Brad just came out."

"Came out? Of where?"

"For God's sake, what has Ohio done to your brain?" says Jenner, exasperated.

"*Excuse* me for not being able to read minds," says an equally exasperated Danielle. "And I'll have you know, Ohio is a wonderful place!"

"I don't know, I might be with Jenner on this one," says Brad, sounding thoughtful. "I went to Cleveland once and almost got mugged outside a church at ten o'clock in the morning."

Before the conversation goes from merely ridiculous to downright tragic, I take the reins. "Brad is gay, Danielle."

She bursts into laughter that lasts so long Brad has to come to his own defense. "It's true. I'm gay. That's why I couldn't go through with the wedding."

Danielle's laughter dies as doubt sets in. "Gay? I don't understand."

"That was my exact reaction, too." I get up from the kitchen table to find another bottle of wine.

"I'm surprised I didn't see it," says Jenner, "but I'm glad you pulled the plug on the wedding, for both your sakes." His voice hardens. "We'll talk about how you should've handled that later."

"I appreciate the support, but I've already put him through the wringer." I lift a bottle from the wine rack on the counter next to the fridge. *Nebbiolo. Nice.* "Besides, what's done is done."

"Right!" says Brad, overly bright. "What we need to concentrate on now is getting her back together with her stepbrother!"

Danielle mutters, "This is the strangest phone call in history."

"We're going to need the full backstory if you want us to be any help," says Jenner, smoothly switching gears. He's always good in a crisis.

I spend roughly ten minutes recounting everything that's transpired between Matteo and me since I met him, including my plans to crash his show at Fashion Week using my new dress designs.

"Hold on," Brad interrupts. "You were gonna make me wear a *dress*? When were you gonna get around to telling me that?"

"At about the same time you got around to telling me the wedding was off," I say sweetly. "Because there's nothing quite like being humiliated in front of hundreds of people while wearing a couture gown handmade for the occasion. You *did* say you'd do anything to make it up to me."

That shuts him up.

"Let's cut to the chase, shall we? How do you feel about him? Are you in love with this man?"

Jenner's question stops me cold. "It would be ridiculous, wouldn't it? So soon after meeting him? So soon after my relationship with Brad ending? So soon . . . period?"

"That's not an answer."

"It would be romantic, not ridiculous," says Danielle. "I knew as soon as I met Brian that he was the one. Took one look—boom. And your kids would be *gorgeous*."

"Whoa! No one's talking about having kids."

Brad says, "She's right. Your kids *would* be gorgeous."

Jenner says under his breath, "Ugh. Breeders."

"Can we move on from the kid talk and the love talk? What am I supposed to *do*?"

"Get your head straight and figure out how you feel. It's not right to pursue him because you're lonely, or because Satan bruised your ego."

"Hey," says Brad, hurt. "Did you nickname me Satan?"

"Yes, and it's an insult to the lord of darkness," scoffs Danielle.

"I think," continues Jenner over the interruption, "you should do exactly as Matteo suggested and take some time. You've endured some of the most traumatic things that can happen to a person, all within the space of a month. You ended a significant relationship. Your father died. You moved to another country. Your business burned down—"

"Your business burned down?" shout Brad and Danielle in unison.

I fish the corkscrew from a drawer and open the wine.

"As I was saying," thunders Jenner. "Even if it were possible for you to know without a doubt how you feel right now, it's impossible to begin a relationship that has any chance of lasting during such a chaotic time in your life."

He's right. My life *is* chaotic.

And the only thing that has kept me grounded has been a man who blackmailed me for kisses and held me up during my father's funeral and threatened to break Brad's legs for hurting me and challenged, infuriated, and excited me at every turn.

I hear my father's voice in my head speaking the last words he'd ever say to me, his final piece of wisdom before he left this earth.

The easier it comes, the easier it goes. The truly valuable things and people will always test your mettle, but every bit of pain will be worth it in the end. Don't give up when something is difficult. Dig in your heels.

"I have to dig in my heels."

Everyone says, "What?"

"It's a long story. Listen—I love you guys. Thank you so much for worrying about me, and thank you for being my friends. But I think I know what I need to do. And Brad?"

"Yeah?"

"You're not totally off the hook, but making this phone call goes a long way."

When he says, "Thanks," he sounds dejected.

"What's the matter?"

"Um . . . I sorta liked the idea of the dress."

I say goodbye and hang up before the conversation can take any more unexpected turns, then dial Matteo's number.

I've got some heel digging to get to.

THIRTY-FIVE

MATTEO

I see her number on my phone, and it feels as if I've been shot through the heart.

No one ever told me this love business would be so painful.

I take a deep breath and hit "Answer." "It's you."

"It's me. Please don't hang up."

"I wasn't going to."

"Good. Because I need to say important things, and I need you to listen."

Frowning at the strange tone of her voice, I stand from the chair I've been sitting in for the past hour and feeling sorry for myself. "Have you been drinking?"

"Yes!" She sighs, going from enthusiastic to wistful. "But not because I needed liquid courage to call you. Because I was depressed."

That makes two of us. I stare at the flames crackling in the fireplace, wishing my chest wasn't so tight so I could breathe.

"Are you still there?"

"I'm here." I lower my voice. "And I don't like the idea of you drinking alone."

"Cut me some slack, Count. It's not every day I get dumped by the man of my dreams. And before you ask, *no*, I didn't get drunk after Brad left me at the altar, and *no*, he wasn't the man of my dreams. He was a fantasy I made up in my head who ticked off a bunch of boxes that didn't matter because they weren't real. *You're* real. You're what I was looking for all along, only I was too busy dealing with all my disasters to realize it."

She pauses for a moment. "Though I have to admit that you're incredibly irritating when you want to be. I've never met anyone who can do smug better than you."

That roar in my ears is my pulse. I can hardly hear her voice above it. I'm not sure how much of what she's saying is the alcohol, how much is the truth, or if I want to know the difference. "I've had a lot of practice."

She laughs. It loosens some of the tightness in my chest. "You get a gold star for effort, that's for sure."

My mouth wants to turn up into a smile, as it always wants to when I hear her voice. Or see her face. Or think of her.

But I meant what I told her earlier. She needs time. I won't be a rebound. I can't be—not for her.

I have to be her everything, or nothing at all.

"M'kay, you're doing your silent smoldering thing, so I'm just gonna go ahead and talk, and you can be over there all broody and non-sharey to your heart's content."

"Exactly how much alcohol did you drink?" I say, worried.

"I want you."

She says it with total disregard for my question, with an abruptness that borders on curt, and with a dark, solemn tone that makes it clear she's completely serious.

Suddenly I'm no longer concerned about her alcohol intake.

"I want you because you're smart, and you're funny, and you're talented, and you respect your mother, and you make me feel capable of murder, and flight."

"Flight?"

"When you kiss me, I feel like I grow wings. It's a cliché, but it's true, so bear with me."

I understand exactly what you mean.

"I want you because I've never met anyone who challenges me like you do. Who looks at me like you do. Who makes my heart stop beating the way you do when you walk into a room."

The tightness in my chest is back with a vengeance. It's in my throat, too. I have to struggle to draw a single breath.

We sit in silence for a while, until she adds, "Also, your hair is incredible."

Now I can't help but smile. "You've been talking to my mother."

"I really like her."

"You sound surprised."

"I *am* surprised."

I chuckle. "She's an acquired taste. But worth it."

"Totally. Moving on." She hiccups. "I have many more compliments for you if you'd like to hear them."

God, she's adorable. And completely drunk. "I'd like to hear you drink a large glass of water, take aspirin, and go to bed."

Her voice softens. "Why don't you come over and put me to bed?"

The thought of her lying naked in her bed makes me groan.

"Was that a *yes* groan or a *no* groan?"

"It was a groan of frustration."

"Drive over here and be frustrated. We can be frustrated together. Until we're not." She giggles.

"I can't be a rebound," I say, my voice thick. "I can't be a place-holder or a crutch until you get your life together. I meant what I said: you need time—"

"What I need is for you to stop telling me what I need and get your ass over here," she cuts in. "What I need is to kiss you and apologize and tell you all about how I was plotting to crash your show at Fashion Week."

Cue the sound of squealing brakes. *Crash my show?*

"Yeah, it was dumb," she admits sheepishly when I don't say anything. "I was gonna make Brad wear a really pretty dress I've been working on—hopefully Jenner and some of his model friends, too, but he wasn't on board yet—and get up on the catwalk with a sign around his neck that read *Moretti Sucks Balls.* Or something like that. I hadn't exactly figured it out yet.

"But you broke up with me, and I realized it was a stupid plan and it wasn't revenge I wanted, it was you. And the way to get you probably didn't involve making a scene at your show."

She's got me completely confused. "Who is Jenner, and why the hell would your ex agree to wear a *dress?*"

"Jenner's my best friend from San Francisco. You'll meet him, he's great. He's coming to Italy for Fashion Week. And Brad's still trying to make amends for the whole wedding debacle."

I'll bet he is.

If she's trying to make me jealous, it's working. My blood pressure just shot through the roof. Though she told me not two minutes ago he wasn't the man of her dreams, she also told me they had "unfinished business." Now she's telling me he was willing to completely humiliate himself in public to make amends for how he humiliated her.

The son of a bitch is still trying to get her back.

I should've broken his legs when I had the chance.

"Hello?" she says, sounding nervous.

"Still here."

"Are you mad at me?"

"No, bella," I murmur, wanting her so bad it's a physical ache. "But you've been drinking, and I already told you I don't take advantage of incapacitated women."

"I am very capacitated," she says, attempting to sound sober. It would've been a passable attempt, too, except for the burp at the end.

Even *that* is adorable.

More proof that I'm totally gone for this woman. That I'm doing the right thing by staying away.

The last thing she needs is another man muddying the waters. She has to decide what she wants for herself.

In time.

When she's sober.

Since she brought up Fashion Week and the show, I'm tempted to tell her about my own plan, but decide now isn't the time.

Besides, I want it to be a surprise. That was my intent from the beginning.

"Go to sleep, bella," I say, though it nearly kills me.

"You're blowing me off *again*?" She sounds outraged and so dejected I have to grit my teeth against the urge to grab my keys, run from the room, and go to her.

"No, I'm saying good night." *Good night, sleep tight, I'm madly in love with you.*

"I can't believe my groveling didn't work," she grumbles to herself. "That was some A-plus groveling."

"It was. Go to sleep."

She sighs. "Fine. But if I die of alcohol poisoning, you can't say I didn't try to convince you to come over here and save me."

She hangs up before I can say another word, leaving me staring at the phone.

Definitely the death of me.

I swipe my car keys from the dresser and head out, growling under my breath.

When she wakes up in the morning, she's going to have worse things than a hangover to deal with.

THIRTY-SIX

KIMBER

I come awake slowly, feeling hot and thirsty. There's heat at my back, and a weight over my waist, and my first thought is that Cornelia's in bed spooning me again.

Then I remember Cornelia's in Milan with the marchesa, and open my eyes.

The weight around my waist turns out to be an arm. A human arm. Judging by the muscles and overall size, it belongs to a male.

"You snore," says a husky voice behind me.

I'm swamped with sweet relief. *He came!* "No, I don't."

"Like this." Matteo breathes heavily in and out, mimicking Darth Vader.

"You're lying! I do not!"

When I hear him chuckle, I want to elbow him, but then I get a kiss on my bare shoulder and melt instead.

"I'll record it next time."

I roll over onto my other side and snuggle into his chest. He's fully dressed, including socks, which I discover when I slip my feet between his.

"You're under the covers with me."

"I am."

"And you have all your clothes on."

"You have a gift for stating the obvious."

If I didn't hear the affection in his tone, I'd slug him, but his voice is so sleepy and warm I sigh with contentment instead and snuggle in deeper. With my eyes closed, I whisper, "I didn't die from alcohol poisoning. Wanna know why?"

His chest rises and falls with his heavy exhalation.

"Because you came and saved me."

"You're deeply strange."

"C'mon. Play."

Another exhalation, accompanied by a kiss pressed to the top of my head. Despite the pain behind my eyeballs, I'm so content I could float right out of bed.

He says, "Yes. I rode in on my stallion and saved you from a wine overdose. I'm a true hero. I deserve a parade."

"At least a plaque," I say, nodding. "Or a commemorative mug."

"I'm angry with you," he says, and really sounds like he means it.

My heart starts to pound. "Because of what happened with Dominic?"

"Because this is the second time I've been awake all night worried about you choking to death on your own vomit."

I wrinkle my nose at the visual. "Ew."

"Precisely. Do we need to talk about this?"

I stick my face into the space between his shoulder and neck and suck in a lungful of his scent. "Before I met you, I'd only had one other hangover in my life. It was the first and last time I drank gin. I was sixteen."

"So you're telling me it's not a habit."

"I'm telling you it's not a habit."

He exhales again, sounding relieved. His arms tighten around my back.

Smiling into his neck, I whisper, "You're very protective for someone who's giving me space."

His voice gets all gruff and growly. "Have you ever heard the expression, 'Don't poke the bear'?"

"Yes. Why?"

"Because you are *poking the bear*."

"I'm sorry." I pause for a moment, then whisper, "But I'm crazy about the bear, and I don't like it when he doesn't want to be around me, so I have to chase after him with a stick and poke him until he pays attention to me again. Even though the egg isn't supposed to chase after the sperm."

Matteo pulls his head away and looks down at me, furrowing his brow. "What the hell are you talking about?"

I don't know anymore. His eyes are so blue they're blinding me. *God, this man is beautiful up close.* "Do you even have pores?"

He blinks. "You're still drunk."

"No, I'm sober. It's just that you're incredibly handsome."

His expression sours. "You're trying to butter me up."

"Is it working?"

"No. I'm still angry with you."

"I thought we made up!"

He looks confused for a moment. "Did we?" Then he shakes his head. "Even if we did, I'm still angry. And you still need time."

"There you go, telling me what I need again. I think you should listen to someone else who's telling you what I need. His ideas are much better."

I flex my hips against the bulge in his pants so there's no mistake about my meaning. Matteo lets out a soft groan and fists his hand in my hair.

"Stop."

"You're in bed with me with a raging hard-on. You don't want me to stop."

I kiss his neck, give it a gentle bite, and wriggle my hips in what I hope is an enticing fashion against him. For my efforts, I'm rolled onto my back with my wrists pinned to the pillow over my head, and glared at.

"I'm in bed with you because you hung up on me after threatening to *die*," he says.

God, he's hot. Look at this gorgeous hunk of a man, so pissed off and sexy.

He grits his teeth. "Don't. Look. At. Me. Like. That."

"Make love to me."

He groans and drops his forehead to my chest. "You want to kill me, is that it? You're hoping to murder me?"

"I can think of worse ways to go." I arch my back so my breasts press against his face.

He makes a sound like he's deeply in pain and nuzzles his nose into my cleavage. "What is this thing you're wearing?"

"A nightie. I put it on hoping you'd come over. Do you like it?"

"It's not a nightie, it's a torture device. I hate it." He lovingly rubs his cheek against it and sighs.

I squirm underneath him, wanting him to release my wrists so I can paw his perfect body. "Let me go," I say breathlessly, heat washing over me.

When he glances up at me, I catch my breath. His eyes have gone so dark. There's a stillness in them, a new danger, and suddenly it's very hard to breathe.

"No," he says softly, as if to himself. "I don't think I will."

He transfers both my wrists to one hand and rips off his belt in a whip-crack move that has me gasping in surprise. He winds his belt around my wrists, ties it off to the headboard, and gazes down at me in hungry silence, inspecting my body.

His lips curve into a ruthless smile.

"Matteo—"

"*Quiet.*"

The dominant tone in his voice shuts me up just as fast as it turns me on. I bite my lip, watching him, feeling my pulse go from a trot to a gallop. I think I might ignite.

On his knees between my legs, he slowly unbuttons his shirt and tosses it to the floor. Looking at his abs, I squirm a little more, dying to feel him on top of me.

He climbs off the bed and casually strolls into the bathroom.

"Hey! Where are you going?"

"Aspirin," he says over his shoulder. "Water."

I drop my head back onto the pillow, close my eyes, and gnash my teeth. From the bathroom comes a low chuckle.

"What was that noise? Do we have two bears in the room?"

"You're so lucky I'm tied up right now," I say, breathing hard with the urge to throw something at him—primarily myself. "If I wasn't tied up, I'd kick your butt. I'd do such a gnarly karate chop on your head, it would fly clean off. I'd—"

"Good thing you *are* tied up, then." He appears at the bedside as quickly as he left, holding a glass of water in one hand and two small white pills in the other. Watching me glare at him, he smiles.

"Is this punishment for believing Dominic?"

"No. This is punishment for making me worry and shaving years off my life with that mouth of yours. Take these." He holds out the aspirin.

I stick out my tongue and let him lift the glass of water to my lips so I can drink. After I swallow, I go back to glaring at him.

He sets the glass on the bedside table without looking away from me, murmuring, "But you know I won't let you suffer too long."

I make an incoherent peep of lust and squirm some more.

He straddles me, kneeling on either side of my hips and planting his hands beside my head. Staring down into my eyes, he says, "Or maybe I will. I haven't decided yet."

Before I can sling a few voodoo curses at him, he lowers his head and sucks my nipple through the nightie, making me arch and gasp.

"Mmm. Lace." He tugs at the fabric with his teeth, scraping it across my nipple, making me gasp again. Then he pushes the nightie down, fills his hands with my breasts, and goes back and forth between them, nibbling and sucking until I can barely draw a breath.

"So pink and hard," he whispers, softly kissing around one aching nipple. "Wet from my tongue. Where else are you pink and wet, bella?"

God please find out please find out and hurry up about it. I don't dare speak, because I'm afraid it will break the spell, and he'll go back to being angry and giving me space.

The last thing in the world I want from him at this moment is space.

He slides his big hands down my ribs until they span my waist. He squeezes, his eyes dark, his grip just this side of hard. I can tell he's controlling himself, he's working hard to go slow, and it thrills me to know he's as excited as I am.

He follows the curve of my hips down to my thighs, then slowly pushes up the hem of my nightie.

"No panties," he breathes, staring down at me with avid eyes. He slips a thumb into my wetness and strokes it up and down as I moan and rock my hips, my nipples tingling.

Looking at me spread open, his fingers between my legs, he grips his erection in his other hand and squeezes it through his trousers.

Wowzers. I almost faint from desire.

He draws his zipper down and pulls his hard cock out of his boxer briefs, fisting it at the base. "You're so beautiful," he whispers, watching me with hooded eyes as I flex my hips in time to the movement of his thumb. "God, you turn me on."

"Right back atcha, hot stuff. I need to touch you."

I strain against the belt, tugging my wrists, but he's got me tightly bound. Why that should be so hot, I don't know, but I can't remember ever feeling this wound up. The air against my skin is excruciating. The sheets under my body are a bed of hot coals.

His hands work both of us until I'm panting and sweating, about to break. "Please. Oh God, please."

"What do you want, sweetheart?"

"Please make me come."

"How? Mouth or cock?"

I let out a low guttural moan, rolling my head on the pillow, and he chuckles.

"Certo. Both."

He lowers his head between my thighs and replaces his thumb with his tongue.

I suck in a breath through my teeth, exhaling hard when he slides a finger inside me. "Ohh . . ."

He grunts into me. It's dirty and hot, and I love it. I love it so much I open my legs wider and rock my hips against his tongue, moaning like a porn star when he reaches up to tweak my hard nipple.

Leather cuts into my wrists. Matteo's rough cheeks scrape against my bare thighs. I'm trembling and panting and desperate for him, for him to fill me, fuck me, tell me how he feels about me as he spills himself inside my body and claims me for his own.

I arch hard against the bed, pulling at my restraints, the ache between my legs gathering into burning hot pins and needles. Almost—*almost*—

As I'm about to go over the edge, his mouth vanishes. Then he slaps me lightly between my legs where his tongue just was, right on my throbbing clit.

I come, screaming.

He grips one of my knees and opens my legs wider, and slaps me again. And again.

And again.

I cry out, the pleasure so intense it's almost pain.

He speaks to me in Italian as I writhe, his tone low and urgent, the words spilling out in a rush that becomes a musical hum in my ears. I'm helpless, lost, jerking and wailing, begging him not to stop in a voice that doesn't sound like my own.

"Beautiful. Beautiful," he whispers raggedly, and slaps me again.

When the last convulsion passes and I'm drenched and limp on the sheets, every part of me aching, I burst into tears.

"Sweetheart, oh sweetheart, oh God, did I hurt you? What's the matter?"

Matteo is frantic, ripping the belt off my wrists and gathering me into his arms. I sob against his chest, clinging to him, until I catch my breath and my tears slow.

He takes my face in his hands. "I'm so sorry! I thought you liked it, I thought it felt good for you, I should have asked—"

"Don't be sorry. That was the most incredible orgasm of my life."

He stills. His eyes search my face. "Really?"

I nod, sniffling. "Yes, really. I think I saw God."

He exhales in relief, squeezing me so hard I think he might snap me in half. "Jesus."

"Him too. There might have also been cherubs."

Matteo starts to laugh, softly at first, then louder. "What am I going to do with you?"

"More of the same, please."

He takes us back down to the bed and kisses me with so much tenderness it leaves me shaking. He dries my face with his fingertips and his lips, kissing away the tears, murmuring such sweet things I feel like my heart could break from hearing them. I wrap my legs around his waist and my arms around his shoulders and tell him to take off the rest of his clothes.

"Oh." He goes still again.

"What is it?"

"I didn't bring a condom."

I understand by the look on his face why not. "Like when a woman doesn't shave her legs before a date so she won't be tempted to have sex."

"Exactly."

I take a breath for courage and say, "I'm clean. I was just tested. So . . ."

His lids droop a little, and his voice drops. "So . . . bare is what you're saying."

I bite my lip, nodding. "As long as you're clean, too."

"I am," he answers instantly. "I have the papers at the house if you want me to go get them."

I give him a look that says, *Shut the hell up.*

He grins. "Okay. Now that that's out of the way." He jumps up, stands on the side of the bed, and strips.

When he's finished and is standing there naked in all his glory, I slowly shake my head in awe. "Wow. Just . . . *wow.*"

"Thank you. I think."

"Get your ass in this bed *this instant.*"

He's a good boy and obeys without batting a lash, jumping on top of me with a fake animal growl and tickling me until I shriek. Then he slides inside me and the shrieking stops, replaced by deep groans.

Into my ear he says huskily, "You're *soaked.*"

"Your fault." I gasp as he thrusts, driving deeper. "Oh God, this is all your fault if you stop I will kill you."

"And so *hot,*" he whispers, thrusting again. "You feel so amazing. You feel like heaven, bella, fucking *heaven.*"

I open my thighs and take him deeper, grabbing him by the scruff of the neck. When my nails scratch his scalp, things turn intense. He bites my neck. I bite his shoulder. His fingers dig into my ass. Mine dig into his back. He starts to fuck me, hard, grunting and hissing out such wonderfully filthy things it makes my cheeks burn.

I love it. I love it all. Every dirty word. Every possessive bite. Every single pinch, stroke, and groan he gives me.

When he shudders, making a soft agonized noise, I know he's close. Close and holding back so I can get there first.

But I want to get there together.

Into his ear I whisper, "I have an IUD. Come inside me."

"God," he says, his voice strangled. "Could you be any more perfect?"

Then I can't think anymore because I'm riding a cresting wave, higher and higher, up into the bright endless blue of the sky. The roar of the wind blocks my ears. The sun burns my face, the smell of his skin sears my nose, and I'm flying.

The wave breaks over me. The roar of the wind becomes the sound of my name as he throws back his head and shouts it, his body tight and straining, surging against mine.

I fall and fall and fall, tumbling, twisting, turning, letting go of my last shred of resistance when he spills himself inside me and cries out something in his language that sounds like a prayer.

THIRTY-SEVEN

We sleep.

I wake with his hand on my breast, his hardness and heat against my back. We make love again, slowly, quietly, on our sides. I'm glad I'm not looking at his face because I'm so emotional I fight tears the entire time.

I never expected to feel so much. My chest aches from holding it all inside. *I love you* is on the tip of my tongue, but I can't say it, even afterward when we're lying entangled with our breath and pulses slowing, sweat cooling on our skin, and he's tenderly smiling down at me with his heart in his eyes.

Love made such a willing fool of me before. I need to be 100 percent sure this time that I'm not being blind.

"You're thinking."

His voice is thick with sleep and satisfaction. He strokes a hand up my spine, burying it in my hair, and pulls me closer against him.

"How could you tell?"

"I smell something burning."

"Ha."

We're quiet for a time, though it feels as if a thousand things are being said. His hands are spinning stories against my skin. His strong, steady heartbeat underneath my cheek is selling promises. His smile is a fairy tale I want nothing more than to believe.

"Tell me."

I sigh, happy and melancholy, peaceful and scared shitless all at the same time. "This might be easier for me to deal with if you were poor and looked like Shrek."

"I'll sell the castle and give all the money to charity," he says promptly. "I'll gain two hundred pounds and paint myself green."

"Good." I hide my face in his chest.

He cradles me in his arms, kissing my temple, nuzzling my ear, chuckling a bit at my stupidity. "If it makes you feel any better, from now on I'll only tell you all the things I find irritating about you."

I jerk my head up and glare at him. "Like what?"

He presses his lips together to keep from laughing. "Your calm, even temper, for instance. Your sweet, loving tongue."

I say tartly, "You thought my tongue was pretty sweet when it was wrapped around your dick."

His eyes flare. He murmurs, "My kingdom for that mouth."

My heart skips a beat. Suddenly breathless, I say, "You don't have a kingdom, Count."

"The hell I don't."

I roll my eyes when his smug smile makes an appearance. "Okay. Sure. You're the king of the fashion world. The ruler of ready to wear. The liege of lederhosen—"

"You know I don't make lederhosen," he growls, rolling me onto my back so I'm pinned underneath him. "And call me *Count one more time . . .*" He lowers his head and nips my breast.

"Ow!"

Warm and soothing, his tongue slides over the place he just nipped. I scowl at the top of his head. "You bit my boob!"

He sends me a smoldering look. With a rough edge to his voice, he says, "You fucking loved it."

My stomach drops, like it always does when he looks at me that way. When he rises up on his elbows and takes my head in his hands, my stomach bottoms out altogether.

"And you love *me*, too. Don't you?"

His eyes bore straight down into me, blue lasers searing my soul, daring me to lie to him.

"I thought . . . you wanted me . . . space."

It's all I can string together. My brain is mush from the way he's looking at me. From his words and his intensity, from the effort of holding back my enthusiastic *Yes!*

"I want you to tell me how you feel about me," he says, looking right into my eyes. "I want you to be brave and put it all out there. To my face this time. We can take it slow. It doesn't have to change anything. But if you don't think this is going anywhere, I need to know. I meant what I said yesterday. I can't be a rebound. For anyone else, yes, but not for you."

I bite my lip so hard it hurts. "I already told you I've never wanted anything as much as I want you."

He waits, unblinking, watching my face.

"And that I'm terrified you'll break my heart."

He's as still as a stone.

Holy guacamole, this guy can be intimidating.

"What else?" he prompts.

"That's not enough?"

"Indulge me."

I moisten my lips, wishing my heart would settle into a steady rhythm. "I don't think you're a rebound."

"You don't *think*?"

Oh shit. Bad choice of words. "I mean I'm pretty sure." When he blanches, I quickly add, "I'm almost a hundred percent sure!"

He withdraws from me like you'd recoil from a big steaming pile of dog doo on the sidewalk. He turns his back to me and sits on the edge of the mattress with his head in his hands.

I sit up, pulling the sheet up to cover my bare breasts, and try not to panic. *He wanted the truth. He asked for the truth!*

Yes, he did, and you're a moron if you think it's what he really wanted to hear.

I whisper, "Please don't be angry with me."

He shakes his head, exhaling heavily. "I'm not. I'm angry with myself."

When he stands and starts to get dressed, the option of not panicking vanishes. "Matteo, please don't go. Let's talk about this."

"Why? Will it change anything?"

"Please, I want you to understand—"

"I understand perfectly," he says, ice crackling in his voice. "This is what I was trying to avoid. This is why I told you to take your time. Then you got drunk and told me I was what you were looking for. You paid me wonderful compliments. You even complimented my *hair*."

He sounds disgusted, as if he can't believe I stooped so low.

"You gave me everything I wanted. You gave me all of you. *You let go.* Only you didn't, because when I asked you if you loved me, you wouldn't say yes." His eyes are fierce. "Not because you couldn't, because I think you do. You *wouldn't*."

"You're the one who keeps telling me I need time!"

"You do!" he thunders. "And you're going to get it!"

I watch in shock as he yanks on his pants and shirt. He stuffs his feet into his shoes without putting his socks on, grabs his keys from the dresser, and stalks out of the room without so much as a *See ya later.*

"Don't you dare cry," I warn myself, listening to Matteo's car engine roar to life outside. "Don't you *dare*."

I go into the shower and stand with my face turned up to the spray so I have an excuse for all the water pouring down my cheeks.

The rest of the morning without him feels endless and empty. My heart hurts. I don't know if I should call him or leave him alone to cool down. I suspect he's right that the only thing that will fix this is a separation, but I hate it.

On the other hand, I've finally discovered what other flaws he has besides a gigantic ego: the man has a temper that's just as fast to flare into dragon mode as my own. I probably shouldn't be happy about it because I can already see a lot of fights in our future that could've been better handled with calm conversation.

But then again, makeup sex is a pretty awesome silver lining.

When I walk into the shop, Clara takes one look at me and starts to judge.

"You chased the sperm, didn't you?"

"Relationships are more complicated than eggs and sperm, Clara!"

"You want a complicated relationship, get a cat. Men are as complex as ferns. Don't overthink it."

She goes back to her embroidery, and I go into my office and do a face-plant on my desk. Ten seconds into it my phone rings.

"Hello?"

"Hey, Kimber."

I flatten myself into my chair and stare at the ceiling. "Hi, Brad. Will you do me a favor?"

"Sure! What is it?"

"The next time I develop feelings for someone, just shoot me in the heart and Super Glue my vagina."

There's a long concerned pause. "I take it the Matteo situation isn't improving."

"Correct."

"Do you want me to talk to him?"

My eyes almost pop out of my head. "Of course not! Was that a joke?"

"I'm just saying, it might help. I can explain to him about your personality."

"What *about* my personality?" I demand, jerking upright in the chair.

He calmly continues on, as if he isn't in danger of being murdered. "The stubbornness. The temper. The way you always have to win. I won't tell him about the gas, though. He's on his own in that department."

I do another face-plant on the desk, groaning. *"How is this my life?"*

"In other news . . ." He pauses for dramatic effect. "I'm moving here."

"Here? *Where* here? I'm very confused."

Brad sighs loudly. "To *Florence*! Isn't that awesome?"

"I can think of a few other words," I say through gritted teeth. "*Why* are you moving here? Your whole life is in San Francisco!"

"No it's not. You're here."

That leaves me utterly speechless. I must have done something really terrible in a previous life for the universe to treat me so cruelly.

Then he adds sheepishly, "And so is Gio."

"Gio?"

"Giancarlo. I told you about him."

It takes a moment to sink in, then I'm astounded. "You're *that* serious about this guy? Already?"

"Oh hellooo, pot," he says drily. "Kettle here. Let's have lunch and talk about the definition of irony."

I see he's developed a biting sense of snark since he decided to come out. Maybe I have Giancarlo to thank for that. Good for him. "What about your parents?"

His voice grows heavy. "They still think I'm trying to get you back."

"Have you thought about what you're going to do about that?"

"Nope. Have you thought about what you're going to do about Matteo?"

"He's giving me space to make sure he's not a rebound. There's nothing to do except make sure he's not a rebound."

"He's *not*," says Brad, as if he's an authority on the subject. "I know you, and I know you have real feelings for him. It might be bad timing, but that's not the end of the world."

"Thank you, Dr. Phil. I wish you would've been this clear-sighted about our wedding."

"Me too. Sorry again, by the way. If we're not doing the modeling thing, you'll have to think of some other way for me to make it up to you."

I'm overcome by a wave of exhaustion. All I want to do is crawl back into bed and hide under the covers until I'm old. "Just be happy. That's enough."

"You want me to be happy?"

He sounds choked up, which makes me even more tired. I can't deal with anyone else's emotional breakdowns right now. I'm too busy handling my own. "I'd hate to think we went through all that trauma and neither of us was better for it in the end. So yes. I want you to be happy. You deserve it."

After a moment of silence, Brad bursts into tears.

"For God's sake, are you taking hormones or something?"

He sobs. "Don't shout at me! I'm emotional!"

"Really? I hadn't noticed." I flop back into the chair and close my eyes. *Maybe it's all a bad dream. Maybe I'm going to wake up any second and it will all be over.* "I have to go now. My straitjacket is calling."

"Fine." He sniffles, drawing in a shuddering breath. "But if you need to talk about Matteo, I'm here."

He hangs up, leaving me wondering if my life will ever make sense again.

For the next week, I bury myself in work. I log in so many hours at the shop, I give up going back to the house overnight and sleep on a cot in the office. Clara keeps me fed. Anxiety keeps me company. Whenever Jenner or Danielle call to get an update on Matteo, I tell them the same thing. "We haven't talked."

I'm beginning to think he's as stubborn as I am.

Then, on the tenth day after our argument, I receive an invitation in the mail. It's on pure-white linen, engraved with gold-foil script. My name is written in calligraphy on a line below the elegant House of Moretti logo, followed by a date, time, and the address of the Royal Palace of Milan, where the showing of their couture collection will be held.

Clara sees me holding it and asks what it is.

"Kimberella got her invitation to the ball," I answer, smiling.

THIRTY-EIGHT

The first thing I have to do is figure out what to wear.

I've never been to an haute couture show, because they're strictly invite only. Even if you're a Saudi princess or Beyoncé, without that invitation in hand, you can't get past the door. The women who wear the world's finest and most expensive handmade clothing are a certain breed, most of whom don't want to be named publicly or, God forbid, photographed. Designers are famously tight lipped about their clientele, too, so the entire process gains a secret, sacred air.

It's a once-in-a-lifetime chance for me to model one of my own designs.

There will be more potential buyers at this show than I could ever hope to reach individually. If I could even somehow determine who they were, which I couldn't. Each designer's list of clients is as protected as if they're state secrets.

Aside from sending clothes to every high-profile celebrity in hopes of having one of them wear something of mine in public, the only way to break into the rarefied society of women who collect and wear haute couture is by word of mouth.

I'll be a walking billboard for my work.

Which means whatever I wear has to be *perfect*. We have only a few days to complete the collection and alter whatever design I choose to my measurements.

The problem is deciding on that design.

"The sequined powder blue with the ostrich cuffs," suggests Clara as I critically eye every dress we've been working on.

"Too dramatic."

"The leather and satin with buckles on the waist."

"Too edgy."

"The red silk with the plunging neckline."

"Too sexy."

"The sleeveless purple with the sheer overlay on the skirt."

I turn to inspect the dress pinned to the muslin form next to Sofia's workstation. Look nine is spectacular, if I do say so myself. It's a deep royal purple with a full satin skirt and a sheer panel attached at the small of the back, designed to float out like a sail with the wearer's movement. The bodice is made of hand-dyed lace appliqued with tiny sequins and overlaid below the breasts with a horizontal wrap of silk to accentuate the waist. The high slit in the skirt adds a dash of sex appeal, but the overall design is elegant and sophisticated.

I clap, hopping a little in excitement. "That's it! Clara, you're a genius."

"I know," she says. "Now what are we going to do about lunch?"

I give her a big kiss on the cheek, then order sandwiches from the deli down the street. After we eat, I go back to work with renewed energy, counting down the minutes until I can see Matteo again.

Three days later, the purple dress is finished, we're putting the final touches on the rest of the designs for the new collection, and Jenner has arrived in Milan. He alerted me of that fact by sending a text that read Elvis is in the house.

When I call him, he picks up on the first ring.

"Moshi moshi."

"Don't tell me you're inside the Japanese guy again."

He sighs theatrically. "Alas, lovely Hiro and I have parted ways."

"But you'll forever honor his memory when you answer the phone," I say, laughing.

"I'm sentimental that way. How are you, darling? You sound better than the last time we spoke."

"I'm a little better, mainly because of the invitation."

I can tell his interest is piqued by the way his tone sharpens. "Invitation?"

"To Matteo's show at the Royal Palace."

"So you won't have to crash the gig after all!"

"*We*, I think you meant."

He sniffs. "I deny all knowledge of your ludicrous scheme and would happily tell that to any concerned authorities."

"Puh. You know I would've talked you into it."

"Of course," he says blithely. "But only because I'm frightened you'll clobber me. I was there when you rearranged Satan's nose, if you recall. How is he, by the way?"

"Still gay. And in love with someone named Giancarlo."

"*Giancarlo,*" purrs Jenner. "How delicious. I think I'm in love with him, too. Pity I'll never meet him. I could avenge your honor by breaking them up."

"Oh, you'll probably meet him. Brad has decided he's moving to Florence to be with the new boy toy. And he's hanging on to me like a bad head cold. I'm sure if I told him I was going to Milan for the show, he and Gio would be on the next train out."

After a moment, Jenner chuckles. "Well, no one can say your life is boring."

I exhale and sit in my office chair, feeling as if I've aged a decade in the past month. "I could do with a little boring right about now, let me tell you."

"What's new with the wicked stepmother and your doggie stepsisters?"

"It turns out she isn't so wicked. God, I have a lot to catch you up on. When can I see you?"

He tells me the name of the hotel he's staying in, then insists I get ready for Matteo's show in his suite because he doesn't trust I'll do my hair right or accessorize properly. It sounds like a fabulous idea, so I agree.

I'll need the moral support. Tomorrow will be two weeks since I've seen Matteo, and I'm more worried than I want to admit about how it will be between us. I miss him so much it feels like a limb has been cut off, but I have no idea how he feels or what he's thinking. He hasn't contacted me since the night he walked out.

I'm terrified he's changed his mind about us.

Even more terrified than I am of him breaking my heart, which says a lot.

"Stop fidgeting."

"Hurry up! I'll be late!"

Standing behind me in the gleaming marble bathroom in his hotel suite, Jenner carefully affixes the comb into my upswept hair, then steps back to survey his handiwork. He nods in satisfaction. "Half-up, half-down. Sophisticated but sexy. Congratulations, you're perfect."

"I'm also sweating through this friggin' dress," I mutter, flapping my arms in an effort to cool myself. The air conditioning is blowing right on me from a vent in the bathroom ceiling, but my body has decided it's time for another searing hot flash.

I know it's hormonal. I'll be seeing Matteo in a short while, and my damn uterus is throwing a rave party complete with flashing lights and disco music. I'm a wreck.

Jenner takes me by the shoulders. "Just breathe, darling. Like so."

He inhales slowly through his nose, then blows the breath out through pursed lips.

"I know how to breathe."

"Clearly you don't. You're hyperventilating." He demonstrates another dramatic intake of breath through his flared nostrils, nodding at me to follow his lead.

"Ugh. Fine." I breathe as theatrically as possible, mimicking him. "Oh," I say several calming breaths later. "That actually works."

He smiles. "Now we're going to practice walking."

"*Walking?* I already know how to do that!"

He arches an eyebrow in disagreement. "When wearing couture, one doesn't simply stomp around as if mashing grapes underfoot. One *glides*." He floats away from me as if on a cloud, his lower legs moving but his upper body completely still. It's quite the effect.

"I'll never be able to copy that, catwalk boy. And thanks for that ego-boosting description of how I move. It was just the shot in the arm I needed."

When I glare at him, he dissolves into laughter. "Oh, Poppins. I tease. Your walk is lovely. I'm only trying to loosen you up."

"Please, no more loosening. It's having the opposite effect. I'm wound so tight I might snap."

"I know," he says softly, coming back to rest his hands on my shoulders. "It all feels a bit déjà vu, doesn't it? The last time we were in a room together prepping you for a big event, it didn't end quite as planned."

"Hopefully this time will be different. Knock wood." I reach out and lightly rap my knuckles against his temple.

"Very funny. At least you're not carrying calla lilies."

"That reminds me. Where's my clutch?"

"Here." He picks it up from the counter, then makes a face at it. "What's in this thing? Rocks?"

"Lip gloss, my phone, and a giant stack of business cards. If all goes well I'll be handing them out like candy."

He chuckles. "I love it that you're going into this with such an entrepreneurial spirit."

I practice the deep breathing again because my heart has decided it would be a good time to pound. "It would be smarter if I were going into it with a belly full of Xanax. God, this is *worse* than the wedding. My nerves are shot!"

I hold out a hand, and we watch it tremble.

Jenner murmurs, "You really have feelings for him, don't you?"

What an understatement. "Turns out that old adage 'Absence makes the heart grow fonder' is true. I just wish . . ."

When I'm silent too long, Jenner prompts, "What?"

I look up into his eyes and say quietly, "I wish it could be easier."

"It?"

"Love. Relationships. Why does it all have to be so confusing and convoluted?"

He sighs, smoothing a hand over my hair. "Because real life isn't a fairy tale, darling, and making a relationship last is hard. Love involves a lot of forgiveness. People aren't perfect. Falling in love is easy, but staying in love is a choice. You have to decide if the ups and downs are worth sticking out because there will be plenty of them. There will be pain.

"That's where we all go wrong, expecting love to be a Hallmark commercial where you run through a field of clover into each other's arms and live happily ever after with no regrets. True love is when you can look at someone and say, 'I know you will hurt me and disappoint me and fail me in a thousand different ways, and I accept that because you make me a better person. Because with you I become whole. Because I'd rather die than live a single day without you, come what may."

I stare at him, blinking back tears so I don't ruin my mascara. "Honestly, you're the last person in the world I would've expected that from."

He swallows hard, looking away. When he speaks, his voice is low and rough. "Not all of us are brave enough to risk our hearts being broken more than once. Not all of us could survive it."

I'm shocked by that. Ten years I've known this man, and this is the first time I've glimpsed the lovelorn side of him. Apparently his revolving door of partners started after a heartbreak so big he couldn't come back from it.

I ask gently, "Are you gonna tell me about it?"

He draws himself up, tosses his head, and forces a bright smile. "Not right before you hop into your carriage to head off to the ball. Come on, let's get going. I have a surprise for you."

"Xanax?"

"Better. A limo. And you don't have to worry about it turning into a pumpkin at midnight. I paid extra for that."

With a furtive swipe of a knuckle at the corner of his eye, he leads me by the elbow from the room.

The palace is a massive blocky neoclassical structure set in the heart of Milan, right next to a white cathedral that looms over it with skyscraping spires. The facade of the palace is spectacularly uplit in washes of red light, making the building glow like a ruby against the sapphire evening sky. Ruffled by the breeze, a row of crimson banners emblazoned with the Moretti logo hangs from the roof, boldly declaring the palace's occupant for the night.

Matteo definitely knows how to put his stamp on things.

My heart included.

As the limo pulls into the palazzo entrance and slows to a stop, I practice more of Jenner's deep-breathing techniques because I'm about to faint from nerves. A uniformed valet opens the door and helps me out, appreciatively eyeing the expanse of bare thigh revealed by the slit in my skirt.

"Buongiorno, bellissima," he says in a husky baritone, smiling at me with smoldering bedroom eyes the color of espresso.

Whew. Italian men. They could get a girl pregnant through osmosis.

I join a flow of exquisitely dressed people entering the palace through a designated door and show my invitation to a burly guard dressed all in black. He checks my name off a list, then nods, allowing me to pass into a spectacular hall echoing with marble and lit with dozens of crystal chandeliers sparkling in icy-cold brilliance overhead. Feeling self-conscious but pleased by all the admiring looks my gown is getting, I follow the crowd up a sweeping red-carpeted staircase to the second floor.

At the landing, I enter another world.

Thick piles of red rose petals are sculpted into drifts along the walls and balustrade. Thousands of red rose heads have been strung together and hang at irregular heights from the ceiling like vines. Glass vases taller than I am are filled with water, red petals, and floating candles, and stand flickering between the drifts, lending everything an ethereal glow. The soft strains of violins play through hidden speakers, and the air is perfumed with the scent of roses and candle wax.

The overall effect is magical, sensual, and breathtakingly romantic.

Tall carved wooden doors stand open to a soaring ballroom, where rows of seats flanking a catwalk lit from beneath in pink lights await. People mill about inside, pretending to glibly chat as they check out who's who and what they're wearing.

Another uniformed guard at the door is checking invitations again and pointing out seat assignments. I get mine—front row center, be still my heart—then take a deep breath, square my shoulders, and enter the room.

And instantly feel the touch of a cool hand on my arm.

"Mi scusi, signorina."

I turn to see a woman standing beside me. She's extremely pale, with waist-length black hair, cheekbones like the freshly sharpened edge of a knife, and eyes that probably don't close all the way when she sleeps because of the amount of skin that has been removed from her lids by plastic surgery. Her dress is a slinky black silk number that shows off a pair of savage hipbones. She looks as if she last had a solid meal in the nineties.

Her companion is a woman who looks exactly like *Vogue* editor Anna Wintour.

I'm so unnerved by the possibility that it might actually *be* Anna Wintour that I try to smile but bare my teeth like a cornered wolf instead. "Yes?"

The woman says something to me in Italian, gesturing at my dress.

"I'm sorry, I don't speak Italian."

Anna Wintour says, "She wants to know who you're wearing."

"Oh! Me! I'm wearing me!" I smile again, aiming for a credible impression of a human this time.

Anna and Morticia share a look. "You're a designer?"

Morticia covetously eyes my dress. I think she wants to pet me, or maybe take me hostage. My ambition suggests we'll accept either.

"Yes. Here's my card."

Morticia takes it, lifts it to her nose, and tries to squint at it. If only she had enough extra skin around her eyes to pull it off.

"Grazie." The two drift away, whispering with their heads bent together.

I suppose that went well, but don't have time to dwell on it, because the lights dim and the music grows louder, indicating the show is about to begin.

Unfortunately, my nervous bladder has decided it's time for a bathroom break.

I look around for a restroom sign, but can't see anything due to the press of bodies and the low lights. People are taking their seats and I should, too, but if I don't find a ladies' room, I'll have to sit through the entire show squeezing my thighs together and praying my Kegel muscles are strong enough to avoid having to make an embarrassing emergency exit.

I head back to the guard at the door and ask directions to the nearest bathroom. He points down the hallway. I take off, holding my skirts aloft as I trot as fast as I can in my high heels.

When I come to the end of the corridor, it splits left and right. There's no sign for a restroom, no lighted placard or helpful attendant, only more yawning hallways echoing with the sounds of the show I'm about to miss.

Did I pass it? Maybe I ran right by the door! Panicking, I decide to head right.

I keep going, passing room after room with closed doors blocked by stanchions with velvet ropes, obviously not restrooms. Just as I'm about to give up and turn around, I spy a set of double doors open at the end of the hallway, spilling out light.

When I run through them, I'm greeted by a wall of portable hanging curtains that set designers and interior decorators use to block off large areas of unsightly space. This particular curtain is crimson, so I know I'm in the right place.

It's weird that the curtains are closed, but whatever. I have to pee.

I part the curtains where I find a break and walk into chaos.

An entire small city has been set up in a space the size of a hotel ballroom. Row after row of gowns hanging from portable racks line the walls. Directors' chairs opposite lighted vanity tables are filled with models in short red robes being prepped for makeup and hair. Designers scurry around a long line of models waiting near a curtained door on the opposite side of the room, fussing over last-minute adjustments. Rock music plays, photographers snap photos, girls take selfies, and assistants shout over one another for pins or scissors or shoes.

I'm backstage.

As if he's a homing beacon, Matteo draws my gaze like a magnet. He stands at the head of the row of models about to go out onto the catwalk through the curtained door, inspecting each gown, accessory, and lock of hair to ensure it's perfect.

My heart throbs to life. I'm seized by the urge to run to him, throw my arms around his shoulders, bury my nose in his neck, and breathe in his delicious scent. I want to touch him so badly, to feel his strong arms pull me close, it's like wildfire in my blood.

Then he moves, the girl at the front of the line of models comes into view, and the fire turns to ice.

The model wears a one-shouldered gown of vermillion silk. The skirt is voluminous. The bodice glitters with sequins. The cut, style, and design are exquisite, and as familiar to me as my own face.

Because the dress is *mine*.

I recoil as if I've been punched and suck in a hard breath, clapping a hand over my mouth. I stare in wide-eyed horror at the girl, my mind blank, a trapped scream trying to claw its way out of my throat.

He said he wouldn't. He promised. No, no, this can't be happening, this is some kind of mistake . . .

My gaze skips to another model, then another, and I realize with a cold sickness that it isn't a mistake.

Every one of the designs from my sketch pad is on a model about to walk through the door. *He used them all.*

Shaking, I take a step back. My legs feel like lead. My head swims. Memories fly at me hard and fast, all the things Matteo said to me. All the beautiful lies.

An animal moan of agony passes my lips.

How did I allow myself to get here, humiliated and used, duped by my feelings, *again*? I swore I wouldn't, I vowed I'd never again be such a blind fool, yet here I am, standing in a gown I made by hand for the occasion, watching a man I adore burn my soul to the ground.

I stumble back, colliding with the wall, gasping for breath because I can't get air, I can't breathe, and if I don't get out of this room this second, I'm going to die.

I spin on my heel and run from the room.

I run wildly down the echoing corridors of the palace, blind to its opulence, pain like poison eating through my veins.

How could he? How could he? How could he?

There's an explanation. He loves you. You know he loves you. Give him a chance to explain.

Are you nuts? Explain what, that he planned this all along? That he couldn't convince you to sell him Papa's business, so he made you fall in love with him instead? That he's the most coldhearted bastard who ever lived?

Just give him a chance!

At the head of the sweeping staircase, I jolt to a stop. I'm breathing hard, shaking badly, and almost certain the contents of my stomach are about to make a large unsightly stain on the red carpet, but I fight the urge to fly down the stairs for a moment, long enough to hear the voice in my head urging me to stop. Urging me to take my seat in the front row and let it play out. To let all the dominoes he stacked up fall.

There has to be a reason he invited me here tonight. In my heart of hearts, I don't believe he'd be so cruel as to give me a front-row seat to his betrayal.

Whatever his reason for doing this, I want to hear it.

I won't run away. I won't punch him in the nose and break all the china in the house. Though there's nothing more I'd like to do than avoid the truth, the reality is that I'm in love with him in a way I never was with Brad.

I'm in love with him. Even if he's made a fool of me. Even if he's lied to me. Even if anything.

I'm in love with him. Come what may.

A terrible decision, really.

You can do this. Go inside and take your seat. Watch the show. Afterward, talk to him. Like an adult. Have it out. Find out the truth. Deal with whatever it is.

"Okay," I whisper, steeling my nerves. "Okay."

I turn around, determined to march back into the show and take my seat, but as soon as I take a step forward, the sheer floating panel attached to the back of my waist gets caught on one of my heels. I stumble, teeter, and flail my arms to regain my balance, but suddenly the world has tilted sideways and gravity is doing its thing and I'm falling backward down the staircase.

My head hits a step.

I see stars.

The last thing I remember thinking before tumbling all the way down the elegant staircase of the Royal Palace of Milan is that even Cinderella didn't have to put up with this much shit.

THIRTY-NINE

MATTEO

Where is she?

For the hundredth time, I peek through the curtains. I see the audience in their seats, I see the photographers lurking in the wings, but I don't see Kimber.

Finally I have to admit defeat.

She isn't coming.

Maybe she's gone back to her ex-fiancé. Maybe she's realized what she feels for me is more annoyance than attachment. Maybe my insistence on giving her space to decide I wasn't a rebound was a colossal mistake.

Whatever it is, she isn't here.

The last two weeks I've spent in agony without her are nothing compared to this moment.

"Matteo! We have to start! What are you waiting for!"

Antonio is beside me, hopping up and down in anxiety. He's already sweat through his shirt. If I don't give the signal to begin, a heart attack could be next.

All the models are staring at me, waiting. The audience is beginning to get restless. I can't put this off any longer.

I jerk my chin at Alexa, the model in the red dress at the head of the line. She takes her cue and glides out onto the catwalk. The model behind her steps up. After a count of ten, I jerk my chin at her, too.

Then I let Antonio take over. I need to go sit somewhere quiet and nurse my aching heart.

I was so excited to see the look on Kimber's face when she saw all her designs on my models making their way down the catwalk. Her dress shop in the States might have been obscure, but with her name featured as the star designer of the House of Moretti's new collection, she'll be famous overnight.

She deserves to be. Her work is some of the most beautiful I've ever seen.

I want her to have everything her father never had. All the money, all the acclaim, all the options that come with success. Her father was a brilliant designer as well, but he toiled in anonymity his entire career. By featuring Kimber's designs in the show, I can honor the DiSanto name and her father's legacy, kick-start her career, and get her headlines that will outshine those from her disastrous wedding, all in one fell swoop.

Even if she's decided she'd rather go back to that idiot of an ex-fiancé than be with me, I can still give her something he'll never be able to.

I can give her the world.

Soon enough, the show is over and I'm out on the stage, bowing and waving to thundering applause from an audience that doesn't include the only person whose opinion matters.

I've never felt so wretched in my life.

FORTY

KIMBER

The relentless beeping is what finally wakes me.

That, and the extraordinary amount of pain I'm in.

I blink open my eyes and fight to focus my vision until a clock swims into sight. It hangs on a wall painted sickly yellow opposite me. The clock ticks cheerfully with noises that ricochet inside my head like gunfire.

Where am I?

I turn my head and am rewarded for the movement by a white-hot spike of pain so intense it makes my vision shimmer. I hear a bellow, and assume either someone has let an elephant loose in the room or that trumpeting sound came from me.

I suspect my little tumble down the palace staircase has not ended well.

"Poppins! You're awake!"

Into my field of vision looms Jenner, looking uncharacteristically disheveled. His hair is mussed, his eyes are red, and his clothing is wrinkled, as if he's coming off a long weekend of heavy drinking and sleeping in his car.

I try, and fail, to ask what's happening. Alarmed by my feeble bleating, Jenner says, "Oh God. Nurse! Nurse! She's awake! She's making strange noises!"

He disappears from view, but returns rather quickly, accompanied by a stern-looking male nurse who shines a bright light directly into my eyes.

"Mrpf!" I protest, scowling.

"How are you feeling, Miss DiSanto?" asks the nurse, in a tone adults use when speaking to infants. I'd like to smash his face.

"Everything hurts." I manage to form the words correctly, which makes Jenner utter a cry of relief. The nurse thinks it's pretty cool, too, because he beams at me.

"Good! That's a very good girl."

If this guy hands me a lollipop, I won't be responsible for my actions. "What happened?"

"You've had a bad spill, I'm afraid."

"How bad?" I try to crane my neck to look down at my body, but discover there's a brace around my neck, preventing me from moving that way.

Terror sets in.

"How bad is it?" My voice is high and pitifully thin. The elephant has left the building.

"You're going to be just fine," says Jenner, in a soothing tone that manages to terrify me even more.

"I'm fucked, aren't I? I'm paralyzed! I'm a quadriplegic! Oh God, just tell me the truth! I'll be in a wheelchair for the rest of my life, right?"

The nurse looks at Jenner with his brows arched. Jenner lifts a shoulder. "If you knew what she's been through lately, you'd get it."

"You're not paralyzed, Miss DiSanto," says the nurse patiently.

"How do you know?" I holler, unconvinced.

He glances down. "Because of the death grip you have on my arm."

I follow his gaze. Sure enough, that's my hand digging into his nice tanned forearm. "What about my legs?" I shout, not letting go. "Why can't I move my legs?"

Jenner says gingerly, "Could be the casts."

"Casts? *Plural?* I have *casts on my legs?*"

"And on your left arm. Apparently your bones are as brittle as a sardine's, love." He adds brightly, "At least you didn't snap your neck!"

"What about my brain?" I ask frantically, struggling to sit up, though it sends stabbing pain everywhere. "Do I have brain damage? Swelling? Posttraumatic whatever? Am I going to need help feeding myself and forget everyone's names and get lost when I go for a drive in my own neighborhood?"

I can tell the nurse is trying not to roll his eyes. "You have no brain damage. The scan showed no evidence of hemorrhage or swelling, and the EEG was normal."

I exhale in relief, flopping back against the pillows, letting out a little grunt when I'm reminded by my nerve endings that I'm not supposed to be flopping against anything at the moment.

"Just relax, miss. I'll have the doctor come in and go over everything with you, all right?"

I feel weepy. In four seconds, I've become overly fond of this male nurse with the strongly accented English and the cowlick that needs a professional stylist to wrestle it down.

"Okay," I say, trying not to blubber. "Tell him to bring good drugs."

The nurse smiles. "I can help you with that."

He presses a button attached to a cord hanging from a metal stand next to the bed, on which also hang two bags of clear liquid. The liquid runs down a plastic tube, ending in a catheter inserted into the vein in the inside of my elbow. Within seconds, I'm infused with a warm, fuzzy glow.

"Oh boy." I laugh, giddy. "Those *are* good drugs. Lord."

"If you need another dose, just push the button." He tucks the cord next to my arm and leaves, pulling a curtain around the side of the bed closest to the door.

"How did I get here?"

Jenner pulls up a chair, sits, and takes my hand. "In an ambulance."

"How are *you* here?"

"Believe it or not, Brad."

I think about that for a while. My brain swims with images of a grinning blond prepster with a broken nose wearing a leisure suit while riding a unicorn. *Oh dear. I'm hallucinating.* "I don't get it."

"The paramedics found your phone in your handbag. Brad was under your emergency contacts."

Note to self: change your emergency contacts. I crinkle my brow in confusion. "How'd they get past the lock screen?"

"Your thumb." He says it like *Duh.*

"So they called Brad. Who was in . . ." I struggle to recall his where-abouts through my lovely drug cocktail. "Florence."

"Yes. He called me, and I got here before he did—"

"Wait, he's here?" I look around, expecting him to pop out from the bathroom waving his hands and yelling, "Ta-da!"

"He was. Earlier."

The way Jenner says that makes me suspicious, but I can't figure out why. I peer at his face. It's slowly getting closer, then retreating, then getting closer again. This is some stuff.

"How long've I been out?"

"Since they brought you in last night."

It hits me with the force of a wrecking ball—last night.

The show.

Matteo.

I let out a little whimper of pain and close my eyes.

"Poppins?"

I whisper, "Matteo. He used my designs in his show."

Very seriously, Jenner responds, "I know."

I open my eyes and look at him. "You do? How?"

He glances at a folded newspaper on the small table beside the bed, but before he can answer, I hear the door open and footsteps entering the room. There are some hushed whispers I can't make out, then from behind the curtain drawn around the bed, Brad appears, hand in hand with a good-looking young man I've never seen before. He has dark eyes and deep dimples, and thick black hair so glorious it could star in its own commercial.

"You're awake!" says Brad, loud enough to make me wince.

"Don't remind me. Who's this?"

Brad slings his arm around the shoulder of the good-looking young man, who smiles shyly at me. "This is Gio."

I know it's probably inappropriate, but I start to giggle. I mean, really. *This* is my life.

"Hello, Gio."

"Buongiorno," he murmurs, all sorts of cute and bashful.

I make eyes at Brad, mentally transmitting *I can see the appeal.*

With a wriggle of his eyebrows, Brad sends back *Right?* Then he goes all businesslike and weird, dropping the smile and the friendly demeanor. "So, Kimber, let's talk."

"Why do you sound like an attorney all of a sudden? Is this about your trust?"

He blinks, caught off guard. "The trust? No, this is about *you.* I wanna talk about how you're doing. What's going through your mind today?"

He has a strange air of expectancy as he waits for me to answer. I look at Jenner, who's gazing back at me, inscrutable as a cat. Then I look at Gio, who's still doing his cute shy thing.

Then I'm mad.

"Cut the crap, Wingate. I'm lying here in pieces. What do you think is going through my mind?"

"I don't know, that's why I'm asking. Last I heard, you and Matteo had separated because he was giving you time to make sure he wasn't a rebound."

You could hear a pin drop the room is so quiet. Except for the beeping of the machine I'm hooked up to, of course.

"Maybe we can talk about this later," I whisper, thinking I should push the red button on that drug-cocktail bag again. My heart needs a stronger dose of numbing chemicals.

Brad and Gio draw closer to the bed. Brad says, "Jenner told us you went to Matteo's show at the palace. So . . . ?"

He leaves the sentence hanging, an invitation to continue. He knows I find it impossible to resist dangling questions, the bastard.

With a great gust of a sigh, I nod. "I did. And then I fell down the stairs."

Brad makes a face. "Back up. What happened in between the arriving and the falling down the stairs?"

"Why are you shouting?"

He makes grabby hands at me. "C'mon. Talk. You'll feel better if you get it off your chest."

I look at Gio. "You know, he was never this kumbaya, touchy-feely, let's-sit-in-a-circle-and-share-our-deepest-darkest when he was with me. You've been a good influence on him."

Gio blushes, which is deeply appealing. "Grazie."

"Watch out for the gambling, though," I warn. "And he can never figure out what he wants to eat at a restaurant. It's the worst. You'll be there all night. You'll age years before he decides on an appetizer."

Brad makes a sound of impatience. "Enough about me, we're talking about you!"

I have to close one eye because the room is gently spinning. "Oh, me? Let's see. Where to start? I was dumped at the altar by my fiancé. Well, you know that part. My father died. I inherited everything. My dress shop burned down. I moved to Italy and took over my father's business. I hated my new stepmother, but then I didn't. My fiancé came out of the closet—oh, you know that, too. Then I fell in love with my stepbrother—"

"What did you say?"

I blink, startled by Brad's loud interruption.

"That last part," he insists. "About your stepbrother."

I think about it, then realize my mistake. "Oh right. My *ex*-stepbrother."

Brad groans, dropping his head back to stare at the ceiling. "What *about* him? The *other* part!"

"The falling-in-love part?" I say faintly, a wash of tears blurring my eyes.

Jenner and Brad shout, "Yes!"

I grumble, "Geez, guys, dial it down a notch. Man down over here, in case you hadn't noticed."

When they both glare at me, I relent. I have no idea what's happening anyway. These drugs are marvelous. "Yes. I'm in love with him. I didn't want to fall in love with him, but how could I not? He's very . . . he's just so . . ." I sigh again, wistfully this time. "*Wonderful.* He's the most wonderful man in the world."

Brad is grinning like he just won a bet. He probably stopped at some gambling hall on the way to the hospital. "So he wasn't a rebound."

"No. Oh. Are you looking for some credit for dumping me so I could find someone better? Is that what's happening here?"

Brad looks vaguely insulted. "Better? I mean, he's a great guy, but *better?*"

Jenner says sharply, "Let's not get off track, Satan."

"You know I don't like it when you call me that!"

"Fine. I'll demote you to Beelzebub. Happy?"

Poor Gio looks totes confused by all the demon references.

"Even if he did use all my designs in his show, I still love him."

That makes the conversation come to a screeching halt, but I'm on a roll now. A drug-induced emotional roll that doesn't want to be stopped, so I blather on, feeling numb and sad and more than a little pathetic.

I wave my good arm through the air. "I know. You don't have to tell me. It's silly. But it's the truth. Even if he's been lying to me, and using me, and planned it all from the beginning, he still has my heart. It's like that thing you said, Jenner, what was it? Oh yes. 'Because I'd rather die than live a single day without him, come what may.' It's not the dresses that are important, or my pride, or anything else. It's him."

I inhale a deep painful breath. "I accidentally walked in on his backstage area when I was looking for the bathroom. I saw all my dresses on his models . . . and I was so angry, and shocked, but most of all hurt. I was devastated. I ran away. Then I got to the top of the stairs and couldn't take another step. I wanted to hear him out. I wanted him to explain because even though I saw it with my own eyes, I didn't believe he'd betray me. My heart wouldn't let me believe it."

My voice breaks. "Then I tripped on the hem of my dress and went ass over teakettle, and that's the end of that sad story right there."

Matteo rips aside the curtain. "Only it's not," he growls, his eyes a luminous, incandescent blue. "It's just the beginning."

I stare at him, more confused than Gio about all the demon talk.

I'm not entirely sure Matteo's really standing there, so beautiful and wild-eyed, so incredibly intense. I'm pretty drugged up. This could be another hallucination. Though he is wearing different clothes from last night . . . but that doesn't prove anything—I had Brad in a leisure suit on a unicorn a few minutes ago.

Then he speaks, and nothing matters except what he's saying.

"I wasn't lying to you. The only thing I planned was to make sure your talent got all the accolades it deserves. Because I love you, too. More than I want my next breath. More than anything. More than life itself, bella, I love you."

"Oh," I say faintly, my heart doing somersaults inside my chest. "That sounds like a win-win."

Matteo and I gaze at each other, Brad does this weird little dance of glee, and Jenner rises from his chair and herds Brad and Gio out of the room, closing the door softly behind them.

Matteo gently clasps my hand, leans over the bed, and kisses me on the forehead. "I thought you'd gone back to Brad," he murmurs tenderly. "I thought you'd decided you didn't want me."

"Oh, Brad's gay," I say happily, hoping I'll remember all this when I'm out of my drug coma.

He chuckles. "Yes, I got that. You enjoyed watching me get jealous over him, didn't you?"

"Yes! Boy, that was fun. Your show was gorgeous. The roses, God. Must've cost a fortune. Was it a success?"

Matteo's forehead creases. He looks faintly alarmed by my cheerful babbling. "The press is calling it my best show yet. Everyone is raving about my collaboration with the electrifying new American designer."

Me, he means. He's talking about me. I grin at him, so joyful I could levitate.

"Did you guess the theme?"

"Um . . . roses are red?"

He kisses me softly on the mouth. "True romance," he whispers, gazing at me with his heart in his eyes. "After us."

"I don't know, we've had a pretty busted-up love story so far, Count."

He kisses me again, making my lips tingle in a wonderful way. "I'd spank you for calling me *Count*, but given your current condition, I'll take a rain check."

"Spanking." I sigh blissfully.

"You're as high as a kite, aren't you?"

"Yes. How come you told me you wouldn't use my designs but then you did?"

342

"I said I wouldn't use them and not give you credit. That's very different. Your name was on the program, in all the promotional materials, everything. I was going to make this whole speech at the end about how love inspired the new collection and the collaboration, but there was an empty seat in the front row, and I was so depressed I dropped it." His voice grows rough. "Are you angry with me?"

I consider it. "Normally I don't like surprises, but this one seems pretty good. Maybe you should tell me everything, starting from the beginning."

He kisses me again, sits on the edge of the bed, and tells me the whole story as he holds my hand, all about how he was trying to get me to fall in love with him from the start by challenging me. Something about appealing to my infamous competitive nature. He never wanted to take over my father's business, or use my designs without giving me credit—he only wanted to aggravate me into falling in love with him and make me famous in the process.

I'm fuzzy on the details, but I think that's the gist of it.

"I can't believe it worked," I say, grinning at him. "I am *so* predictable."

He smiles. "Not exactly. More than once I thought you were going to castrate me."

"How did you find out I was here? Jenner?"

He shakes his head. "Brad called me and told me what happened. He told me you were in love with me but were too scared to admit it because of what he'd done. Then he told me he was gay, and a lot of other things suddenly made sense."

"Whose idea was it to hide you behind the curtain so you could hear my teary confession of love?"

Matteo tucks a lock of hair behind my ear, smiling down at me, so handsome it hurts. "You have him to thank for that, too. He's more clever than I would've given him credit for."

Son of a gun. Brad played cupid with Matteo and me.

Guess he really did want to make it up to me after all.

"Honey," I say, hit by a strong new wash of happy warmth. "I think you sat on my drug button."

Matteo leaps up and looks down. "Oh shit."

"Yeah," I say, beaming, watching the room spin around his beautiful head. "You should probably kiss me before I pass out."

He obliges, taking my face in his hands and pressing his lips against mine. He whispers, *"Ti amo, bella. Ti amerò per sempre."*

"Right back atcha, hot stuff. I love you forever, too."

Hey, I think I'm learning Italian!

I sink into unconsciousness with a body covered in plaster, a heart bursting with happiness, and a huge grin on my face.

EPILOGUE

ONE YEAR LATER

No matter how plump, plain, or poor a man is, the right tuxedo can make him look more dashing than any fairy-tale prince.

Right about now, I'm thinking Prince Charming can kiss Jenner's dashing ass.

Not that he's any of those other *P* words, but the general idea stands.

He steps out from behind the dressing room door in a fantastic midnight-blue silk tux that took me two months to make, and spins in a circle, waiting for my reaction. He's immaculate, the picture of perfection, right down to his gleaming patent leather DiSanto loafers.

I've recently expanded into menswear. You wouldn't *believe* the profit margin in men's shoes.

"Winston Churchill's hairy balls!" I shout, leaping from the divan I've been sitting on as I've waited for him to get ready.

Jenner shakes his head, chuckling. "You're always stealing my best lines."

"I've been saving that one for a special occasion. Today seemed particularly apropos."

He smiles and holds out his arms. "Come give us a hug."

I cross the short distance between us and nestle into his arms, resting my head on his shoulder, being careful not to smudge my makeup on his jacket. We stand in silence for a long moment until he gives me a light squeeze and pulls away.

"Isn't it strange?" he murmurs, toying with the lace on one of the cap sleeves of my dress.

"What?"

He meets my eyes, and I'm surprised to find his misty. "Life. I never would've thought in a million years I'd be here, now, getting ready to walk down the aisle toward the man of my dreams to take vows that aren't recognized by the legal system of this country. If you'd told me a year ago any of it would be happening, I'd have laughed you out of the room."

"You would have *scorned* me out of the room, with withering disdain that would've left permanent scars."

He brightens, as if I've paid him a great compliment. "Yes, I would have. But here we are."

"Here we are." I smile at him, tapping his chest. "Who knew you had a real heart hidden away under all that tin?"

"Tundra," he corrects sourly. "And don't get cheeky with me, darling. It's my wedding day."

"I'll get as cheeky as I want, my friend, considering if *I'd* never broken three-quarters of the bones in my limbs, *you'd* never have met the man of your dreams."

"True." He fakes a groan. "But a *nurse*. I couldn't even land a doctor?"

"The heart wants what it wants," I tease, grinning at him.

"Indeed it does." He swallows, blinking back tears. "Oh, Poppins. This is the happiest day of my life." He pauses for a moment, then says forcefully, "If Toni stops the ceremony to announce he's straight, I expect you to break his nose!"

I burst into laughter, and Jenner joins in. We both know Toni isn't about to have a change of heart, on either his gender preference or his choice of partner. He's been gaga over Jenner since they first locked eyes over my pathetic cast-covered body in the hospital a year ago. Jenner has been equally gaga over him.

Now that's what I'd call a silver lining.

"Are you ready?" I ask.

"I'm ready."

"Chin up. Back straight. Tits out."

"God, you've got a memory like an elephant," he says with affection.

We walk arm in arm from the room, headed toward the staircase.

Over the past few months, all the rooms on the second floor of Il Sogno that had been closed for so many years have been opened and redecorated. The exterior of the house, along with the gardens, has been given a face-lift, too, and even the fountain of Aphrodite and her lover has been restored to working order.

Thanks to the recent success of DiSanto Couture, there's money for that sort of thing.

As Jenner and I pass through the living room on the way to the backyard, the strains of a classical violin trio grow louder. Pachelbel's "Canon in D." When I snort, remembering it was the exact song playing as I walked down the aisle toward Brad, Jenner murmurs, "That ghastly song. We can never get away from it, can we?"

"If I ever get married again, I'll strangle the musician who dares to play it."

Jenner glances at me, a knowing look in his eye, but doesn't comment. He knows I'm not in a rush to walk down the aisle again—present occasion excepted, of course—though things between Matteo and me are about as perfect as they could possibly be. I've learned that happily ever after doesn't have to include a wedding.

All it requires is the right person at your side.

We walk through the open French doors and out onto the lawn. It's a gorgeous day, sunny and clear, idyllic. The guests rise from their chairs as we approach. Matteo is in the front row, smiling, devastatingly handsome in a blue suit and tie. The marchesa is two seats down from him, holding Beans in her arms. When the dog spots me, she bares her teeth.

Toni's waiting for us at the end of the aisle, grinning like mad when he sees Jenner.

The ceremony is simple, moving, and utterly beautiful. I sit beside Matteo and try not to cry, but he keeps handing me tissues for my leaking eyes. Brad and Gio are in the row behind us, and at one point, Brad reaches out and squeezes my shoulder.

They had their civil union ceremony two months ago. The senator and Mrs. Wingate didn't attend, but from what I understand, the blow of their son being gay was mitigated by Gio's family's vast fortune in real estate.

I'll never understand some people's priorities.

When it's all over and we're showering Jenner and Toni in rose petals as they make their way back down the aisle toward the house and the party about to begin inside, Matteo pulls me against his side and kisses my hair. Into my ear, he whispers, "How soon can we get you out of this dress?"

I smile. "Weddings make you horny, do they?"

"*You* make me horny." He presses a kiss to the side of my neck, then says something in Italian. I know for sure it includes the words "lick" and "forever" because I've been studying the language in my spare time.

What little spare time I have. Matteo's show last year rocketed the DiSanto Couture name from obscurity to massive popularity so fast my head is still spinning.

The only downside is that Papa isn't here to see it. He would've been so proud.

"You'll have to keep it in your pants until after the toasts, hot stuff. I've got the best man speech to give. Maybe we can have a quickie in the bathroom between that and the first dance."

"You know I don't do quickies," he says huskily, his eyes burning.

I smile at him and wind my arms around his neck. *Yes. That I know.*

"Hey, lovebirds, are you coming inside or what?"

Along with the marchesa, Brad stands with Gio at the end of the rows of chairs. The two of them are holding hands, smiling at us, and God, life is bizarre. Unexpected, wonderful, and bizarre. I can't wait to see what other twists it's got up its sleeve for me.

"Yes, we're coming."

We follow them in, laughing when Cornelia bounds out from inside and starts to run around us in circles, barking.

The rest of the afternoon is a blur of dancing, speeches, food, and champagne. At one point, late into the evening when everyone is soused and the band is playing a slow song, I see Dominic and the marchesa quietly conferring in a corner. I nudge Matteo with my elbow and lift my chin in their direction.

"You're a better person than I am," says Matteo, watching Dominic with narrowed eyes. "I never would've forgiven him for taking money from your father."

I lean against his shoulder, and he drapes his arm around me. "Though it's my personal specialty, grudges aren't something Papa believed in. I know he would've wanted me to work it out. And Dominic did apologize and offer to pay the money back, so he got credit for making an effort."

Matteo says stiffly, "Until he apologizes to my mother for the way he's treated her, he'll always be on my shit list."

I smile at the man I love. "Why do you think I invited him, Count?"

He slants me a sour look. "What is it you have against my title?"

My smile is brilliant. I turn and wind my arms around his waist. "Nothing at all. I just love how much it annoys you when I call you *Count.*"

"So it's not that you'd rather be a countess than Marchesa Moretti." Wrapping his arms around my back, he gazes down at me with love shining in his gorgeous blue eyes.

I laugh, glancing over at his mother. "I think someone already has dibs on that title."

"And *I* think it's time we had another marchesa in the family," he says softly.

Startled, I look at him. His lips curve up as I stare at him in shock. *Is he saying what I think he's saying?*

"Uh . . . I, uh . . ."

"You 'uh' what?" he teases, brushing his lips against my cheek. "You 'uh' want to see the ring before you decide?"

"The ring?" I say breathlessly. My heart is pounding so hard I can barely hear my own voice over it. My knees are made of rubber.

Matteo turns nonchalant. "Unless you'd rather not. I know you're not that keen about matrimony." He pauses. "It's pretty nice, though. Big."

His lips press together as he watches my expression. He's trying not to laugh, the bastard.

Oh, it's on.

I compose myself, thoughtfully pursing my lips as I fiddle with his lapel. "How big?"

"Massive." He pretends to be thoughtful. "Now that I think about it, it's completely gaudy. You wouldn't want to wear it anyway.

Diamonds that large only attract the wrong kind of attention. People will think you're showing off."

He sighs, looking away. "You'd probably be a target for muggers. You wouldn't be able to wear it in public, that's for sure. Just around the house. No, maybe not even there—the servants would talk, someone would plan a theft. I suppose you'd have to keep the thing locked up in a safe where the light of all those flawless carats can shine without the threat of being stolen. Hey, should we dance?"

"Where is this horrible, gaudy ring?" I shout, breaking. I take him by his lapels and shake him. *"Show it to me now or I'll kill you!"*

He starts to laugh, loudly, grabbing me and pulling me against his chest so hard I lose my breath.

"It's in my pocket, bella."

I start to laugh, too. "And here I thought all this time you were just happy to see me." I shove my hand into the left pocket of his trousers and come up with a small black velvet box. I stare at it, my hands shaking, my lungs constricting, all the blood draining from my head.

Matteo gently takes it from me and cracks it open.

He has to catch me before I fall.

"Jesus," I say, clinging to him as he laughs. "That *is* gaudy. Tell me it's cubic zirconia, I don't want to think you had to put the castle in hock to buy that awful thing."

"I love you," he says, sliding the ring onto my finger. "Will you marry me?"

It is very, very hard to breathe. "I can hardly say no after you bought me the world's biggest diamond."

"My plan exactly," he says, nodding. "But that wasn't officially a yes."

I gaze up into his eyes, blinking a few times to clear my vision from tears. Everything I've ever needed is gazing back at me. "Yes," I whisper, my voice breaking. "Officially, yes. I love you with all my heart."

"It's the hair, isn't it?"

"Shut up and kiss me."

"God, you're bossy."

"No, I'm just really good at digging in my heels."

We share a grin. Then he kisses me to the sound of applause and champagne corks popping as Beans sinks her teeth into the hem of my dress.

ACKNOWLEDGMENTS

As always, huge thanks are owed to my developmental editor, Melody Guy, who is incredibly good at her job and has the patience of a saint. You always make my books so much better, and I appreciate your talent and hard work.

Thank you to my team at Montlake Romance, specifically my editor, Maria Gomez, and the copywriting and proof-editing teams who put in such hard work to make the manuscript shine.

Thanks to all the bloggers who share and support my work, and to my readers, without whom I wouldn't have a career.

Thanks to Jay for everything, always.

I created original pen and watercolor fashion sketches of Kimber's collection for this book, which you can see on my Pinterest page: www.pinterest.com/jtgeissinger.

ABOUT THE AUTHOR

 J.T. Geissinger writes unique, passionate love stories for readers who need more than cookie-cutter romance. Ranging from funny, feisty rom-coms to intense, edgy suspense, her books have sold more than one million copies and been translated into several languages. She is the recipient of the Prism Award for Best First Book and the Golden Quill Award for Best Paranormal/Urban Fantasy and is a two-time finalist for the RITA Award from the Romance Writers of America. She has also been a finalist in the Booksellers' Best, National Readers' Choice, and Daphne du Maurier Awards.

Join her Facebook readers' group—Geissinger's Gang—to take part in weekly Wine Wednesday live chats and giveaways, find out more information about works in progress, gain access to exclusive excerpts and contests, and get advance reader copies of her upcoming releases. You can also check out her website, www.jtgeissinger.com, or follow her on Instagram @JTGeissingerauthor and on Twitter @JTGeissinger.

Made in the USA
Coppell, TX
26 September 2023

22079126R00215